THE STORM

Visit us at www.boldstrokesbooks.com

THE STORM

by

Shelley Thrasher

2012

THE STORM

ISBN 10: 1-60282-780-X
ISBN 13: 978-1-60282-780-6

This Trade Paperback Original Is Published By
Bold Strokes Books, Inc.
P.O. Box 249
Valley Falls, NY 12185

First Edition: December 2012

Credits
Editor: Ruth Sternglantz
Production Design: Susan Ramundo
Cover Design By Sheri (graphicartist2020@hotmail.com)

Acknowledgments

Lee, Jean, and Carolyn helped me get started.

Jennifer, Cheryl, and Cliffi encouraged me to keep going.

Connie and Justine read numerous drafts and helped me focus.

Mama always answered my questions.

Rad provided writing tips, insights, and a chance to share my work.

Sheri designed my beautiful cover.

Ruth edited my book as if it were her own.

Thank you. I couldn't have done it without all you special women.

Dedication

To my grandmother and great-grandmother—oil and water.
To my mother, for sharing her stories of life on the farm.

Dedication

CHAPTER ONE

Early morning, late September 1917
Near the front lines of the Allies in France

"Are you here, Helen?"

"Come on in, kid. I'm due in the surgery unit in fifteen minutes."

Jacqueline Bergeron slipped into Helen Fairchild's tent, relieved to escape the blowing rain. Helen sat on her cot near a tiny fire, with one hot-water bottle on her feet and another on her hands. Though she wore two pairs of stockings and all her wool clothes, she still shivered in the unseasonably cold weather. She'd even wrapped a blue wool scarf over her head and around her neck, so Jaq could see only her kissable lips, small nose, and eyes like slate.

Jaq trembled with more than the cold as she stood on the reinforced door covering one of the two trenches under her feet. During her ride here to unload the wounded men she'd picked up earlier, she'd tried to dredge up enough nerve to confess her feelings to Helen. Otherwise, she'd explode.

She hugged herself and shifted from one foot to the other, wanting to run back to her bloody ambulance. But she held her ground.

"Helen. We need to talk."

Helen looked at her as cheerfully as if she thought Jaq might invite her out for morning tea. Did Helen have any idea what she meant to say? Every man and woman on the base could probably read her intentions.

"What's up, kid?" If Helen knew what she had in mind, her acting skills surpassed Mary Pickford's.

"I've been wanting to ask you something personal, but I don't know how."

"Just spit it out, kid. We don't have any time to waste. You know that better than anyone, don't you?" She laughed, and Jaq almost lost her nerve.

"Are you interested in women? You know, in a personal way?"

"Why, sure, kid. I like women a lot." She still looked like she didn't have any idea where Jaq was headed.

"I mean, do you really like them? More than you like men?"

Helen looked a little startled now but kept smiling. "I'm not sure what you're getting at. I like just about everybody."

Jaq took a deep breath and jumped in. "Have you ever had romantic feelings about a woman?" Suddenly, she felt like she was in over her head and had forgotten how to swim.

Helen went rigid. "No. I can't say I have. Why do you ask?" She was almost frowning now, though she didn't seem angry.

"Sometimes I think about you the way men think about women."

"Oh, you just have a crush, kid." Helen looked directly at her and smiled indulgently. "That happens a lot when you're in a strange situation with none of your pals nearby. You'll get over it."

"So you're sure you don't feel that way about me?"

"Of course I'm sure. I like you a lot, but just as a friend. A close friend, mind you."

She took another deep breath. "Helen, I don't just like you as a friend. And I don't have a crush. I know the difference. I love you. Do you love me?"

Helen froze. Her lips tight, she whispered, "No."

She was so gentle, almost apologetic, the single word shouldn't have hurt so much. But it did.

Helen quickly began to thaw.

"Oh, Jaq, I'm flattered. You're just tired and homesick. Rest a little and those strange feelings you call love will disappear. If they don't, try to forget 'em. You're imagining things."

She stood there mute and shook her head, wanting to crawl into one of the trenches under her feet and never come out. She'd be safe there. No one could hurt her again like Helen just had. The ground was calling her into its warmth and safety when Helen took her hand and pulled her down onto the cot beside her.

"Don't be too hard on yourself, kid. It's not you. It's me. I'm not made like other people. I don't have the type of urge you describe for anyone, either male or female. Never have, never will. I'm married to my vocation. Saving lives makes my life worthwhile. You're a great person, and you have a natural, wonderful feeling. You just need to find somebody like you. Keep looking. You'll bump into that special person, and when you do, you'll know. Forget me. I'm a lost cause."

Jaq felt a little better but didn't believe her. Helen was just being nice so she wouldn't go hang herself or sniff mustard gas. She jumped up.

"Got to go. Thanks, Helen. See you around."

She stumbled through the rows of muddy tents to her ambulance, and as she drove away, the rain still hadn't let up.

Jaq sped back to her base and ran straight to the mess tent. Henry sat there, holding out a precious bottle of whiskey. They always shared their hard-found liquor and discussed what a farce the War was. He treated her like a pal. After she slid onto a rough bench, she emptied the cup he'd shoved toward her. Then another. Nasty stuff. It burned but numbed.

"You ever feel like saying to hell with everything and everybody?" she asked him.

He appraised her with gun-barrel eyes. "All the time."

"Just do what feels good. The rules be damned." She was rambling and didn't want to confide in him, but she was bursting. Her words slid out on her whiskey breath. "It hurts to want someone you can't have."

He nodded, his eyes explosive. "Sure does."

She'd said too much. "I better get some sleep. Got to clean my filthy ambulance later. Thanks for the booze."

He poured another one. "See you. Take care."

She stumbled to her tent and dove onto her cot, still dressed. Thank God her tent mate had left on a few days' leave. She didn't feel like making small talk.

Her heart felt as bloody as the arms and legs of the soldiers she'd delivered earlier. Welcome silence soothed her to sleep.

She woke to ragged breathing, an intruder's eyes on her, the faint stench none of them could wash away. Footsteps. The breath smelled of metal.

Someone large and heavy dropped on her. A man. Plunged his tongue into her mouth, writhed against her, frenzied. She clawed him.

His hand caught her forehead. Her flesh ripped, blood flooded her right eye. She struggled, he panted. His cock swelled against her leg—a short, fat bayonet. She couldn't let him stab her, had to outwit him. She lay still.

"You know you want it," he murmured as he raised himself up, cloth scraping along his legs and hers. His pants were down, her skirt up. It was Henry. He pressed back onto her. She jerked her knee into his crotch, reached just under her cot for the wrench she kept there.

He fell to the ground, moaning, yet scrambled toward her again. She swung, lashed the darkness until the wrench struck flesh. He thudded to the floor and she dashed around him, across the camp to the forewoman's tent, pressing a handkerchief to her bleeding forehead.

"Miss Truman, come quickly. I need help," she whispered as loud as she dared, standing just outside her quarters. Then she rushed inside, shook Miss Truman's shoulder.

Looking dazed, Miss Truman threw on a wrap, lit a kerosene lamp, and hurried beside her back to her tent.

Henry sprawled unmoving. Miss Truman felt his pulse, dropped his arm to the floor. "He's dead. You caught him on the temple." She eased Jaq's bloody handkerchief from her forehead and studied it, then looked at his fallen hand. "And he got you with his signet ring. An eye for an eye, I'd say. I'd better stitch up that gash."

It was wartime. No one would miss him.

Chapter Two

March 1918
Storyville, New Orleans

"Well, blow me. I didn't even know you were married, Jaq."
Willie Piazza fingered the diamond nesting in the hollow of her throat.

"Yep. Last spring in London. My sister introduced us. Lasted one night. Long enough to realize marriage wasn't for me."

She glanced around the nearly deserted saloon in Storyville. The mayor had outlawed prostitution last year and closed New Orleans's most notorious sporting establishments, including Willie's. Too bad. It was a colorful part of the city.

She tossed back her shot of whisky and lit a cigarette. "Can you believe Eric just showed up out of the blue? I'd almost forgotten about him." She jabbed long fingers through her coarse, cropped hair.

Willie languidly stripped off one red kid glove and fondled her hand. "You certainly haven't been acting like you were married since you got home."

A familiar bolt of electricity shot up her arm as she squeezed Willie's bare palm. "No. I haven't. And I've enjoyed every minute with you. But I've got to be out of town awhile."

"What for?" Willie brushed her fingers against Jaq's cheek.

The smoke from her cigarette drifted toward Willie. "Eric promised to help me get our farce of a marriage annulled if I'd do him a favor."

"What's he want?"

"His mother died a few months ago, and his two younger brothers enlisted right after that. His dad's been sick and doesn't have any help, so Eric asked me to drive him up to some flyspeck of a place in East Texas."

Willie drilled her with translucent green eyes. "East Texas? Nothing but hicks and pine trees in that part of the world. Why can't he drive himself?"

"War injuries. He's got a bad leg and can't see well right now. Hurt one of his eyes real bad in an aeroplane crash. Besides, he said we'd just stay long enough to hire a couple to take care of his dad and the farm. The old man must have some money."

Willie took a drag off her Russian cigarette in its long gold holder, then flicked the ash into a cut-glass ashtray. She had as many facets as it did. "You're a soft touch. Hope you don't have to stay too long."

"You and me both."

Jaq jerked her blue-striped tie loose and almost ripped off the collar button. It felt like a damn noose, but along with her starched shirt and black suit, it provided a hell of a lot of freedom. The white collar reminded her of ground razors.

She glanced at the deep V where the tops of Willie's white breasts met before they disappeared into her red velvet dress. She wanted to caress the line where soft cloth met bonbon flesh.

Willie stubbed out her cigarette and said in a voice as smooth as Canadian Club, "I'll miss you."

As Willie slid her tongue over full red lips that set off her creamy skin and stylish blond wig, Jaq shivered with pleasure. Willie knew how to display her assets and acted like Jaq was the only person in the world worth listening to.

She'd miss Willie's supple hands on her body. Being close to death near the front lines in France last year had made her crave a woman's touch more than ever. And now for the first time, a woman had responded to her without guilt or regret. Willie didn't love her, and she didn't love Willie. But she loved the freedom Willie allowed her. She could cry out in release as Willie thrust fluid fingers into her parched body. If she'd allowed herself, she could have sobbed without being afraid Willie would reproach her for indulging her feelings.

"I'll be back before you know it. I just hope Eric keeps his end of the bargain." She drained her glass. "Three's my limit. It's late. I better go. Got a long trip ahead of me."

"If you wish." Willie lifted her crystal glass with strong fingers and sipped her cognac.

Shivering again, Jaq inhaled the rich, full-bodied scent of Willie's Red Moscow perfume. She'd rather still be in Willie's bed instead of leaving tomorrow with a man.

"Come back soon," Willie murmured as Jaq buttoned her collar, tightened her tie, and shrugged on her black trench coat.

"Sure thing."

Settling her worn fedora over her right eye, she stepped out into the damp, muggy air. Gaslights cast shadows along the streets, and the familiar odor of dead fish and black mud made her miss Willie's spicy, floral warmth.

She sauntered through dark streets toward her parents' house. The smoke from her cigarette drifted into the fog as she pondered red velvet and white skin. Damn. Her collar still chafed her.

Good thing it was so late. Mother would throw her out if she saw her dressed like this, like a man. Hard to believe Mother hadn't discovered her nightly masquerades. She was lucky, there, and lucky too that Eric had a sense of humor about it all. If Father knew, he'd probably laugh along with Eric. Well, maybe.

She took her time returning to her bland prison. While she'd been there, her mother had done nothing but insist that she cheer up and act normal, and her father had spent most of his time escaping from the house by going to his office near the docks. Now her so-called husband waited there for her to drive him to the ends of the earth.

Surely she'd be able to relax in East Texas. That's what she needed.

❖

March 27, 1918
New Hope, Texas

Molly Russell sat on a low stool and listened to the soft, drawn-out *coo-oo* of the mourning dove as she pressed her head into Nellie's side and tried to milk her. The sun warmed her arms, and the morning breeze cooled her. Inhaling the sweet smell of golden hay, she stared absently at the dew glinting on a spiderweb in one corner of Nellie's stall.

She hadn't been able to sleep last night and had finally gotten up and worked on a song she was composing. Of course she'd overslept this morning, which set Mother Russell off. "We need to hurry, Nellie."

Yesterday Mother Russell had scolded her for letting the corn-bread burn, and she still heard her caustic words: "Land's sakes, where's your head? Thinking about that silly Easter program, aren't you?" She was probably stewing in the kitchen right now while she cooked breakfast.

"I should get a medal for living in the same house with Mother Russell for all these years," she told Nellie. "If only I'd asked Mr. James to introduce me to her before we said our vows. If he had, I'd most likely be in Dallas right now. Maybe I'd have met someone who loves music too, or found a job teaching it. But then I'd never have come to know you and had Patrick, God bless him."

Nellie moved away and she grasped her tits more firmly. She'd massaged them and now held them gently but firmly, squeezing but not pulling. She'd even rubbed her right knee along Nellie's stomach and hummed her favorite melody from *Swan Lake*, but the cow still wouldn't release her milk. "What's wrong, sweetheart? You seem restless." She put her ear to Nellie's stomach.

"Are you nervous because I'm worried the music program won't go well Sunday? I wish I could take my time with you. But if I do, Mother Russell might storm out here and prod us both."

She enjoyed Nellie's soft brown eyes, smooth skin, and earthy scent. She liked feeling her respond, enjoyed talking and singing to her. They were usually so in tune. "What's wrong, precious?"

She'd bathed Nellie's tits with warm water and handled them until they softened. She'd…Heavenly days! She'd forgotten to feed her.

"I'm so sorry, sweetheart." She moved the gallon bucket, then eased up from her stool. "I'll go get your breakfast. I can't do anything right this morning. Of course, I never can do anything right. I wish I could run away from the farm."

❖

"Molly. Molly Lee." What in tarnation was she doing out in the barn so long?

Mrs. Russell grabbed a long amber bottle from a kitchen drawer and rolled out the biscuit dough on a floured board with hard, fast strokes.

She was glad she could talk to her husband, Calvin, about anything. Even if he had been dead nigh on forty years, looking at the big picture in her room of him wearing his Confederate uniform kept him alive in her mind most all the time.

"I heard Molly get up late this morning, the lazy heifer. Then she lolled around getting dressed. Sounded like she was in a daze, stumbling over everything. I give her the easiest chores on the place, and she can't even get up and out in time to do 'em right," she muttered to him. "Where's that gal's head most of the time? In the clouds, I reckon."

After patting plump biscuits into a greased pan, she shoved them into the hot oven and slammed the door shut with a clang.

"Most likely dreaming up a new piece of music, Calvin." At least *he* understood what she had to put up with. "Says she wakes up in the middle of the night sometimes with a song running through her head, so loud she has to jump out of bed and scribble it down. Thinks she's another Chikovski—some fancy Russian fella she's always carrying on about. Well, if she doesn't bring me some milk pretty soon, I'll Chikovski her."

She stormed halfway out to the barn and called again. "Molly, I know you can hear me. We need some fresh milk in this house right this minute. You best quit lollygagging and get a move on."

A blue jay on the peak of the outhouse raised his crest straight up and squawked like he was mocking her. She threw a stick at him then marched back to the house in the early morning light.

Maybe she'd get a rise out of Molly, the little slacker, but she doubted it. The overeducated know-it-all.

CHAPTER THREE

Jaq tightened her grip on the steering wheel of her black Model T. "Damn. We've been on the road—if that's what you call these washed-out ruts—three days. They're pounding me to jelly."

"Sorry I can't help more. Maybe my leg will be better when we head back." Eric McCade unwrapped the white butcher paper from a wedge of yellow cheese and pulled out his pocketknife.

"How much farther to New Hope?"

He handed her a thin slice with larded cheesecloth still stuck to one end. "I bet you didn't hear me say it's almost four hundred miles all told. Thinking about getting away from your mother, weren't you? She and your pop seemed concerned about you when we left."

"You're imagining things. Now she won't have anybody to gripe at except him. She knows he'll stay at his office even more now, without me to distract her. Just tell me when we'll get there." She bit into the sharp cheese, its pungent, earthy flavor easing her queasy stomach. "How about some crackers? I can still taste that chili from last night." This drive through Louisiana made her appreciate the luxury of traveling by ship and train.

Eric maneuvered several saltines from their waxy package. "Here you go. If we expect to find someplace better than that dump we stayed in yesterday, we need to make it to Natchitoches tonight."

"Okay. How far's that?"

"Forty more miles, give or take."

"I've given you about all I can. Another half day? Then what?" She polished off the crackers and another piece of cheese, dusted the crumbs onto the black rubber floorboard, then pointed toward the half-empty Coca Cola bottle he held between his legs. "Remind me again how I let you talk me into this." She could kick herself. She must have been nuts.

"So many questions." He handed her the Coke. "We'll reach New Hope Saturday. And in case you've forgotten, my darling, you stood before that official last year and promised to love, honor, and obey me."

"Right." The lukewarm drink tickled her nose and washed down the dry crackers and cheese. If only she could wash away such a foolish mistake so easily. "And the next day I told you to forget it."

"But in the eyes of God and the law, we're still one."

"And only one of us is driving." She smoothed the black leather seat beside her. If only it was better cushioned. "Hey, didn't Father give me a swell homecoming gift? I don't care if this Model T's four years old. She could probably do thirty-five or forty on a good road. But our sham of a marriage isn't near-enough reason for me to spend ten hours a day behind the wheel, no matter how much I love her."

Eric gave her more cheese and crackers. "Let's see, then. You're coming with me because you feel sorry for me?"

"Huh. That'd be a cold day in hell. So what if your plane crashed and ended your flying career—for now, at least? You think that'd make me agree? Besides, I'm counting on us not being there long. If you believe I feel sorry for you, you're crazier than I was when I married you." She was lying. The battered man beside her barely resembled the strutting pilot who'd bulldozed her into marrying him just a year ago. Of course, all the gin they'd consumed had helped.

"So you're doing it because I'm still a tall, handsome war hero with a fistful of medals?" Eric cut a thick slice of cheese for himself and stuck it between two crackers.

He was so banged up, she couldn't bear to hurt him. She simply didn't want to be his wife. "Something like that. And we understand each other. You'd do the same for me, wouldn't you?"

"I suppose so. Especially if you'd promised we could annul our mistake." He ate some more, then gathered his crumbs and tossed them toward the steep ditch on the side of the road.

Hell, she might as well be honest. "Hmm. Yeah. That went a long way toward convincing me. But I still love you—like a brother."

He finished the rest of the Coke and threw the bottle out too. "If you'd let me, I'd convince you we could be more than that."

"Nope." She'd learned her lesson. "We tried once. That's enough. I told you, I love women and you'll never be more than a friend."

"Speaking of your so-called love for women, what's with you and Willie Piazza? I spotted you two in the saloon last night when I stopped by for a quick drink. You looked like you could eat each other alive."

"Yep. We'd been doing that quite often. But it's nothing serious. We're just pals."

"Like you and me, I guess."

"Yeah. But she's got the right equipment and plenty of spare time."

"Not something you and I've had much of till lately."

She tightened her shoulders, then released them. All this driving, talking, wandering, and running away had made her quiver inside. She just wanted some peace and quiet for a while.

"Yeah. Well, how about we end this bogus marriage soon?" She stretched one arm above her head, then the other. Disguising herself as a man so she could visit Willie late at night had made her skin prickle. Disguising herself as a wife made her yawn.

If God would just let her get back to New Orleans and become a free woman sooner rather than later, she might think a little better of him. Being tied down sure wasn't what it was cracked up to be.

Molly's right cheekbone ached and her eyes felt grainy as she grabbed an old wooden box. The sweet odor of the hulls and yellow cottonseed meal she scooped into it eased her headache, but it didn't lessen her perpetual heartache. A stubborn refrain, *Why did I marry and move here?* rarely stopped playing in her mind and plaguing her heart.

"Here's your favorite treat, Nellie," she called. "Nice and rich. It'll keep your coat shiny."

Nellie lowed and swished her tail. Usually docile, even she rebelled when she didn't get what she needed.

"Be patient, sweetheart. I can't stand for both you and Mother Russell to rush me. Oops." She'd hit her ring with the scoop. She was all thumbs today.

She glanced down at her left hand. "Oh dear, I knocked the diamond out of my engagement ring."

She pulled on her gloves, dropped to her knees, and ran her hands along the littered ground. Nothing but chicken feathers, tufts of hay, piles of cornhusks, and mounds of dried and fresh manure. Her stomach churned, and she gulped to keep from throwing up.

"Darn. Well, let me finish milking and run a bucketful to Mother Russell. After I wash the breakfast dishes, I'll come hunt my diamond."

She rinsed Nellie's tits then sat on the low stool, her head fuzzy as Nellie munched her breakfast and finally cooperated. The leisurely music of the milk buckets was usually soothing as their treble *ping, peng* gave way to a bass *shhoop, shhuup*. But the twenty minutes it took her today seemed like twenty hours.

She grabbed several flour sacks she'd boiled and poured each pail of milk through one of them into small buckets for sweet milk to drink and into crocks for churning. Then she set the crocks in a washtub, poured water into it, and let each one's cloth covering hang in the water to help cool the milk. The cream would gradually rise. After breakfast she would add some leftover souring cream and a little milk, then churn the mixture into butter and buttermilk. As careful as she was, though, sometimes the milk spoiled.

She hurried to the well, even more jittery, and jerked her gloves on again. Otherwise the rough rope would callus her hands. Her shoulder muscles protesting, she strained to pull an already cold tin full of milk from the deep well for breakfast and carefully lowered the small buckets of fresh milk to chill.

She scuttled to the kitchen but didn't dare spill a drop. "This should be enough for breakfast, Mother Russell." She'd mention her diamond later.

Mr. James walked in from feeding the mules, Patrick dancing beside him. "Hi, Ma. I'm all clean and ready to go to school."

"Good boy." She rubbed his arm and her day brightened. She couldn't survive without him and her music. "You missed a spot."

His sunny expression dimmed. "Gee. Sorry. I tried."

She squeezed his small shoulder. "That's all right. Just run along and wash your neck again before breakfast." She gazed fondly at him then asked Mr. James, "Could you draw some more well water? I need to heat enough to fill the kettle, wash the dishes, and sterilize the pails."

When he returned to fill the reservoir on the wood-burning stove, she was in the pantry looking for some preserves. She overheard him and his mother.

"I declare, James. Don't see why she has to scald those milk buckets every blessed time she uses them. Once a week's enough. Powerful waste of manpower, and well water too."

"You're right, Ma. Like you're always saying, she's gone overboard about germs. I bet she got that notion at that gol-dern university."

She'd heard it all before, but she stopped for the first time that morning, afraid the heavy white sacks of flour, corn meal, and sugar on the shelf next to her might fall and crush her. They'd trap her in this small closet and smother her.

Suddenly she wanted to smash the Mason jars lined up on another shelf. The purple blackberry jam, the light-pink plum jelly, and the crimson strawberry preserves, safe and sweet in their glass jars, would dye the pantry floor. Then she'd grab the tidy white bags that hung over her head and scatter seeds all around her—cotton, squash, okra, cucumbers, peas, and beans.

Did Mr. James and Mother Russell even care if she overheard them? Did they think she was deaf and totally insensitive? *How much longer can I endure her hateful remarks and his refusal to defend me?*

Mother Russell grumbled about how salty the ham was as she sliced it. When she dropped each piece into her black skillet, it hissed. "Downright finicky, that's what she is."

Molly felt like crying. They obviously believed she was worthless. She had to get away.

❖

The bile started rising in Mrs. Russell's throat as soon as Molly confessed she'd lost that dad-blasted diamond. What business did a farm wife have wearing a one-carat ring, especially while she milked the cow?

She ate a biscuit and gravy, two pieces of ham, and two fried eggs but still felt a mite nauseous. Cooking the ham hadn't taken any of the salt out of it. Better kill another hog pretty soon, before it got too hot.

That diamond kept worrying her. Nothing but trouble, just like Molly.

James had been bound and determined to own that ring. Cost him a good bit of money too. But they'd had a bumper cotton crop that year, and he'd felt flush.

The first gal he offered it to lived just down the road. He musta had her in mind when he bought it. He'd been partial to the sweet little thing for quite a spell. Might have made him a pretty fair wife, and she was always batting her eyelashes at him after church. Why, at the New Hope picnic she sat beside him at dinner and let him buy her lemonade and ice cream. She couldn't figure what he saw in the girl though. She always acted like a scared rabbit.

But when he popped the question, she hemmed and hawed, said she was honored and all sorts of nonsense but wanted to move to town and try city life.

He moped around then started sparking a flashy, hard-looking woman in the next county over. Her folks were kinda trashy, and she looked like she'd had plenty of hard knocks. But James took a shine to her and courted her awhile.

She coulda told him right off the bat that'd never pan out. The woman was most likely meaner than a snake when you got to know her. Good thing she turned him down flat after he brought her over for Sunday dinner.

Now Molly sat there cutting her eggs into little bites and eating 'em like nothing had happened. Acted like she'd forgotten she'd been careless enough to lose a diamond in that filthy barn. But it wouldn't do a lick of good to ask her how she coulda done it. She'd have some smart-aleck excuse.

Her mind seemed stuck on James and that diamond, like the day he charged in real excited, saying Molly had consented to be his wife.

She glared at Molly—leaving all that good ham sitting on her plate—and felt like wringing her neck. What a wastrel.

Back then she'd told herself that Molly was just funning him and, sure enough, after a couple of days there came a letter. She'd had second thoughts and was sending his ring back.

She buttered a biscuit and filled it with fig preserves.

James's heart near 'bout broke. Looked like one of the mules had kicked him in the face. Then he musta decided he just wasn't gonna take no for an answer, because he started paying her all kinds of attention. Courted her for quite a spell, then brought her home on a Saturday afternoon and said they'd tied the knot. Coulda knocked her over with a cotton boll.

Hmm. These preserves sure had turned out good.

Molly'd been all dressed up in a frilly white outfit, with matching kid-leather shoes cut to show her ankles. And wearing real silk stockings! Great Scott. She didn't look fit for anything but sitting around all day drinking tea and playing the piano. And that's exactly what she'd do if she had her way.

She sopped her third biscuit in the egg yolk left on her plate. She didn't feel quite so queasy now.

At least she'd taught Molly to milk old Nellie, and they seemed to get along fine. But look what came of that. Now she had to go help her hunt that diamond. Molly would never find it by herself.

Law. She was just about at the end of her rope.

CHAPTER FOUR

D amn horseshoe nails. They ought to outlaw horses from main roads." Jaq studied her right front tire. "Flatter than this river bottom. Glad I brought some of my brother's old clothes to wear."

She gazed up and down the hard-packed highway near the banks of the Cane River. "Doesn't look like anyone will rescue us, so I better fix this. How about getting my tool kit out of the back."

She was sweating after she jacked up the car and wrestled the tire off, but it felt good to get some exercise for a change.

"Say, I've never known a woman who could do that," Eric said.

She straightened up and wiped her forehead with her shirtsleeve. At least he had the grace to praise her. "My brothers taught me. Came in handy driving an ambulance." She ripped the tube out of the tire and inserted a new one. "I'll patch this old tube when we reach New Hope. No sense wasting daylight now."

Fifteen minutes later they leaned against the front fender and gazed at the huge fields. "Those are pecan trees on this side of the road," Eric said, "and cotton fields on that side, in case you didn't know."

She shrugged and pulled a small packet of cigarettes from her front pocket, then tapped one out. She needed a break. "Want a cigarette?"

"One of yours? Nah." He jerked out his own pack and held it up. "Real men smoke Lucky Strikes. Couldn't have made it through the War without them."

Spoken like a typical man, she thought. "Who changed that tire?"

He grinned. "A real woman, I suppose, even if you do wear men's clothes. They've been okay so far. Fooled the drummers and whiskey salesmen at the hotels. I bet those guys would have pestered a looker like you, even with me beside you."

He gave her an appreciative glance. "But you need to start wearing a dress tomorrow. I've already told my aunt and uncle in Logansport that we're married. Besides, it's just fifty miles on to New Hope the next day. You'll have to be Jacqueline instead of Jaq when we get there."

She nodded. The cigarette was loosening her tight muscles, pepping her up. Cigarettes had been her best friend last summer when she returned from a late-night run. After picking up wounded soldiers near the front lines and delivering them to the care stations out of enemy range, she'd needed a boost.

"A drink would taste good about now," she said. She was ready to reach the hotel and have a decent meal.

"We've got half a bottle of Kentucky bourbon left, and plenty more where that came from. We're set if we have to stay in New Hope longer than we planned."

"Heaven forbid." He produced the bottle like a magician, and she took a swig from it. "Ah, that's better. Well, we better get this show on the road. I want to hit Natchitoches before dark."

As they pushed on over the rough highway, she said, "Willie told me a few things about this area. She's quite literary, you know. Supposedly Harriet Beecher Stowe modeled Simon Legree on someone from around here. And Kate Chopin lived nearby for a while."

Eric looked down at his fingernails. "Even I know Simon Legree. But who's Kate Chopin?"

"The author of a scandalous novel called *The Awakening*."

He seemed skeptical. "I never read novels. What made it scandalous?"

"She showed that women experience passion."

"That's nothing new." Eric ran a hand through his blond hair, then lit another Lucky Strike. "I've caused a lot of women to feel passion."

"Uh-huh. Chopin gives the inside story of an unhappy marriage. Her book's about the wife of a New Orleans businessman and her torrid affair with a younger man. I hate the ending."

"She goes back to her husband?"

"She commits suicide. I wanted her to meet the woman of her dreams and live happily ever after."

Eric snickered. "You're a romantic. Never going to happen. What else did Willie tell you?"

"Just that a freed slave inherited her former master's entire plantation near here. He'd fathered a lot of her children, and one of their sons ended up with the place."

"A colored woman and her half-breed offspring owning a big plantation? That's where I draw the line." Eric took a big drink from the bottle. "Coloreds need to know their place and stay there."

Her spine stiffened. "What about Willie?"

"What about her?"

"She's an octoroon and used to own one of the biggest houses in Storyville."

"She's just a whore. She doesn't count."

"A lot of the high-society women in New Orleans used to send scouts to see what she was wearing so they could get in on the latest fashions. She counted to *them*."

"Fashions? Huh. They're silly." Eric picked a piece of tobacco off his tongue and flicked it out the window.

"Is driving four hundred miles and changing a flat tire silly?"

"No." He stared straight ahead.

"Is driving an ambulance in France silly?"

"No."

"Is agitating for women's right to vote silly? You know I picketed in Washington this past fall before I went home."

One side of Eric's mouth twitched. "I don't doubt that. And most men *really* think that's silly."

"Are you like most men?"

He faced her, his expression serious. "In some ways I am. Being away from home all these years has made me a little more open-minded, but I'm still a country boy at heart."

"Well, I hope your heart isn't too country. If it is, you may have to stay in New Hope by yourself."

"What about that annulment?"

"You wouldn't—"

He held up his hands. "I'll give it to you. Let's go get Pop settled. Then we'll drive back to New Orleans before it rains so hard we can't make it."

"I'll hold you to that." She hoped she didn't regret this little adventure.

❖

Molly pulled on her heavy work gloves. If she jammed one of her hands into an old board with a nail in it under all this mess on the barn's dirt floor, she might not be able to play for church Sunday. She couldn't bear to miss accompanying the special trio she'd been coaching since Christmas.

The manure-coated hay almost gagged her, especially after Mother Russell had glared at her throughout breakfast. If Patrick hadn't chirped like a cricket during the entire meal, it would have seemed like a funeral.

She had tried to ignore Mother Russell's hateful glances and forced herself to eat a few bites of egg and biscuit. She'd tried a little ham, but it almost gagged her. She could still hear that poor pig squeal and see the blood on Mother Russell's and Mr. James's clothes when they slaughtered it last fall.

Her stomach felt even more upset now, and she didn't know where to start looking for the diamond. It could be anywhere, especially since Mr. James hadn't cleaned up his mess after he shucked dried corn for the horses yesterday.

After what seemed like hours, Mother Russell spoke up. "Did you notice any chickens in here while you were milking?" She was down on her hands and knees brushing hay and cornhusks every which way.

The dust tickled Molly's nose and she sneezed. She wished she could be inside practicing the piano. "No. I was too busy trying to pacify Nellie."

"Judging by these droppings, they were in here not long ago. If I'm right, one of 'em decided to have a big diamond for breakfast while we were inside eating her eggs." Mother Russell looked disgusted. "I can't find a thing with all this mess on the floor. I bet my right arm a chicken ate it."

She should feel more upset than she did. What was wrong with her? After all, Mr. James paid a lot for that ring and acted so proud of it when he slipped it on her finger, both times. At first she'd been excited because she wouldn't be an old maid. She'd been old—almost twenty-three—and a lot of her college friends had been married for years and had housefuls of children.

Before she'd met him, she'd been majoring in music at a Methodist university near Austin. Being a preacher's daughter, she could go almost for free. But after three years at the university she couldn't ignore the facts any longer. Her parents were struggling financially. She had to get a job and support herself, not selfishly rely on them to buy her clothes and let her become even more cultured.

"Mother Russell, I don't think we'll find my diamond. We've searched high and low. It's just not here."

She hoped she'd convinced Mother Russell that losing the ring had upset her. But the longer she looked and didn't find it, the better she felt.

How strange. When she'd told Mr. James she'd changed her mind about marrying him, she'd felt a little like this. Lighter. Relieved. But he wouldn't listen when she'd tried to explain her reasons.

Mother Russell gave her such a disgusted glance she scooted over to another dark corner, hoping to catch a telltale glimmer.

"Molly, you're not even looking. Pshaw, gal, don't you even care about losing the most valuable thing you've ever owned?" She spat on the dirt floor. "I'll be right back. Got to go feed the chickens. Look sharp while I'm gone. We're wasting time. There's a heap of ironing waiting, with your name on it, and then you've got to get to churning. We're near 'bout out of butter."

Something cracked inside Molly, like an eggshell breaking, and new thoughts began to ooze from it. Half-heartedly searching the ground, she brushed a cow patty, then examined the brown streak of manure on her glove. A diamond wasn't her most valuable possession. There, that was part of how she'd felt when she'd rejected Mr. James's proposal.

She sat down on her milking stool and let a new idea form. Her own self-respect was worth a lot more than the diamond.

She stood and stripped off her spoiled glove. She'd lost her regard for herself the day she'd given in and told him she'd take his ring back. She hugged her realization close. He'd kept pressuring her and she'd simply gotten tired of saying no. What a coward she'd been.

She straightened her wrinkled skirt and walked toward the house. But he'd made their future sound so promising—a little house of their own and her very own piano. On their wedding day he'd said, "As soon as we can, Miss Molly, we'll move into a place in town."

Granted, she had her piano and enjoyed her music activities in the community, but they were still living here on this huge farm with Mother Russell, and she was afraid they were here to stay. She didn't know how much longer she could stand it.

A brand-new feeling bubbled up inside her. It smelled nothing like manure and felt nothing like the filthy ground in a barn. Multicolored, it gleamed like a rainbow after a storm. She stopped in the backyard and gazed at the bright blue sky and the greening trees.

She needed to quit regretting the past and make the best of a bad situation. Crawling around in the barn looking for a diamond she didn't even want certainly wasn't making her feel any better about herself and the mistake she'd made.

Almost lighthearted, she hurried into the kitchen and stirred the coals from the fire they'd used to cook breakfast and added some wood. Then she set two flatirons on the stove to heat. She'd finish her chores in record time so she could spend the afternoon playing her piano.

She should have lost that diamond a long time ago. Mr. James hadn't even bought the ring for her in the first place.

CHAPTER FIVE

Molly sat as straight as a pin while she played the opening hymn for the Easter Sunday service. She half listened to the congregation but paid close attention to the handful of talented youngsters she'd coached all year.

All of a sudden she detected a new sound—a trained, rich alto. Where had it come from?

She caught herself. She'd missed a note. She shook herself and concentrated on the worn black-and-white keys.

While waiting to play the next hymn, she glanced over her right shoulder. Some people who never entered the church during the rest of the year always showed up on Easter. Once-a-year Christians, her papa called them. She scanned the worshippers dressed in their Sunday best and spotted a stranger three rows back, sitting next to Eric McCade.

She tried not to gape. There she sat, a canary among crows, and her black eyes danced as she stared at her.

She must be Eric's new wife. What were they doing in New Hope? A woman that stylish belonged in New York or London, not here. They were probably just visiting and wouldn't stay long.

When the preacher finally finished his opening prayer, the woman quickly blessed herself, the way Catholics did. She'd heard they worshipped statues and had a priest talk to God for them, though maybe that wasn't so strange. She used music instead of words to pray.

Then it was time for the anthem, and she held her breath while her three young singers grouped together in front of the piano. Even while she sat there and directed them, she was aware of the stranger. She accompanied the group softly, trying not to drown them out but to highlight their voices, gratified when they finished without a bobble. Relieved that the performance was over and had been a success, at least in her eyes, she sighed. Now she could start planning the Christmas program.

Unfortunately, only the young people's parents paid much attention to their offering. Mother Russell looked as if she was far away and hadn't heard a note, and most of the others looked bored. Even Mr. James seemed half asleep, though Patrick gazed at her with admiration.

The preacher kept glancing at the newcomer, obviously distracted. And some of the women in the congregation looked upset. She wished they'd pay that much attention to her music. Didn't anyone appreciate how difficult her job was? What would they do if she pushed the preacher aside and shouted that music was just as important as the sermon or the prayers?

Oddly, the woman in yellow had seemed to really listen to her protégés' anthem. Her obvious appreciation made the long hours of rehearsal for this special Sunday more worthwhile, somehow.

Her excitement over the musical event subsided and she relaxed a fraction. After the interminable sermon she would have to play her least favorite Easter hymn, "The Old Rugged Cross," so slow and dreary. Right now she felt like dozing off, but she glanced furtively at the visitor.

Her straight black hair, cut scandalously short, hung right below her ears, and thick bangs brushed the top of her eyebrows.

Why were she and Eric here, and what did Mother Russell think about her and her hair, on Easter Sunday of all days?

Not that she cared. She liked it.

Before the service began, Mrs. Russell swiveled around in her pew and spotted the stranger. "Hannah," she murmured to her daughter, who lived down the road from her and James. "Looks like Eric McCade's brought his new wife home for a visit."

Hannah shielded her mouth. "She better watch out. All the men are staring at her with their tongues hanging out, and their wives look ready to murder her."

Slim pickings, she thought. The good ones had run away to war, including her youngest, Clyde. Sure glad James was too old to go.

She sat there in the front row between James and Hannah, pleating and unpleating the stiff serge of her newest long black skirt. Had to look her best on Easter Sunday, especially since the preacher was coming to dinner.

"Did you ever see the likes? Eric married him a doozy." She whispered so nobody but Hannah could hear her.

Hannah held her hand before her mouth again. "That cropped-off hair's disgraceful."

She nodded and took a deep breath, aiming to mind her own business.

Who'd have thought she'd ever be seventy years old and live to see Calvin and all but three of their eight children in their graves? Still in all, her life had been a real honest-to-goodness adventure.

But Lord have mercy, she was worn out. Why, thirty years ago she could be up near all night tending a neighbor with malaria or helping his wife birth a child. Then the next morning she'd jump out of bed before the rooster crowed and roust the farmhands. Most of 'em lazy as sin, but after her kids either died or married and farmed their own spreads, she had to rely on hired help.

If only Calvin hadn't passed away so young—not that long after they'd settled in Texas. But thank God James had stayed with her all these years.

Damn Yankees! If it hadn't been for them she might be back in the lap of luxury in Georgia instead of pioneering here in East Texas. If the South had won the War, like they should've, she'd definitely be in high cotton right now instead of sitting here all worn out and not getting any younger.

She'd climbed out of bed this morning at first light, like always. By the time that lay-a-bed Molly even thought about stirring, she'd made dressing to go with one of their old roosters she'd boiled all yesterday afternoon.

While Molly finally milked the cow, she'd fixed a big breakfast for the four of them. Then she'd cooked four different side dishes to go with the chicken and dressing for Sunday dinner. Even made a chocolate pie.

What was she gonna do in her old age? Molly couldn't even produce but one grandchild to help around the place.

She squirmed in her pew and shooed a fly away from her nose. She'd spent her life buying up acreage and building her place to be one of the best in the county. But it still took hard work to keep it up, and James had to choose an unfit wife.

Lord have mercy. He'd have done better to pick that short-haired creature in the yellow dress. At least she looked like she had some get-up-and-go.

❖

Jesus H. Christ! What had she gotten herself into?

The farm wives around Jaq glared at her as she sat on the rough bench in the third row of the strange little church. She couldn't help it if their husbands had given her the eye when she and Eric walked in.

She drummed her fingers for a while. Then she elbowed Eric and tilted her head at the preacher, whose eyes were burning at her from behind the pulpit. "What's his problem?" she whispered, but Eric just shrugged.

The preacher rose and read the scripture for the day, still looking at her more than anybody else. Most men were so obvious. In New Orleans and Washington and London, strange guys had stopped on the street and gawked at her.

She'd cut her hair, damn it, so they wouldn't pay attention to her. And she was taller than a lot of them. She'd thought that'd help. Hell. They kept right on.

It was worse in France and Belgium, even with her wearing bloody khaki and being near the front lines. She'd kept a big wrench next to her cot, though she'd never expected to use it. She deserved better after hauling their broken bodies away from the trenches.

The soldiers would yell, "Hey, Jaq, get your ass over here. It's about time you showed up." Some of them treated her like one of the boys—when they were too shot up to walk. But even then they flirted with her.

Being in Europe wasn't all it was cracked up to be. Dodging bombs and watching men die. Scratching lice. Didn't take her long to figure things out. After several months, she'd wanted out, back home to the States. Killing Henry, even if it had been an accident, was the last straw. But she never thought she'd end up here.

She glanced at Eric, who seemed a million miles away. Good thing she was wearing kid gloves or she'd stick a splinter in one of her drumming fingers. She needed to find something to distract her.

She noticed the Easter lilies, dogwood, and fern sitting in front of the pulpit, but she couldn't get her mind off the damn war. When she had to stay still like this, everything she saw reminded her of it.

The sermon bored her. Why had she let Eric talk her into coming?

She glanced at the people sitting nearby. Everybody looked so rigid and wooden, so suspicious and unfriendly. Then she noticed the redhead playing hymns on a battered upright piano.

Suddenly she remembered standing beside her ambulance in France on a cool, clear night last summer. The smoke and noise from the distant artillery had finally subsided, and she'd welcomed the silence. She'd stood there long enough to finish a cigarette and gaze at the stars that penetrated the haze. That was one of the only moments during her stay in wartime Europe when she'd felt at peace.

Why had this country pianist made her remember that moment?

She stared at the woman's long fingers. They appeared elegant and capable, and she stroked the keys like she was making love to them. Pressing gently yet firmly, she seemed to know what each key was capable of and to be able to tease every ounce of beauty from it. And she didn't even act like she was aware of her own ability.

The pianist sat up straight on the hard bench yet didn't seem rigid like the other women in the congregation. She moved her arms and hands fluidly and swayed gently with the music as she played. How wonderful it would be for those hands to touch her shoulder, slide down her arm then around her waist, pull her close, engulf them in a music that sounded more like a hymn to human love than one that praised a God who let innocent men and women die in a senseless war.

The woman's obvious tenderness as she directed the trio of singers made a lump form in Jaq's throat. The pianist seemed to have taught them to express the pure emotion contained in each tone and word. Purity and innocence? Jaq's throat tightened. Those were myths, but this woman and her young charges made her almost believe they still existed.

She took a slow, deep breath, and her drumming fingers gradually slowed to match the rhythm of the song the young people performed. As their voices rang out clear and true, she once again saw Sister Mary Therese in the choir at the academy where she taught fine arts.

She'd been a schoolgirl there, with such a crush on Sister Mary, her favorite teacher. But she'd gotten over that and vowed to never again make such a fool of herself. Who was this woman who attracted her the way Sister Mary had?

Hmm. If Eric couldn't find some help for his father soon, she'd need something to distract her. Maybe she could get to know the pianist's story, but she sure wouldn't get involved with her in any way. She'd learned her lesson the hard way.

Chapter Six

During the sermon, Molly couldn't keep from peeking at the stranger more than she should have. Her distant expression, like a bubble around her, kept people at bay. They still stared, though, as if they'd never seen a beautiful woman, especially one who seemed so confident and sophisticated.

Mr. James sat next to Mother Russell as obediently as Patrick did. Had he noticed the newcomer? He was probably too busy imagining himself as Ajax fighting in the Trojan War or thinking about Boy Jim Harrison. He would rather read his two favorite books, Homer's *Iliad* and *Rodney Stone*, by A. Conan Doyle, than eat.

At forty-seven, Mr. James sometimes seemed Patrick's age; they both kowtowed to Mother Russell. But after a long day in the cotton fields, he often bowed his broad shoulders like an old man. And when he took off his straw hat, his hair was more gray than brown.

Slipping along in his wake, she would never be able to do any of the things she longed to. She was stuck in this isolated community with an aging husband and a mother-in-law who would live forever. Even without its diamond, her ring enslaved her like a manacle. Her unshed tears blurred the notes in front of her as she mechanically played the Easter favorite "Christ the Lord is Risen Today." If only she could experience resurrection—into a new life of freedom.

After the doxology she stole another glance at their visitor. The woman stared at her like a man would, as if she could see through her corset.

Her cheeks grew as hot as the farm kitchen on an August afternoon, and she tingled all over, like she'd heard a beautiful Mozart aria. Why would the stranger affect her that way?

She didn't know whether to frown or giggle, but thankfully she'd finished performing. Otherwise, the tremor in her fingers would most likely make her miss another note. And that simply wouldn't do. Everyone praised her flawless piano playing, which took long hours of practice to achieve. Her music had to be perfect, even if nothing else about her was, according to Mother Russell.

What did the newcomer think about this one-room church—and about her performance? Did the stranger consider her as much of a hick as she herself regarded some country people?

After the service, she pulled on her white cotton gloves and hurried across the church to Mr. James and his mother, who stood in the front pew chatting with the neighbors. On occasions like these, Mother Russell obviously fancied herself a queen holding court.

"Sure glad we got that shower yesterday, aren't you? The potatoes and onions need it bad."

"How many acres of cotton are you planning to plant this season?"

"Think the price of a bale will be any higher this year than last?"

She always tried to be pleasant to the women who flocked around Mother Russell, but they treated her with kind indifference, almost as if she were a simpleton. She didn't have anything to say about crops and the weather, and they didn't mention today's music.

She hovered on the fringes with Patrick and wished at least one of them would comment on her little trio's stellar performance instead of the price of cotton. She felt like throwing down a hymnal, anything to elicit a response, but she refused to give them the satisfaction of asking for their opinion.

As she and Patrick stood there, he gazed up at her with innocent blue eyes. "Mama, can I have a drumstick at dinner? The preacher ate both of them last time he came. He acts like his wife don't cook good."

"Say 'doesn't cook well,' Patrick. I'll try to save you one, but you know the preacher always gets the best pieces because he's company."

Eventually the Russell clan began to stroll toward the back of the church, and she smiled over Patrick's red hair at Mr. James. Then she clasped his arm briefly, though she knew he would escort Mother Russell up the aisle instead of her.

She'd tried to tell him several times how much this gesture humiliated her, but either he didn't understand or didn't listen. Or perhaps he didn't care. He would obviously rather upset her than his mother.

She walked as proudly as possible at the rear of the family procession, holding Patrick's hand as Mr. James and his mother led the way. If she couldn't leave, she would somehow make him recognize her as worthy of his respect someday, perhaps even his equal.

❖

Jaq tapped her foot as she stood near the church's front door. She wanted to examine the redhead up close and see if she was for real. Besides, Eric had run off to talk to his admirers.

Everybody around here most likely still considered him the smartest, bravest, and most handsome man ever, especially the pretty girls. He hadn't lost his blond good looks and strong physique. However, he'd changed a lot since the last time they saw him. This war had cost him plenty.

She watched several couples emerge from the church, the women clutching their husbands' arms when they spotted her standing there alone. How could a woman fall for phony promises, give herself up to a power monger, and then spend the rest of her life worrying about some other woman taking away the man she'd sold herself to?

Thank God she'd come to her senses. She'd been almost as blind as these local women obviously were.

Last year in London Eric had said, "Jaq, marry me and we'll travel everywhere you want to go—Egypt, Russia, India, Japan. Anywhere. We'll always have each other to lean on."

He must have realized how much she loved adventure. For once she'd appreciated her pretty face, because it could have helped her do some of the things she'd always dreamed about.

But she should've known better than to marry him. They'd gotten caught up in all the wartime excitement.

Their first night together—what a disaster. She'd tried and he'd tried, but they just didn't fit. She'd made sure that night was their last.

After the gin wore off, she couldn't fool herself—or him. She'd had to level with him. "Eric," she'd said, as they lay in bed smoking, "I thought things might be different with you, but I don't feel anything when a man touches me. You don't repulse me, like most men do. But I had an experience with a woman when I was a teener and loved the way she felt. I hoped I'd outgrow it, but I haven't."

She thought of Willie and all their nights together. Nope, she hadn't outgrown it.

For a minute Eric had looked hurt, like she'd kicked him in the crotch. Then he took a drag and winked. "We'll keep that to ourselves. No harm done." He'd obviously never had any trouble persuading a woman to share his bunk.

"When this war's over and we can spend more time together," he'd said, "I bet I can convince you to like men more than you think you do."

That hadn't set too well. He didn't know what a hard sell he had in store.

They'd spent the last few days of his leave in the pubs. Someone would yell, "Hey, Eric. Let me buy you a drink." So he let them, again and again. He and she didn't waste a second worrying about the future. The days flew by, and the next thing she knew, he'd flown away.

They'd lost touch except for a few letters. When he showed up in New Orleans, the black patch over one of his clear blue eyes almost made her cry. He'd probably never fly solo again, though his eye might heal in time. And maybe he wouldn't always have to depend so much on a cane.

She'd had to do something decent for a change, help him straighten out his life. Then maybe she'd do the same for herself.

CHAPTER SEVEN

Jaq's kid gloves were coming in handy again. The preacher—he was about her age but acted like he was fourteen—wouldn't let go of her hand or stop chattering. "We're so glad you and Eric attended our Easter service, Miss Jacqueline," he said. "I'm so sorry about what happened to him overseas…"

Would he ever shut up?

He had to think she was an idiot. His words were a smoke screen for the hand almost caressing hers. And his sweating palm had made her black glove slippery. Ugh. She couldn't stand for anyone, especially a man like him, to touch her.

She was about to jerk her hand away from the salivating preacher and go find Eric when an unusual couple marched out the front door. He was tall—at least six feet—the older woman beside him only a few inches shorter. Long black skirt, starched white blouse, and thundercloud-gray hair yanked hard into a tight knot. A black straw hat topped her head.

The minister squeezed Jaq's hand one last time and dropped it when the haughty woman stared at him. She'd patted her weathered face white with rice powder, and her sharp eyes and large ears probably didn't miss a thing. The diagonal gashes in her long earlobes indicated that she'd once worn heavy earrings. Maybe she'd been beautiful back then and thought she still was.

Jaq had seen the queen in a royal parade in London—head high and spine straight, with an air of superiority. This woman must have been her understudy.

Finally, the pianist appeared, meandering after a small group of women and children in the older couple's wake and guiding a boy of about seven. Was she the old woman's lady-in-waiting? Their daughter? A distant cousin? The preacher's sweaty palm had made her even more cynical than usual, and she kept up her guessing game partially to get her mind off him.

But the little boy, plus the cut and fashion of the woman's simple dress, indicated that the young woman was a wife and a mother. She recognized the look. Damn. What a shame.

This woman's clear green eyes drew her in, pulled her nearer, and made her want to dive into them, like Sister Mary's did.

And like Willie's arms did. From the sacred to the profane. She should be ashamed of herself, but she wasn't.

The pianist and the boy stood to the side while the rest of the congregation fluttered around the puzzling older couple. Surely the old woman wasn't married to the younger man. He had to be the husband of the red-haired pianist, though he looked at least twenty years her senior. And the child most likely belonged to them. Damn it again.

"Mrs. Jacqueline McCade, may I present Mrs. James Calvin Russell," the preacher said. "And this is her son, Mr. James."

She stood her ground and pasted on her social smile. Her mother and the nuns had made sure she had an airtight one. She extended her hand as graciously as she could manage—first to the regal woman, then to her escort.

She hoped the preacher hadn't made her gloves too slick. It wasn't good manners to greet royalty with slimy hands.

Mrs. Russell couldn't keep from bristling as she held out her hand to the stranger. Lordy, so this was Angus McCade's new daughter-in-law? He was as unlucky as she was.

She looked kinda like a boy—a wild one, to boot. Those black eyes seared right through you and dragged you in at the same time. Probably made men want to tame her. Well, Eric was the right one for that job.

Her mind was spinning, but she forced herself to smile. In her position she had to keep up appearances.

Though she hated to admit it, Eric's wife was as handsome as he was, him with his blue eyes and her with those dark ones.

Straightening her hat, she let her inner conversation run its course. Wonder what brought Eric back from the War before it was over. That patch over his eye, most likely, and that bad limp. Losing his ma had to have upset him something terrible too. She always did anything he asked and didn't make any bones about him being her favorite. And him not even at her funeral last month. Now all of a sudden he turned up, with a wife. Men nowadays didn't have much sense when it came to choosing a helpmeet.

Something didn't add up. Why wasn't Eric standing here beside her, instead of loitering in the parking lot flirting with those pretty girls? He was behaving like he did before he ran away to race automobiles, then off to the War. Why, he used to act like he thought he was a prince, and nobody disillusioned him.

At least he could come speak to James, who'd put him on a pedestal since he was a youngster. Always called him Ajax and Boy Jim, after some characters he admired in those infernal books he always had his nose stuck in.

She finally quit her woolgathering and paid attention to the newcomer, who shook her hand like she was doing her a favor. "Mrs. McCade," she said. "We're right glad to have you in our little community here at New Hope."

The hussy pulled back her damp hand like a chicken had pecked it and seemed to begrudge every word she spoke. "Thank you, Mrs. Russell. This is a quaint part of the world."

Quaint. My stars and garters. She was the quaint one. Fact of the matter, she was downright queer. "Angus has been bragging that his boy married some pretty little French girl from New Orleans. We didn't think we'd ever lay eyes on you, a well-traveled city girl and all. Why in the world did you and Eric decide to head back to New Hope?"

Again, Eric's wife acted like she'd rather eat mud than carry on a polite conversation. But she managed to sidestep the question with some nonsense and make her feel like a fool for asking.

Fed up, she slipped away and found somebody who'd treat her with the respect she deserved. She couldn't keep from glancing at the outrageous young woman's stomach though, as she passed.

No, she wasn't in the family way yet. She was tall and looked healthy, but her hips were too slim for bearing children, and she was no more fit for farm life than Molly. She had things all backward with her sheared-off hair, short skirt that showed half her calf, and those long bangs.

That girl was an ill wind, as James would say. She shuddered like somebody had just walked over her grave.

❖

Molly and Patrick strolled out the front door of the white frame church and stopped. The new woman stood talking to Mr. James, Mother Russell, and the preacher as if she considered herself their equal. She appeared so self-assured—shoulders thrown back and a faint sneer playing over her red lips. She'd obviously sized up the situation and found no one to measure up to her standards.

But her cheeks weren't as rosy as they should have been. And her lips never blossomed into the type of smile a woman of her age and beauty should possess. Her kohl-circled eyes glinted, as hard as flint.

Molly eased closer. The woman's world-weary expression made her seem older than Molly's own thirty-one years, but she appeared to be only in her mid-twenties. Molly had an urge to touch her cheek, which seemed almost as smooth as Patrick's.

"Come meet your new neighbor, Miss Molly. May I present Eric McCade's pulchritudinous new wife," Mr. James said, trying out a word he'd most likely discovered in a Sherlock Holmes novel. Molly thought he sounded ridiculous.

"Miss Jacqueline, this is my child bride, Miss Molly Lee. She's always ready to help out here at church with the music. Or drive the buggy to somebody's house to give a piano lesson. But she does her share of the chores, and then some. Ma and I can't complain, can we, Ma?"

Mr. James looked at his mother as if for approval, but she kept her back to him. Molly knew she wouldn't agree even if she'd been paying attention.

Grasping Jacqueline's gloved hand, she said, "Welcome to New Hope."

"It's a pleasure to meet you."

"It'll be good to have someone near my age to catch me up on what's happening in the outside world. We live just a few miles from you, so you'll have to visit often."

As she spoke to her new neighbor, she noticed the slightest glimmer of light in her flinty eyes, as though something metal had struck them and caused a spark. But it disappeared so quickly she feared she'd imagined it.

"You've done wonders with that trio," Jacqueline said. "Their voices blend beautifully."

"Thank you for the kind words." She felt taller and held her head a bit higher.

But when she glanced at Mr. James and his mother, she shrank again and lowered her gaze. *Oh, I want to spend more time with her,* she thought. *I like the way she makes me feel.*

The preacher was shifting from one foot to the other. "Mrs. Russell," he said when she returned to their little group, "don't you think it'd be right neighborly to invite Eric and his new wife to partake of one of your delicious Sunday dinners?"

Mother Russell straightened her shoulders. "Sir, since you eat so much every time you dine with us, I doubt we'd have enough to feed even one extra mouth this Sunday. Maybe next quarter, when you come preach for us again."

Then she turned to the newcomer. "Come calling when you feel sociable." She frowned and glanced at their buggy. The preacher eyed her apologetically and simpered toward Jacqueline.

"Thank you," Jacqueline said readily. "Eric and I need to get home to his father."

Without another word, the vision in yellow strode with soldierly purpose to her black Model T, started it with one strong hand-crank, and raced off down the red-dirt road.

If only she were riding beside her.

CHAPTER EIGHT

Eric limped over and climbed into the Model T. He slammed the door as Jaq took off. "Gee, thanks for almost leaving me. Did you forget you had a husband?" He was breathing hard.

"I wish I could," she muttered. "And thanks for deserting me. Do you think I enjoyed talking to that horny preacher and the Russell clan?"

"At least Molly's young and pretty."

"Granted. And a lot more married than I am. She has a little boy, if you didn't notice."

"Oh yeah. Too bad. You could probably seduce her if she didn't. I saw the way you stared at her during church. And the subtle way she looked you over."

"Don't be ridiculous. What about you and all those beauties? I thought you wanted to see your old friends. Those girls were probably babies when you left New Hope."

He lit a cigarette and blew smoke at her. "Not quite. Didn't you notice how everybody looked at me when I hobbled into church? Years ago, before I left, they acted like I was Jesus at the Second Coming. Today they couldn't keep their eyes off my eye patch and my cane."

She gripped his arm a second, concerned. "They were surprised, that's all. I'm sure they still consider you their best and brightest."

"At least those girls do. To all the others I'm spoiled goods. The guy who had to leave the War. A dud, not a hero."

She sped through a green tunnel of newly leafed trees. Unpainted shacks and a few white two-story houses dotted this dense forest, with cattle and new-plowed fields nearby. She needed to distract Eric, shake some sense into him. They had to take care of his father's situation so they could head back to New Orleans. "Say, is this where some of those people at church live?"

He didn't even glance at her or the buildings. "Yeah."

Red-orange earth the color of clay flowerpots stretched out, just waiting to turn green. Eric's father, Angus, had explained how farmers with their teams of mules plowed the weeds under when it dried up enough in the spring. That was better than tanks destroying anything that grew. It was quiet and beautiful here, and obviously fertile, like Molly.

Where had that thought come from? Why had Eric mentioned seducing her? Did he know something she didn't? What kind of person did he think she was?

The huge trees—pines—along the edges of those fields had deep roots, Eric's dad had said. She needed more of those but didn't want to be immovable, like the people around here seemed to be. All except Molly, with her lilting voice.

Eric finished one cigarette and lit another. If he kept acting like this, she'd drive back to New Orleans by herself. But now Mother knew she was married and wouldn't let her rest until she either got unmarried or lived with her so-called husband.

"Damn. This road's rough."

"Yeah, pretty bad."

"These ruts and puddles remind me of all that mud near Passchendaele last summer."

Eric finally showed some interest. "I remember. It rained for three months. I was stationed near there, and it grounded us for days. We sat around itching to fly. Every time it cleared for a few minutes, we took off."

"Where we were, the tanks mired down, clay stuck to everything, and some of our men and animals drowned in the bombed-out craters filled with water. Driving an ambulance in that hellhole was a bitch, especially in the middle of the night."

Eric looked at her with respect. "Luckily, I missed that. Being an ace has its advantages." His eye took on a faraway expression.

"Yep." She nodded, still mired in the past. After her patriotism had worn off, she'd stuck around France because she'd thought she might bump into Helen. God, she missed her—and the excitement of war. She missed Willie too.

Even though she'd just gotten here, it was so God-awful quiet she wanted to scream. She didn't miss the whine of the shells before they exploded, or the wounded men screaming for relief. And she didn't miss living each minute waiting for her next voice lesson with Sister Mary. She ought to relax and enjoy the silence.

She tried to rouse Eric. "That Mrs. Russell sure is a powerhouse," she said. "Bet she'd give the kaiser or the president a run for his money. We should make her a general and put her in charge of all our armies. We'd lick the bloody Boches in a week."

He just grunted, so she decided to ignore him.

Mr. James seemed nice enough, with good taste in women, but he was a mama's boy. And why had he volunteered all that information about Molly's love of music in such a condescending way? Wasn't he proud of her talent?

Molly seemed fragile and sweet. Was she as straitlaced as Sister Mary? That long red curl escaping from her mound of hair, and those soft green eyes...Similar to yet so different from Willie's. She'd probably be a great kisser. It'd be interesting to find out.

No doubt Mrs. Russell kept her on duty around the clock. How did Molly get trapped in that situation?

She glanced at Eric, who didn't look like he'd be much fun while they were here. So Molly wanted to be friends? Hmm. Might be enjoyable.

By God, she could even endure Molly's mother-in-law for the opportunity to spend some time with her—maybe.

After the pitiful dinner Jaq had scraped up for Eric and Angus, with their help, she sat in the front-porch swing and smoked. Slow footsteps sounded inside, and she stubbed out her cigarette and dropped it into an old Coke bottle. She was waving smoke away as Angus eased through the front door. He dropped into a rocker and just sat there awhile before he looked at her.

His thinning hair must have been the color of Eric's once. And he was about Eric's height, but he moved hesitantly.

"Eric's taking a nap," he said abruptly, as if his throat was rusty.

"Yes, I suspect he needs to take a lot of them." She didn't know what else to say.

After a long silence, he gazed at her as if just realizing she was there. "I surely do appreciate you looking after both of us."

She murmured something polite, but he dismissed it with a wave.

"No, I really mean it. I'm in a tight spot right now, but I'll get back on my feet. Eric will too. You're a kind lady to help us out like this."

She started to remind him that she was Eric's wife but wasn't sure what Eric had told him. And he was obviously no fool. They didn't act anything like a happily married couple.

She and Angus sat there a while longer in silence until he said, "Well, I best go rest a mite too. Eric and I need to go see a man about some land later. You try to find something to occupy yourself, you hear? Don't want you to be too lonesome while you're here. Go visit somebody you met at church this morning. That Molly Russell is about the nicest one around."

What a dear man, she thought as he went inside. *Worrying about me being lonely, when he must be grieving his heart out for his wife and boys.*

She tapped another cigarette from her pack. At this rate, she'd run out in a week, and then what would she do? As she sat there and smoked, Eric's earlier remark about seducing Molly began to buzz around her head like a fly. Why were Eric and Angus both pointing her in Molly's direction? Did they think she'd treat Molly the same way Sister Mary had treated her?

Suddenly an image of Sister Mary Therese pulled her into the past, though she'd rather not visit it again. Why keep torturing herself?

Sister Mary sat next to her on a concrete bench in the convent garden, spring flowers blooming yellow and blue. Eighteen, she'd noticed only how Sister Mary's hair and eyes outshone the flowers. "I'm glad you decided to stop skipping school this year," Sister Mary had said.

"Yeah. Mother is too. You must be a good influence." She had promised her mother not to miss any more classes in exchange for taking singing lessons from Sister Mary.

She recalled almost bloodying her fingers when she pressed them into the rough concrete to keep from edging them toward Sister Mary's thigh. "But I do miss spending all day in the French Quarter and Storyville listening to music and taking pictures. Would you like to see my favorite of all the ones I've taken?"

Riffling through the photographs she'd pulled from between the pages of one of her textbooks, she selected one of a dark-haired prostitute wearing an almost-transparent black dress. "What do you think?"

Sister Mary had paled but had questioned her about it. She'd even called it a work of art, which thrilled her. She also remembered exactly how she'd sighed in relief. Any of the other nuns would have ripped the photo to shreds and reported her to the mother superior.

Her legs had burned when she'd looked at the shot. She'd given the woman five dollars to pose for her, and as she and Sister Mary sat side by side and gazed at it, Sister Mary seemed to have trouble catching her breath. The area between her own legs definitely began to throb.

Eventually, Sister Mary said, "You're a fine student and have developed your voice quickly this year." She must have been trying to resume her role as teacher rather than peer.

She had thanked her and said, "You've influenced me more than you can imagine."

Then Sister Mary had beamed, and two of her blond curls slipped out from her wimple. And when Sister Mary patted her back and let her hand linger, she'd sat as still as possible, silently willing Sister Mary to never move it. It radiated heat and made the blood rush through her body so fast she could almost hear it. She began to sweat in spite of the cold concrete she sat on.

She had spent many precious minutes with Sister Mary that spring. Sister Mary's gentle, soothing touch on her arm or head made her dream about that touch every night and crave it constantly. And once when Sister Mary ran her hand over Jaq's cheek and whispered, "What a fine young woman you are. I'd love to have someone like you nearby all the time," she'd almost fainted. She'd treasured that remark and repeated it to herself every night before she went to sleep and every morning when she woke up. And she'd vowed never to wash her cheek.

Sister Mary began to touch her more and more often that spring, and her fingers lingered longer. Jaq had walked around in a daze, marking time when they were apart. Sister Mary was the center of her universe.

One day that April, she and her mother had a huge fight. "Jacqueline," she'd said, "this house is too small for you and me both. I hope you get married very soon and leave me in peace."

She'd run to Sister Mary's room at the academy and tapped on her door, wanting comfort.

"Jacqueline, what are you doing here? I can't let a student visit me." Then Sister Mary had seemed to reconsider. She'd glanced down the hall with a guilty expression, nodded at her to come in, and then closed the door quickly.

She sat in the only chair, and Sister Mary propped herself against her desk, fingering the cross that hung from her rosary. "What is it, *ma petite*? How can I help you?"

As she repeated Mother's words, her voice shook. Then she stopped and gazed at Sister Mary's strange expression.

As if in a trance, Sister Mary had slowly lifted her rosary over her head and laid it on the desk. She straightened the rosary, then restraightened it, looking far away, as if someone had taken possession of her body.

Jaq couldn't speak.

Trembling, Sister Mary had uncovered her head, dropping pieces of white linen at her feet. Her blond hair escaped, and Jaq stared, her hand moving as if in a dream toward Sister Mary's curls. Sister Mary caught it and held it tight. Oh, how thrilling her touch was as she slowly ran her other palm over Jaq's hair. Her scalp prickled under every strand Sister Mary smoothed. Sparks ignited inside her head and shot through her.

Sister Mary hesitated and Jaq had thought she was praying. Jaq was—praying the moment would never end.

Gradually, Sister Mary lowered her hand to Jaq's cheek and inched it around her neck. When she pulled, Jaq flowed toward her. Lost in that intense gaze, she almost liquefied. Sister Mary's soft lips brushed hers and an electric current jolted her, so strong it sizzled.

She hardly felt Sister Mary unbutton her white shirtwaist. God. She could barely breathe as her white cotton stockings, then her long black skirt, fell in a pile at her feet. When Sister Mary slid Jaq's underclothes off with trembling fingers, she grabbed the chair back to steady herself.

Dazed, she stood frozen while Sister Mary stripped off her own gartered stockings and slipped out of her black wool habit and rough underwear. Her white skin dazzled Jaq.

"Twin Eves before the Fall," Sister Mary whispered, but she couldn't process the words.

Suddenly, somehow, Sister Mary lay on the narrow bed in the small room under her, as if expecting something. What should she do? Sister Mary refused to kiss her lips, but when she eased down Sister Mary's body and kissed her ample breasts, Sister Mary seemed to relax. Jaq took them in her hands, gently squeezing then sucking them, and Sister Mary moaned.

Running her hands down Sister Mary's stomach and hips, she held a portion of perfect flesh, then showered it with kisses and moved to the next pleasurable expanse. She inched her way downward, growing ever more sure of her destination—Sister Mary's blond triangle.

It was everything she had seen in her photo, and more. She blew on it, and Sister Mary's hips twitched. She fingered her way through the silky thatch, and Sister Mary jerked. Finally, she thrust her tongue into the fragrant wilderness, and Sister Mary sighed and went still.

She tasted sweet-salty, and as Jaq licked, Sister Mary began to undulate, moving in rhythm with her tongue. She lapped up and down the sides of the hard knot beneath her tongue, then drew it into her mouth, sucking and biting it gently.

Sister Mary writhed and began to pant, and Jaq clung to her for a blissful eternity as Sister Mary wriggled beneath her. Suddenly, with one last upward thrust, Sister Mary shuddered and lay motionless.

Sister Mary's salty essence coated her face, and she felt content. She had apparently pleased her favorite person in the world.

But Sister Mary had jumped up, almost tossing her to the floor. Without a word, she jerked her habit on. Her hands shook as she helped Jaq button her crumpled blouse then shoved her from the room.

The next day at her private voice lesson, Sister Mary Therese had made it clear Jaq would never visit her again. She'd refused to touch her, even when they were alone. And during their final lessons Sister Mary had never looked at her. Worst of all, she wouldn't talk to Jaq except when necessary.

Fortunately, she graduated soon. All that summer, she'd dreamed about taking lessons from Sister Mary again. She walked by the school hoping to see her—even from across the campus. Most of all, she wanted to share Sister Mary's bed.

That fall her older sister asked her to live with her in London, and she'd welcomed the chance to be away from Mother and Sister Mary.

While visiting her aunts in Washington and New York, and then abroad, she'd weaned herself from her total obsession with Sister

Mary. She made herself forget her curls…her breasts…her taste, but the memories still intruded at the most unlikely times. They demanded her attention and drained her. Why couldn't she erase the recollections, rip them from her mind?

Damn it. She'd thought Willie had finally sated her longing for Sister Mary, but here it was again, making her twinge.

Chapter Nine

The preacher had polished off most of the chicken and dressing, and Mrs. Russell was resting on the front porch with the men. She hoped he wouldn't stay more than an hour or so because she needed to put on her old shoes and walk the place, like she did every Sunday. She had to decide what James needed to plow and plant this spring. If she didn't write out the weekly schedule, he'd fool around and forget to do something important. He never had got the hang of planning.

She spit off the side of the porch then wiped her mouth with a blue bandanna. Snuff calmed her down and gave her a lift at the same time.

Her front yard looked mighty fine. She swept it every day with a brush broom and pulled any sprig of grass or weed that dared stick its head up. She'd built her prized flower bed full of daffodils and jonquils out of an old wagon wheel. Had to keep the place looking good so the neighbors wouldn't talk. Her kids and grandkids used to climb the fence and splinter the railings, so she'd whittled the sharp pickets herself. She could see for miles, but her fence kept stray dogs and strangers out. Everybody admired her big house up on this hill.

She pulled a tin canister from her pocket, pinched out another dip of snuff, and spread it under her lower lip with an elm twig. Then she chewed the stick to keep it nice and soft.

Staring up at the big lazy clouds, she sighed. It sure was good to be here, safe in her white wooden house that James built from the ground up eighteen years ago. When he'd finished, he hung his carpenter's apron on a nail in the attic and wouldn't even hammer together a chicken coop now. Musta been a heap of work.

Compared to the log cabin she and Calvin built when they got here from Georgia, this was a mansion. To think she'd lived in that cabin for nigh on thirty years. Yes, sir, she couldn't imagine wanting a better place than this.

If only Calvin was here, rocking beside her. She could barely remember what his hand felt like on her cheek. Come to think of it, she'd trade her fine house for their log cabin quick as a wink if she could have him back.

The screen door squealed on its hinges, and Molly sashayed out. She belonged in the parlor, not on the porch. Always sticking her nose where it didn't belong.

"Patrick, it's time to do your schoolwork," she said. "You've been out here long enough."

"But, Mama, I want to stay. Please? I'm almost seven. The grownups always talk about interesting things. I won't bother them. Can't I just listen?"

"Maybe you could make an exception, Miss Molly," the preacher said.

"If you think it's all right, sir. Now, Patrick, you behave yourself." Molly hesitated, glanced at the empty porch swing, then left.

The next thing you knew, that dry stick would want to sit out here with them on a Sunday afternoon, she thought. Great day in the morning! Then she'd want to read the newspaper first. Not even James got such special treatment.

❖

Jaq sat in her idling Model T at the end of the Russells' driveway, trying to decide whether to motor on up to their house. Was she crazy? Why had she decided to drop in on them without a proper invitation? Well, Mrs. Russell had asked her to visit when she felt sociable.

After her conversation with Angus, she'd become restless and decided maybe she and Molly could have a quiet talk. She wanted to find out how much Molly actually resembled Sister Mary. Hopefully, the preacher had already left. He'd spent last night at the McCades' house and rambled on till nearly ten o'clock, but he hadn't just talked. He'd flirted with her in his indirect, sleazy way.

She'd thought Eric would set him straight, but he'd just sat there. He'd clammed up not long after they'd reached New Hope and he and Angus had talked awhile. Maybe he was missing his mother and his brothers, so she hadn't wanted to intrude. The preacher was harmless, yet he irritated her. Besides, his flirting showed disrespect for Eric, even if their marriage was bogus.

What if she got stuck with the man of God and Mrs. Russell all afternoon? Damn. It'd serve her right for dropping in on them, but that empty house was already driving her nuts.

Why was she sitting here trying to rake up enough nerve to chase Molly Russell? Hadn't she learned her lesson about unavailable women? It was bad enough to be in this out-of-the-way place. Maybe she should mind her own business, not get into trouble by pursuing Molly.

Eric and Angus would be hungry when they got home. She'd have to fix them something to eat—again. Maybe some leftover biscuits and lumpy gravy. Hell. They needed to find Angus a cook and a hired man, fast.

Oh well. What did she have to lose? She was a lost cause anyway, so she might as well do what she wanted to, instead of what other people thought she should. Maybe it'd keep her from being so damn bored, at least. Or maybe it'd keep her from remembering what happened in France.

The preacher reared back on two legs of the ladder-back chair. Mrs. Russell glared at him, and he straightened up.

"Mrs. Russell, Mr. James. I read in the Tyler paper yesterday that Mrs. Minnie Cunningham, that heads that gang of suffrage ladies down in Austin, has struck a deal with the governor. They're gonna let all the women in the state vote in the July primary. How do you like them apples?" He puffed up like he was telling them something they didn't know.

She'd been reading about some hussy named Alice Paul stirring up women all over the country. Got the ones that could already vote out West to set themselves against the Democrats a couple years back and had been nearly driving President Wilson crazy since then. Humph.

Why, the President had enough on his mind without them pitching a fit. Riding around the countryside on a train and wearing their prison clothes. Making speeches complaining about bad food and rats. Spoiled Yankee city women that didn't know a thing about hard times. They deserved everything they got.

All that nonsense just to let women vote. She had twice as much sense as most men, but her ma didn't vote, and neither did her grandma. If that was good enough for them, it was good enough for her.

"Well, sir, I'm too old and set in my ways to get all het up about running to town and casting a ballot," she told the preacher. "One politician is as crooked as the next, so I don't see what all the fuss is about. I've got enough to do here without stirring up trouble like these silly women. They need about five kids each. That'd settle 'em down real quick."

James nodded then shut his eyes and went right to sleep.

The preacher fished around for something else to discuss. "I spent last night with the McCade family and talked to Mr. Angus about his two younger sons."

"Is that right?" she asked. "So you met the new Mrs. McCade then?"

He blushed. "Yes'm. She's an interesting person. Different from most all the women 'round here."

"Ain't that the gospel truth? Anyways, I don't aim to waste my time talking 'bout her. How's Eric?"

The preacher looked sad. "Well, ma'am. I never knew him, but last night he didn't say much. Sat in the corner glaring at me."

"Lordy. That doesn't sound like the Eric I've always known."

"The War's most likely changed him," the preacher said. "He acted like he was mad at the world, and I can't say as I blame him, being wounded like that."

James had waked up and looked worried. "I've always put a lot of stock in that boy. He's the pride of the community."

But she figured Eric'd been through a lot and needed to rest. Then he'd be back to his old self. She changed the subject. "What did Angus McCade say 'bout his two youngest boys?"

"Oh, he was about to bust a gut. Said they're having the time of their lives up at Camp Funston in Kansas, meeting young men from all over the country. But they said it was mighty crowded. Over sixty thousand soldiers, they reckon."

"Land of Goshen," she exclaimed. "That's half the size of Dallas. Have the men been well?"

"The boys said the influenza at Camp Funston was pretty bad, but not to worry about them none."

She smoothed back her hair. It felt oily. She'd better wash it with Borax Saturday. The weather was getting warmer. Maybe she could dry it in the sun.

Just then three big blue jaybirds flew out of the chinaberry tree and landed in a large oak in the unfenced section of the front yard. *Jeeah, jeeah,* they screeched.

She jerked her head up and stared past the white fence and down the long driveway. A T-Model had pulled off the road and sat still with its motor running, wasting gas. Who in tarnation had the gall to come calling without letting her know? Would she ever get to take her Sunday-afternoon walk?

Jaq drove up toward the big house through huge oaks. Then, right before she parked, she spotted a green automobile sitting up on blocks under a shed. What a waste. She ran her fingers through her hair and straightened her bangs.

Mr. James ambled over and opened the gate like an old-fashioned gentleman. "What an unexpected pleasure. Welcome, *Madame*, to our humble abode. We don't get many visitors as comely as yourself. And with such a mellifluous name. The feminine version of Jacques, I believe. And isn't Jacques French for James?"

What an old fuddy-duddy, she thought, though he did seem literate. But what pretentious language.

"My pleasure, sir. I hated to stay closed in on this beautiful afternoon, so I'm trying to get better acquainted with my new neighbors."

Of course Mrs. Russell was frowning. And the preacher leaped down the steps so fast he almost tripped. He stuck out his hand again and she shook it, gloveless this time. It was still sweaty. She wiped her hand on her skirt.

"Reverend, Mrs. Russell, I'm sorry to drop by so unexpectedly."

She sat in the porch swing and fumbled for something to say. "I see you've put your Overland up on blocks, Mr. James. Does it need to be worked on? Maybe I can help."

He turned red and spluttered. "No, it's in perfectly fine running order. Drives like a winged chariot. It's merely that—"

"We need new tires and sure can't get 'em in wartime like this." Mrs. Russell spit a stream of snuff into the side yard. "And the price of gasoline. Pshaw. Twenty-five cents a gallon is enough to harelip the mayor."

"I agree with you, ma'am. In Europe they're predicting the gasoline shortage will decide the outcome of the War. It takes a ton of fuel to run just one tank."

"*Tank.* Have you seen one of those mechanical elephants up close?" The machinery of war clearly fascinated Mr. James.

"I volunteered in the mechanical division of the British Women's Auxiliary Army Corps. In France and Belgium I worked on all types of vehicles and drove an ambulance. I know everything about anything you can steer."

Mr. James and the preacher looked shocked, like she was a freak, and Mrs. Russell scowled even more. "A woman should stay home and write encouraging letters to men like my youngest, Clyde. Or join the Red Cross and make him warm clothes. She doesn't belong near the battlefield. Why, during the War Between the States—"

"Now, Ma, hold your horses," Mr. James said. "This is a new century, the era of the modern woman. We aim to stop all wars forever. *The War to end all wars*, that's what President Wilson keeps promising. So if it takes a little assistance from a few brave individuals of the female persuasion like Miss Jacqueline here, I say hurrah for her."

"Humph," Mrs. Russell responded and shoved a pinch of snuff under her lip. What a nasty habit.

The Holy Joe appeared appalled. He probably believed women shouldn't be anything but objects for him to lust after in secret.

Mr. James seemed like a kid at a Fourth of July parade. And the little boy—Patrick—sat on the edge of the porch, swinging his legs, his expression mirroring his father's.

She pulled her faithful Brownie out of her pocket and held it out to Patrick. "May I take your picture?"

His blush made his freckles stand out as he nodded, then stiffened.

"If you'll lean back against that post and try to forget I'm here, I'll take it when you least expect it."

"Yes, ma'am." He was still rigid.

Mr. James jumped in. "Where did a fair young damsel such as yourself learn the mechanical arts, Miss Jacqueline?" He clearly didn't intend to steer far from the subject.

She was tired of repeating the same old story, especially to men. Most of them were fascinated, but threatened too. Hah. As if she could compete with them in any professional arena.

"My brothers love automobiles—always used to have one torn apart in their workshop," she explained. "They put up with me underfoot, and I learned everything I could."

Mr. James pointed toward the shed and said, "My trustworthy vehicle. What can you tell me about it?"

She smiled to herself. This should be easy. "It's a 1914 Overland touring car, with a four-cylinder engine, poppet valves, and a one hundred fourteen-inch wheelbase. I like its sliding-gear transmission but prefer the more expensive models with sleeve valves."

Mr. James looked like he might fall off the porch. "Uh, very impressive, Miss Jacqueline."

She made the swing glide again because she always felt more comfortable in anything that moved—the faster the better. "I prefer the Model T. Mr. Henry Ford's new mass production has left the competition in the dust. It's the wave of the future."

Mr. James rubbed the back of one of his large ears. "I hate to disagree with such a pretty little lady, but Mr. Ford's mass-production scheme will never pan out. The type of careful workmanship you see exemplified in yonder fine automobile sitting up on blocks will rule the future. You can mark my words."

She kept her mouth shut about Mr. James's prophecy but wanted to say, "If we survive this war and have a future. And if we have enough gasoline to fuel it."

Instead, she stopped swinging and focused on Patrick, who seemed wrapped up in her disagreement with Mr. James. As she finally snapped pictures of him, Mr. James, and them together, she hoped they'd turn out well.

CHAPTER TEN

Cooo, cooo, cooo, a mourning dove called from a pine tree near the frog pond. Molly stood in the kitchen—her hands warm in the soapy water—and automatically washed the goblets they'd drunk their monthly treat of iced tea from.

The dove made her think of her mama, who never let her wash dishes or even work in the flower beds with gloves on. "Here, let me do that. You might hurt your hands," she would murmur in her gossamer voice. "Why don't you run practice the piano?" Mama's blue eyes always gleamed like dew on a sunlit web as she smoothed her black hair back into soft waves that framed her cheeks.

Dear Mama, usually so tired from taking care of all of us, she thought. *Yet she knew how much my music means to me and never let me help much around the house unless she was sick. She's a saint, nothing like Mother Russell—Oh, my goodness. Patrick's still out on the porch.*

She dreaded venturing out there. It reminded her of a war zone, with Mother Russell in command. Her teachers had always stressed that ladies shouldn't discuss such crude, worldly subjects as politics and war.

Patrick was as curious about the War as Mr. James, who'd fought his biggest battle to date with a balky mule in the cotton field. That and his ongoing war with his mother, though Molly was sure Mr. James didn't consider it a war. An unwinnable situation, to which he succumbed long ago.

Most of the year, the front porch served as their entertainment center, but she stayed in the parlor with her piano. As a girl, however, she'd loved to sit out with her parents and listen to her elders reminisce about the old days. The stories about her spirited maternal grandmother, who died ten years before she was born, especially fascinated her. She'd heard them a hundred times.

Grandmother had wanted a home in the country for her and her children and traveled by wagon from Austin to somewhere near Abilene to look for acreage. One Sunday afternoon as she and her husband walked up a hill east of their camp, she stopped and said, "I want to live on this piece of land for the rest of my life."

The next week she developed pneumonia. While a friend rode from their camp to the nearest town to find a doctor, Grandmother died. Ironically, they buried her where she'd earlier chosen to live.

Molly often mused on this story. Her grandmother left six children behind, including Molly's mama, only twelve years old. Still a child herself, she'd had to rear four younger siblings ranging from eighteen months to ten years. Then she'd married and borne five children of her own, only to lose her oldest daughter to diphtheria.

Molly picked up a dirty plate and sighed. Would she ever finish washing this stack of dishes? Would she ever be able to leave the farm?

If only she hadn't accepted Mr. James's proposal. She'd always preferred music to marriage. And her mama had even encouraged her to try a different way of life, to get her education. Education would give her choices, her mama had said. Molly heard her mother's voice as if she'd just spoken: "Choices are sweet. Not all women are meant to be mothers."

Why hadn't she listened to Mama?

As she washed the remnants of cream gravy out of the black skillet, she dreamed of how she would compose light, happy pieces as well as play them. But stuck on a farm, she had to milk the cow and do a hundred other chores before she could take time for her piano. She dried the heavy skillet carefully and rubbed some bacon grease into it so it would retain its hard crust of burned-on grease and not rust. *She* certainly was rusting on this farm.

Eric's new wife Jacqueline seemed as bright and shiny as a new copper kettle, exciting and irresistible. Jacqueline magnetized her, galvanized her, and—oh, she didn't know what else. Made her tingle in places she'd forgotten she had.

Then it came to her. Jacqueline reminded her of Tish, a character in the short stories she loved to read in *The Saturday Evening Post*. Tish and her two unmarried women friends had such exciting adventures and so much fun. They could always find something to laugh about, even when Tish involved them in the most outlandish situations. Completely independent, she did what she wanted. Of course her wealth helped.

Molly finished washing the last pan and stacked it on top of the plates and silverware, then covered them with a clean dishtowel to keep the flies off. Wiping her hands on her green gingham apron, she hurried to the front door to retrieve Patrick.

A low, slightly familiar voice stopped her. Could it be…what was Jacqueline doing here? She had just been thinking about her.

"Patrick, it's time for your schoolwork. No more excuses," she said, as she entered Mother Russell's sacred space, less hesitantly now.

As she greeted Jacqueline and took Patrick firmly by the shoulder, their stunning visitor rose. "I'll help him if you like," she said and smiled.

Well, she *could* smile, and it was most becoming. Molly continued inside with Patrick, and Jacqueline followed like an old friend. Land's sakes, inviting herself in like that. Mother Russell was most likely fit to be tied.

As they escorted Patrick to his room, he kept saying, "Mama, Miss Jacqueline took my picture with her camera. And Pa's too."

Jacqueline helped him with his arithmetic and watched him practice his handwriting, and then Molly assured him that the preacher would leave soon and that she and Miss Jacqueline would go sit in the parlor and talk. She kissed him on the cheek and ran her fingers through his curly red hair before they left. Leading Jacqueline to the parlor, she felt like butterflies were dancing on her head.

She tried to view the familiar room through a stranger's eyes. Of course, her piano passed muster, since it and the one at the church were the only two in the community.

The tufted red velvet loveseat that Jacqueline slumped onto was in fairly good condition, even with its missing button. A lace-covered throw pillow hid that flaw, so perhaps she wouldn't notice. The matching chair, where Molly now sat on its edge, was tolerable. Add the large couch that completed the red velvet set and a hanging framed print of two horses, one black and one white, in a storm, and the parlor might serve.

What could they talk about? She struggled to find a suitable topic of conversation. "If I may be so bold, how did you like the preacher's sermon this morning? He's a fine Christian man."

The woman toyed with the pillow and glanced out the front window. Finally she threw up one hand and guffawed like a field hand.

Molly recoiled. If Mother Russell heard that laugh, she'd wonder what caused it and Molly wouldn't be able to explain.

Jacqueline finally stopped laughing and scrutinized her. "He's nothing but a lecher who should have preached to himself about lusting in one's heart."

Why had she invited Jacqueline into the parlor? She was most unsettling. Again, Molly didn't know what to say.

Jacqueline rescued her. "I apologize. I usually speak my mind, especially now. In Europe last year I saw death almost every day, so I don't worry what people think. The truth is more liberating than little white lies. And when I met you, I sensed you could accept it." Jacqueline's black eyes cavorted like demons.

Molly gasped and drew herself up like she was sitting on the piano bench at church. "You are fortunate that I have an open mind. Your opinion of the preacher would offend most people around here, even if they secretly agreed." She allowed a small smile to surface but reined it in immediately. "Please do not repeat this conversation to anyone."

Jacqueline seemed contrite, though a tiny grin edged her full lips. "Agreed. Let's see. Where did you grow up?"

"In Austin. Papa served as the associate pastor in one of the largest churches there, and he had high hopes for his calling as a Methodist minister."

"Did he succeed?"

A wave of sadness washed over her. "Poor Papa. He had a falling-out with the presiding elder, and neither would budge. In fact, the elder threatened to go to the bishop, and Papa has such a temper. I get my red hair from him."

"Yes, and it's beautiful." Jacqueline stared at her as boldly as she had in church this morning.

The heat began at Molly's fingertips and worked its way up her arms. She flinched when her breasts began to throb as if Jacqueline had caressed them. Her throat tightened, and her face flamed. It probably matched the color of the chair she sat in. She'd never reacted this way to a compliment, much less one from another female.

Who was this queer, dangerous woman, and how could she avoid seeing her again?

❖

Jaq's thighs sizzled, as hot as a summer night in New Orleans. Damn it. Where had her comment about Molly's hair come from? Probably someplace she should stay away from. Sweet Jesus. What was it about women's hair that made her act crazy?

She'd never lost control around Helen—the one woman in France who'd interested her—except that once. Helen had kept her in line with those dark eyes. But she'd sure taken a nosedive around Sister Mary. She'd let unavailable women hurt her enough. She and Willie were strictly pals.

Shaking her head, she asked, "Did you live in Austin long?"

Molly's complexion gradually returned to normal. "Until I was six. After the problem in Austin, the bishop assigned Papa to preach in small towns all over East Texas—Fulshear, Fairfield, League City—"

"That's close to where I grew up."

"And where might that be?"

Molly sounded even more formal and stilted than she had earlier, though her voice was still melodious. Damnation. Jaq hoped she hadn't completely scared her away.

"Galveston."

"Galveston? How long did you live there?" Suddenly Molly leaned forward, elbows on her knees, and lost some of her stiffness, like Jaq'd hoped she would.

"Until the Storm." She still shuddered when she said that word.

"Did you lose anyone?"

Safe, she stared out the bay windows at the branches of the budding trees in the yard. They weren't moving much in the breeze, but her heartbeat revved up like it used to at the front, and memories of the Storm engulfed her.

Smelly, decomposing bodies. Corpses rotting in the streets in September heat, reeking worse than men mowed down in France.

Survivors piled corpses into boats, buried them at sea. They washed back. Workmen burned them like firewood in huge bonfires on the sand. Thank God she and her family—except Grandfather—left the island before those fires started.

Molly had asked her a question, so she nodded, managed to say, "We lost my grandfather." Then memories of the Storm sucked her back.

The wind howled, buildings crashed. Her legs ached even now. Running from one end of the house to the other, she'd prayed, "Please, Mary, don't let a tree smash the roof. Keep a wagon or buggy from slamming through our walls." She'd pressed her ears shut, closed her eyes. The wind still roared.

No birds called the next morning—all fled before the Storm. The calm ocean, soundless. Streetcars lay rammed into buildings. Their green island, brown—muddy floodwater in some places, black sludge in others. A wall of wreckage had flattened everything. Eerie silence.

Then people began to call. "Help me. I can't get out. For God's sake, help." Boats, pilings, roofs, trees trapped them.

Those voices still invaded her dreams. Then when Galveston was silent again, soldiers' moans echoed in her head. She couldn't make them stop.

She glanced at Molly and jerked out of her nightmare.

Molly's green eyes were as peaceful as the center of the hurricane had been when it passed over Galveston that night and gave them a brief respite. Molly gazed at her with such understanding. Had she spoken aloud?

"You lost your grandfather?"

"Yes." The horrible events that she'd replayed a thousand times flashed through her mind.

Jaq had held her older sister's hand and peeked into the hastily dug hole in their backyard. Her father and brothers had wrapped her grandfather in a white sheet and lowered him into it.

The priest had raced through the ritual, but the stench that encompassed the entire island had almost gagged her. Their big live-oak trees had all blown down, so they stood in the blazing sun and the mud. Sweat ran down her sides, and she smelled horrible because she hadn't had a bath in so long. A mosquito kept buzzing around her face, and flies were crawling up her arm and zooming around the sheet where her grandfather lay, stiff and dead. She craved a drink of water and something to eat, but Mother said they didn't have much left, that they had to save as much of it as possible for when they left the island.

"Be still and stop sniveling," her mother had hissed during the funeral. "If you hadn't been so stubborn and run out after Bébé during the storm, your grandfather would be alive right now."

It was all her fault. Jaq had held the pup and petted her and tried to get her to calm down, but Bébé had kept barking so loud she finally put her down for just a minute. When a huge gust blew the back door open, Bébé went wild and dashed out. Jaq had chased her, splashing through the big mud puddles. Just as Jaq had been about to wade after her into the flooded alley, someone grabbed her. It was Grandfather, and he'd kept her from saving Bébé. She'd broken away from him and run back toward their house, crying.

Just as she'd reached the back door, she'd heard a loud crash and turned around. A huge tree limb had crashed right where she'd just been, and all she could see was Grandfather's legs sticking out from under part of it.

He was dead, and Mother was right. All her fault.

Molly said softly, her voice jolting Jaq back to the parlor, "I'm so sorry. You were, what, seven? eight?"

"Six years and three months. It seemed like the end of the world. I'd never seen my parents act like that. I'm sure they tried to hide their fear, for our sake. My sister was ten, my twin brothers eight, and I was the baby. They wanted to protect us, but nobody could."

As she tried to shake off the memories, Molly's small hand touched her knee and she spoke, her voice soothing. "I wish I could have been with you. I was almost thirteen when the Storm hit. The water started to rise and we ran out to the bay and played in the waves. But then it began to flood our yard. The wind kept picking up speed. It blew off roofs and ripped limbs from the trees. All my family survived, but I was terrified."

That's exactly how Jaq had felt, but she'd never told anybody.

"Papa was in Galveston that week because he was scheduled to hold a church meeting there. He waited as long as possible but finally realized how bad the hurricane might be and caught the last train out.

"He told us the wind and the waves had pushed the locomotive off the tracks. He'd managed to get out of the coach and climb on top of a floating boxcar, and he lay there panting and praying it wouldn't sink."

Molly let go of her knee and returned her hand to her lap. Jaq missed their contact immediately.

Molly shifted in her chair. "Papa tried to save a drowning woman and her baby. He held on to the boxcar railing with one hand, stretched out his other arm, and pulled her on top of the train by her long hair. The baby was dead, poor little mite. But the woman lived. They managed to stay on top of that boxcar all night through the Storm, and the next morning some men in a rowboat rescued them."

Jaq was glad she'd decided to visit the Russells, in spite of Molly's mother-in-law. Molly was so beautiful, and she seemed to understand. Holy smoke. She made Jaq feel so much better. But after those revelations, she couldn't be attracted to Molly, couldn't even consider seducing someone so pure and innocent.

Molly scared her more than the Storm had.

CHAPTER ELEVEN

M rs. Russell plopped down on the large couch then arched her back to try to get shed of some of the soreness. If she didn't keep working, the misery hit her pretty hard. The preacher had finally left, but they had an uninvited visitor, so she had to sit some more instead of walking the fields like she'd rather.

"Hot cup of coffee, Jacqueline? That'd be the ticket late in the afternoon like this. Molly, how about fetching some? Make it myself out of white-oak acorns from the yard. Soak 'em a few days to get the tannin out, then roast and grind 'em. Almost as good as the real thing. Sure will be glad when this dang war is over and done with, though. I miss my coffee and especially my sugar."

"Why, thank you." Jacqueline turned to Molly. "I'd appreciate a cup. If you don't mind." As she spoke she locked eyes with Molly and preened like she'd just discovered an egg under a setting hen, all pleased with herself and the hen too. What had those two been cooking up? She'd get to the bottom of this situation in nothing flat.

After Molly left, she gave Jacqueline her best smile. "So, what brings you and Eric to our neck of the woods?"

Jacqueline smoothed the nap of the sofa like it was a cat purring beside her. "He had to come help his father find some decent hired help. Then we can go back to New Orleans."

"Kinda worries me 'bout old McCade's sons being in that big camp. I heard the sickness up there's different from any influenza they ever saw, but it won't amount to much."

"I read something like that too. Do they know exactly what it is?"

"Nope. Sounds more like pneumonia. But when the boys go overseas, no telling what they'll come across. Hope my son Clyde doesn't come down with it."

Jacqueline looked real concerned. "I had a bad case of something last summer. Felt like I'd die. It's one reason I came home."

"Say, Jacqueline. The ladies in our local Red Cross chapter would be pleased if you'd join us at our weekly meeting. Molly goes once in a blue moon, but she usually has some music carrying-on. I could take you, introduce you—"

"No, thanks. I'm sick of this men's war. I've been helping the suffragists fight for the vote instead."

Well, she should have known Jacqueline would be cozy with that bunch of heifers. Maybe she'd come around later.

Molly hustled in carrying a small tray. "Here you go. Two cups of coffee, a glass of water, and some leftover chocolate pie."

She had to strain to keep from scowling. It wasn't right to have to share her sweets with a stranger. As Molly sat down, she couldn't resist jibing her. "Jacqueline and Eric are heading back to New Orleans soon."

Molly's face fell. That'd teach her to give away pie.

So she and Jacqueline had already sparked, she thought. Molly would want to gad about with her. They both needed to tend to their families and do their patriotic duty.

"Don't let me interrupt your conversation, girls."

"We were talking about the 1900 Storm. Jacqueline lived through it, and I was so nearby—"

"Heavens to Betsy, that was the worst hurricane imaginable. James finished the house that year. Did y'all stay on Galveston Island after it blew through?"

Jacqueline looked like she didn't want to talk about it. But then she started in like she aimed to flush it right out of her system.

"After the Storm, we didn't have anything. No telephones or electricity, of course. But no food except what little was left in the house—not even much drinking water. And we were the lucky ones. Some people didn't even have any clothes."

Jacqueline acted like she really didn't want to say any more. Finally, though, she smoothed down her bangs like she was making sure nobody could see under 'em and soldiered on.

"All the bridges were gone, so nobody could get to us and we couldn't go anywhere. We'd have starved if we'd had to stay much longer. But Father found a small boat—he was in the shipping business, and most of his fleet was out at sea. Some men who worked for him rowed us across to the mainland."

Molly sipped her water and looked like she was 'bout to cry. "Thank God y'all were saved."

"Saved?" Jacqueline asked, like she almost wished she hadn't been. "Eventually. But we didn't find anything on the mainland but more dead bodies—people and animals. All the roads were washed out, and the train tracks were twisted like hairpins, some of them around tree trunks. It stank so bad we threw up what little food we'd eaten."

Jacqueline picked up a saucer of pie, then set it back down without taking a bite. Maybe she'd lost her appetite. She kept on talking like there was no tomorrow. And at church Mrs. Russell had thought she was stingy with her words.

She pondered the situation. Come to think of it, that's the way she'd been when she finally found somebody to listen to her about what happened in Georgia during the War.

Jacqueline recommenced. "We walked until my legs almost fell off. Then my brothers took turns carrying me. We saw mud puddles everywhere, but we couldn't drink the water because of all the rotting bodies. Finally, we saw smoke. It was a relief train from Houston, and we ran to it as fast as we could."

She warmed up to Jacqueline. She'd been through some rough patches. Not like Molly, who'd always had her bread buttered on both sides. She knew what it felt like to be hungry, but she didn't let herself dwell on the hard times. It was too easy to get caught up in them and miss out on the good ones.

Might as well let these youngsters know 'bout real suffering. Maybe give Jacqueline a little consolation. She was evidently carrying some mighty heavy burdens.

She cleared her throat. "Well, in 1864 my life was kinda like what you describe, Jacqueline. I lived a good piece west of Atlanta, and my future husband spent all that long, hot summer on the battlefield defending the city." She'd treasured every letter he'd scribbled on a scrap of paper with a pencil and sent her.

"Damn Yankees took all our cornmeal and livestock. Even pulled the turnips out of the ground and stripped the green apples off the trees.

And my poor husband-to-be writing me 'bout how famished out he was for fruit and vegetables. Said he could eat as many of 'em as he could tote. But those Yankees got 'em all."

She didn't know how she'd made it through those bad spells. But she'd been young and full of life, like these two girls.

Just thinking about how hungry she'd been even before those parasites came tromping around, carrying off everything that wasn't fastened down, made her shudder.

She stopped to take a breath and looked around. Molly was staring at her like she was seeing her for the first time, but she acted like she was aching to visit with Jacqueline instead of listening to an old woman carry on. She made herself shut her mouth.

As for Jacqueline, she was most likely so full of misery right now she couldn't abide to hear about anybody else's.

❖

Molly jumped up. "How about a song or two to brighten things, after all this talk of storms and war? When I was a girl and we didn't have quite enough to eat, Mama always said a happy tune would make our stomachs feel fuller."

Mother Russell scowled like she didn't believe her, but she pushed on. She didn't want to depress Jacqueline on her first visit. "How about 'Pack Up Your Troubles in Your Old Kit-Bag, and Smile, Smile, Smile'? Our boys in Europe probably sing it now and then when they get homesick."

She took a sip of water. "By the way, Jacqueline, I've heard a lot of our soldiers are smoking. Is that true?"

"Not only the men, but the women too. You'd be surprised how much a cigarette calms your nerves. You need it over there."

She hurried to the piano stool and raised the dust cover of her precious instrument. She didn't want to think about Jacqueline putting a cigarette between her beautiful lips.

On countless Sunday afternoons she played the piano, alone, to keep up her own spirits. She was less important to her own household than Nellie and the chickens. But this afternoon she felt more alive and more worthwhile than she had since her graduation concert. The red of the velvet loveseat looked brighter, softer, more inviting to touch. The very air smelled sweeter, the mingled perfume of the wisteria and the chinaberry trees outside rushing to her head like champagne.

Or what she expected champagne would make her feel. Of course, the only alcohol she'd ever tasted was the elderberry wine Mother Russell made especially for communion.

Even her well water tasted as if it sprang from a deeper source, with no taint of dirt or rust, as if she had tapped the source of the ancient Greek gods' nectar. And her piano seemed more in tune, its notes rounder and fuller as they filled the room with cheerful sound.

How wonderful to be alive on this Easter Sunday and to have found an exciting new friend. She hoped Jacqueline stayed forever.

Jaq decided to let Molly entertain her; Mrs. Russell could sit there and fidget all she wanted. Sinking into the velvet cushions she opened herself to the music, and soon the bouncy rhythms and catchy tunes almost had her tapping her foot, as Molly played and sang "It's a Long Way to Tipperary" and "Hail, Hail, the Gang's All Here."

War songs like these provoked memories she didn't mind of last spring in France and Belgium, when she'd joined a bunch of adventurous Englishwomen heading to Europe. After they nervously crossed the Channel swarming with U-boats, they'd had to ride in boxcars that usually carried horses. What a stench, but she hadn't minded. She was seeing the world, though she hoped she never had to be cooped up in something like that again.

It sure had felt good to walk the last leg of the trip. The road was muddy, but she and the other women marched toward camp like they were strolling through an English garden. Carrying their kit bags full of personal belongings, they gulped the fresh air and cracked jokes. They were bursting to do their bit against the Germans, but they didn't have any idea what they were heading for.

She stretched out one leg, as she sat safely on the plush loveseat, then sank back into her memories.

She'd taken off her gloves while she marched, and when she'd swung her arms by her sides, the heavy wool of her long blue overcoat scratched her bent fingers. She'd jammed on her round blue felt hat and cocked its wide brim, feeling as jaunty as she hoped her hat looked.

There she'd been, actually in France, and the mud of her ancestors had felt very real under her walking shoes. Slinging her tight shoulders back she'd smiled so wide her cheeks hurt. She'd been that proud to be part of the first troop of British women allowed to serve near the front lines.

She clutched the lace throw pillow beside her and noticed that a button was missing from the loveseat. She was back in America now. That's all that mattered. She just wanted to let Molly distract her. Molly was safely married, even had a kid.

Molly's fingers skimmed the keys, and her eyes shone as she played one song after another.

Was Molly trying to help? She had no idea how much her bad memories pestered her, not just at night, but all the time. On her drive over here, she'd almost forgotten she wasn't in Europe. She'd nearly had to pull off and rest, afraid a bomb would drop or a shell fly overhead and she'd see dead and dying soldiers in the neatly plowed fields.

She'd like to listen to Molly all afternoon, but Eric and Angus would be home soon. She needed to go see about them. They'd suffered a lot more than she had.

❖

I'd give one of my best laying hens for a dip of snuff, Mrs. Russell thought. *Pshaw. It's too late to go walk the fields now.*

She needed to feed the chickens and rustle up some supper. But Molly just sat there playing that piano, lost to the world.

That big stack of magazines on the round table at the end of the sofa sure needed weeding. James and Molly read every copy of *The Saturday Evening Post* to rags, and Molly swore by *The Etude*. Some hogwash about teaching music. No money in that. Next time she built a big bonfire she'd sneak in here and grab a bunch of the old magazines to start it with.

Why, everybody in their right mind knew *Farm and Ranch* was the only fit reading material for landed gentry. She kept all her old ones to thumb back through.

What in tarnation was going through James's head when he up and married Molly? He'd wasted almost every weekend for near 'bout three months courting her, when he should've been home helping out. After these eight long years, surely he'd figured out what was what. Molly would never be fit for life on a farm.

She was just about to get up and leave Molly to her silly piano playing, but Jacqueline stirred, like she was rousing out of a stupor, and Molly stopped making all that infernal racket. Mrs. Russell jumped up, ready to get rid of their company.

Molly was simpering at Jacqueline and saying foolish things. And Jacqueline looked like she didn't want to be getting on down the road but believed she oughta. Finally they quit their palavering.

Jacqueline said, "Mrs. Russell, I appreciate you letting me spend the afternoon with you and your family. And Molly, I've enjoyed our conversation and your music. You have a real talent."

What a bunch of lies. She didn't trust the Frenchies, even if they were America's allies. She rocked from one foot to the other, feeling as restless as a billy goat in rut. "It was right kind of you to stop by and socialize, Jacqueline. I 'spect we'll see you at Sunday school next week? We only have a preacher once in a while."

Of course she had to try to get the last word in. "By all means. Thank you again for your hospitality."

After another month of Sundays, she headed for the front door. "I'll tell James you said good-bye," she informed Jacqueline. "And he said for you to tell Eric not to be a stranger. He's itching to discuss his war experiences. He and Patrick are out back feeding the livestock. Bet the milk cow's wondering where Molly is. Never get much rest down here on the farm." Humph. Unless they were a lazy good-for-nothing like Molly.

Molly chimed in. "Drive carefully. I hope to see you soon."

She walked Jacqueline to her car and hung around her forever. Probably trying to persuade her to spend the night.

She'd almost given up hope of Molly milking the cow, but when she peeked out the kitchen window she spotted the T-Model creeping down the driveway. Molly ambled back toward the house just as slow.

The little sluggard made her see red.

Molly strolled past the sweet-smelling purple wisteria and hummed "Good Night."

Those two words had been so painful when she graduated from college. She'd been inseparable from several of the girls during their four years at boarding school and spent all her free time with each of her favorites in turn. How she'd loved to stay up after hours and whisper with them. They'd cried and laughed together.

While she attended the university and until she married, she exchanged passionate letters with one of the girls, Esther Harris. They'd pledged everlasting love and devotion, but now they wrote each other about everyday affairs. Then, they'd dreamed, even talked about spending the rest of their lives together, but now things had changed.

When Mr. James proposed, she finally persuaded herself that loving a woman like Esther had merely prepared her for life's real purpose—marriage and devotion to a worthy man. Preachers stressed that a woman and the right man would truly become one in body and spirit and share every thought and feeling. Her papa and mama clearly adored and respected each other, so she would follow their example.

But Mr. James evidently hadn't expected such a union. He wanted someone to make him look good in public, give him lots of sons, and help his mother on the farm. When she'd eventually understood that most husbands were like hers, who was probably better than most, she'd tried to reconcile herself to the reality of marriage.

Being with Jacqueline this afternoon, though, had stirred the remaining ember of her grand dream and made it glow.

Maybe she and Jacqueline would become close friends. That would be so much better than the emotional wasteland she lived in now.

She wanted to always feel alive inside—like she did before she married and as she had this afternoon.

CHAPTER TWELVE

"Do you have to chew so loud?" Eric glared at Jaq, dark purple pouches under his eyes. At least he didn't need his eye patch any more.

She murmured something to keep from biting back.

"And quit slurping that milk. I had to get up early, and now I have to go milk—" He drew back his hand as if he might hit her.

She slammed down her glass. "That's enough! I'm not your mother or your maid or—"

"Or my wife." Eric snatched a biscuit and dipped it in his egg yolk like a farmhand. Some of the runny stuff dripped on the front of his blue work shirt, which *she'd* have to wash.

"No, I'm not. And I can't wait to get an annulment. In fact—"

"Sorry, but everything gets on my nerves lately—the clock ticking, the birds singing, the coyotes howling." Eric swiped at the spot on his shirt and grabbed his coffee cup with a shaky hand.

"It's no wonder, as little sleep as you get."

He took a sip and glared at her like she was the enemy. "Have you been spying on me?"

"Spying? If you call having to close my door and put my fingers in my ears sometimes so I can block out the noise you make when you come in late and stumble up the stairs, I guess I have. And even when you finally make it to bed, you sound like you're wrestling with the sheets. That's how they look every morning, when *I* make your bed."

Eric placed his cup on the table more gently than he'd yanked it up. "I'm afraid to sleep. I can't explain it."

"Afraid? Of what?"

"That something will hurt me if I let my guard down. I know that sounds silly." He looked genuinely puzzled, and his pupils were dilated.

"But you grew up here, you've known these people all your life—"

"You never can tell. The minute you turn your back on even something you've done routinely, it can all blow up in your face. Damn it. What's wrong with me? I need to find somebody to help Pop, not be more of a burden. He's got enough problems. I'm afraid I'll let him down like I've done with everybody else, including you."

She really studied Eric. He wasn't a big-shot pilot any longer, but she liked him better now that he was finally leveling with her.

"Don't worry. You've given everybody more than you can imagine. Your dad told me just the other day how proud he is of you. And you aren't responsible for how I feel about women."

For the first time since they'd been in New Hope, he seemed to actually want to communicate with her. He'd been acting strange since he showed up in New Orleans. Something was tearing him apart inside, but what? When they were in London he was so optimistic, so much fun. Hell, he was as serious as a funeral now. He had to be missing his mother more than she'd thought.

He shook his head, as if making an effort to stay focused on her. "So, Jaq, are you okay? Do you need anything? How do you like playing the busy housewife?"

She shrugged. "Having servants most of my life hasn't exactly prepared me for farm life. I'm trying hard not to kill you and your father with my cooking." Maybe her teasing would improve his mood.

His grin looked forced. "It's okay. Just fine." Then his eyes clouded over again.

What was eating at him? Having an injured eye and being half-crippled right now were bound to give him nightmares. Maybe he missed the excitement of the War even more than she did or thought the locals would call him a lazy coward. How ridiculous. He was braver than most men and had the medals and scars to prove it.

He seemed to want to be left alone almost all the time. And she had no idea how to help him open up like he just had. She really didn't know him very well. Most men, except her brothers, were as foreign to her as the Boches—and just as much of a nuisance.

She didn't know what to say or do, so she just sat here. Eric ran his fingers through his shaggy blond hair and looked like he was about to say something else. Then he pushed back his chair, tightened the laces on his heavy work boots, and headed for the door. He paused.

"I got a letter from my pal Dick the other day. If you want to read it, it's on the counter. I glanced at it yesterday. I don't want any reminders of the War, but I want to keep in touch with him." Again, he started to leave, but turned around.

"By the way, why have you been staying here so much lately? Cleaning out my mother's closets, scrubbing the floors. I appreciate all you're doing, but you don't have to isolate yourself just because I don't feel sociable. You haven't even gone back to the church for three weeks."

Then he was gone.

He could be so sweet. That's one reason she hated whatever was happening. Yet he'd been so irritable lately. She didn't know how much more she could stand.

She *had* to stick by him until he and Angus straightened out their lives. He just needed to readjust after all those years of fighting and now losing his mother. She could spend a while supporting him, even if she couldn't be his wife in the bedroom.

She scanned the letter that described some of the adventures Eric's friend had been having. Sounded exciting, if you were several thousand miles away from the action.

Being in the air was a whole different thing from fighting on the ground. Eric probably missed being a pilot a lot, though he wouldn't talk about it anymore. When they'd first met, he'd described one close call after another.

In closing, Dick wrote, "I'll always appreciate you taking time out from flying with the Frenchies to teach me how. You gave me the chance of a lifetime. Every time the boys and I score a round of drinks, I hold up my cup to you." He talked about the other fliers as if they were his brothers. Eric had to be longing for that type of companionship.

She and Eric were both alone now, but living around people she had so little in common with bothered her. It was like being in a foreign country and not understanding a word of the language. If Molly wasn't here, she might break her promise and drive back to New Orleans or head straight to Washington and join the suffragists.

She noticed more than several dirty glasses on the countertop. Eric had evidently brought them downstairs from his room earlier this morning. My God, he'd been drinking more than she'd realized.

In New Orleans, he'd visited the liquor store every day. And he'd spent most of his time in a bar near her parents' house. On the drive up, she hadn't had much room for luggage because of his stash.

Eric had held his liquor well while he'd stayed those few days with her and her parents. When they'd introduced him to their friends, they'd stressed his wartime service but didn't mention hers. It evidently embarrassed her mother. And she'd never even mentioned Jaq's brief suffragist activities.

She lifted the heavy kettle from the wood-burning stove, poured hot water into the dishpan, and sprinkled in some Ivory Flakes. Eric had bought a box for her when she'd asked and seemed glad to do so. They were a lot easier on her hands than the farmwomen's harsh lye soap.

As she swished through the warm soapy water, her shoulders loosened. She'd wanted to go to the church the past three Sundays, but she refused to spend more time with Molly. Molly was so damn innocent, like she'd been before Sister Mary. Hell. She wouldn't be able to live with herself if she took advantage of her. Since their shared revelations about the Storm, she just wanted to know Molly at a distance, to remind herself the world wasn't completely ugly.

Helen had been different—friendly to everyone but singling out no favorites. And Helen always kept her in check. It didn't matter that she was in love with Helen. Actually, being able to put Helen on a pedestal had made her comfortable. She could feel as infatuated as she wanted and not worry Helen would take her seriously, like Sister Mary seemed to—that one time. But if Helen had responded at all…

Molly, though, had practically stood on the running board of her Model T and ridden away with her that Sunday night. Molly seemed to need someone to share confidences with, but damn it—she couldn't be that person.

Her life was too complicated, and she was too susceptible to women like Molly, who'd seemed to understand her feelings about the Storm, played a handful of songs, spent ten minutes saying good night—and penetrated her defenses.

After that afternoon, she'd hummed the songs Molly played and felt warm inside. But the feeling faded in a few days. She didn't need to want what she'd never have. She wasn't a teener anymore.

Molly would always be faithful to her marriage vows, and Jaq refused to be a substitute for a man, a second choice, merely a dear friend. Besides, Molly would never leave her son and sometimes acted like a child herself. Jaq needed an equal, someone to share her adventures, not tie her down.

She couldn't be the kind of friend Molly wanted or needed. She'd eventually taint Molly, like she tainted everyone else she cared for.

No, she didn't want to hurt Molly. But most of all she didn't want to hurt herself.

She wanted the sexual excitement she'd enjoyed with Sister Mary. She craved it. But she wanted to enjoy it more than once, like she had with Willie. Maybe she should have stayed in New Orleans with her, but they were even more different than she and Molly were. Willie was much more independent than she was. She was definitely her own woman and had said something about going to France, alone, as soon as the War ended.

After breakfast, kneeling in the flower bed under the side windows, she watched the swollen white clouds that billowed like smoke. A faint breeze made the pines sway. Her mind went almost blank as she squeezed the moist loam—so soft, so sensual. The red earth, the color of Molly's hair, yielded when she touched it and moved where she urged it, responded to her caressing fingers—

The telephone sounded, three long peals, then a short one, their ring on the party line. Who could that be? She dashed into the house.

"Four-three-one. Mrs. McCade speaking."

"Jacqueline. We've missed you at the church. Oh, I'm sorry. I'm sure you have no idea who this is. It's Molly Russell."

The speaker on the other end of the crackly line finally took a breath.

"Of course, Molly. I recognized your voice." How could she forget it? "So kind of you to call."

"I wanted to make sure you're not ill. And if you're not, would you like to come over tomorrow? The roses are blooming, and I plan to make rose water."

She hesitated, but looked at the moist earth still on her hands... and gave in. "I'd be honored. What time?"

"How about one thirty tomorrow afternoon?"

"That's perfect. I look forward to it."

She gently hung the receiver back into its hook on the side of the mounted box. When she flicked one of the metal bells at the top, its tinkle reverberated throughout her. She was going to visit Molly soon.

Then bells blared inside her head: *You're making a huge mistake.*

CHAPTER THIRTEEN

Molly loved the earthy scent of the starter made from fermented potatoes that would make her dough rise gradually. After she moistened her mixture of flour, salt, oil, and starter with hot water, she rubbed a chunk of lard into her palms, moving her fingers back and forth together to coat them.

She kneaded the flesh-colored dough easily on the ceramic countertop. Usually the chore stultified her, but today she had her mind on Jacqueline's visit. She hoped her guest wouldn't find her too boring. Thrusting the heel of her hand into the elastic dough, she pushed several times, then folded the flattened material toward her and rammed it down and away from her body. What was it about Jacqueline that made her want to see her so much?

After she regreased her palms, she rotated the dough a quarter turn and concentrated on the way it molded to her fingers, stuck to them until she greased them again. The pliable dough gave repeatedly to her touch, flattened then swelled, and with each stroke of her hands it grew more ready to expand. What made Jacqueline so confident? Her beauty, of course. But something else, deep within, that Molly wanted to warm her hands by.

The minutes flew, and she kneaded the sticky substance much longer than necessary. She formed a ball, returned it to the bowl that she covered with a clean drying-cloth, and stuck it in a warm cupboard to rise.

Her lips suddenly dry, she had to drink some water before she spoke to Patrick. "Miss Jacqueline's coming to see me tomorrow." He sat at the kitchen table and crumbled cornbread into a glass of buttermilk. "Maybe she'll still be here when you get home from school. She's a nice lady."

"Yes, ma'am." Patrick emptied the glass and shrugged.

She had fretted about Jacqueline for the past two weeks. When she wasn't at Sunday school the week after they met, she was disappointed but reasoned that Jacqueline was simply busy. After the second Sunday Jacqueline missed, she began to worry.

She reviewed each topic that had passed between them, every nuance of every word. Perhaps she had offended Jacqueline by insisting that they lighten the mood with some music. Her love of music irritated Mother Russell, so maybe Jacqueline felt the same way. But she'd praised the little trio on Easter Sunday.

When Jacqueline didn't show up at the church for a third time, she had decided to take action. How could she entice Jacqueline to visit, and how could she entertain her, not merely sit in the parlor and chat? That Monday morning as she'd glanced out at the rose garden, she'd conceived her idea about making rose water.

It was a pleasant task, not very strenuous, and provided just enough activity to cover any lulls in the conversation. If Jacqueline had truly been offended, or simply didn't like her, she could refuse the invitation and Molly would try to forget her. But if she accepted…She vibrated in anticipation but had no idea why this newcomer affected her so dramatically.

She hadn't slept well, and after she finally dozed off she woke with a start at first light as the rooster crowed and Mother Russell stomped into the kitchen, then clanged pots and pans. She muttered her usual insults—*sluggards, lay-abeds*—and looked startled when Molly appeared much earlier than normal, dressed and offering to help.

The morning had passed as slowly as the ribbon-cane syrup she poured on her breakfast biscuits. Should she call Jacqueline? What if she pushed her even further away for being so forward? What if Jacqueline acted rude, heaven forbid, or insulting? She couldn't eat more than a bite of peas and drink a big glass of sweet milk for dinner, and by early afternoon she was frantic. She *had* to make the call, because she couldn't remain in suspense any longer.

She shifted from one foot to the other as the telephone rang. How long should she wait? Four rings. Where was Jacqueline? Five. Perhaps she was visiting someone else. Six rings. This was ridiculous.

She was about to hang up when Jacqueline answered, breathing hard as if she had run to catch the phone in time. She could barely extend her invitation and was so shaky when Jacqueline finally accepted that she had to sit down on the nearby bench.

Jacqueline would come tomorrow. Mr. James would be out working in the fields, and Mother Russell would be rolling bandages at the Red Cross meeting. They would have most of the afternoon together. What relief. Maybe she could eat a bite of supper and sleep tolerably well.

At supper, Mrs. Russell thought, *My stars. Molly's been moping around the past few weeks, and now she looks like the cat that ate the canary. Can't ever tell with that gal. It's a wonder James hasn't noticed anything. 'Course, he wouldn't see a log truck unless it hit him.*

She spelled it all out for her favorite laying hen the next morning as she gathered the eggs in the hen house. "Molly's been in the parlor every afternoon for days, playing sad songs. You'd think she'd lost her last dollar. Then yesterday afternoon she up and starts banging out some silly tune by that Russian fellow Chikovski. She played it so cheerful-like, even made me feel like whirling 'round the room—if I was up to such tomfoolery."

Easing her hand under the warm hen, she slid out a fine-looking brown egg. "Been noticing too, for the past few weeks she's been sneaking off down to the pond every chance she gets. Walks real slow under the pine trees and looks up like she's talking to 'em. I should've cut those pines down a long time ago, right after we cleared the fields and the home site. Trees like those made good straight logs for our old cabin, and the barn and such like. But let 'em grow and they just shed needles everywhere."

She placed the egg carefully into her straw basket and scooted over to the next nest. "But I got off track. Just having Molly on the place makes me do that. I was afraid she was losing her mind, but just before I thought I'd better have a heart-to-heart with James about her, she perks right up and acts like her little cheerful self again. Sure glad I didn't say anything."

She put another egg in her basket, then headed back to the kitchen, mumbling to herself. "Probably should have dosed Molly with more sassafras tonic. Nothing like a good spring tonic to purify the blood and help make the change from winter to summer. Come to think of it, that's probably what's been ailing her. The sassafras just worked slower than normal this year. I'll double up next year and make her eat plenty of poke salad for good measure. Put her out of her misery, and me too. Worrying about her has worn me out."

Jaq drove an ambulance over a pot-holed, muddy road to the front lines. Women smoked cigarettes, men drank whiskey, and pianos danced toward her on two legs and chased everybody. A spider spun a huge, sticky web around them all and carried them up in the air. It opened its mouth and—

Jaq woke, exhausted, pulled on an old housedress, and stumbled downstairs to fix what passed for breakfast. What a strange dream that was. She drew several pails of water from the well, heated it, and washed dishes. Her hands were callused from the rope and wrinkled from the dishwater. After eons of drudgery, she trudged back upstairs and fell across the bed.

She woke up again with a start and felt her forehead, lingering on her raised scar. Her forehead was hot, she was sick. Maybe she had the flu. Better call Molly and cancel their visit.

The minutes ticked by and she fidgeted, increasingly disgusted with herself. Damn it. She'd driven over muddy roads full of shell holes—with bombs exploding around her and bullets whistling over her head. She'd seen men with their legs blown off and listened to them scream. She'd tried to drive slow enough not to jar them and fast enough to get away from the gunfire. Anything to stop those screams.

All that, but she was afraid to spend the afternoon with a tiny redhead. So what if those green eyes saw her secrets, if Molly scared her spitless? She was a coward, trying to take the easy way out. She'd even made herself sick so she could tell Molly she couldn't come.

Turning onto her side, she propped her head on one hand and stared at the dresser mirror. The image opposite her needled her cringing self.

She was pathetic. Was she afraid Molly could hurt her like Sister Mary Therese and Helen had? Hadn't they taught her anything?

Molly was beautiful, like them. She was understanding, like them. And she was unavailable, like them. Why put herself through the wringer?

But she was stronger now. She could just go tell Molly she wasn't interested. She needed to face this battle instead of run away, like she had from the War and from Washington after the doctors poked feeding tubes down her.

She flopped onto her back. She was no coward. She'd visit Molly just once. But she definitely wouldn't encourage her. Hell, it wasn't fair to lead her on. What they could have would only halfway satisfy them. That was it. She'd tell Molly she and Eric were leaving New Hope soon. Say she'd rather not start something she couldn't finish.

That way, she wouldn't hurt Molly too much. Or herself. It'd be over before it even started.

The kind of childish friendship Molly was apparently angling for was a lie. Women like the two of them were probably just kidding themselves if they got emotionally involved like Molly obviously wanted to. She would rather be shot than participate. She'd learned her lesson.

❖

For the past few weeks Molly had found refuge at the small pine-encircled pond down the hill from the house. Today it provided sanctuary as she waited for Jacqueline. The hours crept by like a child learning to walk.

When she'd risen at first light, she'd been afraid Mother Russell would change her mind and decide to stay home instead of attending the Red Cross meeting. So she'd milked Nellie, helped cook breakfast, roused Patrick, drawn water from the well, heated it and washed dishes, swept the house and the yard, and picked up Mr. James's dirty work clothes.

Mother Russell measured her with granite eyes during this bustle of activity, but she pretended she was always this energetic and even helped Mother Russell hitch the horse to the buggy.

Now she paced the bank of the pond until she raised such a cloud of red dust that she sneezed. One minute she perspired, and the next a cool breeze blew across the water and chilled her.

Why did she crave to spend the afternoon alone with Jacqueline? Would Jacqueline enjoy their visit? How long would she and Eric stay in New Hope?

As Molly wandered among the tall pines, wondering what was happening to her, she peeled off a glove and ran her hand along the thick, rough bark of the tallest tree in the stand to steady herself. She felt as nervous as if she were about to direct the annual Christmas program.

She meandered to the next tree, puzzled. Why was she throbbing all over, her insides trembling, her arms and legs weak? Jacqueline McCade was simply paying a social call. They would make rose water, eat tea cakes with milk, then return to their husbands. Nothing queer was happening.

She sat on a log, peeled off her white cotton gloves and her bonnet, and studied a young snapping turtle lying on a log in the lake, sunning her cold, brown-black body. Molly longed to be as placid as the turtle.

"Miss Turtle, I'm so excited I can't sit still." All morning her legs had rushed her through her chores, her hands working automatically and her mind spinning around the same subject. Jacqueline. Jackie. Jaq. What a beautiful name. She'd thought it and sometimes even spoken it aloud, whispered it repeatedly, enchanted by its music and rhythm. Jacqueline, her new friend.

The turtle raised its large head and, unblinking, gazed at her.

"Would you like to meet her, Miss Turtle? Well, you can't, because I refuse to share her, even with you and the pines. Today she's all mine."

As she pulled her bonnet and gloves back on, the turtle slid off the log and disappeared into the pond.

Should she ask Mr. James to drive her to the insane asylum? She was going crazy, talking to a turtle about a neighbor woman she planned to spend a pleasant afternoon with, then probably wouldn't see again for weeks. She needed to control herself before she went off the deep end.

She couldn't wait until Jacqueline arrived.

CHAPTER FOURTEEN

I'm late, I'm late, for a very important date." Maneuvering her Model T down the bumpy road, Jaq glanced at her new Longines wristwatch. Why would a line from *Alice in Wonderland* pop into her head? Maybe she was going down the rabbit hole. At least she wasn't heading for the trenches.

She'd already encountered new, strange worlds, though she couldn't decide which was the worst. The Storm of 1900, her encounters with Sister Mary Therese and Helen, the battlefields of France and Belgium, and the brutality the suffragists endured haunted her. She wanted to rip them from her mind.

But here she was, getting herself into another disastrous situation.

She was overdressed. Her clothes probably wouldn't even be fashionable in London, but here her outfit would impress, with its new American look. It certainly wasn't appropriate for working in the kitchen, but she intended to awe Molly and show her she was a cut above her. She told herself she was an urban sophisticate who wasn't interested in befriending a nobody destined to spend her life on an obscure cotton farm.

Of course she was lying, but she was desperate. Molly had already claimed more than enough of her attention.

She'd tried her damnedest not to hear the songs Molly played for her on Easter Sunday afternoon, but every morning she woke up humming "Pack Up Your Troubles in Your Old Kit-bag."

Every time she looked out the window and saw a pine sway in the breeze, she wondered what Molly would look like dancing to her own music. Then she had to remind herself that she'd *never* see her move like that.

Even when she drank a glass of water, she sensed Molly nearby. Her soft eyes gazed at Jaq until she slammed down the glass and told Molly to leave her alone.

How had Molly managed to invade her mind in such a short time? She was a sap.

As she neared the outer gate of the Russell farm, she finalized her plan of attack. She'd act extremely haughty. Her sophisticated outfit and ultra-new wristwatch should help. She'd pretend to be bored and indifferent, which would be hard as hell. Then she'd deliver her carefully prepared speech about leaving this hick burg as soon as possible. That should cut the afternoon short.

She'd avoid falling into Molly's eyes, no matter how much they invited her. And she would *not* touch Molly. Not at all. Not even her little finger.

But, honestly, she craved to hug Molly and melt into her. She ached to lose herself in Molly's sweetness.

She'd never do that, ever. She might be entering the rabbit hole, but she was armed.

❖

Molly stood at the front door and watched the black Model T motor up the long, winding, rocky driveway. As it neared, her tension ratcheted as tight as a piano string. If a felt-tipped hammer struck her nerves, they'd vibrate like the highest note on the keyboard.

She chided herself. This was supposed to be a delightful visit with a new friend, not a recital. At least she didn't have to do mindless chores or listen to Mother Russell fuss.

Inhaling the fresh smells of spring in the country, she processed across the porch and down the steps as if marching down the aisle of a cathedral decked with flowers. She mentally heard the swell of a Bach cantata and envisioned vast expanses of stained glass.

She had to jerk herself back to the grassless, hard-swept yard she'd just glided across when she met Jacqueline at the gate. "Welcome. It's been too long," she said.

Jacqueline looked outstanding in her stylish black suit with its long jacket, trimmed with gold braid, and her straight skirt. So military, so trustworthy. And the subtle swirls of embroidery on the sleeves and around the bottom of the knee-length jacket added a touch of softness that the outfit's almost-severe lines initially camouflaged.

She caught her breath and fingered the soft cotton lawn of her simple white dress, with its loose-fitting bodice and comfortable full skirt. She winced. The city mouse might not fancy her country cousin.

❖

Why had Jaq worn this stiff, scratchy wool suit? However, it had helped her almost achieve her objective. Molly visibly shrank from her. But why did this little housewife scare her? The Storm and the War were a long way away, thank God. The rose garden and Molly were right here, a very real threat.

She jerked to attention. Molly had just welcomed her and said, "It's been too long."

"It certainly has." She pulled herself together. She needed to act more mature. Oh, she'd meant what she'd just said. And she'd softened her tone. But Molly had sounded so hopeful and eager, probably like *she* had when she used to visit Sister Mary, when she encountered Helen unexpectedly.

She felt like she'd just lowered her sidearm. So much for being prepared.

"Would you like to visit the rose garden?" Molly asked. "It's one of the few interests Mother Russell and I have in common."

She chattered the entire time they crossed the fenced yard and strolled to the other side of the house. "Mother Russell brought several of these roses from Georgia after the War Between the States ended. Can you imagine traveling all that way with two adults and five children in a covered wagon and carrying rosebushes? She said she had a hard time keeping the roots moist because she stayed so busy feeding and watering her family. Once I overheard her tell her daughter that sometimes she even denied herself water and gave hers to her roses."

Molly laughed nervously. "Of course, I'd probably have insisted on bringing my piano, but that wouldn't have left room for many children, I suppose."

Why did Molly have only one child? Maybe when she knew her better—

The climbing roses Molly pointed out had large, sharp thorns. Jaq was glad she'd worn her leather gloves. Those branches could cause a lot of pain. She'd never risk picking those simple white blossoms.

When they entered the rose garden, its fragrance almost overwhelmed her. She recognized some of her favorites right off the bat—Perle d'Ors and Jeanne d'Arcs. Most of this group had large and small pastel blossoms, with shiny green foliage

Strolling beside Molly, she couldn't keep from telling her, "My mother loves roses too. We used to walk through the gardens behind our home in New Orleans occasionally. She knew the name and history of every plant."

The fragrant roses lulled her into remembering some of the few pleasant times she'd spent with her mother. She'd tour the garden with Molly. After they finished, she'd explain that they couldn't visit like this again. Surely she could do it.

❖

Molly's throat grew tight. She'd been so eager to see Jacqueline she hadn't given any thought to what they could talk about. Apparently she'd lost the skill of social conversation, if she ever had it, because she hadn't been able to come up with anything more interesting than Mother Russell's love for roses. She'd always been so busy practicing the piano and playing for church functions that she didn't have time for much else except her chores.

She didn't have much in common with any of the women at church and had lost touch with all her school friends except one. She was even tacitly barred from sitting on the front porch when Mother Russell presided over company out there. Her heart drummed. What could she converse about now?

When she visited Mama and Papa she never ran out of things to say, but she'd known them all her life. Jacqueline was a near stranger, and although Molly sensed that they had a lot in common, so far they'd only discussed heavy subjects, such as the Storm and the War. She wanted to make Jacqueline happy, not depress her. She'd just keep focusing on these beautiful flowers. Maybe they'd inspire her, or perhaps just the flowers themselves would bring Jacqueline pleasure.

"We need to choose ten large blooms that Mother Russell won't miss too badly," she told Jacqueline, "which is quite a challenge."

"Why?"

"She knows I use these blossoms for my rose water. But she begrudges me each one and acts as if I'm beheading a living creature. That's why I wanted to do this while she's gone."

She shouldn't tell someone she barely knew such family secrets, but Jacqueline didn't seem like she'd spread gossip. She appeared to have more important things on her mind.

"Shall we tour the garden first, then select our victims? I've brought a knife to use as our guillotine and a basket to carry our heads in."

Now Jacqueline winced.

Gracious. She was such a dunce! Jacqueline had actually seen dead bodies, and Molly had put her foot in her mouth when she was only trying to amuse her.

However, Jacqueline was gazing around the garden with seeming interest. "I enjoy working in the flower beds over at the McCade place. Eric's mother must have spent a lot of time there. Oh, look at the Old Blushes. Mother adores these, and I can understand how you could love something this beautiful."

Molly understood the allure of beautiful things. A pretty melody, two or three strong voices blending in song, the sound of the wind blowing through the trees, a woman's dark hair and eyes. Goodness, where had that thought come from? She shook her head and reached for a blossom. "This variety smells like fresh fruit. Shall we sacrifice one for our cause?"

As Jacqueline slowly nodded, Molly snipped a large, fully opened white bloom and wished she had the nerve to slide it behind Jacqueline's ear. The image made her heart beat faster.

The bloom Molly had just placed in Jaq's basket was as white as her cotton gloves. How would those same hands, without the gloves, feel if they touched her that gently? Deep down she'd known Helen would never touch her the way she hoped for, and Sister Mary would never touch her again. Molly was different, though—more approachable. Like Willie, in a strange way. They both seemed to know and accept her without reservation.

Then Molly naively explained that the plant would produce large orange hips in the fall, and Jaq couldn't keep from smiling. *You're a beast*, she thought. *You're just like a man. You can't think about anything but the physical.*

But Molly didn't attract her just on a physical level, like Willie did. Molly emitted a kind of perfume of the soul, which appealed to one of her more subtle senses. Molly lulled her baser self to sleep and awakened a longing for something finer and more rare than she'd dreamed of even with Sister Mary and Helen. And for some unimaginable reason she almost believed that dream could turn into reality. The possibility nearly made her sprint out of the garden, jump into her Model T, and never look back.

Molly cut a huge flat pink blossom, almost the same color as her cheeks, then held it out so Jaq could inhale its spicy, fruity scent. Its fragrance calmed her, charmed her into delaying her escape. She took another deep breath. Would Molly's rose water be half this fragrant? If so, and if she gave her any, she'd be lost every time she wore it.

She stopped and admired some cabbage-like pale-pink blooms, reminiscent of Baroque still-lifes. She'd really enjoyed her art course at the academy, and her voice lessons. The blooms made her think of Sister Mary again. Did she ever take her mind off women?

What did Molly's skin look like in places she'd never exposed to the sun?

She mentally slapped herself. She knew what Sister Mary's looked like, and felt like, and smelled like, and tasted like…

If Helen had even suspected her of having such fantasies about her, she'd have slugged her. But she'd had to go ahead and blurt out how she actually felt and…Helen hadn't reacted as Sister Mary had.

Yet Willie was too real, though she'd taught Jaq how wonderful her body could feel. Molly was just right…except she was married and had a son. After that sobering moment Molly and she stopped in front of a shrub loaded with raspberry-colored roses, and their fragrance threw her into a tailspin.

She slowly peeled off her gloves as they wandered through the garden. One rose, its odor like spicy herbal tea, smelled good enough to drink, just like Molly did. She straitjacketed her imagination, but the strings wouldn't stay tied.

Its petals reminded her of the color of Molly's hair, shining gold-red in the sunlight. But the rose was dull in comparison. Her hair shone even more than Helen's, though she hadn't seen Helen in the sunlight very often without her blue dress hat or her white nurse's cap. And the only time she got a look at Sister Mary's curls was when they sneaked out from her wimple and when they were together that one time. Willie wasn't afraid to unpin her dark hair when she and Jaq became intimate. She'd loved to feel it brush against her skin, like a fur coat.

Finally, Molly stopped in front of a compact bush with sprays of small, sweet-smelling pink blooms. "This is the Cecile Brunner, better known as the Sweetheart Rose."

She almost blurted, *And it reminds me of you and Helen and Sister Mary and Willie, all rolled into one.* But she managed to catch herself and listen while Molly said it could tolerate poor soil and partial shade. Then she took out her Brownie and snapped Molly's picture as she stood next to the blossoming bush, holding the basket of roses.

Blushing like Patrick did, Molly explained how easy it was to care for the plant, but Jaq couldn't think of anything except how much she'd like to take care of Molly. Helen and Sister Mary and Willie didn't need her. They had their vocations. But Molly—as healthy, wholesome, and beautiful as all these flowers—was asking her to rescue her, though she obviously didn't realize it. She could give Molly something not even her music could.

By now, though, she needed someone to rescue *her*. She followed Molly out of the garden and toward the house, her planned speech at the back of her mind. She wanted the afternoon to last forever. And if it didn't? She wanted to see Molly again, in private, as soon as possible.

❖

Molly set her basket on the countertop then laid out their ten large roses. "Why do so many of these roses have women's names?" she mused aloud.

Jaq gazed at her with what she feared was a vacant expression and slowly removed her suit jacket. The kitchen was unaccountably warm for this early in the year.

Molly counted several varieties of roses on her fingers. "Let's see, the Cecile Brunner, the Marie Pavie, the Mrs. Dudley Cross, the Madame Alfred Carrière, and the Madame Isaac Pereire. And that's just a few."

Jaq nodded silently as she rolled up the sleeves of her blouse, revealing muscled forearms covered with fine black hair.

"I can think of only two named for men, which is unusual, because men usually name everything for themselves—libraries, buildings, streets." Molly stopped and said, "Goodness, I sound like a suffragist."

Then Jaq smiled, which seemed to delight Molly.

"I'm not sure about the names. Mother did say that the last one you mentioned, Madame Isaac Pereire, was a banker's wife." Jaq's throat was really dry, so after she sipped the water Molly poured for her she managed to croak out a few more words. "Men probably want to acknowledge the beauty of the important women in their lives. Or maybe it would embarrass them to be associated with the flower's beauty and softness."

"You're right about men not wanting to appear soft," Molly said. "Why, Mr. James is like butter inside, but he always tries to pretend he's all man, whatever that means. As for acknowledging the important women in his life, he'd more than likely name a rose after his mother than me."

Molly didn't sound too happy with her husband, but if Jaq ever had a chance to name roses, she'd call a white one the Lady Molly, because her face bloomed with the open beauty of a flower, she smelled like honeysuckle, and she would be so very easy to touch. She'd name a sunny yellow rose the Helen, for one of the most beautiful women she'd ever known, in body and soul. A pastel would be the Sister Mary, because Jaq still loved her, in spite of the pain, and a large crimson one would commemorate Willie.

While Jaq had been musing, Molly had stuck another piece of split pine into the smoldering embers in the stove. Then she set out a kettle, a bucket of water, a large bowl, a wide-mouthed glass jar, and some cheesecloth.

Jaq helped strip the plump petals from their base. How wonderful to do something with her hands. She rubbed one of the velvety petals between her fingertips and on her cheek. Then, giddy and content, she bit one of the jam-sweet raspberry-colored petals. Molly could probably even hear its sound.

Molly packed two cups full of the petals and emptied them into a crock, covered them with four cups of steaming water, and placed a large tin lid on it.

"Now we'll have refreshments while the mixture sits. In thirty minutes we'll pour our rose water into this jar and strain it through the cheesecloth. I always add some to the cold soap I make out of our best lard and use especially for my hands. And you can take some home. Then we'll both smell like the rose garden for several weeks. After that we'll need to make some more."

So it could remind her of Molly every minute of every day? And then they'd have to do this again? She shook herself out of her mood of surrender.

After she hastily rolled down her sleeves, she pulled on her jacket and gloves and behaved for the remainder of the afternoon. Tonight she'd ask Eric how soon they could drive back to New Orleans.

CHAPTER FIFTEEN

Molly lifted the telephone receiver from its hook and whirled the handle to call the operator. Mother Russell was taking her afternoon nap.

"Number, please."

"Hello, Ethel. Would you ring four-three-one? That's the McCades' number, isn't it?"

"It surely is. Isn't it a shame about Mr. Eric? He used to be so friendly, and now he's holed up like a bear. But how are you doing today? That was a beautiful solo you played at church Sunday."

"Thanks, Ethel. May I ask a favor?"

"Surely, Miss Molly. Anything for you."

"Could you make certain none of the other operators listen in on my conversations? I know you'd never do that, but I don't know the other girls as well as I do you."

"I surely will. You can trust me. Just a minute now, and I'll ring Miss Jacqueline. She'd probably enjoy talking to you. Nobody ever calls her, and I bet Mr. Eric isn't much fun to live with right now. She must be right lonely there at that place with those two men to wait on and no womenfolk around to keep her company."

"Yes, Ethel. That's why I'm calling her. Just trying to be sociable."

There was no reason for them not to spend time together, she thought as Ethel connected them.

"Hello."

Jacqueline sounded sad.

"What's wrong? Are you okay?"

"Oh, Molly. It's good to hear your voice. No, I'm okay. Just a little blue. I'll get over it."

"I'm sorry to hear that. Listen, Jacqueline, I've caught up with my chores, and Mother Russell's going to her weekly Red Cross meeting tomorrow. I've made a pound cake and thought you might like a piece. I've been saving flour and sugar for it. Is that okay? Will you be home in the morning about ten o'clock?"

"Why, Molly, you're a real pal. Don't feel obligated, but if you really want to, I'll be here."

"I'm looking forward to it. See you tomorrow."

She slowly hung up the receiver. Jacqueline had acted a little strange during her visit to make rose water. At first, she'd seemed determined about something, and she hadn't said much the entire time she was there. What had been on her mind? Did she want to be friends or was she merely being polite?

But Jacqueline had just called her a "real pal." Surely that meant something. She hoped...oh, she didn't know what she hoped, but it had something to do with spending as much time with Jacqueline as possible. The prospect made her shoulders tingle and her neck throb.

She shook herself so she could think straight. Mother Russell would be upset that she'd used some of their precious flour and sugar to make a cake and then given some of it away. She begrudged others her sweets.

The candy-like longing crept through Molly's veins again, pumping its syrup throughout her, making her willing to do anything to be near Jacqueline. This cake was the only excuse she could come up with to see Jacqueline. She simply couldn't seem to stay away from her, regardless of the consequences.

❖

Molly hitched Gus and Kate to the wagon, still full of energy and looking forward to visiting Jacqueline. As they plodded down the dusty road, her thoughts drifted to Patrick being at school, then to the day he was born.

"Kate," she told one of the mules, "that horrid doctor smoked cigars from the time he walked into the house until right before he delivered Patrick. I lay there on that rough cotton sheet, my legs spread like a plucked chicken's, and he didn't do anything but smoke and stand out in the hall and talk to Mr. James about the price of cotton. I wanted Mother Russell or another midwife to deliver the baby, but Mr. James insisted that it wouldn't look right, that we could afford to hire a doctor for the birth of his first child. The smell of that cigar smoke gagged me so much I almost threw up, but no one even noticed."

She couldn't shake herself out of the nightmarish experience. "I wanted Mama there, standing beside me and holding my hand. But she was in Dallas, too sick to ride all day. Besides, the roads were too muddy for Papa's Model T.

"Instead of Mama, there stood Mother Russell. She swiveled my way once in a while but seemed to be half listening to the men's conversation. Finally she gave me a hard look and told me there wasn't anything to having a baby, that it got easier. After a half a dozen or more children, like she'd had, I'd be able to get right back to work in nothing flat."

A cloud blotted out the sun. Molly had been so sick after the birth. Clyde, James's younger brother, had paid more attention to her than anyone else had. Visited and brought her flowers from the yard that he'd picked himself, though he was usually uncouth and rude to everybody.

"That doctor finally told me I couldn't have any more children because my womb was infected, Kate," she said. "I didn't know exactly what he meant, but I suspected he'd caused it. He never washed his hands, even after holding those smelly cigars. I bet he doesn't believe in germs any more than Mother Russell does. She says a handful of spiderwebs can fix almost any cut or sore, but all I can think about is the millions of germs wiggling around in them."

Ironically, Mother Russell had saved her. She'd told the doctor to leave and mixed up some herbal remedies out of who knew what. Too sick to care, Molly had swallowed whatever Mother Russell offered, and miraculously, she'd recovered.

The sun stayed behind the cloud and a cool breeze began to blow. "When I felt good enough to care about anything, Kate, I was devastated. I couldn't have any more children! I couldn't sleep or eat because I kept worrying if I was still a real woman.

"Finally I calmed down. I'd always wanted a daughter, but I never wanted a large family the way Mr. James did."

The clouds got darker and it looked like it might rain. She clucked at the mules. "Mr. James was thrilled to have a son, but he was cut up when he heard Patrick would be his one and only child, Gus. I failed him and disappointed Mother Russell too. My last chance to gain her respect evaporated, but that didn't bother me nearly so much as disappointing Mr. James. I felt sorry for him."

When she'd recovered, she finally accepted that she'd never have a daughter, but she could always share her love for music with the children in the community. And that's exactly what she did.

Now some of them had moved to the city and were developing into fine musicians. When they wrote her occasionally about how they'd never forget her, she couldn't have been happier.

The sun came out again and she thought about Jacqueline. She didn't have any children but had risked her life near a battlefield helping others. Having a baby was tame compared to that.

"Jacqueline's brave, isn't she, Gus?"

The mules plodded on, their blinders keeping them from glancing right or left.

"I wish I had her courage. It's taken me eight years just to admit to myself that I've never loved the man I married." At this rate she'd be almost as old as Mother Russell before she could get away from here, if ever.

What would it be like to marry someone she loved? She'd never know. She'd accepted Mr. James's proposal out of fear and self-doubt. Now she was bound up here in this alien place as tight as the ball of twine that Mother Russell kept in the kitchen. Every time they came across even a small piece of string, they wrapped it onto the ball and pulled it taut. It would take a lot less time to untangle that ball than it would to get herself out of this situation that she'd been too weak to refuse.

But maybe Jacqueline could help her. Was that why she was so drawn to her—her confidence, her strength, her fearlessness? Molly wouldn't give up until she found out.

CHAPTER SIXTEEN

Eric had been so drunk and acted like another person, a stranger. Jaq had asked, "Why do you drink so much?"

"None of your business," he'd yelled. "Put a sock in it. Nobody loves a cripple."

Too sore to get out of bed, she needed Helen to nurse her, Willie to massage her. Every muscle ached, her forehead hurt. Could she walk? Should have called Molly, told her not to come over. When Molly telephoned yesterday she seemed different—more outspoken, freer.

Pines surrounded the house, closed her in, cut her off from the world, guarded her. Like she was a prisoner of war. "Eric's sentinels," she whispered. "You don't have to work hard today. I won't escape now. I want to…want to leave."

The wind blew, the pines rocked. Was Big Bertha shooting at them, playing war music? She felt shell-shocked.

"Jacqueline. Oh, Jacqueline."

A voice, from a great distance, sounded over the roar of the noisy guns.

"I know you're here. Where are you?"

The person sounded familiar. Who was it? "Molly. Up here. In the guest bedroom. The door's open."

"Gracious. Are you okay? I can barely hear you."

"Fine."

Molly climbed the staircase, walked down the hall. The boards creaked, groaned. The house moved in the breeze with the pines, made Jaq's head spin. Felt like she was in an aeroplane, taking a nosedive.

"Here."

Molly appeared, her red-gold hair mounded on her head, like a halo. Her pale-green housedress matched her concerned eyes.

"What are you doing in bed in middle of the day? Why, I—"

Her eye hurt. She could barely see Molly.

"What happened to you?"

She pulled the sheet closer. Molly shouldn't see any more of her. She felt weak, too exposed.

"Nothing. I fell down the stairs."

"Well, I never saw a tumble cause a black eye like that. You must have hit the banister on the way down."

"Yes. I hit the banister. Don't worry. How are you?"

She didn't want to talk about herself. Ashamed, she didn't want Molly to ask any questions.

Molly tried not to stare, but Jacqueline looked terrible, lying on the bed with a bloody cloth over her right eye and her forehead—and obviously not telling the truth. She reminded her of a box turtle she'd found in the strawberry patch this morning, nibbling berries. As soon as it spotted her, it slammed its shell shut. She couldn't have pried it apart with a case knife.

For a minute Jacqueline seemed to want to open up to her, like the turtle taking a small bite of that strawberry. Then she closed up. She could almost hear her shell snap shut.

Why was Jacqueline in this room? Eric always slept in the room down the hall. A lot of clothes, obviously hers, hung in the chifforobe, and her toiletries sat on a small dressing table.

Mrs. McCade had taken her to see Eric's room once, when he was overseas. "Isn't he neat?" Mrs. McCade had said as she showed her the bare-looking bedroom. "Eric can't stand a speck of dust on any of his things and has to have everything just so. He likes for everything to be perfect. As a boy he always beat everyone in the community at whatever he turned his hand to.

"Once, he lost a foot race at school. He was hurt—and mad as a hornet. Told me nobody would ever like him again, because he was common now. No, he liked to be a cut above the rest of us. And he kept on racing—horses, automobiles. He always writes me about his victories. He doesn't seem to realize he kills people. No. He just shoots down aeroplanes."

Mrs. McCade had rambled on about Eric, and from what she'd gathered, he was a charmer with a hidden side. But she barely knew him, because he'd left home not long after she moved to New Hope.

When the War came along, he was a famous hero. But if he did this to Jacqueline, she'd give him a piece of her mind, hero or not.

"Jacqueline, did Eric hit you? Is that why you're staying in here instead of with him?"

In response, Jacqueline ducked her head almost entirely under the bloody sheet, just like that little turtle.

She didn't know exactly why, but if Eric had hurt Jacqueline she would…what would she do to a big, strong man? Threaten to beat him up? She couldn't even imagine fighting physically with anyone.

At least she could find out exactly what was going on in this household.

❖

The sheet eased away and a hand took the cloth from her face. No. She didn't want Molly to see where…

Molly was talking. "I won't hurt you. No one will hurt you."

Jaq felt totally exposed and hated being helpless.

Eric had been like a train coming out of a tunnel. His eyes had flashed. He'd called her a pervert. His fist had roared at her.

She didn't want to think, she couldn't think. Her head fuzzy, she floated, drifted somewhere, unmoored, sailing across cold seas on the *Lusitania*, the *Titanic*.

When they'd first married she'd explained she liked women, not men. He'd shrugged, said, "We'll see."

Then she'd built a wall, a thick wall of ice, a huge wall of ice like an iceberg. The *Titanic* had grazed it. But Eric was always a perfect gentleman, even in New Orleans when she told him about Willie.

After they married he returned to his aeroplane. She joined the WAACs, went to France and met Helen. Finally she went home to New Orleans, and he showed up. Why did he come? Why…?

His mother had died…mother died…She'd felt so sorry for him, his eye injured, walking with a cane. She agreed to go to East Texas but insisted on separate bedrooms.

He agreed. "Okay, yes, okay, yes. Go with me now. We'll live separate lives afterward."

They'd had separate bedrooms until early this morning.

"Jacqueline, I don't want to pry. But if you confide in me, I'll see what I can do. The community's very tight-knit, and Mr. James and Mother Russell are influential, so—"

"Oh, Molly. So kind. Don't get mixed up in my problems. Keep them quiet. I'll solve them, for good, soon, very soon. Don't worry."

❖

Jacqueline seemed dazed, and her forehead oozed blood. Molly couldn't force her to make sense or even trust her. But she could try to entice her.

"I've brought you that piece of pound cake I promised. I'll go downstairs and get it—"

"You can't. I won't let you. I'm the hostess—"

"Hush. I won't be a minute. Sometimes we all need someone to wait on us. You'd do the same for me. Rest now. I'll be back before you know it."

As she transferred the cake onto a small white plate adorned with purple violets, she said to herself, "She's in a bad way, and stubborn as one of the mules. Well, she's met her match."

Jacqueline seemed to have dozed off, but she stirred when Molly entered the room. She set the cake and a tall glass of milk down and walked over to her. "Jacqueline, I want you to sit up and take a bite. Have you eaten anything today? But first, hold this clean dishtowel to your head."

Jacqueline took the towel but shook her head, like Patrick when he wasn't telling the whole truth. She probably hadn't had any food since last night. Judging from the dirty dishes in the sink and the burnt frying pan on the stove, the men had messed around in the kitchen. Surely Jacqueline wouldn't have left it in such bad shape. At least someone had milked the cow and left a pail of milk on the counter, though it was already turning bad. Just like a man.

"Here, just a bite. It won't hurt you. That's it. Now a swallow of milk. That's a girl."

She coaxed Jacqueline to eat, and she slowly finished the sliver of cake and milk as if she hadn't eaten in days. She acted a lot like Patrick.

He tried to be so independent, but sometimes he still needed her to take care of him. And Jacqueline needed her...

"Now listen here," she said, "and listen good. You're going to dress and pack a few things and come home with me. If your body looks as bad as the rest of you, you won't be able to climb those stairs for a while."

Jacqueline looked stricken, as if she had just suggested that she walk into the church naked.

"No. Mrs. Russell, Mr. James? Can't impose—"

"Don't you worry. I'll take care of them. Mother Russell won't like it, but she won't want to look bad in the eyes of the community. And Mr. James? He'll hardly know you're there. He's got his own routine and doesn't pay much attention to what goes on in the house. When he's there he's usually in his own little world—reading the paper or dreaming up ways to get rich."

"Eric? Mr. McCade? Need to—"

"If they don't know how to cook, they can learn or starve. If you stayed here they'd just have to wait on you. And I doubt any of you would like that. Come on. Kate and Gus are waiting downstairs."

She wanted to get Jacqueline away before Eric returned.

What a bumpy road, but Molly was so careful. In France, Jaq drove over rough, shell-pitted roads carrying groaning men. Rockets exploded everywhere, the noise of bombs and bullets deafened her.

Finally, she and Molly reached the long driveway. The sun was so bright, too bright.

"I'll settle you in the spare bedroom before Mother Russell and Patrick get home. Here. Hold this clean cloth over your forehead and let me rinse your dishtowel. You need to lie down, see if we can stop the bleeding."

Molly braced her. She leaned on Molly, put her arm around Molly's shoulder, Molly's arm encircling her waist. She forced her feet up the front steps, hobbled down the central hall to a bedroom.

"This belonged to Mr. James's youngest sister, Hannah. She got married and moved out. We use it for a sewing room now, and for guests. It's a little cluttered. Hope you don't mind the mess."

"I'm tired. After I rest I'll help you straighten up."

"Nonsense. Undress and put on your gown. I'll take care of everything."

She pulled her gown from her bag. Molly placed her other clothes in an oak dresser and placed her toiletries on top.

"There. The slop jar's beside the bed. Don't even try to go to the outhouse."

Her face warmed. Molly emptying her slop jar? Jaq was helpless like the wounded men on the front lines. Her upper chest ached, and her hip too. She felt like a mule had kicked her, couldn't unbutton her blouse.

Molly took over. "Here, let me do that."

She tried to lift her arms, sit on the edge of the bed. Molly finished undressing her.

"I'd have hit your husband like he hit you. Did you fight back?"

Was this someone else's body, this mass of pain? Her head pounded, her arms and legs were purple, ugly.

"I need to sponge the blood off you, Jacqueline. You sit here. I'll go get a washrag and some water. I won't be long. You'll feel better when you're clean."

Molly seemed upset, angry.

In the mirror, Jaq saw the bruises on her arms and back. Eric had hit her in the face, and she fell and broke open her wound from France. Everything turned black after that for a while. Then she tried to go downstairs. Eric was a large man with a huge temper. She should never have come to East Texas, but Eric had been so pitiful when he asked for her help.

She'd believed she could help him. She was a fool. How dared he do this to her? But she couldn't strike back at him, not after what she did to Henry in France.

CHAPTER SEVENTEEN

Molly tiptoed back into the room and gasped when she stopped long enough to really look at Jacqueline's back and arms. She must have fallen down that steep staircase, like she said, but why didn't Eric tend to her?

She carefully cleaned Jacqueline's soft white skin, as smooth as the ivory on her piano keys, though much warmer. How could anyone damage such beauty? She was ashamed to enjoy touching this amazing body so much.

She reluctantly finished then helped Jacqueline into her gown and tried to brush her matted hair. The white cloth Jacqueline held still had some red spots, and she was beginning to worry about the wound on her forehead. She took the rag, peeked under Jacqueline's bangs, and saw a strange gash about two inches long over her right eye. She raised the damp bangs and guided Jacqueline's hand up so she could hold the rinsed-out dishtowel in place. Then she ran her fingers through Jacqueline's hair before she stroked it with the brush. Coarse, and dull with blood, as it smoothed out under her hands, it sent an electric charge through her.

Touching Esther Harris in college had affected her like this, though not so intensely. They had planned to live together and both teach music, like their two favorite instructors. Late one night studying for a difficult history test, Esther'd been tired and discouraged, almost crying. She was afraid she'd fail and not be able to return to school the next year. Molly had put her arm around her and would never forget the spark between them. It had felt like the highest note on the organ sounded when she held it down for a long time.

Though she'd wanted to do more than hug Esther, an inner voice kept repeating, *You and Esther are merely playing at life instead of actually living it. You'll grow up someday.*

She'd held out longer than most of her classmates by attending the university for three years, until her financial situation finally caught up with her and she accepted Mr. James's proposal.

As she cleaned Jacqueline's skin and smoothed her hair, her dream flamed briefly, like it had after their first conversation. But the law and, even more important, Patrick bound her to Mr. James.

Shaking her head, she scattered the embers of her illusions and helped Jacqueline settle into bed, still holding the towel in place. But when Jacqueline gazed up at her with soft eyes, her dreams flared again.

She *would* love Jacqueline, for as long as she could. She simply couldn't let anyone know, not even Jacqueline.

❖

Mrs. Russell spotted the mules still hitched to the wagon when she drove up. What in the Sam Hill? Molly knew better than to leave the wagon in her way. If she insisted on sashaying around the countryside like she didn't have anything better to do, at least she could unhitch the mules when she finally decided to come home.

Molly should have been at the meeting today. People were whispering that she and Jacqueline were unpatriotic. Hadn't President Wilson himself said that every able-bodied person should rally 'round the boys who were risking life and limb so far away from home?

Even Alice, Clyde's wife, was there, though she didn't have much spare time. She and Hannah were true farm women, not do-nothings like Molly. When their husbands went away to war, just like her own dear one did, they didn't whine. Instead, they ran their farms, raised their young'uns, and managed to scrape by without a man. It'd been hard, especially since the War had taken all the neighboring hired men, either overseas or to the cities.

She pushed through the back door and stopped. Something smelled queer, like perfume and blood. A stranger was here. Molly was in the kitchen instead of the parlor banging on that silly piano, and she'd shut the door to the guest room. Funny. They usually left it open, especially during warm weather, to let a good breeze circulate. It could get stuffy mighty fast, and it was already heating up right smart during the day.

"What's going on, Molly?" she said, because Molly looked like she was about to cry.

"It's Jacqueline. She's bleeding and I can't get it to stop. Eric must have hit her, and I didn't know what to do except bring her home."

"Bleeding? Where?"

"On her forehead. Can you help her?"

You could bet your bottom dollar Molly couldn't doctor her, so she had to come in all tired from doing her civic duty and find the little slacker in her house worrying about a sick stranger. Lord have mercy.

"Let's go see."

She and Molly found Jacqueline all cozied into Hannah's old bed, making herself right at home. Then she peeked under the towel on Jacqueline's head.

"Looks like it's almost bled itself out, but go fetch the sewing basket and a jar of honey, Molly. And look in the pantry where I keep all my jars of dried herbs. Bring me the one labeled *calendula*."

Molly lit out like the house was on fire, and she cleaned up Jacqueline with the damp cloth so she could inspect the damage. Looked like the gash wasn't new. Somebody that barely knew how to thread a needle had sewed it up with big clumsy stitches a while back, and she must have hit it and broke it open again. No wonder she wore those bangs. It must have made an ugly scar.

"Here's what you asked for." Molly stared at the jars she was holding like they were full of poison.

"Okay, Molly. Go to my room and look through my lace-making equipment. You'll see it in the very top of my old trunk. Mind you, don't meddle with anything else in there. It's private and none of your business. Find some white silk thread and a number nine needle. You know. The size I give you to embroider fancy stuff on linen handkerchiefs after I edge them with lace. I need a little bowl and a teaspoon too."

Molly finally found what she needed. She didn't trust Molly to tie a good strong knot, so she did it herself and commenced to take four tiny stitches for each of the four big ones whoever had messed up Jacqueline's face had made. Didn't want to make 'em too small—might weaken the skin. She did a good job, if she had to say so herself. And Jacqueline didn't let out a peep, though it must have hurt like the dickens.

Molly looked like she'd pass out every time she poked a hole through Jacqueline's skin, but she just stood there and squeezed Jacqueline's hand so hard she was afraid she might have to reset the bones.

After she finished, she told Molly, "Untie the twine from around that herb jar." She took the brown paper off the jar and fished out four or five petals of calendula she'd dried last fall. They were brown now, but back then they were bright as the sun. Most folks called 'em marigolds, but they were the best thing possible to help a body's skin heal.

She crushed them and mixed them with honey then spread them as thick as she could over the place and tied a clean bandage around Jacqueline's head.

When she finished, at least Jacqueline remembered her manners and said, "Thank you, Mrs. Russell."

She sighed. Now she had to go rustle up some supper to feed the extra mouth Molly had saddled her with.

❖

Mr. James arrived from the fields and patted Patrick on the shoulder. "How's my boy? What did you learn in school today?"

"Hi, Pa. I'm learning to read pretty good. Maybe I can read you a story before long. Guess what? A nice lady is visiting us."

Mr. James looked at Molly with a question in his eyes.

"Mama let me carry the lady some potato soup," Patrick said. "She woke up and ate a few bites. Then she went right back to sleep."

Molly tried to explain what was going on, but Patrick was wound up. "Grandma doctored her and said she'll be okay. Mama said she needs to get a good night's sleep and rest here. She can stay, can't she? I'll help take care of her."

She wanted to hug Patrick. "It's Jacqueline McCade he's going on about. Remember her from Easter Sunday? Looks like Eric hit her. You don't mind that I brought her home to stay with us awhile, do you?"

"Well, now." Mr. James glanced at his mama, who stood at the stove with her stiff back to him. "I reckon she needs a little help, and it wouldn't be right if we didn't give it to her. Isn't that what you think, Ma? But it's hard for me to believe Eric would do something like that. Why, he's the most upstanding young man I ever knew."

Mother Russell scowled. "Bunch of nonsense, if you ask me. Folks ought to take care of their own personal problems. Eric won't thank us for getting between him and his so-called wife. I sewed her up, but I didn't invite her in the first place."

"I appreciate what you did, Mother Russell," Molly said. "She's asleep right now, but she looks bad. Probably nothing serious, but I don't want to take a chance."

"Ah, pshaw," Mrs. Russell said. "Just another mouth to feed and extra work for us all. But I can't have the neighbors saying I'm not a good Christian woman. Have to set an example for those that don't have as much as we do."

Mr. James looked relieved. He didn't like for his mama and her to quarrel. In spite of his fascination with war, he was a man of peace.

As she thanked her lucky stars for that, a truck pulled up the driveway. She knew exactly who it was.

The buzzing in Jaq's ears had faded. Now she felt like the voices in the distance came from actors on a stage and she was standing in the wings.

Eric: "Where's my wife? I've come to take her home."

Mr. James: "You're not going near her. What happened between you two, Eric? I'm disappointed in you. Boy Jim would never lay a hand on a woman."

Eric: "You need to get it through your head that I'm nothing like that character you admire so much. I've got a bad eye and have a hard time walking. I'm not worth a plug nickel."

Mr. James: "Calm down, boy. Just tell me what's going on."

Eric: "I've been hitting the bottle more than I should, sir. And late last night I had more than I could handle. I was gassed. Jaq asked me something—I don't even remember what—and before I knew it, I popped her one. I don't know what got into me. I've never hit a woman. She fell and I got out of there before I did anything else to her."

Molly: "She hit her head, hard, and acts like she had a concussion. I don't know what happened, but she was in bed and acting strange when I went to your house this morning. Her forehead wouldn't quit bleeding, so Mother Russell had to sew it up."

Eric: "Good grief. That's why Pop was looking at me so strange all day. He must have helped her. He fixed breakfast this morning—that was a mess. Even made us a lunch. Said Jaq was feeling poorly, but I had no idea how bad off she was."

Mr. James: "Son, I don't think you meant to hurt your wife. But you need to stop looking for your manhood in a bottle. We all still believe in you. You need to heal. Our recruiters would love to have an experienced man like you in our own army to help the new men out."

Eric: "You're right, sir. I'm sorry you had to get mixed up in all this, but I've learned my lesson. No more whiskey for me. Patrick, don't ever do anything bad like I have. And Miss Molly, thank you for tending to my wife. She's a fine woman, and I'd never hurt her on purpose. It's probably better if she stays here for a spell, if you don't mind. You can take care of her better than I can. And she most likely doesn't want to see me. I'll try to straighten myself out, and when she comes back, I swear on my mother's grave I'll never touch her again."

Mr. James: "All right. Everyone deserves a second chance, but I'll be keeping a close eye on you, son. Putting down that bottle won't be easy, but you've got a lot to gain. Just remember that."

Eric: "I will, sir. And thank you again, Miss Molly. Tell Jaq I'm really sorry, but when she's ready it'll be good to have her. You can let her know too that I've decided to go back and outfly Eddie Rickenbacker as soon as I get better. I have to prove I'm still the man everybody's always thought I was."

Jacqueline was glad the play ended happily. How strange to be a character in such a melodrama. Maybe Eric would keep his promises to himself and to her after the way Mr. James had been so firm with him. He wouldn't want to lose face in the community, but she hoped he was just bluffing about going back to war. What would his father do without him? And what about her?

But she couldn't worry about that now. Snuggling into the feather mattress in the next room, she sighed and fell sound asleep for the first time since Eric hit her.

CHAPTER EIGHTEEN

Mrs. Russell stood at the black wash pot in the backyard poking the clothes into the boiling water with her long wooden battling stick. The dirty-looking soap bubbles expanded then burst—kinda like her notions about Jacqueline.

That girl needed to get up out of that bed and start doing for herself. She'd laid around five whole days, and Molly said she just had a touch of fever now. She'd had a powerful thirst, so they gave her lots of water and made her eat as much as she could stomach. She'd cut her stitches out this morning and told her not to frown. Her eye was still purple, but she'd healed fast, probably because she was so young and feisty.

Maybe Eric had straightened himself out enough so she could think about going home.

She *was* pitiful, hobbling like an old woman when she got up to use the slop jar. At least she'd kept those bangs combed back. Her forehead should look better in a month or so, and then she could start hiding her scar again. She kept offering to help but wasn't up to it just yet. She was hurt pretty bad.

"I'm ready," Molly said as she poured the last bucketful of water she'd drawn from the well into the big number-three washtub. "I'll rinse the white clothes now, if you want, and you can start the darker ones. We're running a little low on lye soap. We need to make some more before the next washday."

She wiped the sweat off her forehead and watched Molly fish the steaming clothes out of the boiling water with the battling stick and tote 'em over to the first rinse tub. It took her several trips, and all that time she acted like she ran the place, like she'd grown up washing clothes in the backyard and drawing all the well water they needed for it by hand.

It'd be a blessing when Patrick got big enough to do that chore all by himself.

She'd never been a stranger to hard work. Her pa never could afford any slaves, and since he didn't have anything but girls, she grew up on the end of a hoe. She could chop a row of cotton faster and cleaner than anybody in the county, including her husband Calvin, though he didn't practice as much as she did.

Her back was as strong as a man's, but it sure got sore once in a while. She was getting a little old. Yes, sir, it'd be good to have a big strapping boy to haul the water out of the well instead of having to depend on Molly and mostly do it herself when James was out in the fields. She was getting weary of working like a man.

"How are you this morning, Patrick? Are you enjoying your summer vacation? Why aren't you outside helping your mother and your grandmother?"

"Mama said she'd call me later. She lets me help her get the clothes dry. I like to spread them all over the bushes. It's fun, like a game."

Jaq sat in a chair in the guest room. Molly had tiptoed in as soon as she woke up and said she'd slept on filthy sheets long enough. It was washday, and she and Mrs. Russell had already built a fire, she said. They had the wash pot ready to go. And her sheets did feel dirty. She'd spent a lot of time between them.

Patrick plopped down on the bare feather mattress and stared at her like she was an exotic animal in a circus parade.

"Can I stay in here with you and talk about the War? Were you really over there where they're fighting?"

"Yes, Patrick. This time last year I was in Belgium, close to France. Be glad you're not old enough to be there. The boys on the front lines have to sleep in the mud a lot of nights. And do you know what they have to eat?"

"No, ma'am. What?"

"Well, if they're lucky enough to find an empty house, they cram themselves into a big room. Then they build a campfire and brew coffee and toast bread over it."

"Golly, that sounds like fun."

"It may sound like it, Patrick, but it's not. The boys don't ever have any chocolate pie or buttermilk with cornbread, like you do. One of the worst things is the poison gas the Boches use. They shoot it at our boys in big shells. And if it gets on them it makes nasty yellow sores and hurts their lungs so they can't breathe very well."

Patrick frowned and changed the subject. "Why do you call them Boches, Miss Jacqueline?"

"It's an ugly word for the Germans. Some people say it means cabbage head. I'm not sure how it got started, but a lot of the soldiers in Europe use it, so I picked up the same habit. It really means we don't like the German soldiers and wish they'd go home and leave us alone."

Patrick looked like he was interested, but he didn't seem to believe everything she told him.

"Oops, I hear Mama calling me. I'll be back as soon as I can."

She enjoyed Patrick's company. He seemed bright and caring, like his mother. Mature for his age, but she'd heard that was common for an only child. He was already showing signs of growing up to be as large as his father. Lately, he'd started visiting her every chance he got. He liked to talk about life beyond the farm, especially everything his father had told him about the Trojan War.

Mr. James glamorized war, and she hated to disillusion Patrick. But a lot of the young men—and women like Helen—were in Europe because of that same type of lie. Damn it. She refused to help send Patrick off to another war to be slaughtered. She believed in the suffragists' nonviolent tactic of turning President Wilson's words against him.

Poor Helen had been a diehard patriot, though, so excited about her experience in the conflict. She'd kept talking about all the war stories she'd share with her family and friends when she got home. Nothing seemed to disillusion her, even when she was shivering in the cold and the rain. She thought about Helen for quite a while after Patrick left.

The Russells were good people too. Molly had been an angel. And what Mr. James said to Eric the other night made Jaq feel a lot safer about going back. Mrs. Russell was a cross to bear, most of the time, but she'd done a really fine job tending to her forehead. Jaq hoped her new scar looked better than the one she'd had to live with since last year. Every time she looked at it, she was ashamed of what she'd done to Henry.

❖

Molly spread clean white sheets onto Jacqueline's bed. "Is this old feather mattress comfortable enough?"

"It's like lying on a cloud. I've felt like royalty the past few days, with you and Patrick waiting on me."

"You deserve every minute of it, after what happened. I just wish you could live with us forever."

"I can't remember when I've been happier. I enjoyed visiting my aunts in Washington and New York, and living with my sister in London, but she's so fascinated with high society, just like Mother. She was always fretting about what to wear and why she didn't get invited to this party or that one. I told her she'd just recovered from having her second baby and didn't need to be out running around, but did she listen to me? You seem so devoted to Patrick. It's good to see someone who truly enjoys being a mother."

Molly flinched. She *did* love Patrick and would do anything for him. She'd agreed to this life, and she meant to make the most of it. But if she had it to do over again, she'd choose a much different road, perhaps one with somebody as special as Jacqueline. The very thought made her grab hold of the sheet she was spreading so tight she bunched it into a wad. She had to loosen her grip and press out the wrinkles with her hand. That's what life with Jacqueline would be like, she mused—nice and smooth, instead of the twisted-up mess hers was now on the farm.

But it was so hard for two women to support themselves. Men monopolized almost all the paying jobs and denigrated women's work. Her favorite music teachers at Bowdon seemed to have managed financially, though supposedly a wealthy uncle had left one of them a substantial inheritance.

She'd heard that some women dressed up like men, even lived their entire lives pretending to be men and never got caught, just so they could make enough money to survive on their own. But she wouldn't like that. She liked being a woman, and she enjoyed being around someone who seemed to feel the same way—such as Jacqueline.

"Mother Russell asked me to change your bandage today. Do you mind?" She hoped she could do it right.

"Of course not. But don't you have better things to do, with all your chores?"

I can't think of anywhere I'd rather be. She patted the bed. "It'll only take a few minutes. I've watched Mother Russell, so maybe I'll do a decent job."

Jacqueline's expression encouraged her. "Of course you will. And I'd much rather have you close to me than her."

Then Jacqueline blushed, like she'd said something she didn't mean to.

As they both sat on the edge of the bed and she scooted close enough to take off the old bandage, she smelled the homemade soap they all used here at home. Then, instead of the odor of lard sweetened with rose water, she inhaled a hint of perspiration, as if Jacqueline was nervous. But why would she be?

Molly gently brushed Jacqueline's bangs back and eased the soiled bandage off, barely touching Jacqueline's face, though even that tiny contact made her fingers vibrate. The wound seemed to be healing. She could see the tiny holes the stitches had left after Mother Russell cut the thread out. As she carefully ran a clean, wet cloth over the gash to clear away the flecks of calendula petals that still clung to it, Jacqueline grasped her shoulders, as if she'd startled her.

"Does it still hurt?" she asked.

"Not much. But it's a little tender."

Jacqueline didn't move her hands, and she didn't budge. In fact, she inched a tad closer. They sat unmoving for a while, gazing at each other. Something flowed between them, as strong and sweet as taffy. Molly didn't want to breathe and risk disturbing the connection.

"Do I look too horrible?" Jacqueline seemed embarrassed to ask the question.

Nothing about you could ever look horrible, she wanted to say, but she simply rubbed the back of her hand over Jacqueline's cheek, which was as smooth and firm as an almost-ripe plum. "Not at all," she whispered. "I doubt anyone will even notice your scar after a few months."

Without warning, Jacqueline wrapped her arms around her in a long hug and murmured, "Thank you." She just had to hug her back, and for a wonderful few minutes they sat there with their breasts touching and the smell of clean, sun-dried sheets wafting around them. She didn't remember ever feeling so content yet so on edge.

When they finally pulled apart, Molly was full of an energy she'd never experienced. She wanted to run, to shout that everything in the world was wonderful, especially Jacqueline.

But she couldn't do that. She couldn't slip between the soft sheets beside Jacqueline either, or smooth her fingers over her forehead and heal it completely. If she could work that kind of miracle, she'd turn herself into an unmarried woman.

Sadly she wasn't able to work magic, so she gently applied a new bandage and touched Jacqueline's cheek again. "You're supposed to keep it as clean and dry as you can." Then she left the room while she still could.

CHAPTER NINETEEN

Molly missed Jacqueline so much she ached, like someone had kicked her heart. Patrick looked sad after she went home, while Mr. James seemed the same as ever, and Mother Russell acted positively gleeful.

As she stripped the bed, she spotted a few stray black hairs when she balled up the sheets, and she chided herself. Jacqueline just lived a mile or so down the road, and Molly could telephone her any time. But it wasn't the same as her living under the same roof and being only a few steps away, depending on her for practically everything.

Jacqueline had been even more withdrawn than usual during the first two days she'd spent with them and spoke with Patrick more than anyone during her convalescence. He stayed by her bed for hours and chattered but sat quietly while she slept or rested. At times, Jacqueline had gazed out at the rose garden, though she squinted when it was sunny and said the roses had lost most of their fragrance.

What a strange statement, because the flowers smelled as wonderful as ever. And Jacqueline flinched when anyone spoke in a loud voice. Her dark eyes had looked as muddy as the pond after a rainstorm. She'd gradually improved, though she apologized for being too tired to help much around the house.

Hopefully, she wouldn't push herself waiting on those two men, and Eric would remember that Mr. James was watching him to make sure he quit drinking so much.

Molly needed to keep her eyes open too, or she'd fret herself to death wondering what was happening at the McCades'.

❖

"How about some scrambled eggs for breakfast?" Eric asked when Jaq came downstairs the morning after she got home from Molly's. "I've learned to make a few dishes while you were gone. Sit down and let me show you."

She studied him as he scurried around the kitchen. He wasn't limping quite so bad. What a pair the two of them were.

"Here you go. Eggs, biscuits, and gravy. Pop and I've already eaten." He set a steaming plate in front of her and seemed so proud of himself, she had to give him a small smile.

"Thank you, Eric. I could get used to this."

"Sure thing. I bet I can learn a lot more about cooking." He acted as eager to please as Patrick did.

She ate in silence. Though the food smelled and looked good, it didn't have much taste. But neither had anything at Molly's.

"Jaq." Eric waited until she looked up from her plate. "I can't say how sorry I am. I've never hit a woman and I never will again. Something in me just snapped, and the whiskey didn't help. I'm on the wagon now and feel a lot better. My sight's a little blurry, but I can tolerate the light indoors. Direct sunlight still bothers me."

She didn't know what to say. Should she trust him or should she make him suffer for what he'd done? She knew what it was like to lose control and regret her actions. Boy, did she ever. She thought about poor Henry every day, but that couldn't bring him back. If Eric felt that way for hitting her, he was being punished enough.

"I can't say that I'll forget what you did, Eric, and I'll probably be careful around you until I'm sure I can trust you. But sometimes we all do things we regret. Just be good to yourself and get well as soon as you can. And find your father some help so we can leave here. That's all I ask."

Eric looked like a load had dropped off his shoulders. "I understand. You're a doll. I'll show you I'm not a total dud. Thanks for the chance." He scooped up her dishes and carried them to the sink.

"Not so fast," she said as she rose. "I'm not an invalid either. I can do my own dishes, and thanks again for breakfast. You better go help Angus."

❖

"It's great to see you, Molly," Jaq said. "These cookies are the best I could manage. A glass of milk might make my cooking edible, if you don't mind pulling up a cold tin of it from the well."

"You shouldn't have bothered. I didn't come for the refreshments. Seeing you refreshes me enough."

Molly flushed, and Jaq agreed that their Wednesday visits were the highlight of her week. When Molly wasn't there, she usually sank into a funk. She couldn't think of anything but Molly's soft hands and her musical voice. She didn't want to waste a second. She needed to get enough of Molly to last till Sunday, when she could see her at the church.

She'd told Molly a little about her school days in New Orleans, but today she'd promised to describe some of her adventures after she left there. She hadn't said a word about Sister Mary Therese and Willie because that might shock Molly and scare her away. She enjoyed Molly's company and knew nothing would ever grow beyond friendship, but she wanted to spend as much time with her as she could before she left New Hope. Maybe she'd like to hear about her Aunt Françoise and her Aunt Anna, and her visit with them before she sailed to London.

"Are you comfortable sitting here on the porch, Molly? The breeze is swell this afternoon."

Molly settled into the old oak rocker and looked like she couldn't wait for her to begin. Molly was a great listener, so it was fun to tell her tales. She supposed Molly felt the same way when she played the piano for her.

She slipped back to 1912, right after Christmas, when she'd left New Orleans for good. "Aunt Françoise—she's Mother's younger radical sister—took me to a big suffragist parade in Washington. Miss Alice Paul organized it and planned it for the day before President Wilson's first inauguration because she wanted him to realize how much women want to vote."

"A parade. How exciting."

"Yes, I was young and agreed to go because I was bored, but I'm glad I did. You should have seen all the marchers, thousands of them. And so many floats, bands, and cavalry squadrons. Women from all over the world participated, and a lot of women who worked in so many different jobs did too.

"Miss Paul organized all that in just two months. In fact, my uncle said she'd probably be a better legislator than most of the men she's up against."

Molly jumped up from her rocker. "I wish I could have been there."

"You could have, if you'd belonged to the women's organization that marched in the parade. Every state sent delegates."

Molly sat back down. "Huh. I can just see Mr. James and Mother Russell letting me attend those meetings. They begrudge me the time I spend planning our music programs at the church."

"I bet you could if you really wanted to. But you'd probably have a hard time finding a chapter nearby. Now, if you lived in Tyler, or Dallas, or Austin—"

"Even if Harrison had one, Mr. James would never drive me eight miles there and eight miles back. Saturdays are the only time he and Mother Russell make that trip. I don't even get to go with them unless I want to buy something special at the dry-goods store."

"Why, you ought to learn to drive. Then you could go wherever you want."

Molly looked at her like she'd lost her mind. "That'll be the day. Mother Russell and Mr. James would think I've gone off the deep end. Don't forget, our automobile is still up on blocks. Besides, I tried to learn once. What a disaster."

Molly seemed so down in the dumps that she jumped back into her story to distract her.

"I almost got to meet Miss Paul that day, but a disturbance broke out and we had to leave. Some troublemakers shoved into the parade, but the police didn't stop them. In fact, one of the marchers asked a policeman for help, and he told her he'd break his wife's head if she showed up there. The 15th Cavalry finally came and straightened things out. A couple hundred people were injured, but that wasn't too bad, out of the half a million there. I read all about it the next day in the newspaper."

She put the porch swing into motion then focused on Molly, who looked thoughtful. Was she really wishing she could have been there or glad she'd avoided all the uproar? Finally, Molly said, "I'll go pull up that tin of milk now and bring our refreshments out here. You just sit still."

"But I—"

"Don't be silly. I need to stretch my legs and you need to rest. I'll let you wait on me when you're stronger."

So here she sat in the swing and rocked slowly, watching the puffy clouds drift by and listening to the birds sing. Molly would be back soon. She could wait as long as it took. And after she healed and Eric finished his business here in New Hope, she'd be gone, a free woman once again. What if Molly were free too? But she wasn't, so Jaq tried to keep her hopes from singing like the birds in the trees.

❖

Molly pulled her everyday white gloves from her pocket and loosened the knot that secured the hemp rope. She'd read a brief newspaper account of President Wilson's inauguration and recalled something about a women's parade. But when she'd mentioned it, Mother Russell had scoffed and Mr. James had chuckled and said that nothing would ever come of such nonsense. He'd written them off as a bunch of hysterical women who ought to be home cooking and cleaning.

She'd found it the most interesting news item she'd read since she moved to the farm. She recalled wishing she could have seen the parade. But Patrick had been little then, and she needed to stay home and take care of him, not go running off to Washington, DC. Still, she wished she'd done some of the exciting things Jacqueline had.

But such thinking would only make her unhappy. She tugged on the heavy bucket full of water and the tin of milk. The good Lord had sent Jacqueline to her so she could have both Patrick and an exciting, interesting life. She'd savor every moment of Jacqueline's experiences and pretend she'd been right beside her. She'd take every opportunity to visit with and listen to her because Jacqueline wouldn't be here very long. But she didn't know how she'd cope after Jacqueline was gone. Thank goodness for Patrick and her music.

The heavy oak bucket finally swung into view, and she grabbed it and pulled it toward her. She set it on the ledge of the well, lifted out the cold tin bucket, then dropped the big oak one. After a few seconds it hit the water with a dull *thunk*, which was how she would feel when Jacqueline left New Hope.

She grabbed the cold pail and hurried back into the house. She didn't want to waste any more precious minutes.

❖

"Here you go."

Molly handed her a cool glass of milk and set a plate of cookies next to her on the swing. Then Molly took one for herself and returned to the rocking chair. Jaq wished she'd sit next to her but was just happy that Molly was here.

"Thank you. Are they edible?" She picked up a small one, surprised when it didn't fall apart.

"Uhm. Good."

Molly didn't actually gobble hers, but at least she didn't spit it out. Maybe she wasn't a total failure in the kitchen. Besides, if Eric could learn to cook, so could she.

Feeling more confident, she said, "Let me tell you about the other aunt I visited before I went to London. Aunt Anna's my father's half sister, and none of us ever knew her well because she always lived up North. When I visited her in New York she drove me all over the place in her little old automobile. She taught me to enjoy driving fast."

Molly nibbled another cookie and sipped her milk. She seemed almost sad.

"Why, what's wrong?"

"Nothing. Just that you've been so many places and met so many people, and I've never been out of Texas."

She tried not to smile. "That's exactly how I felt when I met Aunt Anna. She'd been a doctor for twenty years when I visited her and had even taught classes at her medical school."

"My goodness. A real doctor?"

"Yep. But now she works at a laboratory in New York City where she tries to discover new medicines or ways to treat diseases. She and her lab partner, Mr. Park, discovered something called an antitoxin that helped wipe out diphtheria."

"Oh. If only they'd found it sooner, my poor sister might still be alive," Molly said. "That's what killed her when she was in school."

She put her hand on Molly's arm. "I'm so sorry. I'll tell Aunt Anna about her in my next letter. She's made some important discoveries about rabies too, and she and Mr. Park even wrote a textbook that all the medical students have to study."

"What's your aunt's name? Maybe I'll find it in the newspaper sometime."

"Dr. Anna Wessels Williams. If you could see her, you'd think she'd be really stuffy. But, like I said, she loves to drive fast and even goes up in aeroplanes with stunt pilots when she can. She's never married or had any children, but she loves to write when she's not at work. She has a whole drawer full of short stories."

Molly just sat in her rocking chair and stared at her like she'd arrived from another planet. Hopefully she didn't consider her too strange. Her aunts were so different from Mother that at first she hadn't known what to think of them. But the longer she lived, the more she admired their independence and their forward-thinking ways.

CHAPTER TWENTY

Mrs. Russell chucked hen scratch at the chickens. Felt good. The chickens pecked as near her as they dared then scattered as she pelted them again.

Having to put up with Molly and Jacqueline laughing and carrying on made her sick to her stomach. And now Molly visited Jacqueline every Wednesday, so she had to make her share of Red Cross bandages and Molly's too.

She didn't mind helping somebody that really needed it. But after she'd sewed up Jacqueline's head, she should have come around in a few days. Shucks. She'd laid there like she'd fought the Hun all by herself and been shot, instead of just reopening a little gash. She'd get up and dry a few dishes or churn a mite, then start looking peaked and run take a nap.

What if she'd just had a baby and had three or four young'uns hanging on her for every bite they put in their mouths, and a field full of cotton that needed picking, and hired help that needed watching? She'd think worn-out-and-go-take-a-nap. She'd have to be up from daylight till dark, so tired she could hardly put one foot in front of the other. With kids you couldn't ever get enough rest, even when you were ailing.

Molly couldn't keep her nose out of other people's business, especially people like that snooty Jacqueline. They acted like the world owed them a living and thought they were better than folks that had to work hard to make ends meet. Well, this was the last time she'd let some lazy heifer take advantage of her and James.

Molly needed to hunt for her diamond. She'd looked high and low, and once in a while Molly poked around in the hay, kinda halfhearted.

The week after Molly lost it, the Watkins Man came by peddling his wares. Molly had traded two chickens for a bottle of vanilla, some cinnamon and other spices, some ribbons, and some of her precious white gloves.

But just as the man pulled out of the driveway in his wagon, it came to her like a lightning bolt what Molly had done. The diamond was most likely in one of those chickens, and the more she studied on it, the more certain she was. Molly needed her comeuppance for losing her diamond.

To top it off, lately Molly had been acting awfully high and mighty about that newfangled rolling pin Jacqueline gave her. Carved out of wood, it had shiny red handles that'd blind you. Kinda gaudy, and probably didn't cost but a dollar or two, if that. Nothing compared to that diamond.

And to make matters worse, Jacqueline hadn't brought her nary a thing. She'd done the lion's share of the work—sewed up Jacqueline's gash, changed the bandages until she finally taught Molly how to, and took every one of those stitches out. Did a fine job, if she had to say so herself. She'd like to see Molly stitch somebody's forehead. And besides all that extra cooking and washing and cleaning, she'd had to put up with two silly, overeducated women instead of one.

Molly put on airs every time she rolled out some dough with that gadget. At least Jacqueline could have given it to the both of them. Did she think only young people found new and better ways to do things? Molly seemed as proud of that rolling pin as she'd be of one of those ultramodern washing machines with a wringer to run the clothes through. That new rolling pin probably didn't work any better than the old amber wine bottle they'd always used, and a washing machine more than likely didn't get the clothes near-about as clean as boiling them with lye soap.

But when Molly picked up that rolling pin she acted like she could even cook better than everyone.

Humph. She'd been baking before Molly's folks started sparking and never had any complaints. At the New Hope picnic everybody always fought for a piece of her chocolate pie. Molly had some nerve. She'd show her who the best cook was—and whose ways of doing things were best.

❖

Mother Russell was bristling like the old gray goose did right before it chased Patrick and pecked him on the head. Molly had raced out into the yard and beat it off him, but she didn't know what to do about Mother Russell. Losing her temper would only make things worse.

They sat in the yard under a shade tree, shelling black-eyed peas and fanning themselves to stay cool, and Mother Russell gave her a sideways look that usually meant she was up to something. Molly tried to start a conversation about the terrible heat, the hens not laying too well right now, the upcoming New Hope picnic, anything—and Mother Russell positively glowered like she had something to say but wouldn't tell her what it was. Often she was chatty and almost civil, but nowadays she was constantly in a foul mood.

After they finished the peas and Mother Russell went to feed the chickens, she telephoned Jacqueline, as she did regularly.

"Mother Russell's worse than ever today, and I can't figure out why."

"When did she start acting like this?"

She hoped Ethel wasn't listening in. She'd promised she wouldn't, but you never could tell.

"Right after you left, almost a month ago."

"You don't think I stayed too long, do you?"

"Maybe, but why would it eat at her so long? She's just making herself miserable, and us too."

"Don't worry. She's probably in a funk or got something on her mind. She'll work it out when she can. Try to act like nothing's wrong."

"Oops, speak of the devil. Here she comes. Better let you go. I don't want to give her an excuse to be any crankier."

"Okay. I'll call you tomorrow. Talking to you always makes my day."

"I feel the same way. I'm looking forward to seeing you Sunday. Oh, by the way, has anyone told you about the New Hope picnic? It's right before the primary election in late July and almost as important as Christmas and Easter around here. Better think about what you're going to wear. I'll explain later. Got to go. Love you."

Jacqueline hesitated a long moment, then said, "Love you too, Molly."

❖

Jaq hung up the receiver. What should she do? She'd promised herself she wouldn't get involved with Molly, and here she was telling Molly she loved her. And she did. But not like Molly thought.

She traced the smooth surfaces of the cool silver bells at the top of the wooden telephone box. She loved Molly the way a man loved a woman, but Molly probably wouldn't understand. The gulf between them was almost as wide as the Atlantic.

Molly obviously believed their love was pure and beautiful, the joining of two kindred souls, but *she* didn't feel innocent love. She wanted Molly to caress her with those resilient fingers, like she did when she'd soothed salve on the bruises on her back and legs. If she had the nerve, they'd be lying nude on a feather mattress and sinking into it right now. She'd roll over, unpin Molly's waist-long red hair, and let it cover them like a quilt. Then she'd burrow her face between Molly's breasts and never come up for air.

Damn it. She couldn't let herself imagine such things. She'd be totally miserable.

As she trudged down the long dark hall toward the kitchen, she couldn't get her mind off Molly. She was her friend, a naive married woman with a darling son whom she'd begun to be fond of. How could she tell Molly what she really meant when she'd said, "Love you too"?

The tall, still pines outside the kitchen window circled the house and separated her from Molly and the rest of the world. She said to a fox squirrel perched on the limb of an oak tree, staring at her with bright eyes, "I have to live a lie but I can't lie to myself. I love Molly Russell." She shook her head and the squirrel jumped to another limb. "But I can't have her, and I'm not sure what I'd do with her if I could."

"You don't say, Ethel. And then they said what? Well, I never. The viper in your bosom. That's right. I certainly 'preciate you telling me. No, I won't let her know I'm on to her. I won't tell a living soul. Thank you, Ethel. We've been friends a long time and I won't forget this. Bye now."

After she hung up the phone, she flew out to the chicken yard and almost killed a couple of her favorite pullets with flying grain. Then she stomped to the rose garden and deadheaded the roses like she was wiping out a Hun battalion all by herself.

"The nerve of those deadbeat gals, calling me miserable and a devil and saying I'm cranky." She talked out loud as she snipped roses right and left. Wasn't anybody 'round to hear, and if there was she wouldn't have cared. She was that mad. "Molly knows Ethel listens in and hangs on every word people say and then can't wait to call everybody up and spread all the bad news she can.

"The whole community probably already knows every word those two said, and I bet the little dickenses are laughing behind my back and carrying on to beat the band, bragging 'bout what a fool they've made out of me. If they think they're so smart, they've got another think coming. I'll get their goat, if it's the last thing I do. They don't know who they're fooling with."

CHAPTER TWENTY-ONE

Molly hummed as she rolled out a double crust. The first apples of the season had just come in, and she'd picked a bucketful of the prettiest ones for the two pies she was making. Apple pie was her favorite, and she'd discovered it was Jacqueline's too. As soon as she pulled the treats from the oven, she'd pay her a quick visit. She hadn't seen Jacqueline since Sunday, and because Mother Russell had gone to her weekly meeting, she didn't see why she couldn't do what pleased her.

Her new rolling pin was so much easier to use than the clumsy empty bottle Mother Russell always insisted on. She'd never gotten the hang of it, and when Jacqueline presented her with this wooden rolling pin with a red handle, she felt like she'd received a pair of silk stockings. Except her new kitchen tool was much more useful than hose.

Faster than a bottle, it fit her hands perfectly. She'd seen one in the Sears and Roebuck catalogue, but Mother Russell would consider it a frippery.

To add insult to injury, Mr. James would probably agree with his mother about the bottle, so she'd never mentioned it. How Jacqueline knew she'd wanted one amazed her. Just a lucky guess, she supposed, but she wouldn't take the world for it.

As she greased her hands, she remembered spreading salve on Jacqueline's back and legs when she was hurting so bad. She'd tried to be careful and touch only the injured places, but the side of her hand had accidentally skimmed Jacqueline's undamaged skin. Simply thinking about it made her get even warmer than she already was today with a wood fire built in the oven.

What was wrong with her? She squeezed the pie dough into a ball, enjoying its texture, then patted it out and began to smooth it with her rolling pin. The pastry spread so easily. Creating a perfect round, she slipped her fingers under its edges and gently lifted it, cradling it in her hands and flipping it into the pie pan.

Then she peeled the red apples, and the long swirls fell away gracefully to reveal the white meat of each one. Like Jacqueline's skin. She sliced the apples into the pan, stopping occasionally to pop a piece into her mouth. She loved the tart sweetness. Then she sprinkled a precious mixture of flour, sugar, and cinnamon on them, dotted them with butter, and slid her fingers under the second crust and flipped it on top.

Holding the pan in one hand, she trimmed the extra overhanging crust, lowered the pan, and squeezed the crust around the edges of the pie between her thumb and middle finger. A few slits, and it was ready to bake. After she repeated the procedure, she slid the second pie into the oven and went to get ready.

She could hardly wait to see Jacqueline's reaction. She felt as excited as Patrick looked on Christmas Eve when they lit the candles on the tree.

❖

"It's so good to see you, Molly. It seems like ages." Jaq's heart started to dance, like it always did when she was around Molly, though it couldn't manage anything but a boring old waltz.

Molly handed her a pie pan covered with a clean white cloth. "How are you? Feeling better?"

"Yes. A lot. Talking on the telephone isn't the same as actually being together, is it?"

"No." Molly stared, like she wanted to make sure she was back to normal, then moved forward, as if to embrace her.

Jaq froze, holding the pie pan out in front of her. She loved Molly but didn't want to touch her. She was content to fantasize.

Molly looked a bit hurt but held her ground.

She tried to smooth the awkward situation. "What did you bring this time? I have to peek. An apple pie? So that's why you wanted to discuss pies the last time we chatted on the phone."

"I wanted to surprise you."

"Why don't we stay out here on the porch, out of this awful heat? Sit in the rocker while I put this in the kitchen. We'll have a piece later."

The pie smelled as sweet as Molly, with a spicy dash of cinnamon. Thank God, she could smell again. Just inhaling the same air that Molly breathed made her heart beat a little faster. In her imagination, she wrapped her arms around Molly and hugged her close. She ran her hands through Molly's thick hair and stroked her cheek. She wished she didn't flinch at the thought of anyone touching her, even Molly. But she just couldn't let anyone near her yet. Her bruises had healed but the memory of them lingered.

She still got tired easily and had an occasional headache. But she'd taken Molly's advice to rest. In fact, she'd been lounging in the porch swing reading the newspaper Eric brought her yesterday when he drove to town to sell his last load of tomatoes. He was keeping his word and had been even more thoughtful than usual lately, though she was still skittish around him.

"Did you know we've finally got the Germans on the run? Our boys have made all the difference." She couldn't keep from touching Molly after all, so she squeezed her hand and Molly returned the pressure. The familiar heat between them hadn't disappeared, though she tried to dampen it.

"I'm so glad, though the War still doesn't seem very real. It's so far away and doesn't have much to do with me, even though Clyde's over there. But I know it's important to you, Jacqueline."

She'd returned to the swing, so she pushed off in it. If she could keep moving, maybe she'd forget how near Molly was. "We need to show the bullies they can't run over their neighbors and get by with it. Maybe this war *will* actually end all wars."

"I hope so. Perhaps all our boys can come home by Christmas."

Looking at the pine forest, she glanced at a few trees that lightning had struck. *They won't all be back*, she thought. And Helen wouldn't be coming home. Neither would Henry.

She shook her head, but the other topic she wanted to discuss wasn't any more pleasant than the one she kept to herself. Together, they'd surely keep her mind off Molly's sweet lips and her encouraging smile.

"I just read about a worrisome new disease," she said. "The Bureau of Public Health in Philadelphia has sent out a bulletin about something called the Spanish influenza."

"Really. Why Spanish?"

She looked so cute when she was puzzled.

"A lot of people died during a big outbreak in Spain earlier this year. The doctors in France always warned us to watch out for communicable diseases, and it's unusual for influenza to occur during the summer. Come to think of it, I had something similar last summer, then had a relapse."

Molly looked at her with sparkling eyes. "Don't worry. If a disease like that did spread, we're so isolated here at New Hope it would have to look long and hard to find us. Catching the Spanish flu is even more far-fetched to me than the War is."

She chuckled. Molly could always cheer her up. She lazed in the swing, warm inside and out, while they chatted until it was time to eat some pie. Only the long hours she used to spend with her brothers working on automobiles had ever made her feel more content.

"Would you like to hear a new record Eric brought me from town the other day? The old Victrola in the parlor isn't in very good shape. Eric's brothers must have almost worn the handle off cranking it. But it should be okay for a song or two. Let's go try it."

Molly clapped her hands like a child. "Oh, I'd love to. I don't get to hear new songs unless I visit Dallas or buy sheet music in town and play them for myself."

"This one's brand-new and it's called 'I'm Always Chasing Rainbows.' It's hard to make out the words at first, but I've already memorized them. Just ask if you don't understand some of them."

Molly whirled the crank and the song filled the air. While she concentrated on the words, Jaq drifted along with the music. She understood what it was like to always chase rainbows and watch clouds drift by. She'd always chased them, and lately she'd seen a lot of clouds. In a way, having Eric hit her was almost a blessing. She'd finally sat still long enough to see that she'd been chasing rainbows forever. As the song said, all her schemes and her dreams had ended in the sky.

Since she was six years old and the Galveston Storm shook her world to pieces, she hadn't found the sunshine. Instead, she'd found the rain. She'd never discovered what she'd wanted, but she'd kept chasing rainbows, hoping she'd eventually find that elusive bluebird.

After the song ended and Molly left, she walked back outside. The more she sat on the porch in that isolated corner of the world and stared at the pine trees, the more she thought Molly might be the bluebird she'd been searching for. Too bad she would always live in a cage, far away from her.

❖

By cracky, the mules and the wagon were gone. She shoved Patrick toward the house, then hustled around the yard, picking up limbs the last storm had knocked down and carrying them to the burning pile.

She had to speak her mind out loud as she dragged a stout piece of oak. "This is the last straw. I go try to send comfort to our poor boys overseas, and Molly pulls this stunt. Who does she think she is?"

She threw the wood into a pile and hurried to get a bucket of live coals from the kitchen stove. Molly's rolling pin was laying on the drain board and she snatched it.

Out of the goodness of her heart she'd taken Patrick to the meeting with her so Molly could have a little time to herself, and what did she do? Went gallivanting 'round the countryside the minute she left. Most likely over at that Jacqueline McCade's, laughing at her.

She slung the embers into a pile of twigs and small branches and added the larger branches. Then, as the fire gnawed through them, she crowned them with Molly's rolling pin. She stood there a minute, then wiped her hands clean on her apron.

❖

The buggy was already back in place. "Goodness, Gus, I didn't realize we'd stayed so long. The time flew by. Every time Jacqueline and I are together, it's harder to leave. I almost wish something else would happen so I could tend to her. No, I take that back. I couldn't stand to see her in pain again."

Humming, Molly unhitched the mules and led them to the pasture, then headed to the back door. She passed the smoking remains of a fire but barely gave it notice. Mother Russell burned trash all the time. She hated litter in the yard.

"Patrick, I'm home," she called as she entered the kitchen. "Did you have a good time today?"

He came running and hugged her around the legs. "Yes, ma'am. I learned to make a whistle out of a willow branch. Listen."

She was laughing at Patrick's squawks and patting him on the head when Mother Russell sashayed in, tied an apron around her waist, and started fixing supper. "Have a good time wherever you went, Molly?"

"As a matter of fact I did, thank you. Jacqueline caught me up on the news, and I lost track of the time. I took her a pie I made from some of the first apples, and she seemed to enjoy it."

She looked around the kitchen. "Has anyone seen my new rolling pin? I left it out to dry before I stored it."

Patrick looked blank. "I haven't, Mama."

Mother Russell shrugged and began to whistle an old tune from the time of the War Between the States, a sure sign she was in a good mood.

"Maybe Mr. James ran out of drinking water and wandered into the kitchen and stuck it somewhere," she said. "Though I can't imagine him even noticing it. Oh well, it'll turn up."

She helped Mother Russell fix supper, relieved she was finally back to normal.

❖

"Molly, what's wrong? Are you hurt?"

Jaq was ready to slam the telephone receiver back on its hook and run out and jump into her Model T when Molly blurted, "Mother Russell...she burned my rolling pin."

"She what?"

"Burned the new rolling pin you gave me. I can always order another one from the catalogue, but she knew I loved it and deliberately hurt me."

She dropped to the bench under the telephone. "Slow down and explain."

"I missed it when I got home yesterday, and no one seemed to know where it was. So when Mr. James got in, I asked him and he looked at me like I was crazy. Then everything fell into place. The bonfire, Mother Russell's shrug when I asked her about the rolling pin, and her sudden good mood after weeks of being crabby." Molly sounded like she was taking a deep breath.

"What did she say when you questioned her?"

"She just shrugged again, so I went outside right before dark, and sure enough, I discovered one of the red handles in the ashes. When I told her what I'd found, she had the nerve to shrug a third time. Then she frowned and said I'd gotten what I deserved. No explanation, no apology, no nothing. I don't know if I can go on living here. She wanted to hurt me, and she did."

"Did you talk to Mr. James?"

"I most certainly did. Last night right before bed I told him exactly what she'd done, but all he said was, 'I guess Ma had her reasons. We'll just buy you a new one and pretend this didn't happen.' He has no idea why I'm so upset about something so 'trivial,' as he called it."

Molly paused. "He doesn't have to work with his mother all day, every day, like I do. It's like standing next to a cottonmouth and not knowing when it'll strike. I told him I was miserable, but he just brushed me off and said I'd feel better in the morning. Told me he was tired and needed to get some sleep.

"Well, it's morning now and I don't feel a bit better. If I had a decent way to support myself, I'd take Patrick and move to town. Mr. James can stay here with his mother and see how he likes that."

Jaq's blood beat in her head so violently she was afraid the pressure would rupture her scar. Maybe Molly would leave the farm. She'd move to town and Jaq could go visit her and they could…No. Molly would never go over the top like that. She was just angry and fed up. But what if she did? Molly could get a job in town, and after she and Eric got a divorce, she could…But that was just wishful thinking. She had to calm down. "I'm so sorry. Can I help?"

"No, but thanks. I better go."

After Molly hung up, she thought about meeting Helen and how she'd immediately gotten her hopes up that something special would happen between them, just like she was doing with Molly now.

On leave in Dieppe, on a cold June day last year, she'd walked into a small store, hunting a pair of boots. She owned one comfortable pair but needed a spare. She remembered it like it was yesterday.

"*Je désire…Je désire*. Rats. I can't remember the words for heavy shoes," the obviously American woman had said.

"Maybe I can help. I've had to buy some too."

The woman had sighed as Jaq helped her find what she was looking for.

As they'd left the shop, the woman held out her gloved hand. "I'm Helen Fairchild. Let me buy you a cup of coffee."

They soon sat in a tiny café, each cradling a huge white cup. "Can you believe I had to pay fifteen dollars for those shoes? Gee, they're such a queer shape and aren't even very comfortable. But my feet have been freezing since I got here. It's a lot colder and windier here than in Philadelphia. And it rains so much. I'm sure glad the hospital issued us this rain gear and rubber boots. I've practically slept in mine."

The weather had been mild and sunny, but Helen had shivered. "I even bought a knitted underskirt," she'd said. "When we first got our street uniforms they told us we ought to wear them in public, which didn't make me happy. Uniforms seemed so restrictive. But now I'm glad they're made out of such heavy material. Even this silly round felt hat feels good."

Helen's dark-blue uniform with its big shoulder pleats and white-banded collar and sleeves set off her fair complexion beautifully. "Your ankle-length skirt will probably be a lifesaver this fall and winter," she said.

"When we got to London after we landed in Liverpool, everyone treated us grand. They took one look at our dress uniforms and let us in wherever we wanted to go. Wouldn't let us pay for a thing, not even food."

Helen had switched topics so fast Jaq had to think fast to keep up with her.

"All sixty-four of us nurses stayed at The Waldorf Hotel. I even had tea at the Astors' country home. Why, I was beginning to think the newspapers had exaggerated how bad it was over here."

"Wartime London is quite—"

"Then we reached base hospital number ten at Le Tréport. We were expecting several hundred beds but found almost two thousand. So there we were—sixty nurses, a couple dozen doctors, a few dentists, and almost a hundred and seventy enlisted men, who were our orderlies. Two days later, more than five hundred soldiers poisoned by mustard gas arrived. We didn't even know the Boches were gassing our men. And the soldiers just kept coming."

The day she'd met Helen was the highlight of her time in Europe. Helen had been so natural, so open, so optimistic. She'd made Jaq feel as cozy as a cup of hot tea on a winter day did, and every time she'd bumped into Helen on the front, the warmth mushroomed. During her late-night missions in her ambulance she began to think about Helen and even volunteered for some of the more arduous drives in hopes that

Helen might be on duty when and where she arrived with the wounded. She'd hoped and would have prayed—if she'd believed that a God could, would, and should help her—that Helen felt the same way. But, like everything else to do with the War, her dreams about Helen had been shot to hell.

She shivered despite the warm weather. Though she ought to know better, she hoped things wouldn't be as disastrous with Molly as they'd been with Helen. But she couldn't stay away from Molly any more than she could have not volunteered to serve on the front or to help Miss Paul. So she'd try not to get in too deep with Molly, but she'd stay close to her until they had to separate for good. She sighed. She'd do whatever she needed to keep Molly safe from her spiteful mother-in-law and insensitive husband and hope that her own heart survived another ordeal.

CHAPTER TWENTY-TWO

"Are you busy this afternoon, Jacqueline?" Molly hated that she'd had to call Jacqueline on the telephone and ask her for a favor, but she didn't have many options.

"No. The house is as clean as I can get it. What do you have in mind?"

She decided to take a chance. "Could you possibly take Patrick and me to town? I need to do a couple of things. I could try to persuade Mr. James to let me go with him tomorrow, but I don't want to disturb his weekly ritual, and I can't do one of my errands on the weekend. Besides, right now I don't want to spend any more time with him than I have to."

Jacqueline didn't answer immediately.

"You don't have to if you don't want—"

"No. It's not that. I'm just surprised you asked. And glad too. Maybe I can return a little of the kindness you showed me when Eric... you know..."

She released a deep breath. "Oh, Jacqueline. If only you could have stayed with us longer. It was wonderful having you so near. I wish the circumstances had been different, but I loved having the chance to get to know you better. And you've already more than repaid me with your stories. In fact, they're one of the reasons I decided to do what I plan for today. But I need to hurry. Could you pick us up right at one o'clock? That should give us enough time. Do you have enough gasoline?"

Jacqueline laughed. "I have plenty of gas, and I'm always looking for an excuse to hit the road. See you at one."

"Good-bye—thank you."

"Thank *you*. See you soon."

She put on a better dress for the trip and told Patrick to wear his Sunday clothes. No one could change her mind now. She just wished she'd had the courage to be even more honest with Jacqueline about how she'd hardly slept because she was so excited about having her under the same roof and how deeply she'd missed her after she left. Maybe someday she'd be able to fully open her heart to Jacqueline, but as a wife and mother, she didn't feel right doing that now. If she were free, and if Jacqueline weren't married either...the thought alone made her feel as if she'd just run down to the bottom field and back on a hot summer day.

❖

What did Molly have up her sleeve, wanting to go to town on a weekday? All the stores were open Saturday, so she didn't need to buy something, unless she wanted to surprise Mr. James on his birthday. But just last night she'd said she felt like throttling him.

The courthouse and the lawyers' offices wouldn't be open tomorrow. Had Mrs. Russell made Molly decide to leave? Maybe she wanted to look for a place in town for her and Patrick. But how could she afford it? Wouldn't she move to Dallas and live with her parents? She'd never manage on her own.

Jaq's mind whirled as she drove. Red dust flew from the hard-packed road. They'd all need a bath after their drive. No! She wouldn't even think about pouring a bucket of sun-warmed water down Molly's bare back, sliding perfumed soap over it, then under her arm and around to her—

She'd better slow down or she'd have a wreck. There Molly stood on the front porch, wearing white and standing beside Patrick. They were both waving, and Mrs. Russell was most likely lurking in the house or the backyard.

She was halfway up the driveway, and Molly and Patrick had already pushed through the small gate in the picket fence and were hurrying toward her.

"Hello, Molly, Patrick." After Molly settled down beside her, and Patrick sat in the backseat, she quickly turned the car around and made their getaway.

She and Molly chatted about inconsequential things, and Patrick jabbered as they motored past sandhills dotted with green watermelons and straight rows of field corn ready to pick. Black-eyed peas grew on low, vine-like bushes between the cornrows.

She'd learned to navigate through the pea plants during the early morning when the heavy dew soaked her old brogans and long skirt. At first afraid she'd step on a snake, she'd gradually learned to treasure the quiet, cool garden at dawn before the blazing sun sapped her energy. The bloody battlefields of Europe receded, and she embraced a fragile truce with her past.

Wouldn't it be enjoyable to share that special time of the day with Molly? To work side by side and occasionally share a drink of cool well water from a jug under a shade tree. Just thinking about drinking from the same container that Molly's lips had touched made her lose focus on the road and direct it where it shouldn't be. By moving her right arm just a bit she could touch Molly's gloved hand, if she dared. That couldn't compare to a kiss, but the touch would be so much better than her arid dreams.

"What do you think about the election this month, Jacqueline?"

She tensed as if she'd just encountered a copperhead. Molly must have been having a one-sided conversation. Jaq had become so caught up in her fantasies of Molly, she'd ignored the fact that the real person sat next to her and wanted to have a conversation.

"What election?"

"The Texas Democratic primary. Mr. William Hobby is running against Farmer Jim Ferguson, the old fraud. The legislature impeached him just last year. Mr. Hobby took his place, and I intend to vote to keep him as governor."

Molly looked like she'd just climbed a mountain or sailed around the world.

"You're interested in politics? And what's this about voting?" She had been counting on Molly to help her stay calm and relaxed in this out-of-the-way place, not remind her of the dirty world of politics she'd seen firsthand in Washington last year.

Molly gaped at her. "Don't you remember my letter from Esther Harris last month—my college roommate? She and her husband live in Austin. I told you about it."

She remembered that conversation, but at the time she'd tried to ignore it. Molly had seemed a little too thrilled to hear from her old friend, and Jaq had changed the subject. But Molly seemed totally carried away now.

"I got another letter yesterday. Her new friend, a Mrs. Cunningham, head of the Texas Woman Suffrage Association, has convinced Mr. Hobby to let women vote in the primary. Of course, she promised him she'd encourage them to elect him instead of that crook Ferguson."

She'd prefer to pick peas in peace than become involved in political wrangling again, but she humored Molly. "When did all this happen?"

"Just before you got here, near Easter. According to Esther, the big-city newspapers covered the story, but most of the small-town editors conveniently forgot to mention the deadline."

Molly was talking so fast she could barely understand her, so she reluctantly entered the fray. "What deadline?"

"We have only seventeen days to register or we'll lose our chance to vote this year."

"Why just seventeen days?" The thought of meeting a deadline made her tired. She'd rather keep meandering through this quiet green forest in her Model T. She glanced out the window at a lush garden, wanting to stop and pick a few tomatoes. She could taste their tart sweetness, feel the juice run down her chin, but Molly interrupted her fantasy.

"I'm not sure about the short time span. Something about a ninety-day waiting period. A woman is running for state office too, for the very first time. Isn't that something?"

"That's great." Her heart picked up speed. "Why didn't you let me know before now?"

"You need to rest. You've been under enough pressure."

"I'm better now." She began to feel a little of the restlessness that had made her want to drive an ambulance in Europe and become a suffragist. "I can't believe it. Miss Alice Paul has been struggling so long for women to be able to vote, and you already can—without having to march or picket."

Molly shook her head so hard Jaq was afraid her long hair would come unpinned. "But we can't vote in the November election. Miss Paul and the rest of the suffragists better keep the pressure on President Wilson." Then she winked mischievously. "Hardly anyone in Texas votes Republican, though. Whoever wins the primary wins the race."

"Very clever. But tell me. Why the sudden excitement about politics?" Molly appeared to be a different person from the cowed wife and mother Jaq had observed at church not that many months ago.

Molly pushed up her luxurious crown of red hair. "Before I met you, I thought only men—and women like Mother Russell—discussed politics. Such things weren't relevant to me." She looked almost sad then brightened. "But your stories and Esther's letters make me want to learn more about this new world opening up for us. Maybe I can even help educate other women about it. Can you tell me more about Miss Paul?" She tidied a stray tendril.

They passed two barefooted girls wearing patched overalls, one of them obviously pregnant, though she looked about twelve. They were struggling to carry a big bucket brimming with water. Molly clenched her gloved hands like she was feeling the thin metal handle bite into them. "Mr. Hobby wants to increase the age of consent for girls to age fifteen," she murmured, as if to herself.

With a sigh, she wondered why Molly had married Mr. James, but then, responding to Molly's request, she let herself be pulled into her memories.

"What about the first time I actually met Miss Paul?"

"Yes, please." Molly relaxed her hands in her lap and half turned in her seat.

She kept her speed at a steady eight miles an hour, ready to slow down if she had to. She didn't want the red dust blowing through the windows to ruin Molly's white dress.

"When I returned from Europe last fall, my aunt told me she'd picketed the White House. She even spent three nights in the District jail. That shocked me and intrigued me too. I'd planned to stay with her and my uncle awhile in Washington, but pretty soon I got bored. So she encouraged me to join Miss Paul's National Woman's Party."

Molly wiped a trickle of sweat from her forehead with a handkerchief and gawped at her as if she'd flown to the moon. "And you did?"

"Yes. My aunt took me to their headquarters and introduced us. Miss Paul is tiny, not even as tall as you are, and even thinner than when I first saw her, five years ago. But her hair was just as thick and dark, and her eyes glowed even more, like a light shone behind them. She sat at a desk in a dimly lit room, with only a table lamp turned on, surrounded by piles of papers—like a tough executive."

Molly's eyes gleamed. "How exciting."

"Miss Paul asked me, in a deep, rich voice, why I wanted to join their organization, and I told her I'd just come back from where the generals were squandering the lives of thousands of our men for bits of land they lost the next day. I also told her I wanted to do something I could truly believe in."

Molly looked so appalled that Jaq tried to distract her. "She has such interesting eyes, Molly. I wish you could see them. They're green like yours when they shine, but when she's serious they look black and brown."

Molly blushed but nodded for her to go on.

"Miss Paul asked about my health and if I'd picket three afternoons a week. And in case they arrested me, if I'd go to prison and on a hunger strike, if necessary."

Molly paled, but Jaq decided to share the truth with her. Molly could take it.

"She's been in prison a lot of times, you know, and even in an insane asylum. She had a rubber feeding tube forced down her throat during her hunger strikes in jail."

Molly gulped, as if she might throw up, but just sat there with an expression of horror.

Jaq waved a hand in the air. "I agreed to everything, and she told me to report for duty the next afternoon."

"My goodness. She sounds rather brusque," Molly said, after she'd swallowed a few times.

She nodded. "Yes. I felt dismissed, but then Miss Paul rose, smiled, and shook my hand with a firm grip. She seemed to tower over me as she welcomed me to the Woman's Party. Her presence filled the room, and I understood why so many women have devoted themselves to her cause. She's so businesslike yet so warm. We gladly did whatever she asked us."

Molly stared at her, seeming to breathe deeper and sit even straighter than usual. "I'd love to meet her."

She wanted to say that maybe someday Molly could, but the chances were so unlikely, she hesitated. She didn't want Molly to be disappointed or, worse, hurt. And she wasn't sure she wanted Molly to grow aware and jaded, like her. She needed the uncritical stability that Molly provided.

She kept her expression noncommittal. "Me too, Molly, but now you owe a story."

❖

"Miss Paul sounds like she won't let anyone stop her," Molly said, suddenly despondent. Jacqueline hadn't given her much hope of ever getting out of East Texas.

"You're right. Oh—" They crested a rise and Jacqueline slammed on the brakes. "I'm still not used to watching out for these chickens. I hit one a few days after I got here. What a mess."

"James's brother Clyde used to love to run them down. He's cruel to his Negro hired help too. Supposedly, when he was a young man, he beat one of their field hands to death with a chain for sassing him and got off scot-free. I've never liked him, except when he was kind to me after I had Patrick. But back to Mrs. Cunningham. We're close to town, so I'll tell you what I know before we get there."

"We have all the way home."

"But I'd rather listen to you. Mrs. Cunningham was studying to be a pharmacist in Galveston when the Storm hit."

Jacqueline shuddered, though Molly didn't know whether her remark about Clyde or about the Storm caused her reaction. "I'm glad she got out."

"She did but went back and helped with the relief efforts."

"I already like her. Did she earn her degree?"

"Yes. But when she got a job, she made half as much as the men, and none of them had gone to college. So she married and moved to Galveston again. She discovered politics there, when she got involved in a legal battle with a vendor selling tainted milk. So I'm not such a late-bloomer, am I?"

Jacqueline shook her head as they pulled up in front of the county courthouse.

Does she think I'm being silly, wanting to change like this all of a sudden? Molly hoped she hadn't let her anger make her do something foolish.

CHAPTER TWENTY-THREE

By the time they reached the broad marble staircase, Molly could hardly wait to walk up and register to vote in the first election ever open to the women of Texas. Jacqueline had unlocked Pandora's box for her, and she almost wanted to thank Mother Russell for making her so angry that she finally dared to defy everything she'd ever known.

She licked two of her fingers and smoothed Patrick's red hair that looked like a banty rooster's tail at the crown of his head. "Pull up your pants, son, and straighten your collar. You can't go in the courthouse looking like you've slept in your shirt."

He squirmed. "But, Mama, my collar's scratching my neck. You put too much starch in it."

She relented and told him she'd buy him something special later, to take the edge off her scolding. But she was nervous and wanted to make a good impression during her first trip to register to vote. Today was a landmark event.

A middle-aged woman directed her to the tax collector's office, and as she climbed the worn wooden stairs Patrick tugged her hand. "Look, Mama. These steps just keep going up and up. I bet this building's taller than our barn."

"I'm sure it is," Jacqueline said. "Someday maybe you can go to Washington, DC. Some of the buildings there are even taller than this one and made entirely out of marble. They're more beautiful than you can imagine."

He stopped. "Really, Miss Jacqueline? Oh, Mama. Can I go? Can I?"

"Of course. Maybe you and I can both go. But now we need to find the tax collector. He's the first stop on our trip."

"Okay, Mama."

After another inquiry, she found the office and knocked on the tall pine door.

"Come on in," someone squeaked, and she entered, still holding Patrick's hand and glad Jacqueline was by her side. Her stomach twisted up like she was about to play a difficult Chopin nocturne at a recital.

"How can I help you, ma'am?"

She'd hoped she would know the person who would register her, but she'd never seen this brash, pimply young man who looked barely older than Patrick.

"I'm here to register to vote in the upcoming election."

"Vote? What do you mean? Only men can vote in Texas." He stared at her through his thick-lensed glasses as if he thought she'd escaped from the insane asylum.

She stood there tongue-tied, ready to back out the door, but Jacqueline said imperiously, "You obviously haven't been keeping up with the latest news. Let me speak to your supervisor."

The owlish young man paled behind his pimples. "Yes, ma'am," he said, and pushed through the door behind him.

This time an older man, who resembled Mr. James, emerged. "I understand you want to register, ma'am."

She pushed her voice out of her throat. "Yes, sir. If it's not too much trouble."

"Why, no trouble at all, ma'am. You see, you're the first of your fair sex to do so, and that young man doesn't read anything but news about the War. I apologize. Just fill out this form and show me some type of identification to prove who you are and that you've lived in Texas for at least a year."

She felt like he'd slapped her. Filling out the form was easy, though she wondered how many people weren't allowed to register because they couldn't read or write. But identification? No one had ever asked her for that. When she'd enrolled at college and at the university, her papa had signed a paper that he was a Methodist preacher, and that was that. Mr. James had their marriage license, and Molly owned no property in her own name. Mother Russell could register easier than she could.

As these thoughts whirled through her mind like a hurricane, the older man gazed patiently at her.

"My friend here, Mrs. McCade, can tell you who I am and how long I've lived in Texas." She and the older man both turned to Jacqueline.

"Of course I know who you are. But I've only been in Texas since late March. Maybe someone in town—"

Molly snapped her fingers. "That's it. I'll go get Mr. Rosenberg. I've traded at his dry-goods store for years. He'll vouch for me."

Downstairs, as they crossed the dusty, rutted main street and carefully avoided piles of manure, she was glad this was a weekday because it wasn't very crowded and she could relax and enjoy her time alone with Jacqueline. Tomorrow the town would be alive with wagons, buggies, and some automobiles, with men spitting on the sidewalks and throwing sacks of feed for the livestock and flour and other staples for their families into their wagons or trucks. They'd lounge on the streets, catching up on the latest news about the War, and the few women in town would scurry from store to store, buying fabric and other necessities. She seldom went with Mr. James on Saturday. He usually had to buy parts for the plow, or new harnesses for the mules, or other bulky items, and he didn't like to escort her in anything but the buggy or the Overland, when it was in operation.

In the dry-goods store, Mr. Rosenberg readily agreed to guarantee her identity. They were walking up the aisle from his office, when Patrick stopped to look at a neat pile of boys' pants. "Mama, when can I have some long pants like these?"

"Why, I didn't know you wanted any. You're not old enough to wear them yet."

"But by the time Miss Jacqueline takes us to Washington, DC, I will be." He grinned. "They'll make me look all grown up, like I'm fit to go to war."

"Well, I don't know, Patrick. I don't want you to go to war—"

"These are an excellent buy, Mrs. Russell," Mr. Rosenberg picked up a pair of black ones and held them up to Patrick. "They're on sale for fifty cents. I just haven't gotten around to marking them down. Why don't you go over there behind that counter and try them on, boy?"

She put her arm around his shoulders. "Okay. If they fit right and if you promise to save them for a special occasion when you're a little older."

He soon ran back toward them. "Look, Mama. They're just right."

So she said with pride, "Here you go, Mr. Rosenberg. Since I'm exempt from paying a poll tax this year, I have enough money from what I've saved from giving piano lessons." She carefully counted out ten nickels.

Just then, Jacqueline pulled her Brownie out of her big purse. "Before you change back, Patrick, why don't you step outside and let me take your picture. If that's all right, Mr. Rosenberg."

"Sure, sure. I'll go with you."

After Jacqueline finished with Patrick, Mr. Rosenberg said, "Ladies, this is a big day for Miss Molly and all the ladies of Texas, so let me take a picture of the two of you. If I can work this contraption."

She and Jacqueline looked at each other for a minute, then Jacqueline handed him the camera. "That's a grand idea, Mr. Rosenberg. Don't you agree, Molly?"

They moved together and ended up with their arms around each other's waists, Jacqueline a head taller than she was. "Just look down into that little silver box on the left front until you see us and move that lever at the top of the round thing in the middle. I've got it set for instant, so that's how long it'll take."

Standing beside Jacqueline for just a fraction of a second made her skin prickle. The picture would freeze this idyllic moment forever, and she couldn't ask for anything better.

Back inside the store, Mr. Rosenberg rang up her sale, folded the pants neatly, and wrapped them in an old newspaper, which he tied with a bit of string. "Here you go, boy. You'll make a fine soldier. And congratulations. You too, ladies. I hope Congress doesn't drag their feet too long before they let all the women in the nation vote."

Patrick seemed to float up the courthouse steps at Mr. Rosenberg's side, and he immediately ran to the second-floor window.

As she added her name to the long list of men who would be able to vote in the upcoming election, she thought about all the ones in Europe sacrificing their lives for their country. She planned to study the candidates and issues very carefully. Her vote could make a difference to the future of this great nation.

After she registered, Patrick called her over to the courthouse window. "Look at all these wires. They're so thick I bet I could walk on them. Why, I can barely see the wagons passing underneath them. What are they all for?"

"They're for the telephones and the electricity that most people in town have," Mr. Rosenberg answered.

"Why don't we have electricity, Mama?"

"It's too far to string a line way out to where we live. But we have kerosene lamps. They're almost as good, aren't they? Come on, son. We have to do a few other things then get back home. Your grandma doesn't know where we've gone."

"I think I'll live in town when I grow up," Patrick said after they had left the courthouse and thanked Mr. Rosenberg. "Would that be okay?"

She sighed. "It would be fine with me, but you better wait till you're older. Then you can discuss it with your pa and your grandma."

She couldn't think of anything she'd like better, unless it was that Jacqueline and she could live in town too and keep on having their picture made together.

But she shoved such ridiculous dreams to the back of her mind with a sigh.

❖

"I need to go to the drugstore, and then I'll be through, Jacqueline."

"Patrick and I'll sit at the soda fountain and wait for you."

As Molly talked to the clerk near the stationery, Jaq asked Patrick, "Are you thirsty?"

"Yes, ma'am. Shopping and doing courthouse business is hard work."

"It certainly is. How about a cherry Coca-Cola in a nice big glass of ice?"

His grin almost split his face. "Yes, ma'am. I'd like one."

After she ordered his drink, she told him not to move from his stool, that she'd be right back. In the pharmacy area she bought two vials of calendula cream then walked a few steps to the soap section and picked up the largest bar of Ivory she could find. The clerk wrapped everything, and she'd paid for it and slid the parcel into her purse before Molly got back to the soda fountain.

"Let's sit at this little table close to Patrick," she suggested, and Molly sank into a small metal-backed chair. "Did you find what you're looking for?"

She held up a small package. "I found the sheet music for that song about rainbows you played for me, and I bought a bottle of ink and some new points for my pen staff. But they still don't carry lined paper to write music on. I'll have to keep drawing my own lines, and it's so easy to smudge them."

"Why do you need all this?" Molly still surprised her.

"I compose my own songs." She blushed, as if ashamed of her guilty secret.

"That's bloody wonderful. Why haven't you told me sooner?"

"I'm so used to hiding my passion, I forgot that you'd understand. Women don't compose music. We sing and play it, but only men create music."

Molly sounded more cynical than she'd ever heard her.

"And who told you that?"

"Everyone. Even my university professors. And especially Mr. James and Mrs. Russell." She looked almost frightened to even talk about wanting to do something only men did.

"Women don't vote either. Isn't that what people have always told us?" She sat up straight. "Well, that changed today, and it's just the first of a lot of changes. How about an ice-cream soda to celebrate?"

Molly's green eyes sparkled like the sun shining on the ocean. Jaq could sit there and look at them for hours, like she had with the waves on her trips back and forth to Europe.

But they needed to get back to the farm, so she ordered a strawberry soda for herself and a vanilla soda for Molly, and Patrick rushed over with his nearly empty Coke glass. She asked for a refill and a double-dip chocolate cone for him, and they all three drank Coke from the same glass. When he dropped some chocolate on his white starched shirt, Molly didn't even frown, though it took time and patience to make it look so smooth using a flatiron heated on a wood stove. She didn't see a speck of soot or scorch marks. As slick as a button, it shone like Molly's face did when she gazed at him with so much love in her eyes.

When they finally drove home, Patrick immediately pulled off his shoes, saying they were pinching his feet, which were hot, and fell asleep in the backseat.

Molly had calmed down, and the trip flew by. Why did it always take longer to go somewhere than to return? During a lull in the conversation, Jaq asked Molly about her mother. She'd said that her father was a preacher who'd saved a woman during the Galveston Storm, but Jaq wondered what kind of woman would rear a daughter who wanted to compose music and register to vote.

"When I was growing up," Molly said, "we were always poor, but some times were worse than others. One day Papa came home after church and told Mama he'd invited ten people to dinner. Papa never paid much attention to what Mama did in the kitchen, but I was right there beside her as she mixed up a bowl full of biscuit dough. We didn't have anything else to eat. Tears were rolling down her cheeks, but she kept stirring.

"I looked toward the kitchen window, and a bowl of purple-hull peas appeared as if by magic. Mama took it with a surprised expression then accepted platters of fried chicken, bowls of mashed potatoes, and pies that our neighbors passed to her. 'Loaves and fishes,' she murmured, and thanked her benefactors. To her, their generosity was as much a miracle as that of Jesus. But it showed me how good people can be, and that if you treat others with as much kindness as she did, they'll gladly return it." Molly settled back with a soft smile, which tempered Jaq's attitude toward the human race just a fraction.

Deciding to help Eric and come to East Texas might have helped her finally find her bluebird, who seemed to want to escape from her cage. So Molly could compose music? What else was she capable of? Did Jaq really want to find out? If she did, it would only be harder for her to leave Molly alone here.

It was only five o'clock when they pulled up the long driveway, but it seemed like they'd been on a long vacation. While Molly was shaking Patrick awake, Jaq slipped a small package from her purse and handed it to her. "A small remembrance of a special afternoon," she said, and Molly smiled like a daisy. "And please give this one to Mrs. Russell."

"Thank you, for everything," Molly whispered then headed back inside the picket fence with Patrick, who had tied his shoelaces together and slung his stiff leather shoes over his shoulder. He carefully carried his new pants.

How could she bear to desert them? She put her Model T into gear and drove away as fast as she dared.

"Jumping Jehoshaphat. Where in the world have you and Patrick been all afternoon?"

Molly just stood in the kitchen without answering and unwrapped a package from the drugstore. Mrs. Russell could tell from the fancy paper.

"Ivory soap. Why, I never. That stuff's so full of air it'll melt faster than ice cream in August. Sure a waste of hard-earned cash."

Molly held the fancy bar up to one cheek, then sniffed it like a rose. "Jacqueline bought me the soap, and this is for you." That's all Molly said before she handed her a little parcel and headed for her bedroom, clutching her soap like it was more precious than the diamond she'd lost.

"Look, Grandma, what Mama bought me. Some long pants. Miss Jacqueline took a picture of me wearing them. And we went way up on the second floor of the courthouse with Mr. Rosenberg so Mama could vote or something. And I saw all the electric wires. Then Miss Jacqueline bought me a Coca-Cola and a double-dip chocolate ice-cream cone."

Patrick finally ran out of steam and went to take off his Sunday clothes and put his overalls back on. He had chores to do, and Molly needed to get to work too.

Molly was spoiling him rotten. He wouldn't be worth killing if she and Jacqueline kept giving him such extravagant treats. *She's horning in on my territory a little too much,* she thought.

Earlier, she'd felt better than she had in months, but they'd ruined her good mood. Too bad Molly didn't have another rolling pin for her to burn, and she'd probably hide her high-toned Ivory soap so she wouldn't have a chance at it.

But then she opened the little package Jacqueline had sent her and felt ashamed of herself. The first store-bought calendula lotion she'd ever had. Jacqueline had remembered her doctoring. Maybe she wasn't such a bad influence on Molly and Patrick after all.

Chapter Twenty-four

Molly still smarted from Mother Russell's personal attack a week earlier, though her trip to town had helped soothe her. She needed something else to occupy her mind, so she telephoned Jacqueline.

"Are you looking forward to the picnic next week?"

"I haven't even thought about it. Who'll be there?"

"Everyone in the community, plus everyone who's ever lived in New Hope. It's a reunion, though I don't know how many people will come from out of town, because of the War and the gas shortage." She smoothed her shapeless calico dress with one hand.

"With all the heat, not much else is going on, I imagine."

"That's right. Late July and August are usually slow around here." A trickle of perspiration ran down her side. She couldn't find any breeze today in the hall, where she stood holding the telephone. "Cotton's the only crop still growing. And once the farm families lay it by, they'll have some free time. The picnic gives them an excuse to socialize and catch up on the latest news. And the local politicians wouldn't miss it. Everybody will probably be talking about the governor's race and about Mrs. Blanton running for office."

"You're probably right," Jacqueline said. "Some of Farmer Jim Ferguson's cronies will most likely be trying to drum up votes for him, but the women will surprise everyone and vote Hobby into office. Mrs. Blanton has accused her opponent of being connected with the breweries, so she has a good chance of winning too. Can you imagine a woman beating a man for state office?"

Molly felt different about the picnic this year, more important. "The local politicians have always bought everyone lemonade, ice cream, and chewing gum at the refreshment stand, but they've always focused on the men. I'm not interested in their bribes, but I would like to have their respect. Now they'll have to court *me* for *my* vote, since it counts as much as Mr. James's."

"That's right, if they have enough sense to realize you're finally a registered voter. What do you think it'll be like for women a hundred years from now?"

"There's no telling. But it'll have to be better than it is now."

"By the way, what are we supposed to wear to the picnic?"

"I wanted to warn you. Don't let the word *picnic* fool you. When I went to my first one I was embarrassed within an inch of my life." Molly frowned. The memory still bothered her, even after all these years. That incident should have given her a glimpse of the future.

"What happened?"

"It sounds silly now, when our boys are dying overseas, but right before Mr. James and I married, he invited me to go. He didn't say a word about what to wear, though, and I didn't think to ask. Since it was a picnic, I wore a casual outfit that looked like a sailor's suit. It was nice, mind you, but nothing fancy."

"And?"

"All the women wore elaborate hats and dresses, and I looked like a schoolgirl. Mr. James just laughed and called me 'shabby genteel.' But I almost gave him back his ring, again." She'd been so mad at him for not recognizing why she was upset. Being so much younger than he was, she'd tried to compensate for their age difference by acting more mature than other women her age. But he insisted on treating her like a child, which infuriated and frustrated her.

"I wish you had," Jacqueline mumbled.

"What did you say?"

"Oh, nothing."

She *had* heard Jacqueline, though, and she didn't know what to think. Did Jacqueline regard her as more than a friend? If she did, what did that mean? If she hadn't married Mr. James and had met Jacqueline instead, would they have lived together like her two teachers had? Would they have been happy, or was Jacqueline simply whiling away the hours with her until she could leave this tedious place? Molly didn't want to put too much stock in four little words, but she knew she'd repeat them to herself a million times as she went about her unending chores.

❖

Jaq hung up. She needed to watch her tongue. She couldn't let Molly know how she really felt. Their situation was impossible. Wouldn't she ever learn to steer clear of nuns and women married either to their career or to a man? Especially one with a child too. She should have her head examined.

She headed to the kitchen to stir up a batch of cornbread to eat with the peas she'd already shelled and cooked. Thank goodness, she was finally getting the hang of a few basic dishes. As she tied a crisp white apron around her waist, she asked herself why she was attracted to unattainable women. Did she actually *not* want to become involved with anyone, so she chose women she didn't have a chance with? Maybe if she recalled everything she could about Helen, she might discover why such women drew her to them.

She had worked near Helen in late August, almost a year ago, at a casualty clearing station near Belgium, where she'd transported some soldiers. The British had barraged the area with heavy artillery for ten days, and then the infantry marched in. With all the rain and the shelling that destroyed the drainage system, the heavy tanks began to get stuck. She had to be careful not to do the same thing.

She was sitting in the mess tent smoking and drinking tea about five o'clock one morning when Helen showed up after a fourteen-hour shift. Helen smiled as she slid onto the rough bench next to her and stared at her muddy feet.

"Hi, stranger. Good to see you. Golly, I'm glad you helped me buy these boots in Dieppe." She looked exhausted yet ready for more of the same as she ate her bread and jam and drank some tea from Jaq's pot. "We've been standing in the operating room in mud higher than our ankles for more days than I can count." She stuck out a small, clay-covered foot.

"When we first got here, I expected to stay a few days, so I just brought two dresses and two aprons. Gee, you can imagine how long they stayed white."

Blood and mud speckled Helen's apron.

"But one of our majors persuaded a car and driver to go back to Le Tréport and pick up some supplies. He brought me six clean uniforms and aprons, our letters from home, and even some fruit and cake. Say,

I still have a little of that cake. Come over to my tent and I'll give you a piece."

Helen interested her, and she would have given her eyeteeth for any type of sweets and conversation with another American, so she picked up her cup of tea and followed.

On the way there, Helen said, "I like your short hair."

She ran her fingers through it and grinned. "Yeah. Mother's going to have a conniption. I got tired of combing the lice out, so I grabbed a pair of scissors and hacked it off. It's sure easier to keep clean, the few chances I get to wash it."

Helen's small, bare tent had the standard hinged wooden floor. Side by side on Helen's cot, they made their cake last as long as they could. Then Helen shoved the cot to one side of the tent and showed her two holes under the floor. They were about two feet wide, six feet long, and eighteen inches deep. Helen and her tent mate had to lie there under sheet-iron-reinforced boards while the anti-aircraft guns roared and pieces of exploding shells whizzed through the air. Jaq had seen shrapnel like that slice a person in half and shuddered to think of the same thing happening to Helen.

But Helen didn't take the situation seriously. She talked about how exciting this all was and repeated how she couldn't wait to tell everyone at home about it. That, and her conviction that nursing men back to health was life's highest calling, seemed to keep her going.

As Jaq had driven back to base she kept visualizing Helen. She'd stood in those makeshift quarters in her long-sleeved white dress with its muddy hem and filthy apron like she'd just conducted a tour of a mansion.

Maybe that was one reason she chased unavailable women, at least these two. Both Helen and Molly gracefully made the best of a bad situation. They faced different types of threats to their lives yet stayed cheerful and persevered, whereas Jaq became pessimistic and ran away. They had made peace with themselves, but Jaq found only war inside herself. Perhaps she was sabotaging her chances at a permanent relationship yet choosing women who could help her eventually become the type of person who could have one.

She broke an egg into some cornmeal, salt, and baking powder and began to stir some buttermilk and soda into it. All this thinking hurt her head.

❖

Mrs. Russell's mind whirled as she lay abed and listened to her eight-day clock strike. *Bong, bong, bong, bong.* Might as well stay awake, she thought. The rooster would be on duty before long.

Molly sure was a puzzle. Made out for the longest time like she was so meek and mild. Never had a hard word even after she burned Molly's dang rolling pin. If Molly had destroyed something of hers, she'd have snatched her baldheaded. Molly didn't use to have much gumption. Practically cried every time she looked at her sideways, till lately.

She couldn't believe Molly had hightailed it to town with Jacqueline. Then she told James she was going to town with him next Friday to vote in the primary. Lordy mercy. What was the country coming to with women thinking they could help run the government? Miss Rankin was a disgrace, voting against going to war with the Hun.

She could barely make out the oval frame holding the picture of Calvin, but she knew exactly what he looked like. He had a revolver tucked in his belt and a saber pointing straight up by his side. A white shirt peeked out from underneath the standup collar on his gray jacket, and a great big bow in front flopped like a dog's ears. His crumbled-down cap had its bill turned up, and his dark hair showed between it and the top of his small ears.

But everything except his hair and ears was fake. The photographer had painted that uniform. Her soldier boy wore whatever was handy to fight in. Never had a special outfit, but he was a captain in their glorious army and a hero. The day Georgia declared war, all but two of the boys at his college joined the Confederate Army. One of the ones that didn't volunteer was blind and the other didn't have any arms. And out of more than a hundred men, they'd elected Calvin their leader.

"You were a charmer, husband, and all those letters you wrote me while you were on the battlefield day and night trying to defend Atlanta from those dern Yankees helped me decide to marry you. Oh, you were a dreamer. And when one dream failed, I tried to help you find another one. This beautiful, fertile land looked so much like what we'd left behind in Georgia. We couldn't afford to buy two thousand acres like your pa did, though we did all right."

She'd hung Calvin's picture on the wall years ago so she could lay in bed and look at it. His serious eyes were actually that light-blue color, staring at her from under his sparse, straight brows. And his thin lips were usually pressed together and turned down a little at each corner. He looked awfully serious, even before the War, and he should have. When his picture was taken, he was about to leave the peaceful world he knew. Everything changed after the War, and he never got over it. Especially since, out of all his classmates, only sixteen of 'em made it home alive.

She had a spot so soft in her heart for him. Just thinking about the gentle way he used to touch her ears, she still trembled. He was the only one she could depend on to help her through the hard times. Confiding in him had always been her greatest consolation.

"James is changing right along with the world, Calvin. Picking up a lot of new ways of thinking from Molly. Used to, I could tell him what to do and he'd *yes, ma'am* me half to death. Might not do what I told him as quick as I wanted, and might be a mite sloppy, but he did it without any back talk.

"Come to think of it, though, he started acting different when I deeded him his share and more of the place. I made it plain as day that I'd keep full possession and manage the three hundred acres we're living on. He paid me with a promise of love and affection till the day I die, but looks like he's trying to wiggle out of it. Molly's a bad influence. I bet my good eye she's doing her best to get him to leave me out here on the farm all by my lonesome."

She smoothed her sheet. It felt rough as a cob. Took her forever to make a sheet stop being scratchy. Had to boil it in her wash pot with strong lye soap time after time. Molly most likely put the soft ones on their bed and Patrick's. And she'd bet her life Molly'd put the softest ones on Jacqueline's bed when she stayed with them all that time. Left her with the dregs.

"Calvin, why did you have to leave before you told me how to manage your boys? If you were still here, we could make do on our own. Send James and Molly packing to town, if she's so set on citified ways, wanting to vote and such nonsense. If I'd known James would up and marry her, I'd never have put myself in his hands. In spite of everything, I've tried to keep our dream alive. It's bound me to you all these years." She tried to twist her gold wedding band, but it was so tight now it would barely budge.

"When you died so young, something in me died too. Oh, I kept on for the sake of the children, and you too. But every time I lost another one, another piece of me shriveled up and fell off. Now I don't have much left inside except my fondness for James and Patrick. And of course Hannah and Clyde."

She scratched a chigger bite on her waistline. The dratted little critters reminded her of Molly. Good for nothing except to make her itch.

"Husband, I hate to say this, but even James has disappointed me, hitching himself like he did to someone who has no idea what our dream even was, and couldn't care less if she did. Nobody's still alive to know or respect what we intended to do so many years ago when I left everything and set out on foot behind a covered wagon to create a new world. The damn Yankees sure destroyed our old one.

"James is getting to where he thinks he's the boss of this place I've spent the best years of my life building up. And Molly would trade the whole kit and caboodle for a fancy piano. Just don't know where to turn in my old age except to you."

The clock struck again. *Bong, bong, bong, bong, bong.* She hated long nights like this when she couldn't sleep and her mind ticked along with the clock. She couldn't shut it down.

Sure would like a big glass of sweet milk. Her stomach was on fire. If James had just married right—somebody who cared about the important things in life like planting and hoeing and weeding—he could have created a regular Garden of Eden.

Sometimes she got so tired thinking 'bout it all, she wanted to throw up her hands. Had to keep on keeping on, though, trying to teach the younger generation what was really worthwhile.

Wouldn't be long till the New Hope picnic. It'd be good to visit with some of the old-timers. Maybe she could slip away from Molly and enjoy herself right smart for a change.

She rubbed her hands together. Just thinking about the picnic made her stomach feel better.

CHAPTER TWENTY-FIVE

Jaq was ready to take a nap after the extra-long Sunday service and the hot-air politicians' speeches. Eating so much in all the heat around a crowd of strangers had exhausted her.

At least Eric was finally socializing with his home folks instead of only girls, and his father was talking to a group of men. So she slid an old quilt from the backseat of the Model T and strolled toward the woods.

The lemonade stand was attracting a lot of customers, and flies were feasting on the few remains of the uncovered food still spread on the long tables under the big oak trees. What the boys on the front wouldn't give for a plate of leftovers. The tin of tea, can of bully beef, and handful of cookies they had to keep them going in the field for several days wasn't near enough.

She tried to shake such thoughts from her head and spied an opening in the thick woods at the back of the picnic grounds. The community cemetery to her right gave her the willies.

As she neared the woods, she spotted two familiar figures walking toward her—Molly and Patrick.

"Hi, Miss Jacqueline. We've been visiting my grandpa. He fought the Yankees in Atlanta."

"He must have been a brave man, Patrick."

He straightened his shoulders. "Yes, ma'am. He fought the whole war. Then he and Grandma got married. They drove all the way here in a covered wagon. Sounds like fun, don't you think? We go down and visit his grave every chance we get. Especially Grandma. She always talks to him like he's still alive."

She smiled over his head at Molly, the sun glinting off her red-gold hair and her eyes as green as the woods.

"Don't bother Miss Jacqueline," she said. "Of course she thinks your grandpa was a great man."

"That's right. Men like him, and some women too, are doing their best for our country right now. We need to respect them, just like you do your grandpa."

He smiled then spotted a group of his school friends by the lemonade stand. "Can I go visit, Mama? I'll stay close to where Grandma can see me."

Molly patted his shoulder. "Of course. Run along now."

"Yes, ma'am." He raced through the picnickers standing around in small groups.

"Looks like everybody's having a good time." Jaq was feeling more full of pep now. Molly affected her that way. "How have you been?"

Her eyes on Patrick, Molly wiped the sweat from her neck, though Jaq would have gladly volunteered to do it for her. "Oh, fine. Just been getting ready for the picnic. We've been cooking for days now and got up before the rooster did this morning. Other than that, the days all run together, except for Sunday and Wednesday. Each season of the year has a different routine, depending on the crops. How about you?"

Was she imagining things, or had Molly just asked that question as if she really wanted to know the answer? "Well, this is such a new world for me, I'm still trying to figure when to do what. Say, have the politicians been after you for your vote?"

Molly frowned. "You were right. Nobody's said a word. Most of those men are so thick between the ears they apparently don't realize they have any reason to be after me. You'd think they'd be better informed than that." She glanced at the crowd of people standing around in small groups, laughing and conversing.

"What do you think everyone's talking about?"

"Oh, the men are probably discussing their crops, the weather, politics, or the War." Molly shrugged in a most ladylike way. "And the women are gleaning any kind of news they can about what's going on in the world, when they get through chatting about their husbands, kids, and problems on the farm. You'd think they'd compare recipes, since they spent all morning in the kitchen. But we have so few ingredients to work with, especially now with the War on, we usually just cook the same old dishes."

"I certainly enjoyed the same old dishes, especially your apple pie and Mrs. Russell's chocolate one. I've eaten in some fancy restaurants, but home cooking like this beats it hands down. Oh, I'm keeping you from whatever you were about to do. I was looking for a quiet place." She raised her quilt.

With a smile like sunrise, Molly said, "I've already visited with everyone I wanted to, and the singing won't start for a while. I'll show you a nice spot, if you'd like."

"I'd love that." Jaq shifted the quilt in her arms and gazed at the woods. The pines didn't look quite as foreboding as usual. In fact, she could hardly resist the lure of the path into their territory. She hoped she emerged without a scratch.

Molly led Jacqueline down the sandy path to a steep, pine-needle-cushioned hill. Thankfully the trees lowered the temperature, and a spring bubbled through pure white sand near the bottom of the slope.

"You'll never drink better water. Want to try it?" Molly asked.

"Sure. Let's kneel on my old quilt."

Molly formed a cup with both hands and scooped up a drink. "Hmm, cool and sweet." She reached for another handful, then turned to Jacqueline, beside her. "Perfect for such a hot afternoon."

The look Jacqueline gave her, though, made her warmer than before she'd quenched her thirst. Another kind of thirst began to build.

After they bathed their faces and hands, she tried to slow her waltzing heart by saying, "The children come here and slide down that big hill. Let's walk a little farther for some peace and quiet."

But her heart only danced faster when Jacqueline agreed. When they entered a small grove with a clearing in the middle, it fox-trotted.

"I like to come here alone sometimes, especially when Mother Russell makes me so mad I can't see straight." She struggled to keep her voice calm and even. "The wind in the pines always soothes me, and I go back to the farm feeling like I've had a vacation."

Jacqueline spread her quilt and patted a spot. "Sit here. You're not mad now, are you?"

She stretched out and gazed through the sheltering branches toward the blue sky. This was heaven—only her and Jacqueline, no chores and no one to scold her.

"No, not angry. Resigned, almost numb. I've tried to understand and forgive her and, believe me, burning my rolling pin is minor compared to other stunts she's pulled. I don't know what to do, but I can't live with her much longer. She eats at me like a cancer."

Jacqueline gave her a sympathetic look. "I know. Eric doesn't affect me that way or I wouldn't be here. But I don't want to spend my life with him. I feel trapped too."

She had an absurd urge to push back Jacqueline's bangs and check her wound, but she was afraid that if she touched Jacqueline she might not want to stop. The soft breeze threatened to lull her to sleep, yet she felt strangely on edge. Jacqueline lay next to her, close enough that if she turned just a hair and reached out, she could—"How did you meet Eric, Jacqueline?"

That was the only way she could think of to distract herself from her shimmying heart.

Molly's question about meeting Eric sucked Jaq back into the happy days before the War, before everyone began to cross the Channel and either didn't return or came back damaged or changed. She wanted to linger on those early times, spin them out to Molly, relive them, show her how she was before she went to France instead of the coward she was now.

"I met Eric in London. I lived there with my sister a few years before the War began."

Sister Mary Therese invaded her mind. Would she ever forget her? She'd opened up so many new feelings. She'd tried to forget them, but right now they were springing to life. Bloody hell. She could probably seduce Molly with her adventures in a world she'd never known. Sister Mary had taught her how.

She could entrance Molly into a state of desire…No! Desire reminded her of quicksilver—here one minute, transformed the next. Or water. Boiling, it scalded, but then cooled and froze. Without Willie, her frozen longing for Sister Mary and Helen could have destroyed her. Willie had showed her sex without guilt, but that was impossible with Molly. Married, innocent, and trusting, Molly had taken care of her when she was hurt and helpless. She *could* control her desire for

Molly, who would never know what she was missing and would grow old contentedly with her grandchildren.

She could merely entertain Molly, not involve her in the jaded world she'd discovered in Europe. Maybe she could remember herself as she was before then. If she were still that old self, Molly wouldn't shrink from her as she would when, and if, she told Molly who she actually was, what she did in France, and perhaps even about Willie.

She inched away from Molly, made her voice carefree. "Sorry. I got caught up in my own thoughts. It's a long story. Are you sure you want to hear it?"

Molly's curls bounced as she nodded. "Oh yes. Your stories remind me of watching a picture show. Your stories are even better than a movie, though, because they're true."

Her face flamed as she murmured her thanks and then rewound her mind.

Molly lay next to her on her patchwork quilt with a face that begged to be kissed as she described how she'd admired one woman who'd run away from home to drive an ambulance in France and sent her mother a one-word wire that said SAILING. More than tempted, Jaq reined herself in and tried to distract both of them by describing another woman she'd known.

Toupie Lowther had owned a motorcycle and driven a Peugeot, which Jaq envied. She had been organizing a group to go over to France and drive an ambulance, but Jaq had joined the WAACs before Toupie formed her unit.

Then Molly put her hands behind her head, a question in her eyes, and asked why she'd joined the WAACs.

When Jaq mentioned "In Flanders Fields," Molly beamed. "Oh, yes. I read it in the paper and cried."

Her reaction warmed Jaq. The little poem had inspired her to join, and now Molly's face shone with the same idealism she'd felt back then, though it hadn't lasted very long.

"It made me want to pick up that torch the poor men with failing hands were talking about," Molly said.

"That's how I felt." She blew out a sigh. "When I got to Europe, I promised myself I'd answer the dead soldiers' challenge to help fight the Germans."

Then Jaq described the khaki jacket and skirt and tight-fitting cap she'd worn and how she'd envied the women who rode motorcycles because they got to wear tight khaki pants with boots laced over them.

Molly gazed at her with clear longing. "You've led such an exciting life. While you were in Europe, I was milking a cow and raising a child."

If only she could take Molly to Europe after the War, introduce her to friends, show her the sights—damn it. She couldn't even think about it. It wouldn't do any good to wish for what neither of them could ever have.

She inched away from Molly again as she tried to describe what war was really like. But she'd intended to tell Molly how she met Eric. Her sister had introduced them because she thought Jaq would enjoy spending time with someone from the States.

A ray of sun hit her eyes and she shut them so she could concentrate on what she was trying to say. Her thoughts were jumbled and she was rambling and going into too much detail, but being so close to Molly affected her that way.

CHAPTER TWENTY-SIX

Molly loved Jacqueline even more because of the way she'd talked about that poem. She'd been so honorable and idealistic back then and still was, though going to war seemed to have made her lose touch with that side of herself a little.

When Jacqueline mentioned a woman called Marguerite Radclyffe Hall and some books she'd read about sex, Molly jerked to attention. No one said the word *sex* in polite company, but she tried to relax. Mama had taught her to listen first and judge later.

As Jacqueline talked, her dark eyes darted and flashed with life, and her pink-red lips, like a lush rose, drew Molly in. Molly wanted to finger those lips, pull them close to hers, see how they tasted.

Jaq talked about Marguerite's older-woman friend, Mabel, who'd had a lot of affairs, even with the future king of England.

That floored Molly. An affair with a future king? This sounded like a novel. She would never have even daydreamed about something so unbelievable.

As Jacqueline described Marguerite wooing yet being mothered by Mabel, Molly tried to pull herself away from the sight of Jacqueline's seductive lips and picture Mabel. She'd never known a woman who had affairs, at least to her knowledge. Her shoulders stiffened. But if Mabel had mothered Marguerite, she must have cared for her.

She tried to relax as she fixed her attention on Jacqueline's closed eyes and full lips with their Cupid's bow. Those luscious lips certainly made it difficult for Molly to breathe.

Then Jacqueline said something that riveted her. Marguerite and Mabel had become *lovers*. She tried to look nonchalant but grabbed hold of the quilt as if it were the side of a rocking boat on a stormy sea.

She gritted her teeth and grabbed a bigger piece of the quilt when Jacqueline described how Mabel wanted to tell everyone they were as much a couple as Lord and Lady Clarendon, her sister. She'd nicknamed Marguerite *John*, after her grandfather, and herself *Ladye*, to mock her sister.

Surely Jacqueline had made this up. But Jacqueline kept talking, far away in another world that Molly could barely imagine.

It turned out that Jacqueline's friends had nicknamed her too, but Molly had almost reached her limit. She needed to get back to the church. They expected her to play for the—

"Jaq." That was what her English friends called her, and then Jacqueline said that if they ever visited any of her English friends, she would have to get used to that name.

Molly took a deep breath. Would it even be possible to visit any of them? Maybe someday when Patrick was grown and she'd saved every cent from teaching piano lessons, she might be able to...*No*. Jacqueline could leave any day now, and she would probably never see her again. Jacqueline had better, more interesting things to do than go anywhere with her.

Suddenly she quit feeling so panicky and thought about college. She *did* know a little about couples like Jacqueline had been describing. She relaxed her grip on the quilt a fraction. But her two teachers would *never* have been that open about their special friendship. In public they always acted like nothing more than companions.

She needed more time to absorb all this information, so she said, "Do you want to hear something strange?"

"After all this, you can tell me almost anything."

"My real name is Marguerite, though everybody has always called me Molly. But isn't it odd that two women can have the same birth name and one be nicknamed John and the other Molly? A name makes all the difference, doesn't it?" Her remark seemed to please Jacqueline, so she lessened her grip even more.

"If I called you Marguerite and you called me Jaq, would that change how we feel about each other?" But as soon as the words left Jacqueline's lips, she bit them and blushed.

How would it feel to be Marguerite, a sexy Frenchwoman who could stir the heart of a suitor without even trying? She let go of the quilt. What a contrast to Molly the milkmaid and pianist, who could stir only her mother-in-law, usually not in a pleasant way.

She decided to experiment.

"Jaq." She practically purred. "If I were your Marguerite, would you give me flowers and jewelry, and write poems for me?"

Jacqueline blushed and stared at her like she had that first Sunday in church. Then she moved nearer and lowered her head alarmingly close.

She instinctively pulled back, and Jacqueline retreated to the other side of the quilt. She didn't know whether she wanted Jacqueline or Jaq by her side.

She sat as still as if the sun had turned to ice. She wanted Jacqueline, or Jaq, or whatever she decided to call her as near as she was when Marguerite had summoned her. She wanted to hear her sharp intake of breath again, to let those lips come closer until they relieved the pressure building in her own.

But she still needed time. She was about to change her life forever—do something even more radical than vote. Something shimmered between them like heat rising from hard-packed earth during a drought and drew her to Jacqueline, like parched earth calling out for water.

Jacqueline seemed to read her mind because she propped her head on one elbow and continued to talk about John and Ladye, Molly's blood pounding so loud in her ears that she missed a lot. Jacqueline really did know some important people, so why would she waste her time talking to her? She flinched at her own insignificance, but Jacqueline apparently didn't notice. And when Jacqueline later asked if she was tired of hearing her ramble, she told her not to stop. In fact, she almost called her Jaq, just for fun, but their little charade earlier had scared her.

Then Jacqueline described how John had met another woman, and when Ladye had later died, John felt so guilty about taking up with the other woman that she and her new lover went to séances, and John was certain she had contacted Ladye.

Molly sat up, brought her knees to her chest, and wrapped her arms around them in a most unladylike fashion. Her world seemed tiny. How shocking that Jacqueline mentioned the word sex so casually, and John went to séances. She wanted to know more. Papa probably wouldn't approve of such activities, but Mama was a lot more open-minded than Papa, so she guessed she took after her.

But then Jacqueline sat up too and said she liked the way John acted like a man in her relationships with both her women lovers. What did Jacqueline mean? Molly listened even more intently.

"John called herself an invert, a man trapped in a woman's body," Jacqueline said. "She believed she couldn't change the way she felt about women."

But Molly was puzzled and wondered why that interested Jacqueline. So she smiled and asked, "You're not an invert, are you? You're one of the most womanly women I've ever seen." As she lightly said these words, though, the nickname *Jaq* hit her in the head.

Jacqueline eased back down and lay on her side, facing her again. "You haven't seen me dressed in my brothers' clothes and working on our automobiles together. You haven't really seen the way I drive, because the roads around here are too rough to speed on. And you didn't see me in France. I wore men's clothes most of the way up here. They make life easier when you're on the road. The next time you come over, I'll show you what I look like in them."

She couldn't picture Jacqueline as a tomboy, though she'd hinted that she'd been one. She saw only a beautiful, fashionable woman.

"In France, doing your job mattered most. But dressing like a man doesn't make a woman an invert, and working like one doesn't either. The way I feel about women makes me one. That's why I married Eric."

"I don't understand." Suddenly she felt like she was talking to a stranger. "How do you feel about women? And what does that have to do with marrying Eric?"

"I married him because I was a coward. I admired John, but I couldn't face my real self, not like she could. And I couldn't stand to even imagine what my parents, especially Mother, would think if they found out. The books about sex that I read scared me silly. I guess I thought that if I married a man, my deep feelings for women would disappear. Of course that didn't work and wasn't fair to Eric or me because I didn't love him."

Molly understood. She knew all about being unfair and marrying a man she didn't love.

"Oh, Eric was handsome and charming, an admirable hero. I must have thought everyone would consider his wife womanly. He seemed really independent too. We never lived together. He left for the front just a few days after we married."

Molly sighed. The only time she ever spent away from Mr. James was when she visited her parents in Dallas. He certainly depended on the two women he lived with, especially his mother. And she was dependent on him.

"After our first night together I realized I'd made a mistake," Jacqueline said. "We agreed to lead separate lives, but I didn't want to get a divorce or even an annulment because of my religious background, and because of what Mother would say. But now we've agreed to have our marriage annulled when we return to New Orleans. The only problem is, I've met you and I'm even more confused now."

Why did meeting me confuse Jacqueline? She lay back again, wrapped part of the quilt over her, and gazed at the pines overhead. Why couldn't people be more like pines—stable, rooted, sure of where they belonged? Poor Jacqueline, caught in a loveless marriage and mixed up because she loved women.

Though she didn't love Mr. James, and Mother Russell drove her to distraction most of the time, she had her music. Most important, though, she had Patrick. He made everything worthwhile, and he always would.

As she lay there, Jacqueline crossed her arms and massaged them repeatedly. She spoke so rapidly Molly had to strain to catch every word.

"In New Orleans I met a woman who convinced me I'll never change. But I'm not as strong as John. Sometimes I wish I could be like other people. Life would be so much simpler."

Jacqueline's dark eyes flashed like thunderclouds, and the words "I met a woman" ripped through her like lightning, shattered her calm. Thunder deafened her, yet she didn't want to run. She wanted to curl up next to Jacqueline and never leave her. Yet who was this other woman? Would Jacqueline see her again when she returned to New Orleans?

"Molly." Jacqueline's voice drowned out the thunder. "I don't want to feel this way. Sometimes I want to find a doctor who can cure me of my attraction to women so I can live a normal life. That won't include marrying another man—I've learned my lesson. I'll probably spend my life alone, but at least it'll be *my* life. I want to devote my life to a worthy cause such as helping women gain the right to vote, or like my Aunt Anna has with her work in medicine."

Slowly Jacqueline edged nearer, as if she needed to be physically as close as possible before she could say what she wanted. And now she whispered, "Women have caused me nothing but heartache. I left France partially because I fell in love with a nurse named Helen. She took care of me when I was exhausted and ill, and for the longest time she never knew I was in love with her."

The thunder boomed again in Molly's head, and she let it. She didn't want to hear about Jacqueline loving someone else.

"Helen was a true hero. She gave herself for what she believed in—this stupid war that has slaughtered so many young people. She was amazing."

She couldn't block out Jacqueline's words. She felt like she'd rammed a needle under her fingernail and recognized the stinging pain as jealousy. Mr. James had given her the diamond he bought for someone else. Now Jacqueline considered her second-best too.

"I don't imagine you want to listen to me talk about Helen, but she's dead, and I can't get her out of my mind. Mustard gas killed her. She spent too much time working on gassed men, and I guess the overexposure ruined her liver. But I left France before she died then went to Washington and back home. I met the woman I mentioned earlier, and eventually Eric turned up, so I've had problems for quite a while."

Jacqueline eased so close her breath felt soft against Molly's cheek. She'd mentioned that woman again. Who was she and what had happened between them?

"I sure didn't need to meet you right now, Molly. Or do you want me to call you Marguerite? I have to resolve my situation with Eric and decide what to do with the rest of my life. I can't stay here and moon over you. I don't get to see you nearly enough, and I have to grit my teeth when I think about you sleeping with your husband."

Taking a huge breath, Jacqueline looked so serious, as if she were about to plunge underwater. "I love you, Molly, like a man loves a woman. And I'm going crazy because I can't be with you like that."

Slowly, Jacqueline lowered her lips to Molly's. At first, they felt like a snowflake, a butterfly's wing. Jacqueline's cheek touched hers. Where was the sandpaper, the prickly pear she'd come to associate with a kiss? The suede brush? The pine needles? Jacqueline's cheek felt as soft as a downy chick, newly picked cotton, a fuzzy peach.

Gradually the kiss grew harder, warmer, and she tasted the sweetness of chocolate pie, whipped cream, strawberries.

Breathless wonder shot through her. The kiss swept her up like the melody of her favorite piece of music. Rising from one octave to another, she soared on the beauty of the tune, lost in its sweep until her senses became one and she couldn't distinguish hearing from touch or taste or smell or sight. Beneath it all, the bass remained steady, like the beating of their hearts.

Jaq became her world, and the other life seemed far away, as mundane as a milk stool. Molly had become Marguerite, and Jacqueline was Jaq, and whoever she was now wished this moment would never end.

Strength blazed through her. She was a woman. But how could another woman, not a man, make her feel like this for the first time in her life?

She needed to think, wanted to respond—

"Miss Molly, it's time for the singing!"

CHAPTER TWENTY-SEVEN

Mrs. Russell wasn't the least bit surprised when the preacher hollered, "Miss Molly, it's time for the singing! Miss Molly!"

Now where had she got herself off to? Patrick said she'd walked down to the spring with Jacqueline. What were those two cooking up?

They talked every day on the telephone and as long as they could after Sunday school. Then they visited practically all day during her Wednesday meetings. They thought she didn't know, but she knew everything around here. Looked like they'd have talked themselves out a long time ago. How much could a body say to another one? They'd be a lot better off if they did something useful instead of moving their mouths all the time.

"Ma, have you seen Miss Molly?"

James looked a mite embarrassed that he'd let his wife stray and now everybody recognized it. He'd wasted his time standing over there under the shade trees cussing and discussing with the politicians about the Lord knows what, and speaking real secretive-like with a greasy-looking city slicker.

Probably had another get-rich-quick scheme up his sleeve. He was so gullible a six-year-old could fool him, but he never learned. *If Molly doesn't sweet-talk him into leaving me and the farm, he'll hang on my coattails until the day I die, and then heaven help him. He'll be lost as a goose.*

Never mind, here came Molly, huffing and puffing. Musta been down at the spring. "Everybody's waiting for you. They're ready to start the singing."

She looked like she was about to have a sunstroke, the silly thing, running so fast in July.

❖

Molly was breathing hard, and not only because of the steep climb up the hill. Jaq had talked about things she could barely imagine—someone having an affair with a real king, going to a séance. None of the women she knew or the ones in her family she'd heard stories about had done anything nearly as interesting as the ones Jaq described. Maybe women *could* do something besides marry and have children. Perhaps she wasn't so strange after all, with her dream of putting music before raising a family.

But Jaq said she'd loved a woman during the War. She also knew a woman in New Orleans but intended to be alone the rest of her life. All the same, Jaq said she couldn't stand to think of her sleeping with Mr. James.

She wasn't thinking just about them sleeping in the same bed, but about the times they felt of each other in the private way. That word again—*sex*. She could barely say it and didn't think about it very often. Respectable people didn't mention it, but perhaps the word somehow applied to her strange feelings about Jaq. Like when she'd replaced her bandage, or made pie crust or bread. She'd never throbbed that way before, as if something was tickling the bottom of her stomach, not in bed with Mr. James or even the summer before they married. Jaq certainly didn't need to worry about that.

Most of the time, she fell asleep as soon as her head sank into the feather pillow. Mr. James got an itch occasionally, but she hardly had time to respond. In and out. She supposed some people might call that sex, but she referred to it as having relations and thought it was overrated.

When Mr. James had courted her, she'd felt a little tingle once or twice when he took her hand in his large freckled one and rubbed it gently against his jowl. And the times he kissed her before they married, she'd flushed all over, excited that she might soon finally solve one of life's great mysteries—what it was like to be with a man physically—and her heart had raced.

But their bedroom was right next to Mother Russell's, which probably accounted for Mr. James not being as demonstrative after they married as he had been before.

Now she usually lay awake after he started snoring and wondered if this was all there was to it. If so, the girls who whispered about it back in college certainly didn't know what they were talking about. She guessed it could be so much more, but she would never know what that more consisted of. When she had relations with Mr. James, she never had the same feelings she had for Jaq. But her body had betrayed her by making her think she should marry him, and look where that got her. Sex was okay, but not nearly enough reason to live on a farm. She couldn't afford to let herself get carried away with Jaq.

Exactly what did Jaq mean about being an invert? Molly sat down at the piano and played the first hymn automatically. In college, the two women teachers she respected so much seemed to be the happiest couple imaginable. No one ever mentioned the word *invert* that upset Jaq so much. They all simply envied their teachers and accepted them as two loving women who seemed to fulfill each other's every need.

Everyone knew they loved each other, and even that they slept in the same bed. Some people whispered they might have done something similar to what married couples did, though they didn't know any more about such things than she did. What their teachers did in private didn't concern them much, probably because they were just two women.

Looking back, she had to admit that her feelings for the series of girls before she met Esther weren't as innocent as she'd thought at the time. But back then everyone had a crush on one of the other girls. Smashes, they'd called them, and she had some powerful ones before she and Esther found each other. But her feelings for Jaq far overshadowed any she'd ever had for Esther.

When she married Mr. James, she'd believed those feelings for women would vanish: she would love her husband and her children, period. And that's probably what Jaq meant about why she married Eric. Maybe she was simply more honest than Molly.

Evidently for some women those longings for other women never disappeared, and maybe they expressed them physically, which made their love for each other even richer and deeper.

Did Jaq think *she* might be one of those women too? With the way she'd been feeling around Jaq, she might be, but surely not. What would she do? Where would she go? How would she ever find anyplace to fit in?

Suddenly her lips prickled, and when she missed a note she glanced around to see if anyone had noticed.

Her lips were probably as crimson as a fancy woman's. Why didn't everybody stare at her and point? Then the light shone through one of the clear glass windows and illuminated the red canna lilies on the altar. What was wrong with what Jaq and she felt for each other?

She missed another note, but she didn't care. She wanted to be in the clearing with Jaq so she could get to the bottom of all this. But maybe she should spend some time alone and let these confused longings sort themselves out. Then she and Jaq could have a nice long talk, and maybe she could understand what was happening.

Jaq trudged up the hill after the singing finally ended. Passing the spring, she thought about Molly for the hundredth time.

Bloody hell. She shouldn't have lost control. She shouldn't have told her so much. And she sure shouldn't have kissed her. Molly probably thought she was horrible and would never speak to her again. But wouldn't that be for the best?

Why hadn't she kept her mouth shut and her lips to herself? She'd probably just stirred Molly up. Damn. What good would that do? She would be leaving soon…and Molly would be staying. Period. They couldn't do anything.

Better not telephone her for a while. *Maybe she'll forget what I said—and what I did.*

But Molly wouldn't forget a word. And she definitely wouldn't forget their kiss.

Jaq wouldn't either. It had flattened her like a Zeppelin raid.

The next Sunday afternoon, Molly and Patrick wandered down to the pond and stopped to pick some honeysuckle that covered the nearby bushes. She sucked the nectar from several of the tiny pink-and-white blooms, and Patrick said, "They sure are sweet, aren't they? Almost like candy." She thought they tasted like Jaq's lips.

The pine trees in the forest near the pond, so dense its interior was almost black, barely moved in the soft breeze. She and Patrick lay down side by side on the mattress-thick pine straw under the trees that circled the pond and gazed up at them.

"Look at that mourning dove way up on that branch." She pointed it out to him. He could already identify almost all the birds native to East Texas, especially blue jays, mockingbirds, and redbirds.

"Listen to that old crow cawing," he said. "He's sure upset about something. And look at those buzzards circling over there. Must be something dead. I like the way they float around. Wouldn't it be fun to do that?"

"Did you know Miss Jacqueline's husband, Mr. Eric, used to fly aeroplanes in the war overseas? I bet he could tell you all about floating around in the sky."

"Wow. Can we go talk to him sometime?"

"I'm sure we can. He wasn't feeling well when he got home, but I bet he's better now. The next time I talk to Miss Jacqueline I'll ask her about it."

Suddenly, a squawking mockingbird dove down at one of their barn cats, who'd followed them. "It must have wandered too close to the bird's nest," she said. It kept diving at the poor cat, who tried to get away, and Patrick pointed at them and giggled.

"What if that bird was after you, son? How would you feel? The cat's just trying to get away."

"I wouldn't like it, Mama. It'd hurt if it pecked me on the head. Why's it acting like that?"

"It's just protecting its babies, so I guess I'd do the same if something was sneaking around our house looking for you. But it needs to stop now and let the poor cat alone. It's probably learned its lesson."

Patrick looked thoughtful and Molly stayed silent to let him ponder their conversation. She wanted him to realize that life wasn't black and white.

She was almost dozing when Patrick shook her arm. "What does that cloud look like, Mama?"

"A pig wearing a pink dress and high-heel shoes."

He laughed. "It looks like an Easter egg with legs to me. Oh, goody. Here comes Pa."

Mr. James ambled over and sat down between them.

"Will you tell me a story about the Trojan War, Pa? Please. You tell the best stories."

Mr. James acted like he was thinking hard, then said, "Well, you know how brave Hector was, don't you?"

"Yes, sir. He was the Trojans' best, bravest warrior."

"But when he was supposed to fight Achilles, what did he do?"

"He got scared and ran around the city three times, with Achilles right behind him."

"And why did he finally stop and fight, son?"

"One of the gods disguised himself as his best friend, but then he disappeared when Hector needed him, and Achilles slaughtered him."

Mr. James shook Patrick's shoulder affectionately, with an expression of pride. "You know *The Iliad* as well as I do. You'll have to start telling me stories about it and other books now. You're not gonna have to quit school after the third grade, like I did."

Molly shook her head. "Now, Mr. James. Why do you have to dwell on the war part of *The Iliad*? There's a lot more to it than that. What about the way Hector's wife and parents grieved when they learned that Achilles had killed their son? Patrick needs to realize that war brings more death and sorrow than pride and glory."

"Ah, Mama. That's woman talk. Pa and I need to know about fighting."

But Mr. James laid one large hand on Patrick's small one and wrapped his other arm around her waist. "You need to know about fighting, son, but you need to remember that war brings a heap of grief too. Look at how much sorrow it's brought Mr. Eric. It takes a real man to suffer through that type of pain and come out on the other side even stronger. And I think Mr. Eric's that kind of person. I want you to be like that too."

She had to fight back a tear. What a good man she'd married. If only she could love him the same way she loved Jaq.

CHAPTER TWENTY-EIGHT

Molly didn't visit or telephone Jaq for more than a month. She wanted to give herself time to get used to the new name—*Jaq*—and the strange feelings it aroused in her. Though she wasn't nearly as exciting as the women Jaq had associated with overseas or in Washington or New Orleans, she was pretty sure Jaq really liked her. But what she'd said about being an invert still confused her.

Plus, she was scared. Their kiss had shown her in thirty seconds what Jaq's thousands of words had tried to communicate. She might be more like Jaq than either of them suspected. And then what would she do? She craved to see Jaq, touch her. Would she be able to contain herself the next time they met, or would she take her in her arms and...?

Familiar things comforted her. Walking by the pond under the pines alone, she talked to the snapping turtle on the log about her longings. She discussed them with Nellie every morning and evening as she squeezed her warm, elastic tits and listened to the milk ping the sides of the bucket. She strolled through the rose garden and tried to inhale the essence of Jaq along with the fragrance of the roses.

When she finally stood on firm ground again, she cranked the handle on the telephone. Ethel's *Number, please* sounded joyful. And when Jaq finally answered, she sounded joyful too. Molly bit her lip so she wouldn't say anything unseemly for Ethel to hear.

"Molly! I wondered if you'd fallen down the well. It's been too long."

Jaq *sounded* glad to hear from her. Maybe she actually did like her. Or perhaps she was playing with her, kissing her to add excitement to her own life. Jaq probably didn't even think about her when they were apart—considered her a naive countrywoman dying for attention from a woman of the world.

"I've been so busy. I'm sorry for not getting in touch sooner, but you know how it is." There. She didn't seem too eager to talk to Jaq—did she?

After they chatted, she asked, "Would you teach me how to drive your Model T? Mr. James and his brother Clyde tried to give me lessons, a few years after we got married, but I didn't do very well. Maybe you could be a little more patient—"

"Of course. That sounds fine. How about Wednesday at ten o'clock? And, Molly, I look forward to it."

"So do I, Jaq, so do I." There. She'd finally said the new name aloud. Did Jaq mean what she said? Could she trust her? What about the woman back in New Orleans?

She finally forced herself to quit doubting Jaq's words. Afterward, she felt like she'd played a Chopin mazurka with the same passion Chopin must have experienced when he composed it. She danced down the hall and back into the kitchen. She was going to see Jaq again. And Jaq said she was looking forward to seeing her. Jaq didn't sound angry or indifferent that she hadn't called in so long. She really did sound like she wanted to see her and teach her to drive. Molly couldn't wait.

"Humph. Wonder what's going on now, Miss Biddy?" Mrs. Russell slid her hand under her favorite black-and-white speckled laying hen and felt for eggs. The straw nest was like an oven. "You need to get busy if you plan to best the record that hen up in Oklahoma set a few years ago. Three hundred eggs in one year! Great Scott. Didn't that beat the band?"

She deposited two eggs into her basket and strolled to the next nest. "And you, Mrs. Dandy. You've been slacking off too. Best get to work. You're beginning to remind me of Molly, and you don't want that, do you? She's been moping around for ever so long, her mind somewhere else. Never knew her to be moody, but lately she's downright testy at times. Must have more starch in her backbone than I gave her credit for."

❖

Two minutes till ten.

Eric had showed Jaq a letter this morning from a fellow stationed on board the receiving ship at Commonwealth Pier in Boston.

Ten o'clock. Why the dickens wasn't Molly here yet?

He said a bunch of sailors had come down with the usual symptoms of the flu. But it was so bad some of the guys had to transfer from sickbay to the Chelsea Naval Hospital.

Two minutes after ten. She jumped out of the porch swing, rushed into the front yard, and looked down the road. Damn. Nobody in sight.

The sailors swore they felt like somebody had beaten them with a club. That's exactly how she'd ached during those two bouts of the flu in France last summer.

Five minutes after ten.

Last year the disease struck in the summer too. Usually everybody had it in the winter.

Six minutes after. Where was she? Blast it. Had Molly stood her up?

She paced from one end of the porch to the other. She'd never known Molly to be late. Maybe she'd changed her mind. Didn't want to associate with an invert. Maybe—

Gus and Kate finally shambled up the hard-packed driveway.

"Sorry." Molly sounded breathless. She tied up the mules and dashed across the front yard. "Mother Russell was in a foul state of mind today. I had to help her and Patrick get ready. She wanted to know why I was coming over here, asked what we were up to. You'd have thought we were having an affair, the way she was carrying on—" Her face was shining as red as an autumn apple.

"Oh, you know how she is. She probably got up on the wrong side of the bed." Jaq'd been afraid of that. Molly had been thinking that she was an invert, an unnatural creature who needed to be cured or—

"I'm excited about my driving lesson. I hope you're in a better mood than Mother Russell. If you don't feel like teaching me, I won't be able to drive myself around like I want. The War should be over soon. When we can buy gasoline and tires again, these old mules will probably retire from the transportation business."

Molly sounded more self-confident than she'd ever heard her, even when she registered to vote. She'd known Molly had it in her, but it was just beginning to show up. She'd teach Molly how to drive. Then after she left Texas, Molly could go to town and visit. She'd have more in common with some of the women there than with the farm wives.

Molly had mentioned a woman named Tabitha Milner, whose father had been president of Texas A&M. After he retired, the family had moved back to Harrison and Tabitha had helped organize some discussion clubs for women. And when the War started, she'd gone all over the county selling war bonds. That's where Molly had heard her speak—eloquently, she said.

Maybe Molly could join one of those clubs, get to know her better. They'd confide in each other. Molly might even kiss her and—Hell, no!

Molly would never become Marguerite while she was married to Mr. James. And she'd *stay* married as long as Patrick tied them together. If she didn't teach her to drive, Molly couldn't meet anyone in town, she wouldn't secretly kiss anybody else…But did she have the right to hold Molly back?

She shook her head, trying to blow her worries away. She had to help Molly become independent. Damn the consequences.

"Let's go, Molly. First, you need to learn how to start this Model T. But be careful. A crank hit one man in the jaw and he died from complications. Stand close to me. I'll go through the motions without actually starting the engine."

Molly stood so near she brushed her leg as she completed her circling motion. *Ohh.* Her skin was supple through her soft green cotton dress. And when she showed her again, Molly didn't back away.

She ached to cup Molly's leg—instead of the crank handle—in her palm. She wanted to encourage the spark between them, not regulate it with the nearby choke. But she caught herself in time.

Whew. She said the first thing that entered her mind, hoping to cool the air. "Maybe soon we won't have to crank by hand. But for now that's the only way to make this horseless carriage run." She backed away and motioned for Molly to try.

Molly'd paid close attention to her instructions and, after a few attempts, could start the vehicle. Molly looked at her and wiped a gleam of sweat from above her upper lip. "Gracious, that was harder than I thought, but it didn't take as long as hitching Kate and Gus. Now what do we do?"

"Okay, backing up is a challenge. Let me get us out of the driveway and find a straight stretch where you can practice steering and shifting."

They sped along the center of the hard-packed main road, or what most people in the area called the pike. Leaving the farm with Molly at her side—what a treat. They smiled at each other and breathed in the fresh air whipping around them. It was dusty, too, but she didn't care. The sun shone like it was smiling at them, but it didn't scorch her like it usually did. Right now, she was immune to anything unpleasant. If only they could keep going and never turn back.

On the longest, straightest stretch of smooth road in the county, she stopped but kept the engine running. "We don't want to crank this contrary thing again unless we have to, so I'll scoot over as far as I can. Edge toward me and put your right foot next to mine on this pedal. Keep it pushed down, because it's the brake. We don't want the car to run away with you while I walk around to the other side."

Molly's hip pressed against hers, and her own motor began to rev up—so high she had to force herself to check that Molly had her foot firmly on the pedal before she raced to the passenger's side. She made it successfully, slightly out of breath—and not from her sprint.

Trying to calm her heart, which was clattering more than the engine, she kept talking. "Now, take your foot off the brake and press the pedal on the left at the same time. Slowly. That'll shift the car into low gear."

Molly did exactly what Jaq said.

"At the same time you'll need to give it a little gas with that lever on the steering wheel. Nice and smooth."

Molly clearly tried her best, but the auto jumped then sputtered. "Mercy. That's what happened when Mr. James and Clyde tried to teach me. They laughed at me, and I got so discouraged I quit." She looked like she was about to cry.

"Well, you won't get by with that now. You can learn to drive. All it takes is time and practice. You didn't play the piano well the first time you tried, did you?"

She shook her head. "No, come to think of it." Pushing her shoulders back like a soldier adjusting to a heavy pack, Molly opened the door and hopped out. "Okay, Jaq, let's crank it again."

❖

Molly—who had tried to conquer her husband's Overland and failed—could drive.

Jaq had explained how to use the three pedals and the levers so clearly that when they sped down the pike, she didn't even have to press the pedals. Compared to playing the organ, driving was simple.

However, rocketing along, she had to force herself not to stare at Jaq. She kept her eyes straight ahead and anticipated sudden stops. They seldom met another vehicle, but when they did, she moved from the center to the right side of the pike so they could pass. And when the road really narrowed, which it did in spots, she pulled halfway off while the other automobile eased by.

Jaq patiently smiled, so she used all her self-discipline to drive them safely home. She would much rather have stopped and hugged Jaq. She parked beside the wagon at the McCades' house and opened her door with a flourish. Perhaps now Jaq would find her more interesting, though she couldn't possibly compare to her fine British and Eastern friends.

"How about a glass of cider to celebrate your success? I made some the other day, and it's tolerable."

"That sounds wonderful. I'm thirsty. I'll wait here in the swing. I hate to miss any of this beautiful day. And I expect you to keep your promise about showing me your men's clothes."

She moved the swing languidly in the September heat. But the pines stood still, as if the very atmosphere held its breath and waited for something. When Jaq walked back out, dressed as a man, she stared, amazed at the transformation. Jaq was as handsome as she was beautiful, and Molly loved her either way.

CHAPTER TWENTY-NINE

How have you been, Molly?"
Jaq handed Molly a glass of cider and sat in a rocking chair, which she immediately set to moving to distract herself. She longed to sit next to Molly on the swing but didn't trust herself, especially wearing these clothes. They reminded her of visiting Willie.

She decided to forge ahead. "I mean how have you really been? Why haven't you called?"

Molly took a long drink and pushed the swing into a faster rhythm. "Umm, how tasty. You're turning into a good farm wife, even if you look more like a farmer." She paused. "I'm only kidding."

"Of course." She rotated her head from side to side, then forward, and popped her neck. All her muscles were cramping because she was so close to Molly but had to keep her hands away. Abruptly, she said, "I don't belong here, but you don't either."

Molly looked a little startled and changed the subject. "I've been thinking about our conversation at the picnic…and our kiss. It confused me at first, and I didn't know whether to be afraid, ashamed, or embarrassed. Then I realized that no matter what people label us—inverts, or perverts, or whatever—we're still Molly Riley and Jaq Bergeron, two people who care for each other. And it doesn't matter whether we look like men or women."

When Molly said "care," Jaq quivered with affection. Molly had taken care of her when she was hurt, and she wanted to take care of Molly in so many ways. But she also wanted to understand exactly what she meant. When Molly said "care for each other," did she mean love or did she mean friendship? She wanted to ask Molly what their kiss had meant to her, but she was afraid of the answer. Instead, she kept her distance by asking, "Why didn't you use our husbands' names? We're still married, I'm sorry to say."

Molly shook her head and her red curls bounced. "Not in my eyes. I should have said we're just Molly and Jaq, and our fathers' names simply point out where we came from." Her eyes danced. "Don't you see? The names Russell and McCade may show our current situation and tell the world the names of the two men we're attached to—who supposedly protect us from it—but they don't indicate where we're going."

Did Molly actually think they had a chance together? Oh, why couldn't she just ask that simple question? Was Molly as nervous about this situation as she was?

Molly's eyes gleamed with mischief, though, as she said in a playful tone, "I've been talking a lot to my wise friends on the farm."

What was Molly up to? Jaq knew good and well that Molly didn't have anyone to talk to. But if she wanted to beat around the bush, Jaq would play along. "Why, I didn't know you had many friends around here." She forced herself to adopt a light tone similar to Molly's.

Molly sighed with what seemed like relief. "Most people wouldn't understand me when I talk about my friends, but you might. One is very independent, and when she gets tired of listening, she simply disappears. But if the weather's fine, she'll sit in the sun and pay attention to me for as long as I can spare. Just yesterday I told her all about you. How you agreed to teach me to drive and how brave you are—going over to Europe during wartime. She lay there on her log and sunned herself as I jabbered on. Then, with a splash, she vanished."

"Oh," Jaq said. Molly was definitely teasing her. "Who listened to you next?"

She stretched one arm over her head and grinned in an unladylike way. "Well, my second friend never disappears like my first one. She simply stands still and listens while I talk about you. And as I rave about your beauty, she gives me a valuable, life-sustaining gift. We visit twice a day, and the better I treat her, the better she treats me. She's warm and comforting. And though she's been known to kick when she gets angry, she's always gentle with me. I can talk my heart out, and she just looks at me with her big brown eyes and lets me ramble on."

She laughed at Molly's antics.

"Let me tell you about my third friend. In fact, you've already met her and her sisters, who visit only when it's warm. But when they do, they brighten up the place. She and her kind are beautiful, though she does have her sharp side if I don't handle her carefully. I can wander around her abode forever, chatting as much as I want, and she merely perfumes the air and lets me be. Actually, she's the one who let me glimpse how glorious my life could be if I allowed my feelings to flow naturally. She's rooted yet always aspires for beauty. She gives pleasure to anyone who takes time to notice her, yet she can protect herself. And she's not afraid to be herself completely."

Jaq drank her cider, set her glass on a low table beside her chair, and made it rock again. "So, have you finished your tall tales, or do you plan to treat me to another one?"

Molly smiled and glanced up at the pines that grew near the house. "I forgot to mention my oldest and dearest friends, who live all over East Texas. If I ever leave here, I'll miss them the most. They're so straight and tall, and they bend with whatever wind blows them." She wiggled like a child. "Now it's time for you to guess who I've been talking about, Miss Jacqueline."

After dramatically scratching her head and creasing her brow, she cleared her throat and recited in her best schoolgirl voice. "Miss Molly, the answer to your first riddle is a turtle. Am I right? Who else lies on a log and suns herself?"

Molly applauded. "One hundred percent, Miss Bergeron. And your second answer, if you please."

"Hmm, this one's easy. Big brown eyes, gifts twice a day, and kicks occasionally. I'd have to say that's your milk cow, though I've never gotten close enough to ours to be absolutely sure of my answer."

"Two out of two. That's wonderful, missy. Just two more to go." Molly laughed more freely than she'd ever heard her.

"Beautiful, rooted, can be sharp. I imagine that's the roses we visited the day we made rose water. And your tall, straight, flexible friends must be the pines that grow around here like weeds." She finished her answers with a formal bow, as if she'd just impressed the strictest nun at her school.

Molly beamed. "Congratulations. You're the best student in the class. And because you performed so outstandingly, you get a prize." She sprang up, stooped down, and lightly kissed her cheek.

She stopped rocking and drew Molly close. Her cheek flamed. "That's the best prize I've ever won. If all the nuns had rewarded me half so sweetly, I'd have been a much better student. But, seriously, you're not afraid of me because I'm an invert? That's not why you've been avoiding me?"

Molly stared, her green eyes reflecting the color of the surrounding forest and making it seem not nearly so ominous. "Oh, Jaq, I could never be afraid of you. You've brought the world to me and heaped it into my lap like a shower of rose petals. You've listened to me rant about Mother Russell and always taken my side. You've awakened parts of me that I'd forgotten about. And you didn't even laugh when I told you who I confide in."

Molly kept standing by her side, and the smell of rose water and Ivory soap distracted her so completely she almost missed Molly's next words.

"I truly don't believe we should let other people label us. We should just be ourselves, each with our unique mixture of strengths and weaknesses."

She had to grip the arms of her rocking chair to keep from jumping up and taking Molly in her arms. The longer she knew Molly, the more she discovered what a sensitive musician and loving person she was—trying to survive in a hostile environment like an orchid attempting to grow in the desert. But she sat still, forcing herself to listen in spite of the way her flesh itched for Molly's.

"For as long as I can remember, no one cared if we women had best friends. Everyone encouraged our smashes at school. And Mama's told me about some of her friends who turned their husbands out of their beds when a woman friend came to visit. They wanted to spend as much time together as they could, and bed was such a cozy place for intimate talks, she said."

Ah. Why hadn't Molly done that when she'd stayed with her all those days? That would have been so much better than recuperating alone. Molly's confidences and strong arms would have comforted her all night. Her thoughts were irrational, but she was in a strange mood. Molly looked down at her like an indulgent schoolmarm. She'd love to be that teacher's pet.

"Do you think those sex doctors would tell Mother Russell that she's a man trapped in a woman's body?" she said. "She can work as hard as one—split wood, plow fields, and draw well water. And she can certainly boss people around better than most men. Just because she's strong, is she an invert? She can survive in a man's world, but nobody would dare label her. If they even tried, she'd tell them to go to the devil."

She and Molly laughed together. She hadn't felt this happy since she was a child before the Great Storm.

"Strong women are simply that—strong—whether they wear a skirt or pants," Molly said. "They're merely being themselves, not trying to be like men. And if they happen to love other women, that's their right."

My God. She'd ached to touch Molly, but now she craved to understand where such thoughts came from. She wanted to explore her mind as well as her body, and to do that she needed to be with Molly every day. Molly wasn't a child. She was a woman. "When you put it that way, I can see your point," she said. Molly's statement bowled her over. She couldn't be any more astonished if her mules sang "Pack Up Your Troubles" in French. "So you don't think I need to find someone to cure me of my preference for women?"

Molly's eyes gleamed. "It would be a waste of good money, Jaq."

CHAPTER THIRTY

When Molly returned to the swing after standing beside Jaq's rocking chair, she missed their closeness. But if she let herself stay so near, she might do something she'd regret later. So she sat alone again and resumed swinging while Jaq went back inside to change clothes.

Back and forth. Back and forth. The gentle motion almost hypnotized her, and she recalled a line from a letter she'd written Mr. James several months before they married. She could still see her words flowing straight across the page in her small, neat script. Trying to tell him she couldn't keep his ring, she had considered each word carefully before she committed it to paper. *I can't understand why I yield to you, believe that I love you and say so, act so, then doubt my own heart, wonder at my actions when you are gone.*

He'd rushed to the parsonage in town where she lived with her parents. Polite, his hat in one hand and a bouquet of roses in the other, he'd insisted on an explanation. So she'd gently told him again, more straightforwardly. "Mr. James, when I'm around you, I truly believe I love you. But when I'm away from you, I realize I don't love you at all. I respect you and admire you, but that's not enough. Marrying wouldn't be fair to either of us."

At the time she couldn't understand why she resisted his proposal. He was a very eligible bachelor, with a large farm and house. Everyone in town seemed to respect him, but she felt strong enough about the situation to risk being an old maid. She would rather live with her parents and survive on her menial salary as a music teacher than keep his ring. Inside she had screamed, *Something's wrong. I shouldn't marry him.* And now she understood a little of why she'd been so adamant.

But every Saturday during the summer of 1910, he drove the buggy the long eight miles from his farm to the parsonage. Invariably he brought a gift—a lace handkerchief, a bar of perfumed soap, a bottle of toilet water. They sat in the front-porch swing side by side, and he talked about the latest Conan Doyle novel or the stories they enjoyed in *The Saturday Evening Post.*

Each Sunday he'd returned, always carrying his hat and roses. He accompanied her to church and watched her attentively while she played the piano. Then he ate dinner at the parsonage, to which he'd always contributed several dozen eggs, a big mess of turnip greens or green beans, a half bushel of tomatoes—whatever was in season. Her mama appreciated his offerings, and her papa seemed to enjoy Mr. James's news about several wealthy congregation members. Mr. James's social connections apparently impressed him.

During this courtship, alone during the week, she heard a weak inner voice insist, *No, you don't love him.* But eventually, she became accustomed to him, felt secure and safe, and decided she actually did love him. She didn't want to live the rest of her life regretting what might have been, like the country girl in one of the poems Mr. James loved to recite to her. He offered his ring again, and she accepted. After she married him, the small voice had grown silent. Until recently.

Since she'd begun to know Jaq, the voice had piped up again and grown downright chatty. The voice encouraged her to do outrageous things, like kiss Jaq back and register to vote. Its suggestions scandalized her at times, but she gradually welcomed its saucy attitude, though she feared it might lead her into trouble, make her disappoint her parents.

Although she'd lost the diamond, she still wore the ring. Every time she looked at it, she noticed its empty setting. The sharp edges pricked her fingers as she rubbed cream into her hands every night. Somehow the ring made her think about her marriage as often and as deeply as she did before she accepted it. She gradually, painfully concluded that she would never fulfill her dreams with Mr. James. Now she asked herself more and more often what might have been if she *hadn't* married him.

But did all her painful reasoning make her love him? No. Did it make her happy? No. At times she thought of simply taking off the ring and hiding it in a drawer. But her inner voice had gained strength and wouldn't give up as easily again. She had to wrestle with this situation, and the empty ring reminded her of it constantly. With Jaq, she didn't doubt her own heart, but could she trust Jaq? She'd been in love with the nurse called Helen just last year. She admitted that she had been involved with a woman in New Orleans. How many others had she failed to mention?

Now she understood what was missing in her life and what she craved. She wanted Jaq, for life, but she couldn't be unfaithful to Mr. James. She'd rather die than betray her vows.

What if Jaq eventually rejected her and found someone new? Or returned to the mysterious woman in New Orleans? Molly would have thrown away the safety and security Mr. James provided and risked everything for nothing. But, most important, she would have revealed her very being, her hopes and fears, to Jaq.

Was she strong enough to survive if Jaq didn't love her as much as she loved Jaq? Those possibilities frightened her more than the prospect of living on the farm with Mr. James and Mother Russell forever.

Lately she and Jaq had sat quietly, busy with some daily task, and listened to the wind blow the tops of the tall pines. At times, as they shelled peas or crated tomatoes or shucked corn, they listened to the colored people sing during their lunch break or while they worked in the cotton fields. The leader, with his deep bass voice, sang a line of an unfamiliar song, and the others repeated the surging melody. The male voices doubled the female voices an octave below them, and some individuals experimented with the melody, their obbligato adding to its richness. Their music sounded mournful yet strangely beautiful, the voices blending so exquisitely that she held her breath every time she heard their music.

Mother Russell thought it downright queer that Molly appreciated their singing and minced no words telling her so, and Molly knew this was yet another mark against her in her mother-in-law's opinion. But Jaq seemed to value the colored people's songs too and said that in New Orleans, especially walking through the French Quarter, she'd heard all kinds of music. The musicians seemed to compose it as they played or sang, instead of reading from a page of music like she did when she took voice lessons.

Molly pondered this new type of music as she relaxed, under the spell of the sounds that touched places inside herself she rarely visited. Jaq somehow gave her permission to enter such areas, as if they were internal rooms she never knew existed but was now tiptoeing through with a lit candle. She was discovering that, inside herself, she lived in a luxurious mansion instead of a plain frame farmhouse.

The music and her strange thoughts lulled her into a pleasant, relaxed state. At times like this she didn't try to entertain Jaq. Sometimes after they sat in silence, they looked at each other and laughed for no reason except the sheer joy of being together. She'd point out a mockingbird to Jaq, high in a pine, or two squirrels as they chased each other and jumped from limb to limb in one of the large oaks that shaded them. A butterfly floated by or a bee flitted from one rose to another. On a hot day, the katydids and crickets formed a choir and serenaded them with their soothing drone.

In the kitchen, as she churned cream into butter, Jaq might hum a tune, and then she would pick it up and they sang together. They sometimes continued for hours, choosing old favorites and teaching each other new ones. Some, sad and slow, almost made her cry, and the light, happy ones made Jaq's midnight-brown eyes glow. Jaq's alto and her soprano blended perfectly.

Sometimes she told Jaq a secret, one she'd never shared with anyone, and Jaq listened as if she were the only person in the world. But she didn't want to simply share her secrets; she wanted to learn Jaq's. The day they'd talked about the Galveston Storm marked the first of their confidences, and they gradually risked more of themselves. They discussed their families, schooling, and attitudes toward religion. She'd never known a Catholic and wanted to learn about Jaq's church.

And she wanted to know about the strong women Jaq had met during her years abroad. Even though she feared she'd never be able to meet them, at least she could know them vicariously. Their stories would warm her long after Jaq left New Hope.

When Jaq returned in her housedress instead of her male attire, Molly didn't know which outfit she preferred. Jaq had looked striking in her shirt and trousers. Daring and jaunty, she made Molly's heart sing like a tenor soloist hitting rich, full notes. But in her dress, Jaq brought out the high soprano of Molly's feelings, like birds trilling in the gauze of dawn.

The voices that blended inside her made her want to rush into Jaq's arms, but she couldn't lose control like that. She had a husband and a child. As the old saying went, she'd made her bed and now she had to lie in it. So, instead, she stretched her arms along the back of the swing, inviting the world into them the only way she could.

❖

Molly sat in the swing and looked sad, happy, uncertain, and afraid all in a few seconds. And throughout, the sun reflected off her red-gold hair. Sweet Jesus, she was beautiful.

Jaq wanted to sweep her up and carry her up the steep staircase to her bed. She'd tremble a little, a question in her eyes. But Molly would trust her—to kiss her gently at first, then more passionately...to slowly unbutton her soft white dress, slip it from her shoulders, and let it drop to the floor. Molly would let her kiss each arm. Neither the sun nor a woman's lips had ever touched them, she was sure. Then Molly would let her gradually slide her slip up until Jaq uncovered her virgin stomach and covered it with her lips. They'd be flaming, but Jaq would try not to burn her.

Molly would probably be startled when she picked her up again and laid her carefully on the narrow bed. And she'd surely say, "Jaq, I shouldn't." But Molly would let her do what she desired, because she desired the same things. She could seduce Molly. Her craving—she'd just seen it in Molly's eyes—would be Jaq's ally.

And Molly's white breasts...Dear God, how they made her heart pound.

After she praised Molly's breasts with her hands as well as her lips, she'd slide Molly's panties over her willing hips. Molly's hair would outshine the sun. There Jaq would stretch out as if they were lying in a hammock on a hot summer day and leisurely finger her. Molly would tremble so beautifully beneath her hands, for no one would ever have touched her as she would.

Molly would throw her head back and moan, "Jaq, we shouldn't," as she neared. But she wouldn't mean what she said. After a long, enjoyable wait, Molly would finally open herself wide and welcome her.

Then—

She shook herself. She had to grip the oak arms of her rocker until they almost splintered, but she controlled herself and began to tell Molly the stories about John she'd requested. If she didn't talk, she'd act like a fool.

CHAPTER THIRTY-ONE

Listening to Jaq allowed Molly to participate in a world she'd only read about. She didn't want to be near the fighting in Europe, but she'd always dreamed of seeing London, Paris, and Vienna. They seemed totally unattainable. Only the wealthy traveled to such locales, but Jaq's stories made the places real. They gave her the courage to try to be the independent woman she'd always longed to be and that Mama encouraged her to be.

Looking around at the McCades' farm, at the red earth that had been her reality for eight years now, she knew she would miss it if she left... But she was fantasizing again. She'd never get away from Mr. James. She was his child bride, married to this land, tied by vows and by blood, and Patrick was her precious link to this small community. She would never desert him. And how could she take him with her, with no money, no freedom? She was better off here.

Suddenly the pines—always so kind and sheltering—loomed, threatened to suffocate her.

As Jaq handed her a full glass of cider, two of her fingers grazed Molly's hand. A glissando of heat shot through her as Jaq said, "Now, where was I? You asked about John."

Jaq described John's appearance and personality, but Molly could barely concentrate because she was so busy memorizing the texture of Jaq's dark hair and the contours of her sculptured face. What if they were only fantasies? She could still dream. If only she could run her hands over Jaq's face she'd absorb every inch of every detail—the straight nose, the arched eyebrows, the scar above it. She barely kept herself from doing just that.

Jaq sipped her drink and looked pensive as she described how John's mother had never treated her well. Strangely, Jaq had mentioned her own mother only once, to say that she loved roses. Had Jaq's mother treated her well? If not, did Jaq have an invisible scar inside her because of that? Molly ached to even consider the possibility. If her mama didn't love her, she didn't know what she'd do. She almost reached over to the rocker and wrapped her arms around Jaq, but what would Jaq think? And more important, what would she do? Would Jaq kiss her again like she had at the picnic? And would she let her? The very idea made her dizzy.

She forced herself to focus on Jaq's description of the year John and her cousin Jane spent taking a road trip through the American South in a one-pistoned Tin Lizzie. John had dressed like a man, smoked cigarettes and cigars, and told everyone to call her Radclyffe.

Molly quivered with excitement. She felt as if she'd just visited another planet, where women counted for something and did exactly as they pleased, like men. How wonderful that such women existed, and even more wonderful that a woman very like them had kissed her.

Sweat trickled down Jaq's sides under the loose housedress she'd thrown on after she'd changed from her men's clothes. But not only the heat was making her perspire. She had just told Molly how John's first lover, Ladye, had made it known that, after she died, she wanted John to live with the woman with whom she was having an affair.

Jaq couldn't imagine letting Molly go like that, even if she was dying. But she had to. She and Eric would surely return to New Orleans soon, where she would become a free woman. She couldn't come back here, and Molly couldn't leave. So what did such freedom mean, if she and Molly weren't together?

She'd done exactly what she'd feared and tried so hard to avoid. She'd become so entangled with Molly she'd have to cut herself away from her like she was slashing through the jungle with a machete.

Damn it. She had to face the facts. She had absolutely no claim on Molly. She had to follow Ladye's example, and hopefully she'd be strong enough. She'd have to deny her feelings and leave Molly here, no matter how much the sacrifice hurt.

❖

Molly wondered how Ladye had felt when she'd realized John was involved with another woman. Jealous, angry, afraid, accepting? Probably all of these, but her love for John tempered her emotions, and she had released John gracefully. Could she follow Ladye's example? Did she have any choice?

She stopped shelling peas and tried to be as honest as she could. She *would* leave New Hope when Patrick married. But she couldn't ask Jaq to put her life on hold and wait that long for her. She wasn't even sure if Jaq would want her to leave the farm with her right now. After all, she was seven years older than Jaq, with a child to take care of. No, she had to let Jaq go. That was the only way.

She picked up a pea pod and started shelling again. For Patrick, she could stay in New Hope. For Patrick, she could live with Mr. James, who was a good man, even though she didn't love him. For Patrick, she could even live with Mother Russell, though she ached when she considered her future.

❖

Jaq hoped Molly realized she was a lot like the strong women whose stories she seemed to love hearing about. And Molly was as interesting and even more appealing because she didn't have a clue how special she was. Loving Molly had helped her forget the past. After she left New Hope, she wouldn't be fit to live with for a long time, but she'd never forget Molly or regret what they'd had together.

Molly, standing with her hand on Jaq's shoulder, shook her from her memories and said, "I better go."

She sighed, grateful for her touch. How many more would she be able to enjoy before she left here, left Molly? She didn't like to think about it.

"Mother Russell will expect me, and I need to go see about Patrick. I miss him when we're apart too long. Thank you for teaching me to drive and for the stories. They've given me a lot to think about." Molly climbed into the wagon and pointed Kate and Gus toward the Russell farm.

Jaq stood in the road and watched until the wagon disappeared from sight, and then she trudged back toward the empty house. Could she and Molly possibly have a future together, or would she be another Helen and ultimately reject her? Molly had come back after their kiss. What did that mean? Helen had been straightforward and said she wasn't attracted to women, and that was that. But Molly hadn't made such a clear-cut statement. She seemed to accept that two women could love each other.

If Molly let her guard down, would Jaq lose control and become another Sister Mary? God forbid. But Jaq hadn't been able to stand her ground against her feelings for Molly so far. She'd better talk to Eric about leaving East Texas sooner rather than later. She couldn't bear to do something as foolish—and marvelous—as make love to Molly. That would only hurt them both.

CHAPTER THIRTY-TWO

Jaq sat holding the pink telegram Eric had just crumpled and thrown to the floor. His father sat in the kitchen, his head in his hands. Eric had stormed out, and she hoped he didn't get drunk. Smoothing the wrinkled paper, she wished she could do something to help relieve Eric's and Angus's suffering. She hated to feel so helpless.

She fixed a plate of food and placed it in front of Angus, though she knew he wouldn't eat. That was all she could do, so she returned to the front porch and sat in the swing. The weather had cooled a bit, and the usually blue sky was overcast. A slow rain fell and compounded the grim mood that had settled on the McCade house.

She stared into space for a long while, contemplating the lives this war had wasted. Sighing, she opened her latest letter from her Aunt Anna, in New York City. Maybe it would help distract her from the news they'd just received.

September 19, 1918

Dear Jaq,

Sorry I haven't written in so long. I trust you're enjoying your stay in the country. It seems like the ideal place to regain your health—if you don't go too stir-crazy. I've been working all day and writing every night, as usual.

I took an unexpected trip yesterday that I thought might interest you, especially in light of your bouts with influenza that you described to me last fall during your brief visit.

William and I left before sunrise, and I drove us out to Camp Upton on Long Island—seventy miles one way. We reached the army camp about noon. It's in the pine barrens of central Long Island, a huge, raw-looking, isolated place thrown up last summer, swarming with mosquitoes.

In a gigantic room there, of the eight rows of cots, with about twenty in each row, only one bed was empty. All the young men there wore long white gowns, and some breathed through white gauze masks. I soon learned this was one of several convalescence wards.

Two doctors hurriedly took us to the area where the actively ill men lay. Some cried out in pain, and some were strangely blue in the face. After the doctors described the patients' symptoms, we swabbed the throats and nasal passages of several men and preserved each sample in a glass tube to take back to the lab with us.

Then our hosts led us next door to the morgue, where they were autopsying a handsome young Texan. He'd recently died of influenza, and aside from his skin's blue pigmentation, his strong body looked untouched, possibly because he'd died quickly. Everyone wanted to know what caused his death.

The doctor conducting the autopsy cut into the soldier's chest with a scalpel and shears, removed the chest plate, and revealed dark red lungs. When detached, both the lungs remained expanded and didn't collapse as normal ones should. As the doctor sliced one open, a mass of fluid gushed out. Of course I took a sample.

But here's the strange thing, Jaq. A battle seemed to have raged inside the soldier's lungs, and the invader won. The young Texan's defenders were dead and had clogged his lungs. Just before he died, he must have been short of breath, then felt as if he was suffocating or drowning. I couldn't help but wonder if the internal struggle actually killed him. If his defense system hadn't put up such a fierce struggle, he might still be alive

I asked one of the doctors if this was the worst case he'd seen, and he said this was typical. So, my dear Jaq, I thought you should know about this in light of our conversations about your illness and the War. The one in Europe isn't nearly as terrible as the one that took place in this poor boy's lungs. At least the Allied forces can see the Germans approach. I don't want to alarm you, but no one has a chance against an invisible enemy as predatory as this new form of influenza.

You can take heart because your cases in Europe last summer and fall probably immunized you to this mutated form. But stay isolated in

the country, and don't let any of your loved ones near a crowd until we
can find a cure for this horrible disease or it disappears on its own.
Your loving aunt,
Anna
P.S. I've been so busy I forgot to mail this for several days. Sorry.

As soon as Molly heard the news, she telephoned Jaq, who sounded very down in the dumps.

"I guess you've heard Eric's brothers died in the Argonne Forest," she said. "Eric's driving to town to register for the draft tomorrow, then on to Dallas to go with his cousin, who's finally old enough to enlist. Eric can't stay away any longer. His leg has completely healed, he's regained his sight in his bad eye, and he says he's licked his drinking problem. He's sure the US will accept his services."

"He has to be devastated about his brothers and sick of sitting on the sidelines," Molly said. "I'd almost rather see him go back to war than to the bottle."

"I agree. I begged him not to, though. My aunt wrote me about a horrible new type of the flu that's beginning to hit the big cities hard. And this means I won't get to leave here as soon as I hoped. I'll have to stay and help Angus until Eric returns from wherever they send him. Oh, I'm ashamed to be so selfish." Jaq sounded like she might cry.

Though inwardly Molly rejoiced, she forced herself to say, "I'm sorry you can't go as soon as you want. Everyone's saying the tide of the War has turned in our favor. And maybe they'll station Eric nearby."

"Yes, but if I know Eric, he'll insist that his aviation skills will help win the War quicker. He'll want to help train new pilots, and with his record, they'll station him wherever he wants. Even if the War ends soon, he'll probably be involved in the aftermath. I'm afraid I'm stuck here until the men begin to come home and the labor shortage eases. Eric and I won't have a chance to annul our marriage until who knows when."

"Jaq, I'm so sorry. Listen, Patrick will be thrilled when he finds out Eric's enlisting. He wants to talk to him about flying. Why don't I bring him over when Eric gets home from Dallas? Maybe Patrick can help us soften him up so we can talk him into getting home as soon as possible."

"It's worth a try, though it probably won't work. He's so stubborn. But maybe we can talk him into requesting an assignment here in the States instead of abroad."

Until then Molly had never realized how desperately Jaq wanted to get on with her own life. But now she was determined to help her leave New Hope, no matter how much she wanted her to stay. She would encourage Patrick to treat Eric like a war hero for signing up, but the prospect of living here without Jaq tore her apart inside.

She had been entranced with Jaq since she first saw her at church wearing her bright-yellow dress. A canary among crows, she had thought then, and now she knew how true her vision had been. Jaq had enlivened her, put her in touch with the larger world, made her feel again.

But Jaq could fly away at any time, and Molly would never see her again. The prospect made her tightening throat ache and her arms feel shaky. She would be even more alone than before, now that she knew what life could be like with Jaq. She'd be left without anyone that she totally fit with or belonged to. Only her piano, her music pupils, and Patrick would ease the pain. He was worth it, she kept reminding herself.

Jaq got up earlier than usual to fix breakfast. Angus wanted to try once more to convince Eric not to register.

They were sitting at the table eating biscuits and gravy when Angus said, "Son, you've been in this war since the beginning. Don't you think you've done enough?"

But Eric was mulish. "I know what I'm doing, Pop."

She tried to warn him. "My Aunt Anna said a bad strain of influenza is killing people, especially in the big cities. Everyone should stay away until it dies down."

They all argued until she almost screamed. She was more than ready to see Eric go when her Model T chugged out of the driveway at six o'clock.

Molly and Patrick planned to arrive about four o'clock the day Eric was due back, so she and Molly could spend some time together first. That would be the highlight of her week, because she planned to clean house the rest of the time. She'd even decided to fry a chicken and fix mashed potatoes and gravy for their welcome-home supper.

She worked steadily for a couple of days changing the beds, sweeping and scrubbing floors, washing the windows, and dusting. All that time, she couldn't keep her mind off Molly. What would they be doing if she were here?

On an ordinary day they'd sleep late then stroll to the barn, arms around each other's waists, Molly's head on her shoulder, watching the birds and the squirrels. Molly would have to milk their cow because that's one thing Jaq simply couldn't master. She hoped she could manage the few days Eric was gone. And from the way Molly talked about Nellie, she enjoyed their daily communion. Jaq could feed the chickens and gather the eggs. That seemed easy enough. But as long as she was dreaming, she wished she'd come into a fortune. Then she and Molly could do exactly as they pleased.

So, since they had money, they'd sleep late because they'd stayed up late the night before kissing and...When they finally dragged themselves from their big double bed with its thick feather mattress, they'd smell bacon frying. They'd kiss—long, deep kisses—then slowly dress. Neither would have worn a stitch to sleep in. They wouldn't want anything to come between them. She'd run a comb quickly through her short hair but take her time brushing the tangles from Molly's luxurious mane—so long she could sit on it—and kiss her neck between each stroke. Molly would be wearing only her chemise, so Jaq would pause to run her fingers over the buttermilk skin of Molly's shoulders and arms, unable to resist her taut, cushiony body.

By the time they dressed and drifted downstairs, their hired woman would have fixed breakfast, with fresh eggs and hot bread. They'd smear butter and strawberry jam on generous slices and feed them to one another, laughing between bites. Jaq would have churned the cream for the butter while she listened to Molly play the piano, and they would have made the jam from tart, sweet strawberries they'd grown and picked together.

They'd work in the flower beds and tend their vegetable garden, where they grew lettuce and spinach. Their hired man did all the heavy work, and they'd all live together happily ever after on the farm, while Patrick (she'd almost forgotten him) grew into a fine young man, met the girl of his dreams, and set up housekeeping just down the road.

The house seemed to glow with her fantasy as she scrubbed and cleaned, preparing for Molly's visit. But it would never be real. She quickened her pace, barely managing to keep herself from giving up hope and just leaving.

Now what did Molly have up her sleeve? Mrs. Russell watched her help Patrick shed his play clothes and put on his Sunday best. She'd been dolling up and said Jacqueline had invited her and Patrick to supper. Something about Eric enlisting.

Losing both his brothers was a crying shame. But Eric's stunt left Angus McCade holding the bag. He didn't have nary a soul to help him harvest the fall crops now.

Hope he didn't expect Jacqueline to give him much of a hand. She wasn't good for anything except mechanicking and fixing a few light meals and keeping house. Speaking of the house, she'd heard tell Jacqueline could sure keep it a heap cleaner. Flat-out refused to milk, Ethel said, though she'd churn when she had to.

Well, if she wanted any butter to spread on her bread, she'd have to climb down off her high horse and make her arm start moving.

Thankfully Patrick was only seven, Molly thought. What if he were eighteen and wanted to sign up for the service too and drive to Dallas? How could she let her baby, the only one she'd ever have, go? The idea of him leaving her to risk his life for his country horrified her.

She'd known Mrs. McCade only from an occasional visit. Always so proud of Eric, but she'd doted on all her sons. The younger two had helped steadily around the farm and would have married soon and settled nearby, raised good crops and sons of their own. The salt of the earth, they lay in foreign soil now, their mother in her grave too.

Molly's older sister had died also, when she was just a few years younger than Eric's brothers were. She'd caught diphtheria when Molly was a child. Extremely religious, almost a saint, her sister saw the best in everyone and forgave them almost before they did anything to hurt her. The illness came on quickly, from some of the other students at school, they thought. She was hot to the touch for almost a week and grew weaker as she lingered, until she finally passed away. At least she'd died at home, with her family, instead of in some faraway country, alone and probably terrified.

Molly's parents hadn't let her near her sister during her illness. But when she lay on her deathbed, they let Molly say good-bye. Her sister had suddenly looked around the room and said in a beautiful voice, "Don't you see them, Papa? Don't you see them? The angels standing around my bed? They've come to take me home."

Everyone was crying, which upset her, but she couldn't decide if her sister was hallucinating because of her condition or if she actually saw angels. The peaceful death, and the fact that her parents had protected her so thoroughly from the ugly parts of the disease, hadn't prepared her to know how she would react now if someone she loved died. She hoped she wouldn't have to find out for a long time.

❖

I declare, the world's gone crazy. Mrs. Russell ruminated as she hoed the dry soil around her rosebushes. If the Frogs and the Krauts wanted to kill each other off, let 'em at it. Just warring over a little strip of land not much bigger than this county. Bunch of foolishness, sending the boys away when the old folks needed them on the farm.

Praise the Lord, James was too old to join up or he'd be riding alongside Eric, who didn't have any business leaving home again. At least James had a speck of sense. Knew he had a young son, an old mother, and a worthless wife to support, so he couldn't gallivant off to war in a T-Model with the rest of the boys, who didn't think about anything but glory and shiny medals.

They didn't remember the big fight against the Yankees—a righteous one. Some nerve those Northerners had, thinking they could dictate how everybody should live from way up there in Washington. That monkey-faced President had no more idea about Georgia folks than he could fly. And it took him four long years of making all loyal Southerners suffer like they were savages before the soldier boys finally had enough. Eventually some of 'em realized fighting's nothing but terrible destruction and heartache for all involved, 'specially the women and children.

Yep, she was powerful glad Patrick was too young and James was too old for this gol-danged silly war. Sure hoped Clyde made it back in one piece.

Chapter Thirty-three

Jaq was exhausted, especially after the ordeal with the chicken. Eric never seemed to have any trouble wringing a chicken's neck, so she hadn't thought she would either.

She'd spent a good twenty minutes chasing the best-looking fryer in the yard before she finally cornered him and grabbed him with both hands, one over each wing. Then she eased him under her left arm and held him against her side so she could grab his neck with her right hand. She was afraid he'd peck her or she'd feel so sorry for him she'd let him go and open a quart of canned peas instead.

But, by God, she'd thought about how good he'd taste and how impressed Eric and Angus, and especially Molly, would be that she'd prepared him. So she grabbed his neck, closed her eyes, and started swinging him like she was cranking her Model T. When he whirled as fast as she could manage, she popped her wrist and snap—the chicken's headless body flew across the yard and tried to run back and join the other fryers.

Chilled, she stared at it. Blood covered the front of her dress, and as she wiped at it she thought of Henry after he slipped into her tent. His blood had drenched the ground...

She rubbed her scar as a wave of compassion for him hit her. The horror of her actions gripped her. How easily things died. Men too.

❖

Molly knocked on the front door and Jaq called, "Come on back. I'm busy cooking. But I'll be through soon."

In the kitchen, at first she saw only Jaq's back as she stood at the stove busily dropping pieces of chicken into the skillet and jumping back when the hot grease threatened to spatter her. But when Jaq finally turned around, she burst out laughing. The fancy lady from New Orleans, used to having servants wait on her, stood there with bloodstains on the front of her housedress and chicken feathers in her hair.

"From the looks of it, the chicken lost the fight, but just barely," she said to Patrick, who looked from her to Jaq with a puzzled expression.

"Mama, she's pretty even when she's all messed up, isn't she?"

Jaq beamed. "Thank you, Patrick. And for that you get a teacake and a glass of milk. And your mother gets nothing." Jaq playacted a frown, and she laughed again.

"Sit down at the table, Molly, and help yourself to the teacakes. I was kidding. You're certainly getting to be a big boy, Patrick. Did you help your mother drive the buggy?"

He was already halfway through his cookie. "Yes, ma'am. But I want to learn to drive a Model T. Will you teach me?"

Jaq forked a piece of chicken and turned it over. "You bet I will. As soon as you can reach the pedals."

As Patrick chattered, Molly let her mind drift. What if Jaq never moved away but stayed in New Hope so she could watch Patrick grow up and actually teach him to drive? Molly would be able to talk to her on the phone every day, see her at the church, and visit when she could escape from Mother Russell's constant demands. She and Jaq could drive to town occasionally to shop and have an ice-cream soda at the drugstore, and maybe they could even join one of those new women's clubs in town that Tabitha Milner had told her about, where they discussed great works of literature. Wouldn't that be exciting?

But she couldn't possibly expect Jaq to live in New Hope, so she pointed her dream in another direction. "If you could live anywhere in the world, where would it be?"

Jaq stood by the stove and turned the pieces over, to make sure they browned evenly and didn't burn, then finally glanced at her. "That's a hard question. London's okay, but it's too cold and damp and gray. I spent half my time inside, waiting to see the sun. And New Orleans is too hot and humid. Washington and New York are exciting, but I'd have to choose Paris." She put a lid on the skillet. "What about you?"

She slowly bit her teacake. "I've always wanted to visit Vienna, because so many famous musicians lived there. But I don't suppose I'd run across Mozart or Beethoven on the street now. And I'd like to see Athens. I enjoyed reading the ancient Greek tragedies when I was at the university, and I'd love to see the Parthenon. As for living somewhere else, I've never been anywhere except Texas so that's hard to say. Why did you settle on Paris?"

She wanted to learn everything she could about Jaq before she disappeared.

❖

Patrick was squirming in his hard-backed chair, so Jaq asked him, "Would you like to go upstairs and look at Mr. Eric's treasures from some of his travels, Patrick? They're in the room at the end of the hall on the right. Just be sure to put everything back, all right?"

He jumped up. "Yes, ma'am. It's okay, isn't it, Mama?"

"Yes, son. We'll be right down here if you want us." As he left, Molly smiled and said, "You're good with him."

"As the youngest child, I didn't have anybody to look after. But my older brothers and sister treated me well, so I guess I want to return the favor. He's a sweet boy. You've done a great job."

"Not if you ask Mother Russell." Molly frowned, and Jaq didn't blame her. Her demanding mother-in-law could upset anybody. "Thank you. I don't know how I'd get along without him. But what about Paris? Have you been there too?"

"Yes. The War's made it dirty and hectic, but I like the openness, the acceptance of all types of people, even the ones like me."

Jaq's arms prickled with embarrassment and excitement as she said the words. She didn't want to remind Molly that she was different, that she loved women. But she had to be herself and try not to think she was strange or even sick. Molly had helped, and she was determined to go the rest of the way on her own.

"Did you visit Paris while you were in France with the WAACs?"

"Yes, briefly. Right before I went back to London and sailed home. I adored it, even though it was in shambles. The people's open-mindedness, their appreciation for a good meal and a fine glass of wine coupled with their spirit of freedom and intellectual inquiry, made me want to stay much longer. I'd heard of a couple of American women who've lived in Paris for ages and wanted to meet them, but unfortunately they were temporarily in another part of France."

She sighed, thinking of the excitement that seemed to radiate from the city she'd fallen in love with. If she and Molly could be in Paris together her life would be complete. "I felt so at home there. I speak the language well, and the Parisians made me feel at ease. I promised myself that I'd live there someday. And maybe I will, after the War ends. I understand that other women like me have formed a little community there, so I might even meet someone as understanding and accepting as you over there."

As soon as the words left her mouth, though, she knew she'd never feel as deeply for another woman as she did for Molly. Molly had eased past every barrier Jaq had set up. So natural and unassuming, Molly had calmed her fears and helped her realize that she could be herself.

She wanted to do the same for Molly, to hold her close, to treasure her sensitivity and help her leave this place where people didn't appreciate how special she was. But Molly was as stuck here as an automobile with four flat tires, and Jaq didn't know how to help her drive away.

❖

The possibility of Jaq meeting someone else to confide in and laugh with made Molly almost sick to her stomach, but she couldn't encourage Jaq to stay in a loveless marriage just because she wanted her nearby. With her looks and charm, Jaq could easily find someone else, and she should thank her lucky stars for Mr. James. At least he didn't abuse her.

She had to resign herself to the reality that though Jaq could move to Paris, she would never leave East Texas. She had roots in this community as deep as the long taproot on a pine. She couldn't leave Patrick, and Mr. James would certainly never let him wander around the world like a vagabond. No, she had to stay here, and she had to let beautiful Jaq sail away to Europe and meet someone else.

Right now, though, they needed to create another memory. She wanted to squeeze a year into each minute they had left to be together, so that an hour would stretch to a span of sixty years of living together and loving each other. "Do you need any help with supper? I can make some biscuits."

"Yes, thank you. Be sure to cover your pretty dress with that big blue apron."

She wrapped the large apron over her next-to-best dress and scooped some flour into a large bowl. Wouldn't she and Jaq have fun if they could stand beside each other in the kitchen every day, just peeling potatoes or making biscuits. An occasional glance, frequent laughs, and sitting down together to share what they created were what counted. But she had to stop thinking about the future and concentrate on the present.

The present. Molly anatomized Jaq's every move. Jaq finished peeling the potatoes and rinsed them then put them into a boiler and ladled well water over them. She placed them on the stove and stood there with a lid, so as soon as the water started to boil, she could cover the pan and move it to a cooler area.

Fine black hair covered Jaq's lightly muscled forearm, though her skin was very white. Her strong arms and capable hands could fix an automobile, pluck a chicken, run down Molly's—

Oh stop. She didn't want to preserve that thought. She'd blush every time she'd recall it. She'd want Jaq so much she'd refuse to let her go, and she had to.

She must.

❖

After Jaq hurriedly changed clothes and stood stirring the cream gravy, Patrick rushed into the kitchen. "They're here. I just heard them drive up. I put everything back exactly like it was, Miss Jacqueline. I'm going to see Mr. Eric, Mama."

The door slammed, and Jaq frowned as she turned to Molly. "I wish I could be that excited to see Eric. Patrick's a real joy. You'll have to bring him with you more often."

Molly nodded as Eric strutted in, his arm draped across Patrick's shoulders. "Pop's worn out and said he's going straight to bed, but look what came busting out the door and jumped all over me. I wouldn't mind having a big, fine boy like this to meet me every day. What do you say, Mrs. McCade," he said with a saucy grin, "think we could manage to find one like him somewhere?"

Eric had to be teasing, so she grinned back and picked up her Brownie from the sideboard. "You two come outside with me and let me take your picture before it gets too dark." After they finished she told Eric, "I doubt if we could find another one. Boys like him don't grow on trees."

Eric ignored her and reached into his pants pocket. "Let's see what we have here. What do you think, boy? Would you like this shiny nickel?"

Patrick hung back and looked up at Molly. "Is it all right, Mama? That's a lot of money."

She hugged Patrick. "It's okay, son. You can show it to your pa when we get home. Tell Mr. Eric thank you."

Jaq couldn't resist, so she made Patrick pose again, with his nickel and his big grin.

Eric was in a better mood than she'd ever seen him, definitely better than since they'd been in New Hope, so she tried to enjoy his high spirits. Maybe it was best for him to join the service. She hoped his good mood hadn't come from a bottle, but he didn't smell like it had.

During supper Eric sat next to Patrick and described his adventures at the recruitment stations, directing most of his comments to him. "We went to this big schoolhouse in Dallas, and my cousin had to get undressed and stand in line forever. And after the doc said he was in good shape, he had to dress and line up again and hold his hand up in the air and swear he'd be a good soldier. I waited out front most of the time, with more guys standing around than you could shake a stick at. Some of them in Dallas were coughing, and in Harrison too, when I had my physical, but the doc said I'm as fit as a fiddle now, and…"

Jaq recalled her Aunt Anna's warning about the influenza when Eric mentioned the crowds and the men coughing, but the trip did seem to have done him a world of good. Maybe her aunt was overreacting.

Patrick seemed totally taken in, and even Molly appeared to enjoy Eric's company. But when she and Patrick left soon after supper, Jaq was so sorry to see them go. She and the McCades had heard far too little laughter in this house. Only when Molly visited did the place fill with music and merriment. But she couldn't come often or stay nearly long enough to satisfy Jaq's craving for her presence.

The house seemed to shrivel. The wind died, and the pines surrounded her like a heavy curtain that smothered her and provoked memories that refused to leave her in peace.

❖

A cool breeze caressed Molly's arms as she held the reins and half listened to Patrick chatter and the mules clomp back toward the farm. She shivered. If—no, *when* Jaq left New Hope, she wouldn't return.

Molly had fallen for her so gradually she only now realized how desolated she'd be when Jaq no longer lived here. The sweet sounds of violins and the beauty of the melody had lulled her so completely that before she knew it she had been pulled into the symphony of feeling that Jaq had created in her. Now it was nearing its climax, blaring French horns and trumpets announcing Jaq's necessary departure. Everything would be over all too soon except for the brief finale. Then the music would end, the musicians would put away their instruments, and the music hall would be as empty and quiet as death.

When that happened, Molly would slowly place her heart into its velvet-lined case, close the lid, and lock it. She flicked the reins and stared into the dark forests that lined the road.

CHAPTER THIRTY-FOUR

Molly trembled in the October breeze as she trudged out to the barn to milk, her forehead warm. Resting her head on Nellie's side, she slowly pulled the cow's tits.

"Patrick hasn't been himself lately, Nellie. His cough worries me. I suppose we had too much excitement at Jaq's. We better go to bed early tonight."

Then she felt herself falling away from Nellie, tumbling into a nightmare of Papa in the Galveston hurricane. Drowning, her body drenched, her lungs exploding, she clutched something. She kicked to propel herself away from the green-black depths and her nose burned, her lungs shut down.

Jaq placed a damp washcloth on Molly's forehead. The aftermath of Eric's special supper replayed constantly in her mind, like the familiar old nightmare of running away but never escaping.

Coughs like machine guns had wakened her. "Here, Eric, take this spoon of honey." She'd rushed from room to room, up and down stairs till dawn. "Angus, try this cough syrup."

Jumping out of bed, dashing downstairs, they'd worn themselves out. Eric twisted, turned in bed, like he was clawing a living creature inside his chest. Sweat soaked Angus's sheets.

She'd bathed their blue faces, their chests. Offered sips of water—they pushed it away. Coughs turned to gurgles. Eric and Angus drowned in their own juices.

Eric sprawled across his bed, one arm flung above his head, the other clutching his throat. Blood covered everything—sheets, pillow, floor. Eric dead in an instant, dead and growing cold, like—No! Just like Henry. Eric's blond hair matted, blue eyes staring, accusing.

"I killed them," she screamed. "I destroyed them both. Like Grandfather."

It came back to her in a storm. Her mother accusing her of causing her grandfather's death. The sound of the wrench as she lashed out at Henry. She shook away that horror, gazed at Eric again—prone, face blue, chest and the once-white sheets red.

I've killed him too, without a wrench.

He might be alive if she'd given in, been a true wife to him, given him a son. He wouldn't have reenlisted. But she'd been willful, as Mother had always accused her of being.

She sat on the porch and craved a cigarette. She'd quit months ago when her supply ran out, would rather smell Molly's freshness than smoke and ashes. The wind moaning through the pines broke the hush, a welcome companion.

She'd disliked Eric and Angus at times, felt like a prisoner. But they weren't bad men. Death had felled them like trees during a hurricane. The silence around her when the wind stopped was as loud as after the Storm.

The next morning, she telephoned one of Eric's uncles in a nearby town. "I know we've never met," she said, "and I hate to tell you, but Eric and Angus both died from the Spanish flu last night."

She never wanted to give someone such news again.

They came and helped with the funeral. They wanted to go to Dallas, where Eric's uncle and cousin had died too, but were afraid. Aunt Anna was right. They all had to be careful. The flu could wipe out the entire community in a week.

Two days after the funeral she was at the cemetery, trying to make sense of what had happened. Gus and Kate ambled up, pulling the wagon loaded with a coffin. The buggy followed, and Mrs. Russell climbed out. The preacher, with a small group of mourners who looked like family members, conducted a brief service. Several men lowered the pine coffin.

Mrs. Russell's dry eyes glinted like the steel of a Confederate sword. This woman had endured war as intimately as she had, and she felt a momentary kinship.

But where were Molly? And Patrick? And Mr. James? The death of the McCade men had inundated her. Who was in the pine box? *Don't let it be Molly.* She and Patrick had been so full of life when they'd eaten supper together.

If she hadn't been so hell-bent on leaving East Texas, Molly and Patrick would have stayed safely at home. They wouldn't have visited the McCades when they delivered the flu.

She had said she loved Molly, but she hadn't called to ask about her and Patrick. She'd exposed them to a terrible disease then hadn't even considered that they might be in danger.

She stared at the wagon again to make sure it didn't contain another coffin, but it was empty.

The small group clustered around the small grave. The chill wind—the first cold snap of autumn—made her shiver, but Mrs. Russell's iron expression made her cringe. "Who is it?" she asked a stranger at the back of the small group as gently as she could and held her breath.

The young woman, obviously one of the family, sighed. "Uncle James. I'm sure sorry to hear about old McCade and Eric. They deserved better."

"Thank you. But where's Molly? And Patrick? Why aren't they here?"

"They're back at the house. Almost lost them too. Aunt Hannah's staying with them. Grandma's too worn out. Molly doesn't know about Uncle James yet."

"Can I help? It's so lonely in the McCades' house now. I need something to do."

"That's right neighborly of you, Miss Jacqueline. Grandma will make a ruckus, but she'll appreciate the good deed."

She'd sat beside Molly's bed for two days and nights, willing her to feel better, as Molly had done for her when she was injured. Molly had braved her mother-in-law's anger by inviting her to stay. She could still feel Molly's touch as she'd cleaned her wound and rubbed salve on her. If only Molly would open her eyes, speak to her—but she just lay there, as white and fragile as a gardenia blossom. Patrick was still sick too, and she couldn't bear the thought of losing either of them.

"I'm sorry, Molly," she said as she held her limp hand. "It's all my fault. I should have listened to Aunt Anna's warning. I should have insisted that Eric and Angus not go to Dallas, and I should have never let you and Patrick near them."

How could she tell Molly about Mr. James? Would Molly be strong enough to take the news?

She'd never dreaded anything more, but a green shoot of hope broke through the brown dirt of her solemn mood. Mr. James was dead. *Molly was free.* She could leave the farm and Mrs. Russell now, take Patrick with her, and do whatever she wanted. But what would that be?

Would Molly blame her for Mr. James's death? Would Molly react to her the way her mother had reacted after her grandfather was killed during the Storm? Jaq couldn't imagine Molly acting like that, but Jaq had killed Mr. James as surely as she'd killed Henry and the others. She couldn't bear to hear Molly lash out at her like Mother had. She wanted to remember Molly as kind and gentle, not angry and vengeful.

Someone pulled Molly's hair, dragged her from the dark water. Clutching her pillow, she burst into light. Jaq stood over her, brushing her hair—a weeping angel.

"What's happened? Why am I here?"

"Thank heaven you're finally awake. I've been so worried. If something had happened to you too—"

"What do you mean? Has Patrick—"

Jaq's desolate expression puzzled her.

"It's Patrick, isn't it? Where is he? I need to see about him. Help me. Please take me to him."

She tried to rise but sank back onto the feather pillow. Vaguely she recalled slipping off the milking stool and lying there until strong arms carried her to bed. She'd hung like a sack of potatoes, murmuring, "I'll tend to the milk later."

She'd just needed a short nap, then she'd separate the milk, clean the buckets…Mother Russell would make a cutting remark about letting the milk sit, but…Patrick, where was Patrick?

She drifted into the roiling water again, the current tossing her like a jellyfish. Still she clung to something, refused to let go. Strong fingers pried it from her, and she spun toward a dark vortex. A soft hand stroked her hair, kept her from drowning.

❖

"Whoa, Nellie. Come back here and let me milk you. I know you're used to Molly's soft hands, but you'd better get used to mine. Humph. You'd think after almost a week, you would be." She jerked Nellie's tits so hard and fast the streams of milk almost turned the bucket over.

"I'd never tell a living soul, Nellie, but I wish the good Lord had taken Molly instead of James. I felt right sorry for her when she was out of her mind with the fever, talking about her pa and some train and begging him to take her and save Patrick. She musta thought she'd lost Patrick but didn't even care if James or me was sick."

She eased close to Nellie and fell into the soothing rhythm of milking. "If it'd been me laying there out of my head, I'd have been worrying about Calvin. He was such a good man, God rest his soul. If the War hadn't come along, he'd have graduated from that college he thought so much of and probably be president right now. At least he'd have made a professor so he could've kept his nose stuck in a book, instead of fighting on the front lines in Atlanta, then trying to make ends meet in this new, strange place." She switched to another tit, and a stream of warm milk hit the bucket like a shot.

"Losing Calvin was the worst thing ever happened to me, but something tells me Molly won't feel that way about James. Of course, now that Patrick's the only grandson I have left to carry on the family name, I intend to do everything in my power to keep him close. Even if it means having to put up with Molly the rest of my life. Sure will be different around here without James, though."

She finished milking Nellie and sat staring at the milky foam. A tear crept out the side of one eye, and she let it roll down her cheek.

"At least Clyde's still alive and kicking. Hmm. Maybe he'd want to pair up with Molly when he gets home. Help him get over losing his wife and kids to this dern influenza, and give Patrick a ready-made pa. Maybe I can make that happen, Nellie."

Another tear sneaked out, and this time she swiped it away.

"Yes, sirree. That'd be best for everybody involved."

CHAPTER THIRTY-FIVE

Molly stretched as the coo of a mourning dove outside the bedroom window woke her. She'd had such a good night's sleep, but what had been happening? How long had she been asleep? She recalled milking Nellie and feeling exhausted. She must have been sick.

She rolled over to slide out of bed and saw someone sitting across the room, her head propped on one hand, seemingly asleep. Jaq. How wonderful to see her. But what was she doing here? She had to talk to Jaq, to make sure she was okay, to touch her...Her feet hit the creaky boards of the bedroom floor, and Jaq's head snapped up.

"Jaq. What in the world? Where is everyone?"

She looked like she wanted to run away. "Patrick's in his room, and Mrs. Russell's in the chicken pen."

"Well, where's Mr. James? What's today? Is he in the fields? I expect he's had his hands full with the cotton picking—"

"Molly, I have to tell you something. We've been waiting until you gained some strength, and Mrs. Russell wanted me to break the news."

She glanced out the window, Jaq's tone filling her with dread. "What news? Has he—"

"He died of influenza three weeks ago, and they buried him a few days later. They couldn't wait any longer. His last words were, 'Take care of Patrick.'"

Now she remembered thinking Patrick had died...but it had been Mr. James. She'd been a terrible wife, regretting marrying him and not even caring that she'd lost the diamond he'd been so proud of. Memories of their courtship, their conversations, and his kindness flooded her. How could such a gentle man simply vanish like that? What kind of a God could be so cruel?

How could she raise Patrick by herself? What would she do now? She sobbed, and the coo of the dove she'd heard earlier became the shriek of a hawk.

❖

Jaq caught Molly before she fell. After tucking her into bed again, she hurried out to let Mrs. Russell know what had happened.

"How did she take it?"

After she explained how Molly had reacted, Mrs. Russell frowned. "That gal needs to get up and go back to work. Patrick needs her, and her fainting and falling out sure won't help him get over losing his pa. The two of them should be over the worst of the flu now, and I thank you kindly for helping with them. It won't be easy without James, but I'll make do, like I always have."

Her face looked more lined than the last time Jaq had paid attention to her.

"Molly and Patrick musta caught the influenza from Eric and Angus, and brought it home to James. All the papers have been telling folks not to go anywhere near big cities like Dallas and San Antonio. And they've been saying that most of the ones dying are men between twenty and forty-five. Mighty strange. Usually the old folks and the youngsters die. Anyhow, you'd think Eric and Angus would have been more careful."

She tucked up a stray hank of hair that had escaped from the tight knot on the back of her head.

"I know losing James is hard on Molly, but after my husband died I didn't lay around and feel sorry for myself. Had to keep going for the children."

Mrs. Russell's unfair accusations made Jaq bristle. Molly had just regained consciousness after a near-fatal illness and didn't give any indication of feeling sorry for herself. Judging from Molly's shocked expression, she was concerned only with Mr. James and Patrick. "We all have to deal with loss in our own way, and I don't know what Molly's is. But she's stronger than you think. She'll pull through."

Mrs. Russell jumped up and stalked back into the house, but Jaq gazed toward the field where some of the few men still alive, both black and white, picked cotton.

So many men dead. All her fault. If she hadn't—

"Jacqueline, telephone," Mrs. Russell yelled from the house.

No one knew she'd been staying over here except Mother. She hurried inside, knowing that her mother would telephone her only if she had bad news.

Her hand shook as she took the receiver that Mrs. Russell held out. "Hello."

She was right. "Oh, no, Mother. Not him too. I'll be there as soon as I can. Good-bye." She slowly placed the receiver on its hook, rushed down the hall to Molly's bedroom, and peered inside. Molly hadn't moved. Had she had a relapse? How long would it be before she roused again?

She turned to Mrs. Russell, who stood behind her. "It's my father. Mother says he's been really sick. I need to leave right now and drive home. I don't want to disturb Molly. I'm sure she still needs to rest. Please tell her good-bye for me and explain what's happened. I'd appreciate it if you'd give her Mother's number and ask her to call me there in about a week." She scrawled it on a lined sheet of paper.

As she drove to the McCades' house, her mind spun faster than the flywheel on her Model T. Would Mrs. Russell give Molly her message and her phone number? Surely she wouldn't be so cruel not to. Why hadn't she stayed and explained to Molly why she had to leave so suddenly?

She stopped in the McCades' driveway, tempted to turn around and do just that. But what if Molly refused to see her? What if Molly blamed her for causing Mr. James to die and putting Patrick in danger? Molly would probably be in a better mood to talk after she'd recovered from the flu completely and mourned for Mr. James.

If she didn't hear from Molly in several weeks, she'd assume the worst about Mrs. Russell and call Molly. But now, she had to leave. She ran into the house and closed all the windows and doors. Then she pulled on trousers and a man's shirt, loaded her Model T, and was on the road within an hour. As she drove past the Russells' house, she had to force herself not to turn into their driveway, but seeing her dressed like this would only antagonize Mrs. Russell. No, it was better to wait, she kept telling herself all the way to New Orleans, hoping she hadn't been a coward but knowing that she had.

❖

Does he expect me to come trotting down this driveway like a pony? The day after Jacqueline left, the mailman sat at the Russells' mailbox and honked his horn nonstop. When Mother Russell got there, huffing and puffing, he handed her a letter. "This here's for Miss Jacqueline. I heard she left yesterday, and I didn't know where to forward it to."

"I'll take care of it." She snatched the letter from him and studied it as she plodded back up to the house. It was written in a strange hand, and the return address was Homer, Louisiana. After she eased the envelope open she pulled out a long letter written on the fanciest lilac stationery she'd ever seen. Even had a sweet scent to it.

She read through it right quick, just to get the gist of it and make sure it was worth sending on, and almost dropped it. Why, it was from some colored hussy named Willie. She said she'd left New Orleans and gone to Louisiana to visit her ma, and after the War ended she aimed to go to France, where folks would treat her decent in spite of her great-grandmother being a slave. What a downright foolish notion. Everything would be a mess overseas for quite a spell.

But something else about the letter nagged at her, like a bad smell coming from the outhouse, so she read it again, slower this time. This Willie kept talking about how much she'd miss Jacqueline, how sweet she smelled, how soft she felt—like they'd been…sweethearts, or some such. Her breath stopped, like one of the mules had kicked her in the chest.

That was it. She'd always figured something wasn't right with Jacqueline, but she hadn't been able to see it because of that pretty face. She'd heard folks whisper about women who liked women more than they did men, in that kind of way. Gol-darn it, if this Willie and Jacqueline weren't that kind of pervert, she'd eat her own hat. And here Jacqueline had been trying to influence Molly to be just like her, right under her nose.

She stuffed the letter back into its envelope. "Law me. I'm sure not gonna call Jacqueline about this letter or give her phone number to Molly now," she told herself. "She's a worse influence than I ever suspected. I'll keep this right here in the bottom of my old trunk. I'd rather let Molly and Patrick associate with the devil himself than with that abomination."

❖

Molly didn't hear any birds, only silence and an occasional frog's mournful croak. Where was Jaq? She'd been here both of the other times she'd waked up, but now the rocking chair she'd sat in was as empty as Molly felt. Had Jaq taken care of her the entire time she'd been sick? She seemed to have, but Molly couldn't be sure. Maybe she was exhausted and had gone back to the McCades' for a rest. Pretty soon she'd drive up and Molly could breathe easy again.

As she slowly washed her face in cold water, she glanced in the mottled mirror above the china washbowl. Her hair looked like weathered pine straw, her eyes the color of dust. She pulled on a simple housedress and wandered out the front door and into the rose garden. The roses, all the same dull color, had lost their odor, like Jaq had complained of when she was laid up. Their thorns even looked bigger and sharper than usual.

She trudged aimlessly down to the pond. As she approached, the snapping turtles slid into the water with a quiet splash. The pine trees had lost most of their needles and resembled toothpicks holding up the gray bowl of a sky.

Finally, she meandered toward the barn, to the pigpen where Mother Russell and Patrick were slopping the hogs.

"Sure glad you finally decided to get up, Molly. It's not easy for me and Patrick to do all these chores by ourselves."

Mother Russell's words barely registered as she walked into the kitchen and slipped into her apron. Mr. James was dead. Had Jaq deserted her too? What would happen to her now without either Mr. James or Jaq?

Her mind fluttered like the wings of a moth trapped in a Mason jar. She could leave the farm. Take Patrick and go live with her parents in Dallas until she got a job. But she was so tired.

Maybe Jaq would ask her to go away with her. If she did, it might be better to stay here until she and Patrick both regained their health. But did Jaq truly want them? Mother Russell said Eric and Angus had died, so maybe Jaq was back in New Orleans now with the woman she knew there, planning to go to Paris with her.

Molly took a deep breath as she began to wash the dirty dishes piled in the sink. She needed to settle down, to wait and see if Jaq got in touch before she decided what to do now.

❖

Jaq fingered her scar as she mechanically drove toward New Orleans. Mr. James, Eric, and Angus would still be alive if she hadn't gone to New Hope. Henry would still be alive if she hadn't gone to France. And even Grandfather might still be alive if she hadn't run outside after her dog.

Mother was right. She should never have gone out in that storm, but she hadn't listened. And she should never have left New Orleans. If she'd stayed there, married an upstanding citizen and had his babies, her life would be smooth right now.

She drove until she was exhausted and stopped at a hotel. After a big meal she went to her room and fell into bed. She didn't look forward to returning home. She'd rather be back in New Hope taking care of Molly and Patrick. She missed them so much she'd almost turned around a dozen times and driven right back to New Hope.

How she'd love to see Molly come running toward her as she drove up, to see her soft smile and her gleaming eyes. But had the smile and the gleam died? She had to find out, but she needed to wait until she felt like she deserved someone as wonderful as Molly and to be sure that Molly didn't blame her for what had happened.

CHAPTER THIRTY-SIX

The deserted streets gave Jaq the willies when she finally arrived in New Orleans. She thought about Galveston after the Storm as she headed for her parents' home on St. Charles Avenue.

Her mother looked much the same—tall, slender, immaculate—but welcomed her so warmly Jaq almost expected her to hug her. She wore her hair in a different style. As far back as Jaq could remember, her mother's maid had tugged her long black hair back and up over her ears and spent hours curling it with tongs into fancy creations, especially when she dressed for a dinner party. What a waste of time. But now it covered her ears and was pulled back gently to follow the shape of her head. With its soft, natural curl, it had to be a lot easier to fix.

As they sat in the parlor, her mother immediately said, "*Mon Dieu*. It looks as if both your brothers, they are safe. Surely the War, she will end soon, and they will return to their wives and babies." Then she blurted, "Earlier this month, your father had to go to the docks to meet a steamer that left Boston two weeks earlier."

"Yes, Mother. Doesn't he do things like that all the time?" Why mention something so mundane?

She set down her cup of tea more forcefully than usual. Mother never lost her temper. "*Oui*, but this time three passengers, they died during the trip, and fifteen became ill, as did six crewmen. All of them, they complained of a bad cough and pain all over their bodies. Your father should have turned around at once when he heard the news. But, of course, man that he is, he went aboard to meet the man with whom he had an appointment."

Jaq sipped her warm tea. She must have inherited her stubborn streak from him, but that was nothing new. Mother had pounded that fact into her head forever. She supposed she'd had to discover it for herself. And her mother was most likely right about something else. That steamer probably brought the epidemic to New Orleans, and even Father's obstinacy couldn't hold out against it.

"Me, I have never witnessed anyone so ill," her mother said, seeming chilled in spite of the warm, humid weather of late October. "His fever. Ah, his forehead practically scalded my hand. He threw his nightstand and his chamber pot across the room. Later he told me he had thought the two of them were ridiculing him for being so weak. Can you imagine? That's when I telephoned you. I could not stand it any longer."

She tried to laugh, but her quavering voice revealed everything Jaq needed to know. Mother, always so strong, had feared the man she'd lived with so long. Her mother moved closer to the light on the end table, which illuminated the new lines in her once-smooth complexion, the black smudges under her dark eyes.

"His fever, how do you say it, finally broke last night, and he is resting easier today. Me, I am so glad you are here. And I am sure he will be also. I need you to help me keep him away from the windows. All month the priests have been driving their horse-drawn carts down St. Charles, calling for everyone to bring out the bodies of their family members who died during the night."

Her mother rose and paced back and forth. Jaq should have been here sooner. How had her mother managed? "Why didn't you get in touch with me before now? Did the doctor help you with Father?"

"Bah. When he first became ill, one doctor told me to sprinkle sulfur in my shoes and put silver dollars in my pockets every morning to kill the germs. If the silver dollars changed color, the sulfur was working, he said. I did not try his ridiculous remedy because I was too busy taking care of your father. And most of our neighbors who did died anyway. I wrote you several letters but finally decided to call. I am tired."

She sat back down and frowned. "Before the influenza arrived, they told us our climate would prevent it from appearing here in the city. Ha. Soon people who had been healthy one day were dead the next. The young and the old were not hit the hardest, but strong, healthy young people."

"Yes, I know," Jaq said. "It was the same in Texas."

For the first time her mother looked at her and said, "I was so sorry to hear about Eric and his father. How are your friend Molly and her son?"

"She's better. But she needs time to recuperate, like Father. I left her this phone number, so if she calls, please let me know."

"Of course, Jacqueline." Her mother smiled and drew on her best social manners like a pair of gloves then began to murmur platitudes.

After her long trip, Jaq just wanted to sleep. It was All Hallows' Eve, and she'd seen enough ghosts and goblins to last a lifetime, though tomorrow she planned to resurrect one more that had troubled her too long.

Jaq rose early the next morning and drove up State Street toward the new location of the academy she'd once attended. It felt strange not to ride the streetcar, then walk through the French Quarter to school. She hadn't been the only one who left the old campus when she graduated. That same year, all the nuns and the academy itself moved from the old convent to this new site.

She parked in front of the cream-colored main building then strolled past small red cedars and magnolias in the inner courtyard. A few students, wearing their familiar uniforms, had clustered in front of the Nuns' Mausoleum. The ten nuns who came to America in the 1700s lay inside it, taking their well-deserved rest from the hard job of establishing the first school for girls in this uncivilized part of the world. Suddenly she was proud to have been part of such a significant institution, even though at the time she'd wanted to be anywhere else.

After she followed the students into the temporary Shrine of Our Lady of Prompt Succor, she sat near the back and lost herself in the familiar atmosphere. All good Catholics were supposed to attend the All Souls' Day Mass, and even though she hadn't been a good Catholic for years, she'd decided to try to be one for a change. Besides, she wanted to see if Sister Mary Therese still taught at the academy. If she did, would Sister Mary affect her like she once had? Would she be able to speak to Sister Mary?

They were supposed to reflect, give thanks, and remember their loved ones now in paradise. So she managed a brief prayer for Eric and Angus, for Mr. James, and for Henry and Helen. She doubted if many people were in the churches throughout the city, for according to Mother, many were still hiding from the flu.

The famous statue of Our Lady stood in front of the shrine. Her gold robe shone too brightly for Jaq's taste, the baby in her arms looked too smug, and evidently this time she hadn't given New Orleans prompt succor like she supposedly had from past hurricanes, fires, and wars.

But in spite of her objections to Our Lady's appearance and shortcomings, she prayed earnestly for Patrick to recover quickly and dwelt on Molly during the remainder of the Mass. They'd each lost a husband, but her loss didn't begin to compare to Molly's. Mr. James was kind and tender, though patronizing. Molly and he had shared a son, which had to have created a bond that would be agonizing to break. When she recovered enough, would she call? And even if Molly did call, could she talk to her without suffering the worst kind of guilt?

The sound of the small chorus roused her and she glanced toward the singers. Surely she'd see Sister Mary Therese. She'd been the assistant director six years ago, but now an unfamiliar woman led the girls. Jaq sighed at the reprieve.

After the Mass ended, she stood in place and watched the small number of students and sisters file past. She recognized none of the students, of course, but a few of the nuns nodded. Sister Celestine, the prioress, who came last, stopped and half smiled. Her pince-nez sat crooked on her nose.

"Jacqueline Bergeron. Thanks be to the saints. I've prayed to see you again, and now God has answered my prayers. Would you be so good as to visit with me for a few minutes in my office?"

Puzzled that the prioress even remembered her, much less wanted to talk to her, she nodded.

Sister Celestine chatted as they strolled across the courtyard toward the main building. Once in her office, she slumped into her desk chair and motioned her into the chair in front of her. Jaq knew it well, for she had once received several reprimands there as she tried to sit still and be respectful. This time she had no trouble doing either.

Judging by Sister Celestine's thin gray hair and marked stoop, she'd spent the past month serving the sick and dying in the infected city. The last time Jaq saw her she'd had dark hair and sat as straight-backed as the chair Jaq perched on.

"How have you been, Jacqueline? Your mother tells me you have seen the world."

"Yes, ma'am. More than I bargained for."

"As have I, my dear." She shrugged and let out a deep breath.

"What's it been like in New Orleans? Mother told me a bit, but I'm sure you've seen more than she has." She couldn't help herself. She felt like a kid tearing at a scab on her arm to see if it was healing.

"We've done what we can to help people through this epidemic. I suppose you've heard some are calling it the Blue Death? The purple blisters, the terrible earaches and headaches, and finally blood oozing, even shooting from the nose, ears, and mouth. And all the while the patient gasps for breath and turns dark blue for lack of oxygen. The ones with those symptoms never live."

She knew them well. That's exactly what had happened to Eric and Angus. She trembled.

Sister Celestine shifted in her chair. "The individual deaths have been horrifying. As have the way so many people reacted to this disease. At first the rich blamed the poor, and the poor blamed the rich. Then people blamed the Germans, the Negroes, the Jews, and any other minority group they could think of. Sick people starved because those who were well panicked and refused to go near or give food to anyone with even one ill family member. And others would have nothing to do with any of the orphans. We have done what we could, but several of the sisters have died."

And she'd thought things were bad in New Hope. Aunt Anna hadn't exaggerated. Those living in a small community or town evidently hadn't suffered nearly so much as those in the large cities.

Sister Celestine seemed eager to share her burden. "Eventually, though, as more people realized that only the influenza was to blame, some of them, white and black, banded together and worked side by side. Of course, the undertakers still had to hire guards to protect their valuable coffins. Who would have thought they would be in such demand? At times when we didn't think we could continue, the children helped keep us from despair. They made up little poems and songs. *I had a little bird. Its name was Enza. I opened the window, and in-flu-enza.*"

Jaq smiled in spite of herself, but one question wouldn't leave her alone. "You said some of the sisters died. Anyone I knew?"

The prioress opened her mouth to speak, frowned, closed it, replaced her pince-nez and adjusted it, and finally seemed to reach a decision. "I take it you have not heard?"

"Heard what?"

"About Sister Mary Therese. I know you especially admired her. That is why I asked to speak to you."

"Did she...was she one...?" She gripped the slick, varnished oak of the chair that supported her.

"No, child. It is not what you think. It is...actually...worse." The sister hesitated, as if wanting to spare her.

What could be worse than dying from the flu? "What happened? I have to know. Please."

Sister Celestine jerked off her pince-nez and folded her hands in front of her on her desk. "After we left the old convent in the French Quarter and moved here, Sister Mary Therese was never the same. She shut herself away and rarely spoke. At first I thought she was merely having a difficult time adjusting to the move, but she failed to improve." She had laced her fingers together and was squeezing them so tight they looked like the blood had drained from them.

"She did not appear for early chapel one morning. I sent one of the sisters to see if she was ill, and the sister ran back with a horrible expression and pulled me toward Sister Mary's room. When I entered, I saw her bare feet rotating slowly. Somehow we cut her down, but of course we were too late. And then we had to return her body to her parents without even saying a Mass for her eternal soul." Her eyes shone with unshed tears, and she swiped at them as she replaced her pince-nez.

"Why?" She grabbed her own left wrist and clamped down on it until she was afraid she'd bruised it.

"We have no idea. Perhaps she told her confessor, but whatever led her to take such an extreme measure must have tortured her like the flames of hell. I only wish her suffering had ended then, but we both know it has merely begun."

She had to get out of there. Sister Mary Therese's blue eyes and blond curls were shriveled now? She couldn't bear the thought.

Feeling as cold as the stones of the archway she hurried through after she quickly said good-bye to Sister Celestine, Jaq almost stumbled down the long flight of stairs from her office. Somehow she drove back down State Street and rushed into the room she had slept in as a schoolgirl. Sister Mary Therese would never sing again.

As she lay there and wondered if she'd caused her death too, all her bitterness dissolved in the tears that wrenched her. She'd never considered how Sister Mary must have felt after their lovemaking. Her own pain had enveloped her so fully she hadn't been able to look outside herself.

This morning she had gone halfheartedly to the Shrine of Our Lady of Prompt Succor to pay her respects to her loved ones now in paradise. She dared the church to tell her that Sister Mary Therese was in hell. She was in a place where women could love one another freely and openly. She was in the type of heaven Jaq vowed to spend all her energy making into a reality on this earth.

And she could begin by asking Molly if they could make a life together. Actually formulating the thought made her hesitate. Would Molly be able to withstand the strange looks that people would give them when they learned that the two of them were raising Patrick together? Were Molly's feelings for her strong enough to defy everything she'd known and been taught? What about her family? How would they react?

If she even suggested such a life together, would Molly reject her like Sister Mary and Helen had? Molly might already be thinking about looking for another husband. After all, a boy needed a father, didn't he? A new husband could rescue Molly from the farm and Mrs. Russell, move her to Dallas or Austin, where she could have a life more suited to her interests and accomplishments.

But wouldn't it be heavenly to be able to offer Molly what a man could?

She lay still for a while then wiped away her tears. She was as good as any man. Better. And Molly loved her. She felt it with her whole heart. She'd give Molly a little more time to recuperate, then she'd call her. No, she'd write her. But wouldn't it be better to discuss something this important face to face?

That was it. When her father felt better, she'd drive back to New Hope and bare her feelings to Molly. She didn't know whether the prospect thrilled her or frightened her.

CHAPTER THIRTY-SEVEN

"Do you miss Pa a lot?" Patrick asked her as they sat side by side on the porch swing the Sunday before Christmas.

"Of course. Don't you?" She put her arm around his shoulder and pulled him close. He still felt bony since being sick.

"Yes, ma'am. I sure do. I miss him bringing me a box of Cracker Jack and a Dr. Pepper like he used to every Saturday when he went to town. And letting me have the first piece every time he cut a watermelon. But I miss his stories most of all. He sure could tell some good ones. Will I have to quit school like he did?"

Startled, she said, "What makes you even mention quitting school?"

"Grandma said I might have to, if you don't find me another pa. She said I'd have to help out here on the farm all day. Is that so?" His expression was so earnest she wanted to kiss his smooth cheeks.

"Would you like to have a new pa?"

"I don't know. Grandma says I need one. She said maybe Uncle Clyde might be good. What do you think? He'll be missing Aunt Alice and his two boys when he gets home from the War. That Spanish flu sure did kill a lot of folks around here, didn't it?"

"Yes, son. A lot of good people. But your Uncle Clyde might miss his family so much he'll want to be by himself for a while."

"Is that what you want, Mama?"

She didn't know what to say. She refused to let Patrick miss out on an education, but she certainly didn't intend to let Mother Russell railroad her into marrying Clyde, even if Patrick did need another parent. Although Molly would never forget how well he treated her when Patrick was born, she had absolutely no desire to marry another man.

"Right now I'd like to get my strength back and help you start feeling like your old self again. Then we'll see what happens. Your Uncle Clyde won't be home for a few months yet."

She did miss Mr. James—his kind blue eyes, his warm bulk beside her in bed on a chilly night, and even his soft snores. She grieved that death had claimed such a good-natured person. She could cry for him.

But she mourned dry-eyed for Jaq.

She couldn't tell Patrick what she really wanted. Mother Russell said Jaq had helped take care of her and Patrick until she received an important phone call and had to leave. But why hadn't she stayed long enough to say good-bye, or left a note or a message, or a phone number?

She couldn't tell Patrick she missed Jaq so much she was afraid her bones might melt, that she might dissolve like fog if she didn't hear from her soon. Her heart was a stone stranded at the bottom of a deep well, with no way to retrieve it.

Had Jaq meant what she'd said? Or had she simply been using Molly to pass the time until she could leave New Hope? Was she lying in the arms of that woman in New Orleans right now, the one she'd mentioned a few times, laughing about the little country girl she'd been able to twist around her smallest finger so easily?

Ever since Jaq had told her that Mr. James was dead, then left her all alone, the days had been monotone. Occasionally she overheard a distant melody, glimpsed a flash of color, but the ache that spread throughout her kept her senses blurred.

As the pain dulled, she might forget her losses for a second, then recoil from the quick memory that Mr. James was dead and, even worse, that Jaq had deserted her without a word. Mr. James hadn't chosen to leave; Jaq had. Mr. James couldn't come back; Jaq *could*. But what were the chances of that? About as small as the odds that she might pull her own heart from the well where it lay underwater.

The women at church, even Mother Russell, seemed to sympathize with her. But she couldn't admit to anyone, even Patrick, how much she missed Jaq.

Only her pain kept her company, almost like a living creature. It existed even between her and Nellie, who should have been able to comfort her with her warm hairy side, her soft tits and eyes.

Not even the Christmas carols she loved could make her feel better. She kept her distance and existed in a gray land with no music, no odor, no taste.

"Why did you leave me, Jaq?" she would whisper as she milked Nellie.

When she visited Mr. James's grave she cried for him, but she also gazed toward the woods where she and Jaq had gone that picnic afternoon. She thought about Jaq's stories, her driving lessons, their trip to town, their kiss. Who cared if the women voters had helped elect their favored candidates? Being able to vote meant nothing without having someone to live for. She wanted Jaq. She would become a cipher, vanish without her.

She pulled Patrick even closer and stared at the dim afternoon sun that barely warmed the gray, cold day. She wanted to rest her head on his and weep forever, but her heart lay stranded like a solitary pebble dropped on a vast desert.

❖

Jaq laid her fountain pen down, slowly folded a letter, and placed it on the pile in her desk alcove. The stack contained one for every day since she last saw Molly.

But she couldn't send them. She was another Typhoid Mary. Someone should quarantine her indefinitely too. How many people had she killed unintentionally? Grandfather, Henry, Eric, Angus, Mr. James, and Sister Mary. She should add Helen to the list and was surprised Molly and Patrick weren't on it. Almost everyone she'd ever loved or been close to had died or disappeared. She couldn't bear to endanger Molly and Patrick, to put them in death's crosshairs again. Molly needed to forget her and find a new, safe life.

It had been two months, and Molly hadn't called. She and Patrick needed to recuperate, and she needed to grieve for Mr. James, who'd been a good husband, as far as that went.

Jaq had been busy too—helping Mother care for Father and doing most of the housework until some servants resurfaced after the threat of the influenza epidemic receded. At least she'd learned some useful skills in New Hope.

But she wanted to talk to Molly. With Mr. James dead, maybe...

She could have discussed the situation with Willie, but she'd left town. Jaq had eventually written Aunt Anna and had finally received a reply today. She slit the envelope open and began to read.

Sunday, December 22, 1918
New York City

Dearest Jaq,

I've been rooted here in my morris chair, my shoulders and arms so heavy I've had to strain to leaf through a newspaper and hold my cup of coffee. We beat the Kaiser, didn't we, but the Spanish flu defeated us.

I have real coffee today, and its fragrance tantalizes me. Was able to actually buy a small can of Folgers yesterday afternoon and look forward to an abundance of sugar and flour, as well as tires and gasoline. With the soldiers beginning to return, we should have plenty of manpower before long.

Unfortunately, the news in the Times dampened the good mood my coffee created. An estimated three million have died these past three months, and the influenza is still racing along Alaska's northern coast. Some are saying that it's five times deadlier than the War.

I know what you mean about being a Typhoid Mary. Not only did I fail to determine the cause of this outbreak, but I also couldn't discover a cure.

I'm still wearing my old chenille robe, and my hair's down, so let me try to respond to your latest letter, dear Jaq. I'm certainly no authority on relationships, never having achieved a lasting one of my own. But if I were you, I wouldn't let Molly slip away. She sounds like a good match for you. Let her continue to regain her health and put her past behind her, but keep your heart open. When she's ready, you need to be ready for her. It won't be easy for her to leave everything she's known and venture into a new way of life with you, especially with a young son to care for. But I have faith in you, and in her, if she's the one you really want.

You're not a Typhoid Mary. Your mother was wrong to blame you for her father's death. She probably spoke out of shock and grief and doesn't even remember her words. You're an adult now, so try to look at the situation objectively. You're a small cog in this great wheel of life, and although it may feel as if you can cause others to die, you can't. No more than I can blame myself for causing the death of millions by failing to diagnose and cure this epidemic. It's tempting for both of us to assume such self-importance, but we need to let it go and do what we can, instead of burdening ourselves with what we can't.

The world will go on. The War's over and the politicians are haggling over the terms of the armistice now. Though the French and the British want to punish Germany harshly for their aggression, President Wilson is determined to be less punitive. I hope he can prevail. Women have almost achieved the right to vote, thanks to Alice Paul and her faithful followers. Your father is recovering from the flu, and I'm sure you played an important role in that victory. Let's enjoy our gains.

Most important, don't be afraid to love, my dear. So keep Molly and her son safe in your heart until they come to you.

Your loving aunt,

Anna

Warmed by her aunt's wisdom and optimism, she folded the letter and slipped it into its envelope. She'd let it keep her company as she waited. Maybe Molly and Patrick would become part of her life after all, but was she really ready for that? She knew what she wanted, but she had to be practical.

How would she provide for Molly and Patrick? She had some money her grandmother had left her, but that would cover only her expenses. She couldn't expect her parents to take the three of them in. That would be unbearable. She supposed she could get a job working on people's cars. That was about her only skill, but would anyone trust her to do what they expected a man to?

Did she want to stay in the South? Being in Europe, especially Paris, had given her a taste of a much freer way of life than she could ever expect to experience here. At least that's how it seemed. She really wanted to explore that possibility, but could she expect Molly and Patrick to leave everything they'd ever known and pursue some vague notion of freedom halfway around the world in a country devastated by four years of war? Molly and Patrick had both said they wanted to travel, but living somewhere so foreign would be so very different from a pleasure trip.

Could she live in Paris without Molly and Patrick? Suddenly she wished they were all back on the farm together, with everyone still alive and Mrs. Russell still making their lives miserable. Compared to being alone in Paris, those recent days seemed like a pleasant dream. She needed to talk to Molly. This was too much to decide by herself. She'd waited long enough. Father seemed to have recovered. She'd make the long drive back up to New Hope as soon as she could.

CHAPTER THIRTY-EIGHT

On St. Valentine's Day, Molly gazed out the window at the garden. A year ago she and Patrick had spent part of the morning cutting seed potatoes into pieces, each with a sprouting eye. Afterward she'd knelt with the sections piled in a bushel basket beside her and carefully placed a piece, eye up, into the furrows Mr. James had plowed. Then he had come along behind her and covered the potatoes with soft red dirt.

Each sprout nestled in the ground, slowly pushed its blind way upward, and emerged into sunlight in several weeks. But now Mr. James rested in the same ground as the potatoes. Surely his soul was making a similar journey into a brighter world.

This year it had rained practically nonstop, and had since last fall. She'd welcomed the gray, wet days. Every day she'd asked herself why Jaq had disappeared without a word. Was she enjoying herself so much with her lover in New Orleans that she'd totally forgotten her?

A vase of jonquils and hyacinths sat on the dining-room table. She hadn't realized the flowers were already blooming. She usually filled the house with containers of them, but Mother Russell had evidently gathered this spring bouquet, their blooms so much paler yellow than normal.

She'd been almost thoughtful since Mr. James died, though she sporadically urged Molly to buck up. But these spring flowers communicated that necessity whereas Mother Russell's words didn't.

Wandering into the living room, she slowly opened the piano, which she hadn't touched since October, and fingered a few keys. She even picked up the sheet music for "I'm Always Chasing Rainbows" that she'd bought when Jaq drove her and Patrick to town. The tinny tone of the piano sounded strange; the usually smooth ivory felt rough and foreign.

Suddenly she remembered something Jaq had mentioned last summer, though it seemed a lifetime ago. Talking about the music she had listened to in New Orleans when she was young, she'd said it sounded like the musicians were composing as they played or sang, instead of reading from a page of music.

Molly hadn't understood that concept and had tucked it into her mind to ponder. Now its meaning sprang to life.

She picked out the tune again, without looking at the sheet music. She usually played it in a quick, lively manner, but now she let her sorrow wash through her and well up through her arms and hands onto the keys. She played the same notes as she had earlier but could almost feel Jaq's presence. She saw her dark hair and eyes, felt the scar on her forehead she tried to keep hidden. She smelled the rose water they'd made together that glorious day and heard her voice as she shared her adventures. But most of all she tasted Jaq's lips on hers, the most exhilarating sensation she'd ever experienced.

She played the familiar tune again, and it came out differently—as if it had a life of its own, as if the piano was playing her, adding notes she'd never seen written down but that somehow sounded right, like the field hands' constantly changing rendition of "Swing Low, Sweet Chariot." It became in turn a spiritual, a sonata, a symphony, and a simple song for Jaq, as she played it repeatedly.

She glanced at the paper and pen she used for writing music, lying unused on the back of the piano. She might compose a new song and call it "The Storm," to commemorate her first lengthy conversation with Jaq last Easter.

But then she closed the piano's cover, sighed, and walked to the front porch, where she sat and gazed at the distant trees. Her new music, from her heart instead of her head, relieved a little of the loneliness she'd lived with since Jaq went away. But only the wind in the pines played the kind of music she could hear and lulled the storm that had raged in her since Jaq left.

❖

Jaq watched her mother stoop over a rosebush in their backyard, one of the rare moments she stooped for anything. Wearing a heavy apron and leather gloves, she pruned the plants to make sure they grew exactly as she wished and that they bloomed their hearts out.

This was the first day Jaq had felt like getting outside since she'd collapsed at the end of December. She'd been planning her trip back to New Hope when suddenly she developed what the doctor diagnosed as the influenza that had killed so many. With her high fever and resulting weakness, she'd had to stay in bed for more than a month. Now, she seemed to be slowly beginning to return to normal, though her mood and that of New Orleans in general was still somber. She felt exhausted, like everyone she knew seemed to be.

Now, with winter on its way out and spring trying to make inroads, she sat in a chair on the lawn and watched her mother for a while. Then she ventured out to where she'd accumulated a small pile of thorny limbs. She'd never paid much attention to her mother's St. Valentine's Day ritual, but her experience in the rose garden with Molly had sensitized her to the flower.

"Why do you insist on doing such backbreaking work, Mother? Are you the world's expert on roses?"

She glared. "I am the world's expert on *my* roses." She straightened, then stretched her back from side to side. "I have never known you to show any interest in what I do out here. You must be bored and feeling better."

"Yes, I am."

Her mother slipped her sharp shears into her apron pocket. "Ah, *ma petite*. I do not mean only your fight against the dreadful influenza. Even before you became ill I noticed how you lay around the house day after day, lost in a dream. He was a fine young man. You loved him very much, no?"

"No! Yes! I mean I don't know—"

"Shh. It is all right. I myself knew a man like him once. In France, before I met your father. He will always be with you, in here." She took off one glove and put her bare hand over her heart.

"Mother. You don't understand—"

"Your mother understands everything. You have to learn to endure your loss and accept what you cannot change in life."

Mother would never understand or accept the real causes for her grief, but for the first time Mother had shown an interest in her feelings.

"May I help you prune your roses? Can you teach me how you make them so beautiful every year?"

"*Oui*. With all my heart." She smiled so genuinely Jaq hardly recognized her. "At this time of the year, I always cut away all the dead canes and twiggy stems. For that I must use the sharp shears." She pulled hers out of her pocket again and snipped them in the air.

"So you trim them every year?"

She took off her other leather glove and stood beside one of her favorite bushes. "Yes. But you must be careful with the very young plants. Roses need time to grow before you cut them back. Not until their third year. You should be patient and observe a young bush, especially a variety unfamiliar to you. Decipher her pattern of growth. Does she want to bush, to stand straight and tall, or does she want to arch and lean gracefully? You must not destroy a rose's natural grace. If you chop an elegantly arching shrub to a stubby plant, you will have butchered it."

"Mother, you certainly chopped me to a stubby plant when I was too young. Remember what you said to me at Grandfather's funeral?"

She paled. "Do you still remember that horrible day, Jacqueline?"

"I'll never forget it."

"Ah, you can't imagine how often I've regretted my hasty words. I would cut out my tongue and lop off my fingers before I would say such things to you again. I can't excuse myself. I thought perhaps you would forget, that you would heal."

"I was a serious child, Mother. I took what you said to heart and still blame myself for Grandfather's death."

Her mother dropped her shears and put her hands over her eyes with a sob. "My poor Jacqueline. The Storm killed him. You did not. Never. You were rambunctious but never cruel. I blamed everyone and everything for his death for a long time. But no one was at fault. Only I, for making you believe such a horrible thing about yourself. You are so brave. Always going into the unknown, where your heart leads you. I wish I had your courage."

Jaq put her arm around her mother's shoulder and comforted her as her mother had failed to comfort her as a child. "Don't cry. You'll smear your makeup." She chuckled. "Besides, your words can wound, but they can heal too. I'll keep them in mind and let them erase the scar your earlier ones left. Now, why don't you show me how to trim a plant properly?"

Her mother wiped away her tears and smiled hesitantly. "If you insist. Let us work on this Archduke Charles together." She picked up her shears then rummaged in another apron pocket. "Here. Take my extra pair. You do not need the gloves, for the bush has almost no thorns."

"Isn't this one of your favorites, a China rose that smells like bananas when it blooms?"

She nodded in approval. *"Oui."*

"A friend of mine told me almost all our roses in the West came from China. She said before we discovered that type of rose, ours bloomed only once a year, in the spring. Is that right?"

"That is indeed correct." Her mother's eyes had grown large, and now they narrowed. "And who is your friend?"

She stiffened. "A woman I met in Texas. One of Eric's neighbors. A farmer's wife who loves to play the piano. She and her mother-in-law have a beautiful rose garden. She gave me a tour one day."

Her mother scrutinized her briefly then shrugged a bit too nonchalantly. "She must be a remarkable woman. Someone who loves music and grows roses in such an uncivilized part of the world."

"She is, Mother. Oh, she is!" She couldn't stop her enthusiasm and was afraid she'd given herself away.

"Is she your friend Molly, the one you said you gave our telephone number to?"

"Yes, Mother. She's a good person, and I've worried about her."

"Why haven't you telephoned her?"

She shook her head. Why hadn't she? "I want to give her time to get well. Her husband died, so I'm sure she's upset about that. I don't want to intrude on her grief." She didn't tell her mother how she'd planned to go to see Molly to discuss the possibility of a future together.

Her mother measured her with her exacting gaze. "If she is your friend, you should call. It's long past time to do so."

"I will. But what about my lesson?"

She tried to calm herself as her mother showed her where and how to prune the rosebush. As she talked about how this variety was called the chameleon of the roses, Jaq thought about contacting Molly. Did she dare? Would Molly want to hear from her, or had her life already taken a new direction? Her mother was explaining how the sun's heat changed the chameleon rose from light pink to deep red, and how it could grow in almost any environment and be trained into almost any shape.

Was she that adaptable? And was Molly? Could they take Patrick from his familiar life on the farm and raise him in a new environment? Didn't he need someone to teach him how to be a man?

Finally, her mother said, "I want to confide something in you. I love the Archduke Charles rose best because my grandmother used to grow large hedges of it in France. The man I mentioned and I liked to stroll through Grandmother's garden and smell them. He was the heart of my heart, but I married your father instead, because my parents wanted me to."

So her mother had a secret love but married to please her parents. Maybe that's why she'd just said she wished she'd had more courage. Should Jaq try to forget her love for Molly, or should she take a chance? Did she really want to? Wouldn't a child slow them down? Could she still picket in Washington or live in postwar Paris with a woman and a child?

Her mother's words strengthened her. She *would* call Molly. At least that would be a start. Then perhaps she could take the trip up there that she'd planned. Maybe Molly could become more than a sweet memory, a lost love Jaq would regret forever, like her mother did.

Jaq was disappointed but not surprised when Mrs. Russell, and not Molly, answered the telephone. After exchanging pleasantries about her father's health and the state of the farm, Mrs. Russell told her that Molly was getting married, that Patrick needed a man in his life. The wedding would take place as soon as Molly's fiancé came back from overseas. Mrs. Russell certainly sounded happy about that. As for why Molly hadn't called her, she could almost see Mrs. Russell shrug and scowl as she'd said, "I don't know why she hasn't phoned you. Just not in the mood, I suppose. You never can tell about her. I'll be sure to tell her you called."

Jaq dropped the receiver, then slowly picked it up from where it swung back and forth by its black cord. She felt like she was hanging by the neck from the gallows, suffocating. As she stared at the receiver, out of breath, she rolled it between her palms. So cold and hard.

During all the hours she and Molly had spent talking to each other last year, the telephone had bridged the distance between them and Molly's voice had breathed warmth into her. But Mrs. Russell's words had cut the phone lines between her and Molly, left her with nothing but a silent black object. *Number, please*, said the disembodied voice of the operator.

She replaced the receiver in its cradle and crumpled into the straight-backed chair next to the telephone. How had she misjudged Molly's feelings so completely? She had seemed so certain that she wasn't happy being married to Mr. James. But if she hadn't had to live with Mrs. Russell would things have been different? And if the man were younger, more willing to live in the city, would Molly have been satisfied?

But Eric had been younger, with no desire to live with his mother, and he had been willing to live anywhere in the world. Yet she hadn't been happy married to him. No, Molly didn't seem to fit with a man any more than Jaq did, just like she didn't fit on the farm. Something wasn't right.

Patrick needs a man in his life. Those words had frozen Jaq's tongue and her brain. Did Molly think Jaq couldn't give Patrick the kind of life that a man could? But when the three of them went to town together, she could have sworn Molly would have loved to be with her, wherever they went, and that Patrick would too.

Who was this man who had been overseas and was due home soon? Molly had never mentioned anyone except Mr. James's younger brother. What was his name? Clyde? Could this be Mrs. Russell's idea? She certainly wouldn't want Molly to stay, but Patrick was another story. He could help on the farm, keep Mrs. Russell's way of life alive. But would Molly sacrifice herself for Patrick by consenting to marry another Mr. Russell?

Jaq felt like jumping into her Model T and driving to New Hope right this minute. But what if Molly was marrying of her own free will, without any interference from Mrs. Russell? She'd try one more way to contact her, and if she got no satisfaction she would make the long trip up there and find out exactly what was going on.

CHAPTER THIRTY-NINE

Jaq contemplated the two cartridges of exposed film—the one of pictures she'd made in New Hope and one she'd brought back from Europe. In England, she'd had her pictures developed in a shop, but at her parents' house she could do it in her father's darkroom.

He'd taught her how right after he gave her a camera for her sixteenth birthday. After that, every time she could save fifty cents, she bought a cartridge of film and wandered through New Orleans snapping pictures. Especially after her experience with Sister Mary, she'd spent hours alone in the darkroom, savoring the smell of the acid fixing powder and the long, lonely wait time for her creations to emerge.

She held her newly developed shot of Helen up to the red light. Helen stood in the mud, her outfit as white as possible, a smile brightening her face. What a waste. She could have had a long and useful life.

And there stood her Model-T ambulance. She'd taken the picture one day after she'd spent two hours cleaning the vomit and blood from the inside and the caked mud from the outside. The sun had beamed down, and she'd had more than her usual three hours' sleep.

The one picture she took in Montmartre made her homesick for Paris. If only she and Molly and Patrick could live there.

And here was one of Willie in her red velvet dress. Her steady green eyes and strong fingers had helped her get ready for Molly. Maybe they'd meet again someday.

Now for the second roll. She gazed at Molly in the rose garden and in the rocking chair on Eric's front porch. Then Patrick on the porch with Mr. James. That shot, and the one of him and Eric, Patrick grinning and holding up his nickel, unleashed her tears as she printed several copies of all of them.

Back in her room, she placed the new photographs on her childhood bed and knelt before them. She wanted to remember at will, like she did when she chose which pictures she wanted to develop and print, not have memories attack her. Spells like that drained her. If she could keep the past at a distance, separate herself like she could from the pictures on her bed, maybe she could free herself from its power.

And if she could accomplish that, maybe, just maybe, she could forgive herself for the damage she'd caused so many others. She'd been wondering why good people had to die while bad ones survived and prospered. So many deaths. Had she really caused them, was she that important and powerful? If she could figure that out, perhaps she could make her peace with the past and move on.

She slid the photos of Patrick with Mr. James and Eric into an envelope, addressed and stamped it, and mailed it to Mrs. Russell. She hoped she'd show the pictures to Molly and Patrick. And at least Mrs. Russell would have something to remember Mr. James by. And maybe Molly and Patrick would remember her.

"Did we get any mail today?" Molly called from the kitchen where she sat churning, when Mother Russell pushed through the creaky front door.

"Nothing you'd be interested in. Just my *Farm and Ranch* magazine. I'm going to read a spell, then take my afternoon nap."

She thought she saw something brown, like an envelope, stuck inside the magazine that Mother Russell clutched as she rushed into her room and slammed the door, but she didn't pay much attention. But Mother Russell had certainly acted strange, all hunched over like she was hiding something. What on earth could it be?

"Mama, Grandma, somebody's coming to see us."

Patrick jumped off the front porch and sprinted through the raindrops out to the gate, with Molly and Mrs. Russell right behind him. Molly stood to the side as Mother Russell passed her, calling, "Clyde. You've finally come home."

Long and lanky, needing a shave and carrying a battered suitcase, he unwound himself from the bed of an old truck. "Thanks for the lift. See you around, fellows." Then he dropped his suitcase and held out his arms.

He looked forlorn as he hugged Mother Russell and Patrick, then Molly. He was probably thinking he'd rather have his arms around his own wife and children. But they were gone, and this was the only family he had left except his sister Hannah. Molly almost felt sorry for him.

"Hello, Clyde. Welcome back," she said as they walked to the porch, though she didn't feel very cordial.

"Here, you sit here in the swing next to Molly," Mother Russell told him. "I'll run in and get us something to drink. Come help me, Patrick."

Amazed that Mother Russell had offered to fetch refreshments instead of ordering her to, Molly sat stiffly beside Clyde. She tried to think of something to say to him as he settled in like a lump, nothing like the lively mischief-maker he used to be. But if he expected her to chatter inanely like his poor wife used to, she'd have to disappoint him.

After what seemed like forever, Mother Russell bustled back carrying a tray loaded with tall glasses of cold buttermilk and some biscuits and fig preserves. "Have a bite to eat, Clyde. Molly and I'll make you a big supper tonight after you tell us all about your adventures overseas. She's quite the cook."

Molly couldn't believe her ears. In all the years she'd known Mother Russell, not once had she praised her cooking.

Clyde still didn't have much to say, even though Mother Russell kept prodding him. But when Patrick looked at him with adoration, he seemed to soften and described what it was like to sail back on a big ship with thousands of men. He sneered when he described how everybody but him got seasick.

She half listened. He resembled his mother and acted like he thought he was a cut above all the men he'd served with. And he certainly had her hurtful tongue. But she paid attention when Mother Russell said, "Why don't you stay here with us for a spell? You could use the company and we could use the help. You could sleep in one of the rooms in the attic. That's where the hired help stay." Why would she invite him to stay here when he already had a place of his own?

"Yeah, Uncle Clyde," Patrick said. "It'd be nice to have another man around the house."

Patrick's words really set off the warning bells in Molly's head. They seemed like something he'd heard Mother Russell say more than once.

Clyde nodded as if he was doing everyone a big favor. "If you'll let me sleep in the guest room, you've got a deal, Ma."

She smiled like a Cheshire cat, and right then Molly knew something was up.

"I got one of the hired men to put new tires on the Overland, and it still runs like a top," Mother Russell said. "Why, Molly here has learned to drive. She carries me into town of a Saturday, when the road's not too muddy."

Molly was really getting the message now. Every time she'd driven Mother Russell to town, all she'd heard were snide remarks and orders for her to slow down or speed up or drive in the center of the pike so she wouldn't bog down.

Clyde laughed. "Molly driving? When James and I tried to teach her, she ended up in a pasture with the front bumper hugging a tree."

"I had a better teacher this time." She used a sharp tone, tired of him still making fun of her about that after all these years. He and Mr. James had been so impatient they'd confused her and made her nervous.

"You don't say." He looked at her with something that resembled respect, yet could have been either disbelief or contention. "I'll have to get you to run me over to the house so I can get my truck. It should still be in pretty good shape. It's a man's vehicle, fit for real work. And fine-looking too, especially with the Rebel flag painted on the tailgate."

Maybe he wouldn't stay long, but Mother Russell had apparently set her sights on just the opposite. Well, she could hope all she wanted to. Molly didn't intend to fall for another Mr. Russell, but she needed to come up with a plan of her own instead of sitting here and letting Mother Russell try to shove something down her throat.

If only Jaq would telephone. She could hardly think of anything but hearing Jaq's voice. She'd a million times rather be with Jaq than anyone she could think of, and she needed to stop pussyfooting around and let her know it.

CHAPTER FORTY

"Where did I put that last sheet of music I wrote yesterday?" Molly mumbled to herself. "Surely I didn't wad it up and throw it in the trashcan. I've been so addled the past few months, I wouldn't be surprised."

She dug through the big trash bin near the back door, all the way to the bottom, surprised to find a big brown envelope folded about six times into the size of a ruler. Undoing it, she noticed the New Orleans return address. And the handwriting. Why, it was Jaq's. She'd recognize it anywhere. Why was the envelope here, and what had been in it?

She carefully memorized the return address and put the envelope back where she'd found it. Then she began to search for clues to this mystery.

Two days later, she found a contract deeding all the farm property to Mr. James, signed by him and Mother Russell. It was buried in a neat stack of papers in the top left drawer of her private desk. The news astounded her. She owned the farm. She could order Mother Russell to leave. But what would she do with this place? She didn't want to stay here, and she wasn't totally heartless, no matter how badly Mother Russell had treated her.

The day after that, on a Sunday afternoon while Mother Russell was out walking the muddy fields with Clyde, she found a letter addressed to Jaq in the bottom of Mother Russell's trunk. What in the world? It was from a woman named Willie, most likely the one Jaq had mentioned.

Jaq, if I let myself, I could develop some powerful feelings for you, and I refuse to do that. Mama lived her life for a man she can't even be buried next to, and I've always promised myself I'd never follow her example. When you read this letter I'll soon be on my way north, and then I'll head across the ocean to a place that treats colored people like human beings, not freaks of nature, and that won't look down on me because my great-grandmother was a slave.

She was colored? Or perhaps half colored? Molly already had powerful feelings for Jaq, and she wanted that type of acceptance too. If she had to leave this part of the world to get it, she was willing to do so. That would be the best legacy she could give Patrick—not to live a lie. But did Jaq feel the same way? Did she want an older woman with a young son to care for?

She straightened the contents of the trunk and felt a little bad for snooping. But Mother Russell didn't have any right to this letter, so she kept it and looked around the bedroom she so seldom entered. The picture of Mr. James's papa hung on the wall, like it always had. It seemed like he was staring at the well-worn Bible that lay on the small table next to Mother Russell's bed. She picked it up. Several pictures were stuck in between the pages of Revelations.

She cried as she gazed at the likenesses of Mr. James and Eric and Patrick. So that's what was in the envelope she'd found in the trash bin. Mr. James looked so tall and strong and wise, there on the porch beside Patrick. She couldn't deny that she missed him—his stories and his kindness. But marrying him had been one of the biggest mistakes of her life, just as Jaq said she'd been wrong to marry Eric. But if she hadn't married Mr. James, she wouldn't have Patrick. She touched Patrick's image lightly, grateful she still had him with her after that terrible influenza. With a last look at Mr. James, she sighed, slid the photographs into the Bible again, and put it back where it belonged.

It was almost time for Mother Russell to get back from her walk with Clyde, so she went into the parlor. As she played a loud Chopin prelude with its clashing chords, she thought, *Jaq sent those pictures. She's still thinking about me. I've got to talk to her face to face. I've got to find a way to get to New Orleans, and I will, if it's the last thing I do.* Then she played her new composition, "The Storm," pounding out the notes. She didn't know what she'd do, but she had to do something.

The next morning at breakfast, she said, "Mother Russell, I've decided to go visit Eric's aunt and uncle in Logansport tomorrow. They were so kind when they came to visit during my convalescence. Don't you remember how they asked me and Patrick to come see them when we got better? It's slacked off enough for the roads to dry out a little. There's no telling when it'll start pouring again. We'll just stay a couple of days."

Mother Russell frowned, but she'd been unusually accommodating since Clyde's return. "I guess you've earned yourself a little vacation, Molly. Clyde and I can manage on our own for a while, so you go enjoy yourself while we stay here and do all the work."

Molly grabbed everything she treasured, which wasn't much, and threw most of Patrick's belongings into a small bag. Wherever they ended up, they could buy more. She was certainly glad she'd never mentioned the five dollars Mr. James had been putting in a cigar box every Saturday since their wedding day. He'd accumulated almost seventeen hundred dollars and called it their mad-at-Ma money. Well, she was certainly mad.

She could leave here and support herself and Patrick on that savings and what she could earn from teaching music lessons. If Jaq hadn't meant what she'd said, or at least hinted at, she could move to Dallas and make a life for herself there. But she'd go to New Orleans first. If Jaq thought half as much of her as she did of Jaq, they belonged together.

Jaq had hoped she'd get some response to the pictures she'd sent, but nothing came.

"I've tried everything I can think of, Mother, and I can't get in touch with Molly." They were supposed to be eating a leisurely breakfast, but she sat drumming her fingers on the table. "I need to get away from here. I want to get on with my life."

"Well, the estate you inherited from Eric will certainly help you do that. That, on top of what your grandparents left you, should set you up nicely."

"Yeah, I can't believe how wealthy Mr. McCade turned out to be, in addition to all that acreage. If I ever want to sell it, maybe it'll be worth something someday. But right now I'm content to rent it to some enterprising young family who'll treat it well."

She had been involved in legal matters lately, though she'd let their family lawyer work out all the details.

"After I sign the final papers next week, I'm planning to drive up to Washington. Miss Paul still needs some help, though I suspect the hardest part of winning the right to vote is behind her. Then I might head back to New York and maybe on to France and see what's going on over there. I'll leave my automobile with Aunt Anna."

She didn't tell her mother that she was going to detour through East Texas and talk to Molly, like she'd been wanting to for months.

"I'll worry about you, Jacqueline. And I wish you didn't have to go alone."

So did she. She'd dreamed of having Molly and Patrick with her, and maybe she could. If she'd guessed right and Mrs. Russell was trying to keep Molly and her apart, she'd show Mrs. Russell a thing or two. But maybe Molly had found someone else to take Mr. James's place. Since her talk with her mother in the rose garden, Jaq had finally realized that she hadn't caused all those people to die. Dropping the burden of her long-held belief had made her feel lighter than she had since she was a child before the Storm.

She couldn't think of anyone she'd rather make a life with than Molly, but if she had to, she could make it alone. She just hoped she wouldn't have to.

❖

Molly drove carefully from New Hope to Logansport, hoping it wouldn't keep raining. While she'd visited with Eric's aunt and uncle, she discussed her interest in the state of Louisiana, especially the state of the roads that led to New Orleans. And when she left their house early the next morning, she headed east instead of west.

"How would you like to go see Miss Jacqueline?" she asked Patrick.

"That'd be swell. New Orleans is a lot bigger than Harrison, isn't it?"

"It certainly is. I imagine they have wonderful ice-cream sodas there."

"I can't wait to get there and see Miss Jacqueline. She's nice."

She couldn't believe she was running away, and she guessed she might be stealing the Overland. But if Mr. James had owned it, didn't it belong to her now? She wouldn't worry about that now. She just wanted to see Jaq, had to see her with an urge so strong it'd take more than a long drive like this to stop her. If only Jaq felt that way, she wouldn't worry about anything else.

Had Jaq written to her and had Mother Russell intercepted the letter and hidden it, as she had the photographs? If she had, what had Jaq said? She might have gone to see that woman named Willie and reunited with her. They could be planning to go to France together, since that's where Jaq had said she'd like to go. Or maybe Jaq had other girlfriends and was amusing herself with them right now.

But Jaq hadn't sent those pictures all that long ago, and she'd been in New Orleans then. Molly needed to stop creating monsters in her mind and trust her feelings for Jaq. If she was wrong, at least she would have escaped from Mother Russell and Clyde. But she hoped with all her heart that she was right, that Jaq cared for her as much as she cared for Jaq.

❖

Late in the afternoon after Molly left for Logansport, Mrs. Russell went into Molly's room to look for the broom. That gal was always forgetting to put things back where they belonged. She glanced around but something didn't seem right, so she checked closer. Molly had taken practically everything, including all her music-writing junk. The same thing in Patrick's room.

She rushed into her own bedroom and checked her desk and Bible, but nothing was missing. Then she dug to the bottom of her trunk to check on the letter the postman had given her for Jacqueline. It was gone. Molly must have figgered out what was going on.

"Clyde!" She hollered out the window, and he came hotfooting it up from the barn.

"What's wrong?"

"Molly's run away. She's kidnapped Patrick and stolen the Overland. No telling what else she took. And to think I trusted her. Get in your truck and go find her. And don't come back until you do."

"But Ma, it's raining—"

"Don't *but Ma* me. I want her and Patrick back here. And if she won't come, bring Patrick. Drive over to Logansport this afternoon. You know where Eric's uncle lives. Surely you can track her down. And if you have to go all the way to New Orleans, because I reckon that's where she'll wind up, you'll most likely find her at this address. Here. I've written it down for you."

"But Ma, it's almost dark and—"

"Don't waste any more time. Skedaddle. This is as important for you as it is for me."

❖

"I'm worn out, Mama," Patrick said. "Why couldn't we stop in that town with the funny name back there? It was pretty. You said we could stay in a hotel."

"Don't you want to see Miss Jacqueline, son? Let's drive a little farther today, and then it won't take us so many days to make this long trip."

She had planned to spend the night in Natchitoches, and she'd looked forward to doing a little sightseeing in the old Louisiana town. She and Patrick had been walking down Church Street when she spotted Clyde's truck parked in front of the courthouse. Thank goodness for that silly Confederate flag on the tailgate. Mother Russell must have discovered that they'd run away and sent him after them.

She didn't want Patrick to know what was going on, so she pretended everything was fine as he said, "Okay. I wish I could drive too, so I could help you out. I'll remind Miss Jacqueline to teach me."

She'd never been so tired. She had to get some rest. She'd tried to memorize the directions from Logansport to New Orleans and hoped she'd jotted them down right, but she couldn't keep up this pace all the way to New Orleans. She couldn't stay in a hotel now, because that's the first place Clyde would look. A woman traveling alone with a child would be easy to locate.

It was almost dark and had been pouring rain all day. She could barely see the outline of the huge trees on both sides of the road. Then she spotted a big house sitting a ways off the road and remembered Esther Harris mentioning a friend of hers, Florence, who had married a Mr. Conway and settled in a big plantation south of Natchitoches. Maybe she could stop here and get directions to her house.

She knocked gently, not knowing what to expect. An older, white-haired woman opened the door, and when she explained who she was looking for, the woman said, "Well, my dear, you've reached the right place. I'm Florence Conway. Won't you come in out of this bad weather?"

After she and Patrick were settled and had eaten a huge meal of leftovers, she put Patrick to bed then sat with Florence in the parlor. It turned out that her husband had died the preceding year too, of a cerebral hemorrhage. "I've raised eight sons and a daughter," she said, "and now my friend Caroline and I plan to restore this old run-down plantation and turn it into a refuge for artists in the area. From what you've told me about your love for music, you're my very first artist guest."

The next morning over an early breakfast, Molly explained her situation, surprised at how understanding Florence was. But they were both educated women, so they spoke the same language.

"I have friends scattered from here to New Orleans," Florence said with a smile, taking off her wire-rimmed glasses and rubbing her eyes. "We'll help you reach your friend Jacqueline."

Molly drove away from the plantation humming, having made a new friend. The sun had even peeked out. To think that she could have made it this far by herself. Every day she got a little nearer to Jaq, and every day her heart beat like a bass drum, pulling and pushing her toward the woman she loved.

CHAPTER FORTY-ONE

"Y̶ou miss Molly, don't you, Nellie? I'm ready for her to get back too. My hands are cramping." She stretched out her aching fingers and wiggled them.

"Who'd have figured she'd pull a stunt like this. Running away with Patrick! When Clyde catches her, he'll bring her home and we'll get back to normal. Sure hope she didn't poke around and see that deed. If she had a mind to, she could snatch this land right out from under us and leave us on the side of the road. Something must have set her off, though, to make her light out of here with nary a word."

Nellie mooed, and she started milking again.

"My husband and I worked like slaves, day and night, to make this land ours. I've watered it with my sweat and the lives of my husband and most of my children.

"It's people like Molly that drug us into the War Between the States in the first place. Always building up the Greeks and Romans in their minds like they had a corner on things—a perfect society with all the frills. That's what the plantation owners and their fancy wives who had slaves at their beck and call did. All those lazy women thought everyone should play the piano and read all the classical books, sew fancywork, and dress in the latest Paris fashions. From the very beginning James must have thought Molly fit the bill as a planter's wife, and that's why he wouldn't take no for an answer. Wanted to live the way his pa did before we lost the War, with her the proof he could do exactly that."

She finished milking and picked up the heavy buckets, then turned back to Nellie. "I don't aim to let any smart-aleck girl waltz in here and spend more time on the piano stool than this milking stool, then steal my property just because James was unlucky enough to die and I was foolish enough to sign a gol-dern deed giving most everything to him. She can keep Patrick and that automobile, but I want my land.

"I sure will miss Patrick though, and I won't be able to do what James asked me to."

❖

Jaq closed her worn leather suitcase. She was traveling light because she didn't want to have to worry about managing a lot of bags on the liner to Europe. Her stomach fluttered with excitement, as it always did before she set out on a new adventure, but the excitement came mainly from thinking about the first stop on her long trip. Hopefully Molly would still be in New Hope and would welcome her with a kiss and a promise to go with her. She could picture the surprise on Molly's face and her gleaming eyes as she stopped at the Russell farm. The thought of any other reception made her scalp tingle.

Of course it would be good to see her aunts and Miss Paul again. They'd almost won the fight for suffrage, so she'd probably sail for France this summer. But would she sail alone, or would Molly and Patrick stand beside her on board the ship and watch the Statue of Liberty fade into the distance?

They'd both talked about visiting Washington with her, and Molly had seemed to think that a trip to Europe would be a dream come true. If she couldn't have them along to share her adventures, would she enjoy this trip, or would she do nothing but long for Molly? Had being with Molly ruined her? She couldn't imagine laughing with anyone else the way she and Molly had, or simply sitting or working near one another as their long silences calmed them both and bound them even closer.

The doorbell rang and she stopped fastening one of the straps on her brown bag. Who could that be this time of the day?

"Please come in," the maid said. "Mrs. Bergeron will receive you in the parlor."

"Jacqueline, you have company," Mother called. "You'd better come quick."

She raced down the stairs and couldn't believe her eyes. Molly wore the same green dress as she had last Easter, the day Jaq had first seen her. Where had she sprung from, like a sapling in spring, fresh and willowy and oh, so lovable? Jaq wanted to rush to her, to take her in her arms and never let her go.

Patrick stood beside her, in his new long pants, beaming. "You better teach me how to drive pretty soon, Miss Jacqueline. Mama just about wore herself out getting us down here. It rained almost the whole way. We got stuck three times."

She rushed to the door and, sure enough, the Overland sat in front of the house, spattered with mud. "What on earth, Molly—"

"I'll go away if you don't want me here, Jaq. I have some money—"

"Go away? I haven't thought of anything but being with you since I had to leave New Hope. Father was sick and you were unconscious and I gave Mrs. Russell the phone number here...She didn't give it to you? That's why you haven't called?"

"That's not all she didn't give me," Molly said, and told her everything that had happened.

As they were talking, Jaq's mother took Patrick's hand and led him to the kitchen, and the doorbell rang again.

Clyde stumbled in. Sometime later, after Molly and Jaq informed him that Mrs. Russell had no claim on Patrick, but that Mrs. Russell could keep the farm and he could have the Overland, he left.

And they were blessedly alone at last.

Molly stood still for a minute, then sank onto the sofa. "Well, that certainly turned out a lot better than I thought it would. Did you mean what you said about not thinking about anything but being with me, Jaq?"

She sat beside Molly and took her hand. Slowly peeling off the white glove, she raised Molly's hand to her lips and savored its fragrance of rose water and Ivory soap. She couldn't focus on anything but how this hand and its mate would feel as they stroked her all over. "I don't think I'm capable of thinking of anything else."

Molly removed her other glove and ran both of her hands through Jaq's hair, as if she were playing the piano, her long fingers drawing the music from the depths of Jaq's being where it had lain forgotten for most of her life. Then Molly lifted Jaq's bangs and ran a strong finger over her scar. "It's almost faded completely, Jaq," she murmured. "No need to hide that beautiful forehead any longer."

Waves seemed to crash through Jaq and wash her clean. The Storm, Sister Mary, Helen, the War, Henry—everything that had haunted her floated on the waves and disappeared into something much larger than she was. She looked at the front window, and the sun streamed through.

Taking both of Molly's hands in hers, she asked the question that had been on her lips for months. "Would you and Patrick like to go up East and on to Europe with me, Molly? And wherever else we want to go or be for the rest of our lives?"

Molly gazed at her for such a long moment, Jaq almost couldn't bear it. Would she say no? *Please say yes.* Time disappeared and only Molly's lips existed. *Say yes.*

"Well." Molly's eyes glistened. "If you're sure you don't have any other women stashed away, vying for your attention."

Jaq grinned. She supposed she had that coming. "I'm sure."

"And if you're sure you won't think I'm a country bumpkin when we meet all those sophisticated women in Europe."

This time Jaq beamed. She loved Molly's gentle teasing. "I'm positive."

"In that case, we'd love to go with you."

"And be with me forever?"

"I can't speak for Patrick, but I can't think of anywhere else I'd rather be forever. I love you, Jaq darling."

The storm inside Jaq vanished as a calm she'd never before experienced engulfed her.

"And I love you too, Molly. With all my heart."

AUTHOR'S NOTE

The Storm began as a family memoir, and a lot of the characters that appear in it are based on actual people. Molly and James Russell, inspired by my maternal grandparents, did live on a farm with my great-grandmother for many years, and prior to that my grandmother did attend the university and study music, which helped her cope with her mother-in-law. My grandfather had a third-grade education, loved *The Iliad*, and built his mother a house.

Mrs. Russell, modeled after my great-grandmother, did travel from Georgia to Texas after the Civil War, and almost all her memories of her husband and her life as a single mother are historically accurate. In addition, my grandmother's father did save a woman during the Galveston Storm, and her grandmother did die young in West Texas. Patrick is patterned after one of my maternal uncles, Wendell, who had a hard life, so I decided to give him a brighter one in fiction.

Our collection of family letters dating back to 1864, several of which were written on the battlefield near Atlanta, Georgia, was invaluable. Oral history from my mother and her seven siblings, two of whom were college librarians, provided the majority of the stories included, such as my grandmother returning my grandfather's ring, her first attempt to learn to drive, the death of her older sister, and her always playing the piano at church and planning the special music services. My great-grandmother really did burn her new rolling pin. Reunion picnics such as the one described are still common in East Texas.

Three of my characters from the world outside East Texas appear by their real names: Anna Wessels Williams, Helen Fairchild, and Willie Piazza. Anna W. Williams did try desperately to find a cure for the influenza pandemic, but failed. As far as I know she had no relatives in Louisiana, but the rest of the information about her in the book is based on fact. A pioneering US medical researcher, she left a large collection of papers ranging from 1846 to 1954, currently housed in Radcliffe Institute's Schlesinger Library at Harvard. Helen Fairchild did serve as a nurse during World War I and lost her life in the process. She left a hundred pages of letters to document her experience in Europe, available online thanks to her niece, Mrs. Nelle Fairchild Rote. Finally, Willie Piazza, an octoroon madam in New Orleans, did reputedly go to Paris after World War I ended.

Two of my minor characters, Eric's friend Dick and Florence Conway, who helped Molly reach New Orleans, are based on the pilot Eddie Rickenbacker and Cammie Garrett Henry, best known as a patron of the arts during the Southern Renaissance of the 1920s. Her extensive collection of manuscripts, both fiction and nonfiction, regarding the history, culture, and literature of Louisiana, is housed at Northwestern State University in Natchitoches, Louisiana, in the Cammie G. Henry Research Center. Eddie Rickenbacker's autobiographical *Fighting the Flying Circus* provides an exciting glimpse into the experiences of the US's most famous WWI ace.

Jacqueline Bergeron McCade is entirely my own invention, though her stories about Radclyffe Hall, Ladye, and Toupie Lowther (reputedly the model for Stephen Gordon in Hall's *The Well of Loneliness*) are accurate. Jaq's alma mater in New Orleans is based on an actual school there, but Sister Mary Therese and Sister Celestine are products of my imagination.

Several poems posted on my website provide additional information about my family's history. If you would like to know more about the local or family history touched upon, feel free to contact me at sthrasher39@gmail.com.

About the Author

Shelley Thrasher, world traveler and native East Texan, has edited novels for Bold Strokes Books since 2004. A PhD in English, she taught on the college level for many years before she retired early, and still teaches one fine-arts course online. She has published numerous poems and several short stories and essays, as well as one scholarly book. Shelley and her partner Connie, with their two dogs, cat, and parrot, live near Dallas in the piney woods of East Texas, where her first novel, *The Storm*, is set.

Learn more about her and her writing at www.shelleythrasher.com.

Books Available from Bold Strokes Books

Crossroads by Radclyffe. Dr. Hollis Monroe specializes in short-term relationships but when she meets pregnant mother-to-be Annie Colfax, fate brings them together at a crossroads that will change their lives forever. (978-1-60282-756-1)

Beyond Innocence by Carsen Taite. When a life is on the line, love has to wait. Doesn't it? (978-1-60282-757-8)

Heart Block by Melissa Brayden. Socialite Emory Owen and struggling single mom Sarah Matamoros are perfectly suited for each other but face a difficult time when trying to merge their contrasting worlds and the people in them. If love truly exists, can it find a way? (978-1-60282-758-5)

Pride and Joy by M.L. Rice. Perfect Bryce Montgomery is her parents' pride and joy, but when they discover that their daughter is a lesbian her world changes forever. (978-1-60282-759-2)

Timothy by Greg Herren. *Timothy* is a romantic suspense thriller from award-winning mystery writer Greg Herren set in the fabulous Hamptons. (978-1-60282-760-8)

In Stone: A Grotesque Faerie Tale by Jeremy Jordan King. A young New Yorker is rescued from a hate crime by a mysterious someone who turns out to be more of a *something*. (978-1-60282-761-5)

The Jesus Injection by Eric Andrews-Katz. Murderous statues, demented drag queens, political bombings, ex-gay ministries, espionage, and romance are all in a day's work for a top-secret agent. But the gloves are off when Agent Buck 98 comes up against The Jesus Injection. (978-1-60282-762-2)

Combustion by Daniel W. Kelly. Bearish detective Deck Waxer comes to the city of Kremfort Cove to investigate why the hottest men in town are bursting into flames in broad daylight. (978-1-60282-763-9)

Silver Collar by Gill McKnight. Werewolf Luc Garoul is outlawed and out of control, but can her family track her down before a sinister predator gets there first? Fourth in the Garoul series. (978-1-60282-764-6)

The Dragon Tree Legacy by Ali Vali. For Aubrey Tarver time hasn't dulled the pain of losing her first love Wiley Gremillion, but she has to set that aside when her choices put her life and her family's lives in real danger. (978-1-60282-765-3)

The Midnight Room by Ronnie Black. After a chance encounter with the mysterious and brooding Lillian Gray in the "midnight room" of The Griffin, a local lesbian bar, confident and gorgeous Audrey McCarthy learns that her bad girl behavior isn't bulletproof. (978-1-60282-766-0)

Dirty Sex by Ashley Bartlett. Vivian Cooper and twins Reese and Ryan DiGiovanni stole a lot of money and the guy they took it from wants it back. Like now. (978-1-60282-767-7)

Raising Hell: Demonic Gay Erotica edited by Todd Gregory. *Raising Hell*: hot stories of gay erotica featuring demons. (978-1-60282-768-4)

Pursued by Joel Gomez-Dossi. Openly gay college student Jamie Bradford becomes romantically involved with two men at the same time, and his hell begins when one of his boyfriends becomes intent on killing him. (978-1-60282-769-1)

Young Bucks: Novellas of Twenty-Something Lust & Love edited by Richard Labonte. Four writers still in their twenties-or with their twenties a nearby memory-write about what it's like to be young, on the prowl for sex, or looking to fall in love. (978-1-60282-770-7)

The Storm by Shelley Thrasher. Rural East Texas. 1918. War-weary Jaq Bergeron and marriage-scarred musician Molly Russell try to salvage love from the devastation of the war abroad and natural disasters at home. (978-1-60282-780-6)

Ladyfish by Andrea Bramhall. Finn's escape to the Florida Keys leads her straight into the arms of scuba diving instructor Oz as she fights for her freedom, their blossoming love…and her life! (978-1-60282-747-9)

Spanish Heart by Rachel Spangler. While on a mission to find herself in Spain, Ren Molson runs the risk of losing her heart to her tour guide, Lina Montero. (978-1-60282-748-6)

Love Match by Ali Vali. When Parker "Kong" King, the number one tennis player in the world, meets commercial pilot Captain Sydney Parish, sparks fly—but not from attraction. They have the summer to see if they have a love match. (978-1-60282-749-3)

One Touch by L.T. Marie. A romance writer and a travel agent come together at their high school reunion, only to find out that the memory of that one touch never fades. (978-1-60282-750-9)

Night Shadows: Queer Horror edited by Greg Herren and J.M. Redmann. *Night Shadows* features delightfully wicked stories by some of the biggest names in queer publishing. (978-1-60282-751-6)

Secret Societies by William Holden. An outcast hustler, his unlikely "mother," his faithless lovers, and his religious persecutors—all in 1726. (978-1-60282-752-3)

The Raid by Lee Lynch. Before Stonewall, having a drink with friends or your girl could mean jail. Would these women and men still have family, a job, a place to live after…The Raid? (978-1-60282-753-0)

The You Know Who Girls: Freshman Year by Annameekee Hesik. As they begin freshman year, Abbey Brooks and her best friend, Kate, pinkie swear they'll keep away from the lesbians in Gila High, but Abbey already suspects she's one of those you-know-who girls herself and slowly learns who her true friends really are. (978-1-60282-754-7)

Wyatt: Doc Holliday's Account of an Intimate Friendship by Dale Chase. Erotica writer Dale Chase takes the remarkable friendship between Wyatt Earp, upright lawman, and Doc Holliday, Southern gentlemen turned gambler and killer, to an entirely new level: hot! (978-1-60282-755-4)

Month of Sundays by Yolanda Wallace. Love doesn't always happen overnight; sometimes it takes a month of Sundays. (978-1-60282-739-4)

Jacob's War by C.P. Rowlands. ATF Special Agent Allison Jacob's task force is in the middle of an all-out war, from the streets to the boardrooms of America. Small business owner Katie Blackburn is the latest victim who accidentally breaks it wide open, but she may break AJ's heart at the same time. (978-1-60282-740-0)

The Pyramid Waltz by Barbara Ann Wright. Princess Katya Nar Umbriel wants a perfect romance, but her Fiendish nature and duties to the crown mean she can never tell the truth—until she meets Starbride, a woman who gets to the heart of every secret, even if it will be the death of her. (978-1-60282-741-7)

The Secret of Othello by Sam Cameron. Florida teen detectives Steven and Denny risk their lives to search for a sunken NASA satellite—but under the waves, no one can hear you scream… (978-1-60282-742-4)

Finding Bluefield by Elan Barnehama. Set in the backdrop of Virginia and New York and spanning the years 1960–1982, *Finding Bluefield* chronicles the lives of Nicky Stewart, Barbara Philips, and their son, Paul, as they struggle to define themselves as a family. (978-1-60282-744-8)

The Jetsetters by David-Matthew Barnes. As rock band the Jetsetters skyrockets from obscurity to superstardom, Justin Holt, a lonely barista, and Diego Delgado, the band's guitarist, fight with everything they have to stay together, despite the chaos and fame. (978-1-60282-745-5)

Strange Bedfellows by Rob Byrnes. Partners in life and crime, Grant Lambert and Chase LaMarca are hired to make a politician's compromising photo disappear, but what should be an easy job quickly spins out of control. (978-1-60282-746-2)

Dreaming of Her by Maggie Morton. Isa has begun to dream of the most amazing woman—a woman named Lilith with a gorgeous face, an amazing body, and the ability to turn Isa on like no other. But Lilith is just a dream…isn't she? (978-1-60282-847-6)

Summoning Shadows: A Rosso Lussuria Vampire Novel by Winter Pennington. The Rosso Lussuria vampires face enemies both old and new, and to prevail they must call on even more strange alliances, unite as a clan, and draw on every weapon within their reach—but with a clan of vampires, that's easier said than done. (978-1-60282-679-3)

Sometime Yesterday by Yvonne Heidt. When Natalie Chambers learns her Victorian house is haunted by a pair of lovers and a Dark Man, can she and her lover Van Easton solve the mystery that will set the ghosts free and banish the evil presence in the house? Or will they have to run to survive as well? (978-1-60282-680-9)